Also by Meg Henderson

THE LAST WANDERER

Meg Henderson

Flamingo
An Imprint of HarperCollinsPublishers

Flamingo
An imprint of HarperCollins*Publishers*
77–85 Fulham Palace Road,
Hammersmith, London W6 8JB

Flamingo is a registered trade mark of
HarperCollins*Publishers* Limited

www.**fire**and**water**.com

Published by Flamingo 2002
9 8 7 6 5 4 3 2 1

Photographs; The publishers would like to thank the following for permission
to reproduce these images within the text: pvi, Scots fishergirls at work in
Great Yarmouth, courtesy of the Eastern Daily Press: p417, © Kieran Murray.

A catalogue record for this book is available from the
British Library

ISBN 0 00 226188 x

Set in Bembo by Rowland Phototypesetting Limited,
Bury St Edmunds, Suffolk

Printed and bound in Great Britain by Clays Ltd, St Ives plc

*For Michael Currie, Coxswain of the Mallaig Lifeboat,
native of Barra, gentleman, philosopher and former fisherman*

I

It seemed to Angusina Polson that her memories of ninety years ago were nearer and more vivid than her recollection of what had happened in the last ninety seconds. And she wasn't Angusina Polson from the Shetland Isles; she knew that. She might be a daft old woman losing whatever mind she ever had, but she knew she was Angusina Hamilton and she lived in Acarsaid, had lived there for many a year, though she couldn't rightly recall how many. She had carried Aeneas's name far longer than she had her father's, but she still thought of herself as Angusina, or Ina Polson, daughter of Magnus and Dolina from Lerwick in the Shetland Isles. Why was that, she wondered? If it was a judgement on her years with her husband then it was an unfair one, because Aeneas had been a good, steady man.

Once, in Yarmouth, when she was worlds younger, Ina and the other herring lassies had gone to see a fortune-teller in a fairground booth. They were a bunch of giggling, shoving lassies out for a laugh, not really believing a word of what they were told about meeting tall, dark, handsome strangers, but wanting to, as long as the others didn't know that they did. The gypsy woman was as dark and wrinkled as a fortune-teller should be, the lines on her face intensifying every time she put her left hand to her mouth and inhaled deeply from the stub end of her cigarette. She clasped Ina's right hand in her own, stared at it intently for a few seconds, then looked at her solemn-eyed before saying, 'You'll marry someone you already know and you'll live across the sea from your home. You'll be content, but you could've done better, and you won't have many bairns.'

Coming from a time and a background where big families were the norm, with women having a bairn a year – or every two years if they were lucky – Ina would have no trouble with the notion of not 'having many'. Not that she had been fooled by any of it, but looking back it was true that she had lived across the sea from her home and she had been content, too, mostly, with Aeneas, even if she did still feel more like the lassie she had been born than the wife she became. Feeling guilty, she would go over it in her mind many times, each time defending Aeneas against a charge that hadn't been made, answering a question that hadn't been asked. Constantly thinking about it didn't change the truth, though; Hamilton she was, but Polson she had been born and, deep down, like a brand burned into her soul, Polson she would always be.

The memories came in no particular order, all jumbled up and out of sequence and more like visions, or waking dreams, than memories. Sometimes she spoke with people she had grown up with in Shetland. Then her daughter Margo would appear, and sometimes Rose, her youngest granddaughter; all of them together as though they had known each other all of their lives. They hadn't, of course, being separated not just by distance, but by many decades. None of it made any sense, except to Ina, because they were her memories. There was something she should remember about Rose but she couldn't quite recall what it was; no matter, it would keep for another time. Most of the memories came from a time when she felt she belonged in the world – unlike now, when it plainly belonged to someone else and made so little sense to her that she sometimes wondered not only whether it belonged to others, but whether it was a different world entirely; maybe she had fallen asleep in the Milky Way and wakened up in another galaxy. Maybe that's what it was. When she tried to retrieve those very early memories they came in snatches. She had a few snapshots in her mind of her much older brother, Sandy, and more of her sister Ella, though she couldn't remember her sister clearly in her younger days; Ella was younger than Sandy, but she had still been seven years older than Ina.

Now that Ella was in her mind she knew there was another connection with Rose, but whatever it was would have to keep for another time, too, because it had slipped from her memory as quickly and easily as it had come into it. She hadn't got to know her sister till they were herring lassies together; maybe after that, really, to be truthful. Ina's own fault, not Ella's, she thought sadly. Ella, poor Ella, she would think, then she would think again and ask, 'But was she really? Hadn't she got what she wanted, what she truly deserved eventually?' Even if it had come at a price, it was one Ella was prepared to pay – and she had never regretted it. So Ella was in her memories, at a distance sometimes as she had been when Ina was a bairn, and closer at other times, as she became later; though she was long gone now. So, for that matter, was the main companion of Ina's early years: Danny, her elder brother by two years. Danny, caught with her in the painful debris of their mother's grief. She recalled her mother's eyes: beautiful blue eyes, Dolina had; deep pools of sadness and, at times, of resentment, too, she sometimes felt. It was when she thought of her mother that Rose would be called to mind. She thought there was a connection, something about the eyes, though Rose's were brown and not blue. What was it? No, it had gone again.

Ina's mind would drift happily to the stars above her native Shetland Isles, a hundred bits of rock suspended far out in the North Sea between Iceland, Norway and Scotland. Only fifteen of the isles were inhabited, and Ina's home had been in Lerwick, on the biggest one, in the east of the part that was called the South Mainland. She had no idea why, but from her earliest days she had taken note of the skies overhead and the familiar but brilliant show that appeared every night. She had been in other places in her life where it was easy to identify the sparkling, faraway planets in their distinctive patterns as they shone brightly against a blue or black backdrop, but it was different in Shetland. There the sky never quite darkened, no matter what the season, but there were no street lights either, nothing to distract from the show up above. The air was clearer, cleaner, too, and you could see more than the major constellations that everyone knew about. Between them were millions of other diamond glints invisible to the eyes of those trapped in other places, as though some great hand had created Orion, the Great Bear, Gemini and the others and, having some stardust left over, as a parting gesture had thrown it into the air over Shetland to fall where it would, so the constellations rested not on the background of blue velvet that people talked about, but on one twinkling with billions of smaller stars, like dew caught in a spider's web.

When she was a bairn she would sometimes wake in the night, open the window and just gaze at it spellbound, lost in the silent glory of it, amazed that others could sleep while the stars travelled across the sky till they melted in the dawn sun. She didn't think there was anything odd about her fascination because her father, Magnus, shared it, so at first she assumed everyone else did too; and by the time she was old enough to realise that they didn't, she was also wise enough not to mention it.

Not that she had much to fear from the teasing of other bairns; she had spent most of her time with Danny. The two younger Polson bairns were bound together by Dolina's loss. So Ina Polson was known all over Lerwick as a boy's girl rather than a girl's girl. Ina Polson could hold her own in any skirmish; but still, the less ammunition you gave the little minds the better, that was how she saw it. She had always been like that, she was never one for close friendships; with them, but from a distance. There was a saying that it was possible to be lonely in a crowd. Well, for Ina it was possible, preferable even, to be *alone* in a crowd; she got on with the others well enough, but she had always liked her own company, too. She would watch the bairns at school, see how wrapped up in each other they were – in tight twos, mainly – and she knew that she would never have any need of that closeness. Then would come bitter hurt when a third inevitably came between once best friends, as they moved on and formed other best friendships, then others, gradually outgrowing each other. It was the normal way of things, though not being aware of this they always behaved as though they had been betrayed. But Ina had never been like that. Ina had Danny and she had her father and she hadn't needed anyone else. Except her mother, of course, and she knew that was a lost cause, even if she always did secretly hope.

Even when she went with a group of bairns – who lived, like the Polsons, 'out by the Burgh', fishermen's bairns – to Clickimin Loch, where the earth was damp and the wild flowers flourished, the others would run around and play while Ina collected the flowers and grasses to take home and press in a book, carefully recording the names underneath: forget-me-nots, marsh marigolds, raggy willies, curly dodies, white and red clover. Nature was her main interest. She wasn't clever at school, Mr Carnegie had told her mother; there was no chance of her ever going to the institute for more learning once she reached fourteen. She remembered Dolina looking at her and there he was again. Angus. Angus would've been clever, that's what Dolina's eyes said when they looked at her; Angus would've gone to the institute, then on to university in Aberdeen or Glasgow. But Ina wasn't Angus; Ina wasn't clever.

Not that it mattered: soon after that Dolina had fallen and broken her leg and, as there was no money for medical attention, the leg hadn't set properly. The others were all married or working and the family couldn't afford to lose a wage, so Ina stopped what schooling she had been getting at the age of thirteen to help her mother keep house. Education for lassies mainly consisted of 'housewifery' anyway, the inference being that, unless they were clever, they weren't fit for

5

anything more than marrying, having a family and being tied to the kitchen for the rest of their lives. Not being clever, Ina was no exception. Housewifery wasn't what she wanted to do, but on the other hand school just wasn't her thing either, as they said nowadays, so better to be at home where she was needed than at school.

In the summer school started at 9 a.m. and finished at 4 p.m., but in winter the bairns were let out at 2 p.m., because it was growing dark in Shetland by then. She hated the regimentation of it; the bairns were made to march about like soldiers in two lines, marched out across a field and made to do exercises, touching their toes, stretching. Anyone who ran was severely belted by the headmaster, ever skulking in the wings for the opportunity. Mr Carnegie was a mean little man who seemed to wait with bated breath for the chance to use the four-pronged leather tawse, a man who looked down on the Shetland people and their bairns. They weren't allowed to speak their own dialect, there was the tawse for that too. 'Normal people don't say "tattie",' he would intone. 'We say "potato",' leaving the bairns in no doubt that Mr Carnegie regarded himself as one of the normal people.

He lived in the schoolhouse, separated from the school itself by a high wall, with his wife, son and daughter. The girl, Isobel, was the same age as Ina, but wasn't allowed to play with the local bairns, though sometimes she would sneak out if they peered over the wall, encouraging her with hooked fingers. Isobel would look around with furtive glances for the first sight of her father, knowing that she too would get the tawse if he found out, which he sometimes did. Ina could see her now, all these years later, a pretty girl with a pink face, brown eyes and the most beautiful golden ringlets, staring out from behind the window, wondering if she dared take the risk and escape her prison. She did eventually, and in circumstances that would appal her father so much that he would leave Shetland and never come back. Now what was the boy, her brother's name? No, it had gone. No matter. And though it was true that Ina had never been clever at school, she could name every flower that grew on the land and draw detailed pictures of them in bloom, and she could sketch every star and their positions in the sky. But that didn't count as clever.

Ina was the youngest of eight bairns, four girls and four boys, counting Angus, the one between her and Danny; he had been stillborn a year to the day before she had drawn her first breath in the first decade of the twentieth century. Later in life she would wonder if the loss of the brother she had never known was the reason, or part of the reason, why she had been such a tomboy. Maybe it had been down to more than just spending her time with Danny; perhaps she had in some way been trying to make up to her parents for their dead son. They had called her Angusina in his honour, but it had always made Ina feel second-hand, as though the birth of a fifth son would have been infinitely more welcome than a fourth daughter; but they had had to make the best of what they got, and that had been Ina. Certainly those who had known her mother before the loss of the boy said that Dolina Polson had never been the same afterwards. Not even the birth of the small but healthy Angusina had made up for that, and neither could Danny, the healthy son born the year before Angus.

Losing a bairn did that to some women, of course, and even with seven healthy bairns, Dolina never truly got over the loss of her fourth son. She would visit the bairn's grave in the small local cemetery at least weekly, carrying a bunch of wild flowers and returning tearful, and all through her childhood Ina remembered her mother looking at bairns who had been born at the same time as her dead son and saying wistfully, 'Our Angus would be that age now,' or, 'Angus would be doing this or that now.' This led to the stillborn boy still existing in some parallel universe inside Ina's head as well as her mother's, so that Ina had a clear image of him through ages he did not inhabit, an image based on what her

7

other brothers looked like and her belief that he would have resembled their mother.

In her imagination he would smile silently and with a slight self-consciousness at her from a distance, this growing, dead boy, as though he agreed with Ina that the situation was unfair. He too knew he could never fall from his mother's grace, because he hadn't lived and so would never commit the normal transgressions of childhood that would have annoyed his mother or made her angry, and so he would remain forever perfect. Likewise Angus would never visit upon Ina the usual brotherly mischiefs and casual unkindnesses, so in her imagination he was a nice boy who felt sorry for her and wished he could help. This made her grow up resenting not being as good as him in any way, but without resenting Angus, and feeling slightly guilty that she had lived and he had not, as though she were somehow not just inhabiting his name, but also his life.

It was a cruel twist of fate that Ina had been born on what would have been Angus's first birthday, and every birthday for as long as she could remember had been a sad day, marked by her mother's tears, a day when she felt her guilt at usurping her brother even more keenly. No one celebrated birthdays in those days, there wasn't even as much as a card, but Ina's was marked in the Polson household as the day Dolina's son had died. Even when she started school she didn't get this huge step all to herself, with Dolina remarking wistfully that Angus would have been at school for a year by now and would probably be reading by himself. Each time her mother said something like this Ina would feel bad, as though nothing and no one, especially not her, could ever make up for living instead of him, and in her head Angus would look at her, smile shyly and shrug his shoulders, as if telling her that he knew how she felt, but there was nothing he could do. Perhaps, too, that feeling of being second best was why Ina was always on the defensive, always ready to take on all comers, to stand up for herself – to stand alone if need be. Danny suffered, too, for not being Angus. Though they never discussed it, Ina knew that was what had forged the strong bond between them, the one born the year before and the other born the year after Angus, the ones who missed out on Dolina's love because they were there and he wasn't.

Not that she was unloved by her father. If anything she was Magnus's favourite, and he always made a special effort with her out of pity, she thought, because Dolina couldn't. He never said this, of course, but Ina knew, and instead of feeling better she felt worse. It was almost as though he had unwittingly acknowledged that Dolina had reason for withholding affection from her daughter and he felt sorry for her. So it was always there, the shadow of the boy called Angus, barring her way to her mother in particular, casting a shadow over her father's affection. She wished she had been given her own name as well as her own birthday, whatever that name would have been, though she never voiced that thought. Certainly there were no more Polson bairns, and delving deep into her memories and thoughts all those years later she would wonder if that was because Dolina's grief had barred the bedroom to her husband as surely as her heart had been barred her two youngest bairns.

Sometimes she wondered if she had got it all wrong, if in fact the entire family had been affected by the loss of Angus, when Ina had thought it had hurt only her and Danny. She began to think this many years later when she was a mother herself and was trying to make sense of her own daughter, Margo, and how she had turned out. But the more questions you thought you'd answered, the more there seemed to be. Just as you thought you had the thing sorted, when you'd chased it to its source, you would find another puzzle waiting there patiently for you, like a fankled skein of wool with so many twists and turns that it could never be undone and you had to abandon it or it would drive you mad. Sometimes you just had to switch off your head and leave it, especially now that her head was so much older and, she admitted it, more easily confused. Anyway, it was just possible, she supposed, that she had tried to make up to her parents, her mother especially, for their lost boy, by sometimes behaving more like Angus might have than Angusina. It gave her a sense, too, of wanting things to be different, or to be somewhere else, in another life where she wasn't faced daily with this undeclared contest she could never win. She would daydream about what it would be like in a place where Angus had never existed, and maybe that was why she looked beyond her allotted horizons. That and the stars, of course, existing somewhere far away, nightly opening up the promise of distance and travel. There was a universe, she slowly realised, beyond where she lived.

Ina, like the other Polsons and most of the other islanders, had reddish fair-hair, pale skin and grey eyes – Viking colouring – and they were determinedly proud that they were more Scandinavian than Scottish. Indeed to call a Shetlander 'Scotch' was the deepest insult imaginable, as mainland Scots were acknowledged to be the scum of the earth. The Shetlands had been given to Scotland as a royal marriage dowry but that didn't mean the Shetlanders were Scottish. As Magnus Polson said, 'If a cat has kittens in a fish box, you don't call them kippers'. Not only did the Scotch look and behave differently, but they spoke oddly, too, though if you listened hard you could make out some of the things they said – not that you would ever admit that, of course.

Native Shetlanders had once spoken a Scandinavian language called Norn, but that had died out after the Reformation when bibles began to be written in English, and it was finally seen off by the Union of the Crowns and the influx of lowland Scots who appeared on the islands. For as long as anyone living could remember, Shetland had its own part-Scandinavian, part-Scottish version of English, though the advent of schooling governed from mainland Scotland had brought with it attempts to make the local bairns ashamed of their own language. That the same verbal cleansing had been visited on every bairn in every area of Scotland wasn't known to the Shetlanders; even if they had known, it would have meant nothing to them. It was none of their business what was happening in a foreign land, and that's what Scotland was to every Shetland mind. People with names beginning with Mac or Mc were 'Scotch', even if their families had been in Shetland for generations, and they were always slightly suspect; so too were those who had come north to find work in the burgeoning fishing industry, who ate creatures like crabs, limpets and mussels; things the native islanders regarded as beneath them and fit only for baiting nets.

In the winter Magnus would take his family to gather whelks, walking miles along the beach at low tide, turning over stones in the pools. If they were lucky they might have the use of a boat, but mostly Magnus would carry sacks of whelks over the hills on his back. Then they'd be weighed in pecks and bought by the local shops for vouchers that could be redeemed for groceries or provisions. No decent Shetlander would ever eat such things, but the 'Scotch' did, so that should tell anybody what they were like. They were all in the fishing and lived 'ootby the Burgh', in Burgh Road on the outskirts of Lerwick, along with those regarded as 'mixed breed', who had 'Scotch' as well as Shetland blood, and Magnus Polson being a fisherman, though a full-blooded Shetland fisherman, his family still lived among them, even if they didn't trust or like them. The people who lived 'ootby the Burgh' were regarded by those who lived 'inby the Burgh' as rough and ready, so fights between the bairns at school were common-place, in which the 'inby' bairns called the 'ootby' bairns names and received a hiding in reply. Rough and ready they were, as proudly as they were Viking.

Almost everything in the diet of those days was salted. Magnus, Danny and Ina would catch fish with a hook on a piece of string at the South Mouth of Lerwick Harbour and carry them home in a basket, to be gutted, split and soaked in a tub of brine for forty-eight hours before being laid out on planks of wood in the sun and wind to dry. Then, to make them edible, they had to be soaked in water overnight and boiled the next day, but there was no alternative in those days before fridges and freezers. The Polson bairns, however, ate better than many others, because their mother came from farming stock and her family and friends would come visiting with food to sell or barter. If Dolina had no money she exchanged salted whitefish or herring for potatoes, butter, eggs and buttermilk, so with meals of salt fish or salt mutton her family had potatoes with their skins on and melted butter poured on top.

As a change from salt fish they would sometimes get three-pence of scrap meat from the butcher, which would make enough stew to last two days; or they would eat salt mutton, if they had been able to afford a half-crown for a small lamb the previous October, or five shillings for a bigger one. Even the smallest bairn in Shetland knew how to feel a lamb to judge how much flesh was on its bones. Between October and Christmas the lamb was fattened up, then taken to the slaughter house to be killed and dressed. As you took it in the lamb was given a number, and two days later you went back with a basket, quoted the number and were given the butchered lamb. They would have a pot roast and some chops while the meat was fresh, and salt the rest for later, soaking it in brine for twenty-four hours then hanging it out to dry.

Nothing was wasted: you even got the lamb's skin so that you could take it to the Sutherland Wool Mill in Brora, where the fleece would be spun into brown, black, white or fawn wool for knitting. Everyone knitted in Shetland, bairns learned as soon they could pick up the wires, or needles, playing their part in keeping the family alive. In those days when there were no state handouts or benefits, every penny counted, even if they never actually saw one. Mittens, socks and intricately patterned Fair Isle jumpers were exchanged by the local shops for the inevitable vouchers: money only changed hands when wages earned by the family went to pay for goods bought on credit during the week, and often there wasn't enough to pay more than part of that.

It was a poor life, she supposed, but they didn't know any other; what the Polsons had was no different from all the other families around them. Knitting wasn't only part of daily life, it was part of their survival from one week to the next. 'Makkin,' it was called, and even if you went out to see a friend of an evening, your mother would shout, 'See and take your makkin with you.' Everyone who could afford it had a sheath, or leather belt, to support the three or four long needles needed to knit a big Fair Isle jersey, and those who couldn't improvised. They would gather the feathers of a skorie, a young gull, tie the stems up tightly in a bunch, secure the bunch around the waist with string and stick the needles in the stems. The lassies would gather in one another's houses, telling tales, gossiping about the things young lassies always gossip about, telling jokes, and all the time there would be the click-click of the needles as they laughed and teased each other about who had their eye on which laddie.

Another good time for 'makkin' was on a Sunday. Shetland was solidly Protestant in those days, and Sunday was regarded strictly as a day of rest, except for three visits to church in their Sunday best. Ina hadn't minded the summer services at the Mission for Fishermen at four o'clock every Sunday, because she loved music and the fishermen were fine singers, but there were also visits to be paid to the kirk, the Congregational or the Baptist or one of the others, and her mind was never really on it. You could listen to music on the wireless on a Sunday and you could knit, but beyond that there was nothing to do but long for Monday morning. On Monday her father would either be off to sea or the factory in Bressay, and their hours of star-gazing together would be over till he came home again. Often in her life she had the feeling that somehow she could never entirely win, she mused;

13

maybe it was punishment for resenting those endless visits to the kirk on all those Sundays.

Every morning her father was at home he would lay the fire using wood gathered from the shore or from the docks and dried. On top of that he would put coal, if the family had been able to afford a half-hundredweight from Hay's coal dump. Sometimes they would be lucky and find free lumps that had come from the huge coal hulks that arrived to deliver fuel for the steam drifters, but usually they burned peat cut from Free Hill, where anyone could have what they needed at no charge; all they had to do was cut it and carry it home. Ina and Danny were the usual volunteers to go with Magnus. They were always trying for Dolina's attention, she supposed – or she was, at any rate. She and Danny never discussed it, so Ina didn't know what he was thinking. They carried the peats home in a kilshie, a basket. Sometimes her back was red raw with the kilshie scraping her skin, but she never said anything. Attention wasn't the same if you had to draw it to yourself, she always thought.

Unlike the rest of the family, Dolina Polson was dark-haired and blue-eyed. In Ina's mind her mother's looks became part of her unattainable quality. When she was very young and had no understanding of how losing a bairn could affect a woman on a very basic, almost primeval level, she had assumed that part of the reason her mother mourned Angus so deeply must have been because he resembled his mother rather than the rest of the family, as indeed he did in the picture she carried of him in her own mind. She had found a shard of a mirror once on the shore and kept it under her bed, taking it out when no one was about and staring into it longingly, hoping that one day her eyes or her hair might change colour. If only she had dark hair, she reasoned, if her eyes were blue, maybe Dolina would notice her more and think of Angus less. There was never anything to suggest that this might be the case, but she remembered trying throughout her childhood to come up with the right combination to unlock the secret entrance to Dolina's closed heart, and that one was as good, or as bad, as any.

Years later she wondered whether that was why Danny had been such a good boy, too. She didn't think of it till her role as wife and mother had proved obsolete and she'd taken to reading books. Danny was a kind lad who would do anything for anyone, and maybe, she thought, his unfailing kindnesses had been his attempts to earn his mother's approval. There was that time one of his school pals had fallen out with his parents and taken to living in an old boat lying at the docks. It was Danny who had taken Davie coats to sleep under, and even his own dinner, as he tried to persuade the boy to go home and make it up with his parents. Danny was always helping people; he was the one who tried to settle fights in the playground, so that the other bairns came to rely on his negotiating skills, and whenever there was a dispute the cry would go up, 'Where's Danny Polson?' Funny when you thought about what lay ahead.

With her father, Magnus, attention and affection came without his bairns having to earn it. He always had time for his youngest two, telling them tales of how his family had become fishermen when, like many others, they been turned out of their crofts during the Highland Clearances, finding themselves of less value to the lairds than sheep. Many had gone abroad – to Canada, Australia and New Zealand – taken away in ships on voyages lasting many weeks. Only half would survive. Some went of their own accord, if having no choice could be described as their own accord, while others, regardless of age and health, were violently forced from their homes and put on the big ships, clutching what little they could salvage and watching their homes burn as they left the land their families had worked for generations.

Ina's great-grandfather and two of his brothers had decided to stay, however, their families living on the shoreline as the menfolk took to the sea to feed them. Many did that, men more suited to the land than the ocean, and often they didn't come home again. There were no trees on Shetland, so wood had to be imported from Holland to make open-decked boats, clinker-built with overlapping planks, sitting low in the water and pointed at both ends, like Viking ships. They were called 'sixerns', because they had a crew of six men rowing, but as these first fishermen became more experienced, the size of the boats increased. It made sense: the bigger the boat, the more nets could be carried, and the more nets, the heavier the catch. Nets were lowered into the water and kept afloat by ropes with corks dotted along their length, and the larger nets by tarred floats, or buoys, made from the inflated bladders of pigs or bullocks, or the skins of sheep or dogs; on the East Coast dogs were specially bred so that they could be converted into floats.

Disasters were common, and no family Ina knew as she grew up was left untouched. There was the great storm of 1832, when seventeen sixerns and 105 men had been lost, and another in 1881, claiming ten sixerns and 58 men, including her Polson grandfather and three of her uncles; death at sea was part of life in Shetland, as it was for every fishing community. And in those early days men were accosted by Royal Navy ships and press-ganged, taken from their little boats at sea, or while they were ashore in some port away from home. Sometimes they would arrive home many years later, but having dreamt of returning home since the day they had been taken, once ashore they found their experiences had changed them and they couldn't settle with the families they had yearned for. Others were never heard of or from again, because most died of their injuries during the attack, from the conditions and treatment aboard the big ships, or in battles that had nothing to do with them.

One of her great-grandfather's brothers, Andro, had been left for dead when the Navy had taken the other five men from their sixern. The big ship with the full sails had happened

16

upon them while they were fishing and had sent a smaller boat out, ordering the Shetlanders 'in the King's name' to come aboard. It was a legitimate way of recruitment, and fishermen could buy permits exempting them from the activities of press-gangs, but few bothered, firstly because the Navy didn't always take any notice of such niceties, and secondly because, even if a permit might have protected them from being dragged off, there was little money for such things. The Shetlanders on Andro's boat fought back – though there was little they could do against guns and cutlasses. Meanwhile the Navy men, thinking they had killed Andro, and therefore having no use for him, left him lying in the boat. He was later found by another sixern from Shetland, surviving to see his home more by luck than anything else, and even nearer to death than when the Navy men had left him.

'He was covered in blood, his own as well as his lost shipmates', and barely conscious,' Magnus would tell his bairns, 'and once he had recovered he found he had a great fear of going to sea in a small boat again. So he borrowed what money was in the family and went to Canada, to a place he had heard of from earlier emigrants: Nova Scotia, "the Land of Trees". He never came back to Shetland.'

'And did he send word that he was well, Da?' Ina asked at this juncture, as she always did.

'He did, he did,' Magnus replied quietly. 'He had a good life out there, and because of him we have family there now.'

Ina and Danny would lie on their backs alongside their father, staring up to the sky, lost in the world above and the one that Magnus had created in their minds.

'There are so many trees in Nova Scotia,' Magnus would tell them, 'that you can barely walk through them, so they say, and when you look up you can't see the sky like we can now, only the high branches of these big trees all crowded together, and it's so dark you can't see a foot in front of you.'

He shook his head. In treeless Shetland the concept of a forest was hard to imagine. 'Just think on that, now,' he mused, chewing on a grass stem. 'And Uncle Andro always said if any of us ever wanted to join him in Canada he would make them welcome. Even if the people he lived among were mainly Scotch people, he said, they were different when they were away from home, better somehow, though each kept to their own. He has a debt of gratitude to the whole family who helped him escape there by giving them what money they could,' Magnus would nod solemnly. 'And though he's long dead now, his family know this, and would honour it, too, because that's the kind of people the Polsons are. You could turn up at their doors and say you were a Polson from Lerwick and without asking a question of you they would take you into their homes and do everything they could for you.'

Danny liked the family stories best. Ina had always known that he wasn't quite as keen on the stars as she was, but he stayed for the rest of Magnus's performance just to be near him. After exhausting family history for the time being, Magnus would chew on his grass stem for a few silent moments, gaze once more up to the sky and say, 'You see that star up there, the one at the tip of Ursa Minor, the one they call the Little Bear?'

The bairns followed the pointed stem of grass.

'Follow a trail in the sky from the two stars to the right of Ursa Major, the Great Bear, to the one on the right of Ursa Minor. It's called lots of names,' he continued, 'the Pole Star, the North Star, Polaris, and when the Egyptians were building the pyramids they called it Thuban. Just think of that, the pharaohs of Egypt looked at that star all those years ago, just as we are doing now, and there will be a fisherman somewhere out at sea at this moment looking at it or for it, because as long as you can see the North Star you can plot exactly where you are.' The three stared heavenwards and shook their heads in wonderment.

'And,' Magnus said, 'even though we're watching it together now, it might be dead. Imagine that now, it might not exist at all, even though we can see it sparkling away for us. It's so far away from Earth that the light takes a long, long time to get to us here. We might now be seeing it as it was when it was still there. Isn't that strange, now?'

Ida would stare at the star. 'How far away is it, then?'

'Well, I can't say exactly, Ida,' Magnus would reply. 'Millions of miles, certainly. You see the moon up there yonder? It's 230,000 miles away from us, so you can just imagine how far away the stars are.'

Two hundred and thirty thousand miles. It was too vast a distance to contemplate, especially when she found the 211 miles to Aberdeen more than she could cope with, so the moon must be nearly as far away, Ida would muse, as Uncle Andro's family in the Land of Trees.

'And did you know,' Magnus would continue, 'that Jupiter weighs more than all the planets put together, including the Earth?'

The bairns would shake their heads again in a show of united wonder. They did know, of course, because Magnus's facts about the planets were frequently discussed.

'And that Saturn is so light that, if you put it in water, it would float?'

The three would shake their heads in yet more wonderment, then Magnus would test them on their knowledge.

'Where is the Earth in relation to the Sun?' he would ask.

'The Earth,' Ina would say, 'is third from the Sun, Da.'

Magnus would nod contentedly.

'And what's the order of the planets?'

'The Sun, Mercury, Venus, Earth, Mars, Jupiter, Saturn, Uranus and Neptune,' Ina would repeat from memory, exchanging a secret giggly look with Danny when she came to 'Uranus', because their father didn't approve of nonsense where learning was concerned. No one knew about tiny Pluto in those days, and oh, Magnus's excitement when it was discovered in 1930. Even if he couldn't see it, it was as if he had found the answer to all the questions in the universe, and the knowledge that it was there pleased him every bit as much as his youngest daughter's shared interest in the stars. That year, 1930, was also the year that Magnus had lost a son.

In those early days of the fishing when her great-grandfather had started out, open boats meant that the fishermen lived and worked exposed to wind, rain and hail, always liable to be swamped by the waves. Gradually, as they learned more about the sea and their trade, part-decked and full-decked boats evolved, and different kinds of boats entirely appeared, with nets designed to go after specific catches. There were some fishermen, like one of Ina's brothers, who went further afield to work as sealers and whalers, catching what was known as 'sea pork'. They came back with tales of the shrill, plaintive cries of the whales as they were 'driven like a flock of sheep to shallow water on a sandy shore', and described how 'the boats push in, stabbing and wounding in all directions', as the creatures finally died 'in water dyed red with their blood.'

Fishermen in other areas went after the poor man's food – oysters, or crabs, lobsters, clams, or salmon – but Magnus Polson went after white fish, which meant he had to find work during the summer months when there were none to be caught. Then he worked in a factory on the tiny island of Bressay, outside Lerwick Harbour, coming home at week-ends, and those were his times with Danny and Ina and the stars. The factory produced fertiliser, and when the boats came in loaded with herring, the ones at the bottom would be crushed and inedible, so these were sold to the factory for processing, along with other fish that wasn't good quality. The resulting smell was terrible, so terrible that Magnus Polson wasn't allowed into his home when he arrived on a Friday evening. The family would make him stand outside to strip off his working clothes so that they could be soaked in the washing tub to be ready for work again on Monday morning. Ina could almost smell it now, all these long years later, picturing Magnus pretending to forget and trying to come indoors as she and her brothers and sisters pushed him back out, holding their noses, giggling and shouting, 'Stand outside! Get your clothes off!'

He had been a nice man, her father; he had always made her laugh. That was probably why she had always had a fondness for men who could make her laugh. They said women married men like their fathers; maybe that had been her mistake – if she had made a mistake with Aeneas, and she wasn't saying she had. Ina smiled to herself. The truth was that the man she had married had been more like her mother, though she hadn't realised it at the time. Was that what the gypsy woman in Yarmouth had meant all those years ago, she wondered? 'Ach, away with you, old woman!' she chided herself. 'Next you'll be believing in fairies!' From the doorway behind her fireside armchair she sensed her daughter, Margo, listening as she worked about the kitchen and watching her with Dolina Polson's eyes. 'She'll be saying the old one's finally losing her marbles,' Ina thought, and hoped she hadn't actually said it aloud.

2

Ina had loved all the seasons on Shetland. In summertime it never quite got dark, and even in those days without street lights it was possible to walk about with no difficulty at midnight. 'Simmer dim', that special high summer light was called, and even once the Sun had dipped below the horizon in the middle of the night it still didn't get dark. Instead a lilac twilight bathed the islands before dawn sunlight returned, bringing a new day. But perhaps Ina loved winter most of all, with the snow sparkling on the frosty roads and almost rivalling the stars in the sky for beauty. She was spellbound watching the mirry-dancers, the bright lights that she'd heard other people call the Northern Lights or Aurora Borealis, and in the clear, quiet air you could even hear the red flames swish-swishing across the sky.

The snow was so deep and stayed on the ground so long that they were regularly snowed-in for weeks at a time, with the entire population on the big sledges every family had, the metal runners polished to make them go faster, weaving in and out of the horses and carts till three in the morning sometimes. They would find the biggest hill and push off, knowing that they couldn't stop till they reached the end or met some obstacle. Once her brother, Danny, had found a horse in the way and just closed his eyes, so that he was the only one who didn't see himself going straight between the animal's front and back legs. And there was a really big hill three miles long that everyone had to try, though the long hike up pulling a sledge, even one with very highly polished runners, could exhaust you before you got to the top. Then would come the exhilaration of the wild, exciting descent that somehow seemed to pass in seconds, followed by that long, long climb back up again.

These days everything was shop-bought, even sledges, though there were few enough of even the modern, plastic variety about. It had to be skis and snowboards for this generation. Not that you saw much snow in Acarsaid, where she lived now, but you saw folk on the TV and wondered what pleasure they got from things they hadn't made themselves. Look what they'd done to Up Helly Aa. She'd seen a news programme about it from Shetland last January and she could hardly believe it: it was all glitter and polish these days. Though TV was one invention she did approve of. Now that her legs no longer worked properly and her memory sometimes played tricks, too, the TV had opened up the worlds that she had never quite managed to visit. During the first moon landing she had sat in her chair, wrapped in a quilt, and watched Neil Armstrong take his gigantic step for mankind and envied him so much it hurt. There were lots of astronomy programmes to see, and in those nights when she didn't sleep as long or as deeply as she had when she was younger, she had discovered a whole new universe in programmes for the Open University, without dancing, singing fools appearing just as it got interesting. She could see up close the familiar constellations her father had taught her all those years ago, and she'd find her eyes tearing up, hearing his voice instead of Patrick Moore's, pointing out supernovas and meteor showers. And now here she was, tears starting again just thinking about him; she would have to stop or her daughter, Margo, would tell the doctor or the grandbairns, with that Dolina shake of her head, that she'd been crying over nothing again.

Where was she? Up Helly Aa, that was it. It too came ready-made these days. When Ina had been a bairn it had been a different kind of a thing altogether, as different from what they had now as chalk and cheese. Up Helly Aa was a

23

Norse festival, a homage to their Viking ancestors, held on the last Tuesday in January to brighten the depths of winter. All the men would dress up in fancy dress – she remembered seeing one who'd made himself look like a box of Scott's Porridge Oats once; she thought of him every time she saw an advert for them on the TV and she'd laugh. Up Helly Aa was a men's only affair and they'd organise themselves into about twenty squads of twelve or fourteen men and march through the town with flaming torches till they came to the Lochside, where a specially built replica of a Viking longboat had earlier been towed. The men would sing 'The Norseman's Home', and then all the torches would be thrown into the air to land on the boat, like streams of fire in the dusk, until it had been consumed by the flames. After that the squads of guizers would make their way through the town, their own fiddle and accordion players accompanying them all through the night, stopping at all the halls and big houses on the way so that everyone could have a dance. The women, though, had to pay for tickets; nowhere was big on female equality in those days, and Shetland was no exception.

The small boys of Lerwick had their own version of Up Helly Aa earlier in the day, they even had their own longboat to burn, but she had seen it on TV recently and the guizers no longer dressed up like cereal packets, they all wore identical Viking outfits with shiny breastplates and horned helmets. They were like theatrical costumes; the whole thing had become a well-organised spectacle for tourists. Well, tourism was big business these days, she knew that, but though the fishing had all but gone, the place was awash with oil money, so what need did they have to change things that had existed for generations and once meant something, just to attract outsiders? She no longer lived there – hadn't even been back since the 1950s – but she still felt they had lost something important when they moved Up Helly Aa upmarket.

It was the same with everything these days. Easter: there

was another case in point. Some bairns in her day boiled eggs and painted them, but the Polsons boiled theirs with a piece of red paper to dye them, then they'd roll them down a hill. The egg that rolled the furthest won, but there was no prize – they'd eat them with bread and butter. There were no chocolate eggs in those days, either; not that she wasn't partial to a bit of chocolate, but they seemed to get bigger and more elaborate every year. Did anyone dye or paint their own eggs these days?, she wondered, and laughed at the thought of how a modern bairn might react if they were handed a hen's egg and expected to be content with that. Birthdays were the same: the presents and cards got more ornate and expensive all the time. When she was young no one celebrated birthdays at all, and at Christmas and New Year they danced in Market Square; that was it. At Hallowe'en nowadays bairns no longer knew what it was to dress up and do a turn. If they celebrated it at all their outfits came straight from a shop, bought ready-sized and complete.

Everything was ready-made these days, Ina thought. She tried to remember when she had last seen a woman knitting. There was a time when every female knitted as soon as she could hold a pair of needles, but these days handknitting seemed to be a reminder of a poorer age and was therefore shunned. They always said they hadn't time, or they had never learned, but Ina always suspected that the real reason was that no one wanted to be reminded of where they had come from. Poverty was a stigma, and making your own or your bairns' clothes was seen as something only the poor did, because they couldn't afford anything 'better'. By 'better' they meant shop-bought tat, Ina thought; inferior machine-knitted rubbish from the sweatshops of the Third World where people were indeed still trapped in poverty. She had seen programmes about it on TV, and would shout at the screen as she watched, much to the amusement of Margo and the others, but that was their ignorance, not hers, she had decided. 'Look at the old one,' they would say indulgently, 'still a firebrand!' as though she was some kind of dinosaur, and she would wonder to herself how this could have happened, how she could have raised a family so unaware of what was going on around them. They were wrong anyway, Ina Polson was no dinosaur, she just thought more than most of them were prepared to; thinking for yourself wasn't encouraged in today's world. It was a strange world to be sure, one where she didn't belong any longer. She was glad she wasn't long for it.

Ina had gone to the fishing on the autumn of her fifteenth year. Lowestoft it was, on the southeast of England, when herring shoals were reaching Smith's Knoll off the East Anglian Coast. The shoals started their long, slow migration in the North, with the Shetland waters fished in March–April, so there was a tradition of herring lassies being Scottish because they were on hand at the start of the season. From there the lassies followed the boats that followed the herring, from Shetland to Wick then on to Fraserburgh, Peterhead, South Shields, Scarborough, Great Yarmouth and Lowestoft. The heaviest and best catches were landed there because the herring were at their peak, fat with milt and roe.

Ina had been more restless than usual that autumn, after her brother, Danny, her closest companion since the day she was born, had joined the Merchant Marine the year before. She missed him and envied him in equal measure. There had been quite a stushie before he left. It had happened on Christmas Eve and Isobel Carnegie, the headmaster's daughter, had managed to evade her father and join the others dancing in Market Square. Ina noticed her dancing with Danny, but she was never quick on the uptake about romances; unlike other lassies of her age, she somehow didn't seem to think in that way. It was only later she understood that Isobel had been sneaking out to meet Danny for some time. Danny hadn't mentioned it to Ina, but then Danny wouldn't, she knew that, it was how he was too, and though both he and Isobel were in their teens, her father still wanted her to have nothing to do with the inferior Shetlanders who had provided him with the best living in the area for years.

That Christmas Eve Danny and Isobel had decided to brave Mr Carnegie, but when Danny asked for permission to court his daughter the headmaster erupted with a fury not even those who determinedly called potatoes 'tatties' had ever seen. Danny was thrown out with some roughness, and Isobel was banished to her bedroom for what seemed likely to be the rest of her life, and not long after that Danny departed for a life on the seven seas. Ina was less concerned about his broken heart or Isobel's and more about the injustices of life. Males could travel the globe, but not females, and the unfairness of that ate at her as she worked about the house with Dolina.

Her chance came like a ray of sunshine on a stormy day, that was how she remembered it: one moment dark and forbidding, the next golden and bright. All of the family were involved in the fishing trade in some way or other. Sandy, her older brother, was a cooper, making barrels for the salt and the fish, and for years he had travelled south, following the fleet every season. But now that he had married, he and his new wife wanted to settle at home. His wife was one of the gutters on their sister Ella's crew, which left Ella, the packer and effectively the boss, short of a worker. Instantly Ina was determined to fill the vacancy. Ella was quite a lot older than Ina; in her early twenties and already married to a crofter. It wasn't unusual for women to leave their menfolk behind to carry on working poor crofts while the women made the money that could mean family survival. There was something more with Ella, though; everyone knew that. It was never put into words, or certainly not words ever spoken in Ina's hearing, but there was a tacit understanding that Ella was more than happy to leave Ronnie at home for the herring months.

The man from Bloomfield's, a curer based in Yarmouth, arrived in Shetland every year to recruit replacements for those who had gone elsewhere and, despite Dolina's misgivings, Ina signed the contract and gleefully accepted five shillings in return. She had been doing housework for two solid years and anyone could have told you that Ina Polson was no homebody, that all her life she had had her eyes firmly fixed on those faraway stars and brighter horizons. The truth was that she would've paid the agent five shillings to take her, if she'd had it, that was; never in her entire life had she had even one shilling to call her own, in that she was no different from any other lassie of her era. Knowing this, Bloomfields paid for her 'oilies', the oilskin skirts and rubber boots that were the uniform of every herring lassie, her mother couldn't use lack of money as an excuse to stop Ina from leaving home because there would be no financial outlay. The firm would also pay for her kist, or trunk, containing her clothes, working and best, as well as the ever-present 'makkin', her knitting. It would take twelve hours by boat from Lerwick to Aberdeen, then another ten or twelve hours to Yarmouth by train, with 'Reserved for Bloomfields' on the carriage window – every curer had their own coaches – followed by more long hours on a milk train to Lowestoft. Once there, she knew, she and the other lassies would have somewhere to stay, in a bothy or a lodging house, but she was in the experienced hands of the other lassies who had followed the herring for years and years before she joined them and if all else failed the Red Cross, the Church of Scotland and the Mission to Fisherfolk were always on hand.

When Ina arrived on that first morning after the long, weary journey, she was surprised to see that there were women of seventy and more still following the herring, mostly from the Western Isles, where Gaelic was the first language, the language from Ireland that hadn't reached Shetland and would probably have been run out of town if it had. The others were by then old hands and had everything well organised, even down to the purchase of a portable gramophone, a pricey item in those times, and when they had to stop at a station for a couple of hours for a connecting train, the gramophone was set up and the lassies danced with the porters on the platform. Someone had managed to lay hands on a songsheet of some current favourite for a couple of pennies, and the lassies would sing as they waited; there was always a lot of singing. At the stations a woman came along with a trolley selling sandwiches and tea, but to cut costs they brought their own sandwiches from home and just bought her tea – tuppence it cost, tuppence a cup. The trains were filthy, though, if you banged on the seat dust flew up in clouds, and they were so slow that you could lean out of the window and carry on a conversation with people working in the fields as the steam engine painfully pulled its clanking carriages along the track.

Every season they stayed in lodgings, three or six to a room. They slept three to a bed and used their kists to sit on because there was no space for chairs. For washing there was a ewer and a basin, and the landlady lifted all her carpets off the floor before they came, putting down old mats instead, keeping her carpets for the summer visitors, who did not routinely drop fish scales on them. Before the fishing started in Lerwick each spring, the lassies would work on the big stock boats that arrived with barrels of salt for the curers whose stations were all around the harbour. Every curer had a wooden stage jutting out into the harbour where the fish would be landed, and the stock boats would go from one to another first, delivering their orders. As the stevedores brought them out of the hold the lassies would roll them up to the station using putters, implements like shovels, only with a point at the end, where the coopers waited to stack them up three or four deep, ready for use once the herring arrived. When Ina started working on the stock boats in Lerwick before leaving for Lowestoft that first year, they were paid fourpence per barrel, so they waited till the stock boats arrived next time and went on strike. The bosses called them Communists and Bolsheviks, every bad name under the sun, but they had to pay up another tuppence a barrel. It was one of her proudest moments; it made her feel that she had some power, and it made her laugh, too, to see the bosses so enraged and so beaten by a bunch of lassies.

There was no time for training and Ina found herself thrown straight in to work that first morning. Watching the speed of the lassies she was instantly frozen with fear – she would never be able to work at that rate – and felt like catching the next train back to the safety of home. Then she thought again: the *boredom* of home, and just got stuck in. The trouble was, she thought helplessly, that everything was happening at once and so quickly that it was hard to pick up one part of the job because another was taking place while you were still trying to absorb the first part. She watched the drifters deliver fish in baskets to the edge of Bloomfields' quay, where they were dumped into a long, sloping, communal farlin, or trough.

As she worked, Edie, the other gutter, gave her a running commentary. 'First you have to rouse them, Ina,' she said, turning the fish in salt, 'then you gut them.'

Ina watched Edie's hands move but it was so fast that she couldn't see what she was actually doing. She had learned to gut fish when she was a child, everyone in her community did, but Edie's hands were no more than a blur so Ina couldn't see the technique she would have to learn.

'See?' Edie asked.

Ina was horrified, suddenly realising that Edie had deliberately gone slowly with her demonstration and she had still missed it. Looking up at her, Edie laughed out loud, then the other lassies round about looked up, hands still flying, and the laughter spread through the yard like a breeze. Ina blushed red with embarrassment, but she knew they were laughing because they all knew how she was feeling, they had all once been in the same position.

'Look,' Edie smiled, going as slowly as she could, 'you just

30

put your knife in at the throat there.' She stopped to pick up a fish and position it in Ina's hands, which made her feel even more of a fool. 'Then you nick it under the throat – no! Not from throat to belly!' Once again laugher rang out. 'Just a wee nick, that's it, and pull the guts and gills out through that, then you throw the fish into the tub.'

Ina nodded and picked up another fish.

'You'll learn to do it quicker, of course,' Edie murmured meaningfully; the slower she was to pick it up the less wages the crew would have to split between them. 'But before you throw it in the tub you have to learn which tub.'

Ina nodded as though she had known this all along, instead of assuming you filled one then another.

'There's one tub for matties, one for mattfuls and one for fulls. That's small, medium and large, see?'

Ina nodded again, conscious that, like the others, she was already covered in blood, guts and scales and was glad she had listened to them when she was getting dressed in her working clothes. Under her oilskin apron she had three jumpers and a skirt that she had been told to keep shorter than the apron to protect the hem from the mess, and it was best if the apron overhung her rubber boots, so that when it was washed down before meals or at the end of the working day, the filthy water wouldn't run inside and swamp her seaboot stockings; not, of course that any plan was foolproof, as she would learn from experience, water, blood, guts and scales could find their way into every crevice. Oilskin jackets with hoods were provided for wet weather, when the herring catch was always heavier, but in summer they could do nothing more to keep cool than roll-up their sleeves and accept the inevitable sunburn.

'You're in for a hard time, Ina,' Edie mused, looking at her and shaking her head. 'You're like the rest of God's chosen, white skin and red hair, Shetland lassies always burn worse because we're fairer.'

From further along came a cheerful shout from another

lassie. 'Aye, well, you're that proud that you're Vikings, serves you right!'

'I'd rather burn as a Viking than be a black-hearted Gael like some folk!' Edie shouted back, and the others laughed out loud, but even as the teasing insults flew, Ina noted, their hands never missed a beat, the work went on at breakneck speed as usual, and she wondered if she would ever be as good as them.

At her side Edie glanced at her. 'Don't worry, Ina,' she whispered. 'We all have to start somewhere, you'll pick it up in no time.' Then she raised her voice, addressing the 'black-hearted Gael' contingent more than Ina. 'You're a Shetland Viking,' she said loudly, 'you're already better than any of these other folk!'

In time, experience would teach Ina all the other problems faced by herring lassies. Salt sores were a constant bugbear, caused by the salt rubbing into the skin on their fingers, so they tried to protect them with 'cloots', strips of unbleached linen wrapped around the fingers and tied with other strips of rags or cotton. Not that it worked perfectly. The forefinger was the worst; if you got cut with a gutting knife it was most likely to be there, so you always wore a thicker cloot on that finger, and there was always a Red Cross or Church of Scotland dressing and first-aid station nearby to tend to the ulcers, sores, splinters from the wooden barrels and frequent cuts that were part of normal working life. Sometimes she would be standing there, her hands working with a life of their own but stinging with the pain of ulcers and cuts that would leave scars on her hands for the rest of her life, and she would wonder if this was really all that freedom from home could offer. There were moments when dragging the peats home in a kilshie, her back aching and raw, seemed like heaven compared to gutting fish, but they soon passed, because she knew this was only the first step away from home, so it was all worth it.

The first year that she went away they had lodgings with

Mrs Christmas in Nelson Road, down by the seafront, ordering groceries from the shop at the corner and paying for them when they got their wages, and the butcher boys and baker boys were prepared to deliver orders to their digs while they were working.

Mrs Christmas, like all the landladies, took up her good carpets while the herring lassies were with her, putting down old mats and only replacing the carpets when the summer visitor part of her trade arrived. The funny thing was that Ina and the others could smell the unwelcome evidence of her cat everywhere in the house, yet they couldn't smell the fish off themselves that made the cat follow them around.

They were content enough with Mrs Christmas, even with her disgusting cat, but the following year she couldn't take them, and their search for other digs brought them to King Street, where Mrs Brown opened the door. There were few tall people in those days, but Mrs Brown was smaller than most, so tiny that as she opened the door they almost asked to speak to her mother. She had fading, short fair hair in tight curls that made her look as though she was wearing a judge's wig, a small wrinkled face and kindly bright blue eyes. Her mouth moved constantly, whether from unspoken thoughts or an attempt to keep her teeth in, it was never clear. That day she was wearing a brown skirt to her ankles so that her feet were hidden and she seemed to glide along on castors, a brown cardigan that fell past her hips and swallowed her wrists and a blue blouse underneath that was the exact shade of her eyes. Everything looked too big for her, which it undoubtedly was, but they were never to see her wearing anything else, and her hair was always perfectly in place, though it would be many years before Ina discovered that Mrs Brown did indeed wear a wig.

'How does she have time to get it like that?' she would wonder, and the other lassies would giggle. 'I mean, first thing in the morning to last thing at night it never changes.' It would be a long time after the herring industry had gone before her sister, Ella, told her that they had all been giggling at *her* and how she never saw things in front of her nose.

They struck it lucky with Mrs Brown, because the tiny landlady was a kindly soul who helped them in any way she could, whereas there were others who did no more than take the money. She saw them as 'her lassies', and did them little kindnesses like helping them with their washing, and she made their meals too, though that had unfortunate consequences on one occasion. Usually their meals comprised of the groceries they had ordered, but one lunchtime Ina had taken home some salt herring, and that night they arrived back at King Street, tired and hungry, to be met as usual by Mrs Brown.

'I've made your tea,' she smiled, her blue eyes twinkling.

Ella and Edie exchanged glances.

'I thought you took some salt herring back?' Ella whispered to Ina.

'I did,' Ina replied gently.

'Did you order anything else from the shop then?'

Ina shook her head.

'Just you go on up to your room and I'll bring it up,' Mrs Brown said, and when she did their worst fears were realised. Mrs Brown, knowing nothing about fish other than how to cook it, had been unaware that salt herring had to be soaked first to remove the salt, so she had fried it as it was. Ella, Edie and Ina glanced at each other in horror. Mrs Brown was kind to them, she looked after them better than anyone else would, the other crews were always asking them to let them know if a room became free in the King Street house. They were fond of her and couldn't bear to hurt her feelings, but just as surely they couldn't eat the poisonous dish. All they could do was accept the inedible offering with every indication of gratitude and lots of 'Yum yum' noises till the door closed behind Mrs Brown, then they collapsed in a giggling heap, each one trying to stifle the noise of the other in case nice Mrs Brown heard them.

'What'll we do?' Ina asked, gazing aghast at the fried herring.

'We'll just have to get rid of it without her knowing,' Ella laughed, lying across the bed and holding her sides.

'But we've got nothing else, and I'm hungry,' Ina complained.

'Well, you eat it. You can have my share as well,' Edie giggled, sending Ella into another spasm of laughter. 'Ssh!' Edie said, trying to stifle her own laughter.

'I'm not eating that,' Ina replied. 'Nobody could eat that, but I'm hungry.'

'So you said,' Edie said tartly. 'You keep saying that as though there was a way out. Do you think a great big cooked ham will appear before us if you keep telling us you're hungry? We're all hungry.'

'Well, what'll we do?' Ina persisted.

'We'll have to smuggle the fish out and do without anything to eat tonight,' Edie said.

'But –'

Edie held a hand in the air. 'Don't,' she whispered with feeling, 'tell us again that you're hungry, Ina, we know!'

All this time Ella was rolling about on the bed laughing.

'And you,' Edie said, 'put a sock in it.'

So they wrapped the fried fish in paper and told Mrs Brown they were going for a walk, then they dumped their meal in a bin and returned, going to bed still hungry rather than hurt their landlady's feelings. For the rest of their time working together they stayed at the King Street house, but never again did they bring home salt herring for their tea.

And there were those cold, cold times in Yarmouth when nothing could protect you from black frost and your clothes were frozen stiff when you put them on. You had to break the ice on top of the barrels before you could fill up after the pickle had been drained off, then you had to stand with your hands inside the freezing barrels to get them used to the cold so that you could work, the tears running down your face.

35

There were times, too, when it rained, and the herring catch was heavier and so you had to work longer and faster to keep up, and your clothes got soaked, no matter how hard you tried to keep them dry, and with nowhere to dry them and no heat either, the next day you just had to put them on wet again. And strangely enough they never had colds: despite the weather and the lack of even basic comforts, they stayed healthy. They were a hardy breed, the herring lassies.

At Bloomfield's in Yarmouth the packer in the crew worked outside, but the gutters were protected from the elements by a roof, and the farlins had shutters built up on one side that were opened and tied up so that the herring could be dumped in. Across the top was slung a string of electric bulbs so that the long line of lassies could see what they were doing, and as they threw the roused and gutted herring into the five tubs they worked with, a cooper would come round every now and again with a measuring stick to check that they had got it right. They usually had, though: sizing fish correctly was born of experience they had gathered in their families and communities all of their lives.

As soon as one tub was full, the crew of three would carry it out to the packer's box, where she would pack the fish into barrels holding a cran, a thousand herring, calling the cooper after the first row to make sure it was tight enough. They would be packed in alternate rows with a scoop of salt between, first belly down, then belly up, finishing with a row belly up, so that no matter which end the barrel was opened there would be a row of gleaming silver bellies on show.

When the Russians were buying at the end of the year it meant even more work, because they liked their herring packed in a certain way. They would walk along the barrels, sticking a hand in and bringing out a herring from the middle, and if there was any trace of gut remaining they would disqualify the whole barrel. Once they had made their choice the barrels they wanted had to be repacked in the design they liked, with the bellies of the top fish squeezed into a diamond shape, so that when the lid was lifted they would see a layer of silver diamonds. Forty-eight hours after the coopers had put lids on the finished barrels, a hole would be drilled in the side to drain off the dissolved salt and fish juices, the pickle being greatly prized by the Russians as a sauce to dip bread in. This process also resulted in the herring shrinking, so it would be refilled with fish barrelled at the same time, some pickle would be poured back in, and the barrel would be resealed and stacked in the yard.

The end of the working day came when there was no more fish to barrel, and that could mean working from 6 a.m. till 9 p.m., depending on the catch. Then everything they had worked with had to be washed down with buckets of water – tubs, boxes, cloths, oilies and boots – and the yard hosed down; but the last thing each gutter did before leaving was to hide her knife somewhere other people couldn't find it. For all of this Ina's crew earned a basic wage of fifteen shillings a week, plus three shillings a barrel between them. Half their basic wage went to their landlady for their digs, leaving them the other half to spend on food, with their barrel money collected at the end of the season to take home to their families. So there wasn't much left for spending – not that they had time, anyway.

She enjoyed the life, though; it got her away from Shetland. She was always one of the last to go home at the end of the season, along with Ella. Everyone knew that Ina and Ella could always be counted on to take odd jobs to stave off the return journey to Lerwick a little longer, and for her part the absence of Danny was one reason for that, especially once he had gone for good in what was regarded as the scandal of Lerwick. He had been doing well in the Merchant Marine, seeing foreign parts that Ina hankered to see. Much as she liked being a herring lassie, she would have loved to travel further afield, but knew Yarmouth was likely to be the limit of travel for a Lerwick lassie. Danny wrote to her faithfully, describing the different sights he had seen, the things he had done, sharing all his new experiences and adventures, but it wasn't the same as being there herself and she still envied him. Then came a letter from her brother, Sandy, with news that Danny had returned on leave, collected Isobel Carnegie, and the two had run off together. The place was in turmoil, apparently, the ministers of all the local kirks calling down God's damnation on them both, while Dolina threatened that he would never darken her doorstep again, and blamed Magnus for filling his head with wild stories of his family.

Ina could hardly believe that her placid brother, the playground arbiter, could have hatched such an outrageous plan, and she anxiously waited for a letter from Danny explaining all. It seemed that, after being rebuffed by Mr Carnegie when he asked for permission to court his daughter, Danny had kept in touch with Isobel by letters sent care of Davie, the boy who'd lived in an old boat at the harbour all those years ago, the boy who had been kept warm and fed by Danny. They had planned the whole thing in detail. Isobel had been given permission to travel to Glasgow to spend a holiday with relatives, something that pleased her father, who lived in fear of his offspring fraternising with the locals. The plan was that she would spend a few days in Aberdeen shopping, then travel on to her relatives in Glasgow. By the time the relatives had contacted Mr Carnegie to report that Isobel hadn't arrived, she and Danny were man and wife and were on their way to Canada. Canada! Where else would Danny go? He was taking his bride to Nova Scotia, 'Land of Trees', where Uncle Andro's descendants would do what they could for the young couple.

Ina was delighted, but the family back home in Shetland were overcome with shame that a son of theirs could have done anything so devious. His name was not to be mentioned ever again and Mr Carnegie was so overcome by the thought of his daughter marrying into the rubbish he had tried to educate that he left Lerwick with his wife and son and never returned. Ina longed to hear every detail of the great adventure. They were both in their twenties, and Isobel had been all but imprisoned by her father all of her life, so Danny had liberated her and taken her off to a new life. They were now living with the other Polsons in Canada, so they really did exist, her father hadn't just been telling stories, and the episode brightened Ina's life as much as it shamed the rest of the family. Her sister, Ella, she recalled later, had neither supported nor criticised her younger brother over the exploit; she had kept her own counsel.

Apart from the burst of excitement over Danny and Isobel's elopement, Ina's memories of those days were of being too tired on her day off every Sunday to do more than sleep and maybe go for a walk, or perhaps do her knitting. The lassies were too exhausted to even go to the local baths for a proper wash during the little time off they had, so they were resigned to smelling of fish. Occasionally they would go dancing, but the heat made the smell even stronger, though the lassies lived with it as a fact of life and hardly noticed it. And she remembered the fun, singing in the back of the lorry that collected them for work at 6 a.m. and took them back to their digs when the herring were finished, and not singing at work because they were too busy trying to fill barrels and enhance the money they would take home to their families. There were diversions too, like the time in 1930 when the Prince of Wales came to visit their yard after he had opened the new Haven Bridge. It just so happened that there were lots of herring, so the lassies had to keep working which was just as well because he swept through without talking to anyone, with the crowds of photographers snapping away and bumping into boxes of herring and making a mess as they chased after him. One gate had been specially decorated with flags for him to walk through, but he looked bleary-eyed, as though he'd been at the drink all night and just wanted to be away from the place, and as he walked through the wrong gate, the one that hadn't been decorated, they all laughed, fish to be gutted or not.

The one thing she always made time for was looking at the stars, and she had managed to save enough for a telescope. Not a big, expensive, real telescope, of course, but a small, folding plastic one; still, it brought the stars slightly closer. Spending money on something her mother would have considered a nonsense made her feel guilty, then her guilt made her feel angry, before she swung back to guilt again; but the thing was done. Her sister Ella would watch her going out on her own to gaze at the stars, her telescope concealed somewhere on her person and whisper to her, smiling, 'There she goes, the lassie with the stars in her eyes.' Ina would laugh to herself; if anyone had stars in their eyes it was Ella. Ella's guilt money was spent on penny novelettes, little stories of love and romance between titled ladies of great virtue and dashing heroes with even grander titles. The ladies would eventually be seduced by the heroes, but it would always be described in poetic, flowery terms. Ella and the other lassies would take turns at buying the latest, and the little booklets would pass from one set of eager, fishy hands to the next, till the pages fell apart. It wasn't an enthusiasm Ina shared, and when she said this she was made to read one, 'to show her', the others said, but it just seemed silly to Ina and she couldn't understand her sister's fascination for what she considered to be rubbish.

Ella had married Ronnie when she was seventeen years old. It was how things were in small communities: they married young with the blessing of the kirk because, the ministers said with heavy, dark emphasis, marriage kept them out of trouble. Ina had never understood that, either, but everyone else seemed to. Once, when she was a child, she had heard a minister say this and had asked Dolina what he meant. Her mother had replied that she would understand when she was older, only she hadn't, and she often wondered how old she would have to be before someone explained. Ella and Ronnie had no bairns, which was unusual, to be sure, but it happened; anyway, Ella was away from home for long spells at the herring and didn't seem to mind. She never mentioned her husband during those months away, gave no indication that she missed him, and in fact seemed happier and freer than when she was at home, so Ina didn't really understand her need for heady romance. Then she thought again of the other lassies who loved the penny novelettes and noted how many of them were married, and it struck her that the married ones indulged in fantasy more than those who were still single, and she wondered what that said about married life.

At the weekends the pubs lining the riverside would be open and crowded with fishermen. Shetland was dry, so there were no public houses but, even if there had been, no woman would have dreamed of going in one. Away from the islands, though, Ina felt daring. One Saturday evening she and a crowd of other lassies were passing the White Lion at the top of St Peter's Road in Yarmouth and one of the others had looked inside and commented, 'The White Lion's black tonight,' meaning that it was full of dark-clothed fishermen. Ina stared in at the figures through the haze of cigarette and pipe fumes. The place was alive with people, male people, enjoying themselves. She was young; she wanted to do something, anything. On a whim she took another step just beyond safety and propriety, and to this day she could still see the shocked faces of her pals. Ella tried to catch Ina by the arm; the other girls stared after her, their eyes wide and their mouths saying a shocked 'Oh!' in unison. Ina had no idea what had possessed her, but once through the door she decided, 'In for a penny, in for a pound,' and shook off Ella's restraining hand. Once inside, though, she had even less idea what to do, and desperately scanned the faces till she recognised a fisherman she had seen about the place. Eddie something, that was all she knew about him, except that he was a Yarmouth man, a native of Skye and the engineer off the *Ocean Wanderer*, a boat from Acarsaid on the north west-coast of Scotland and one of the best known and respected boats in the industry. She knew he was from Skye because he had once made some saucy remark to them in Gaelic as he passed and Ina had angrily told him that they were Shetlanders, they didn't understand his Irish language. It wasn't the reaction Eddie expected from any of the lassies, because he was darkly handsome and he knew it, such a huge flirt that every new lassie had him pointed out to her as a hazard to keep an eye on. Neither was it the reaction the other lassies expected to Eddie, he had a charm they all found difficult to resist and whenever he was around there was a little thrill in the air, so Ina knew that they were now listening to every word.

'It's not Irish,' Eddie replied in English. 'I'm a Skye man and it's Gaelic I was speaking. Are you ignorant or what?'

'Huh,' Ina said, her eyes still on gutting the fish that slipped through her fingers as quickly as anyone else's by that time. 'It's you that's the ignorant one, that's where your filthy language came from, Ireland.'

'My, but aren't you a sweet wee thing,' he said sarcastically. 'I'll be warning the *Ocean Wanderer* lads off coming this way, that's for sure, they might die of too much sugar.'

A muffled, excited giggle passed along the gutters working at the farlin.

'And what,' Ina said clearly, 'makes you think we'd have anything to do with anyone off the *Ocean Wanderer*? Sure everybody knows your skipper is the blackest-hearted creature in the fleet, so his crew can't be much better.'

'I'll grant you Sorley Mor isn't a man for casual chit-chat,' the big man replied, smiling at her. She heard the smile in his voice as he spoke and when she slyly stole a glance up at him she was furious to see his eyes full of amusement. 'But I think I'd rather spend time talking to him than you, Miss Bitter.'

'Then go,' Ina said tartly. 'Who is forcing you to stay?'

As he sauntered off the lassies chatted about him.

'He fancies his chances, that one,' said a voice. 'A real ladies' man, he'll never settle down, too many sweeties in the shop to try.'

'You're right,' another lassie said. 'It would take a brave lassie or a stupid one to take that one on.'

But though the lassies were wary of Eddie and his undoubted charms, they always smiled when they saw him, even as they warned each other off him. Standing at the bar that night he looked at Ina, then at the bunch of dumbstruck lassies at the door, scared to cross the threshold in case the floor should open up and suck them under to who-knew-what fate. He grinned.

All the *Ocean Wanderer* lads were there, even the skipper, Sorley Mor, and Ina saw Eddie drawing their attention to her. Well, she wasn't going to turn tail and run back out. She'd never live it down if she did.

'Can I get you something?' Eddie asked Ina politely.

Ina took a deep breath, trying to appear all assurance and ease, as though this was something she did every day of her life: stormed pubs, consorted with virtual strangers, while downing strong liquor.

'I'll have a port and lemon, thanks,' she replied haughtily, and at the door the eyes of the others opened wider still and their hands flew to their throats to stifle their gasps. Ina had never had an alcoholic drink in her life, but she had heard the racier females talking about port and lemon. It was the only drink she knew by name that women drank. Other women, that was.

Eddie looked as though he was about to laugh out loud. 'You're sure?' he asked.

'And why wouldn't I be?' Ina replied.

Eddie placed the glass of dark stuff in her hand and looked at the door. 'And you, ladies?' he asked.

All of the lassies turned and ran except Ella, who hesitated for a moment then walked in. 'I'll have the same, thanks,' she said tartly, catching her younger sister's nerve, her face flushed and her eyes dancing with excitement and fear.

Ina took a sip. It was the worst taste she could remember. Even eating Mrs Brown's fried salt herring would have been nicer, she was sure, but she knew this Eddie was watching her, ready to laugh; and for that matter so now were the other fishermen, their eyes full of amusement. There was nothing for it, she would have to drink it, so she threw the rest of the horrible stuff down in one desperate gulp that made her eyes water. Ella watched her and decided to do the same.

Eddie looked around the bar, exchanging smiling glances with the other fishermen. 'My, but I can see you ladies are seasoned drinkers,' he said pleasantly. 'How about a whisky this time?'

Ina and Ella looked at each other. Ina would've taken it to prove she could, but Ella's eyes were pleading with her to refuse, so reluctantly she did. 'This is our sixth tonight,' she lied, 'better not overdo it. We don't want sore heads in the morning . . .' Then she hesitated before adding what she hoped was a worldly wise '. . . again.'

'Well, I admire a woman who can take her drink yet knows when she's had enough,' Eddie told her, solemn-faced, and with that Ina and Ella left with as much composure as was possible for two Lerwick lassies who knew they would throw up as soon as they got outside and away from the amused glances of the fishermen. As the door closed behind them they could hear the men laughing, first loud then low, then loud again, as the door swung this way then that, but they were too intent on making it to safety to care. Then they laughed, too, hanging on to each other till they couldn't laugh any more. After that came reality and fear, of course, that someone would tell Magnus and Dolina back in Lerwick, ensuring that a thrashing would await them however long they were away from home.

'And Ronnie will give you a thrashing, too!' Ina told her sister breathlessly. 'Two beatings for one port and lemon that you couldn't even keep down,' she laughed. 'Doesn't seem fair, Ella!'

And Ella had laughed back. Hadn't she? She was so clear in Ina's mind, the double of herself, as all the Polsons were of each other: reddish fair hair, grey eyes. She was more handsome than herself, Ina freely admitted, but no one could avoid coming to the conclusion that they were related. Two peas from the same pod, so alike that you would've assumed they were close enough to know each other inside out, that the two Lerwick sisters who spent so much time together would have had no secrets. But she was right, wasn't she? Ella had laughed?

How many times had she gone over that moment, frame by frame in the intervening years, trying to pick up some message and wondering how she could have missed it and what events that act of bravado had set in motion? What would have happened if they had walked in another direction and hadn't passed the White Lion that night? Would things have worked out differently? It had been the same night the gypsy woman had told their fortunes. As they walked towards that fateful meeting at the White Lion, they were all giggling over what the old woman had said, but all Ina could think of was what she had been told. 'You'll marry someone you already know and live across the sea from your home. You'll be content, but you could've done better, and you won't have many bairns.' She hadn't paid any attention to what the gypsy had told Ella.

3

Everything depended on whether there were herring to catch: too much and you were exhausted, but at least you would have more barrel money to take home; too little and you had to find other jobs to tide you over. There was always filling up, of course, but when that was done you had to clean the offices or maybe work for a day with one of the kipperers, like Sutton's. The curers needed a lot of herring: if there was only one or two cran it wasn't worth the bother to the curers, but the kipperers would take them, and in those days there was no machinery, so the herring had to be gutted by hand.

That's how Ina met Aeneas. He was a manager with Sutton's, a familiar sight about the place, buying up what the curers didn't want. The other lassies laughed at him, he was such a serious wee man, neat and tidy in his checked three-piece suit, his collar and tie and his flat cap and – despite the dirty work he was involved in – highly polished brown shoes. No one could understand why he bothered; everyone else had working clothes and they didn't care how mucky they got, but not Aeneas. They discussed how he could manage to keep the gloss on those shoes: did he have replacement pairs hidden about the place to change into several times a day? They were used to rough-and-ready sorts, like the fishermen they met from all over, the Scotch and the Irish gutters and packers who gave as good as they got.

Aeneas Hamilton was pleasant enough, but he didn't flirt with them; he only had time for business. An old man before his time, they said, though he was still in his early twenties. That was Ina's first memory about him, that she felt a mild annoyance with the other lassies because they joked about him between themselves, offering odds on who could get him interested. It wasn't that *she* was interested, she just didn't see what was so wrong with a man who attended to business and, in truth, she found some of the banter a bit near the knuckle at times. Not that she understood much of it, but she knew by the tones of the voices and the kind of laughter – and, even if she couldn't understand precisely what was being said, she knew it was smut, and she didn't much like that. If Aeneas wasn't that way inclined, well, that was something in his favour, she thought, though she knew better than to say so to the others.

Sometimes he used to ask if any of the girls wanted a few weeks' work with Sutton's if Bloomfield's was slack, and they'd always accept because the alternative of cleaning offices was too much like the housewifery that they had all escaped from. There was kippering work on offer at the end of the season, too, and though the others only sometimes accepted, Ina and Ella always did. With the money they bought presents to take home along with their barrel money, making up for their guilt at spending on their separate passions. They would go down to Woolworth's (there was a British Home Stores in its place these days), where everything was threepence or sixpence, or to Peacock's Bazaar, long gone now, too, so she'd heard: it was a furniture shop now. At the warehouses down Howard Street you could buy a big jar of broken toffee or rock wholesale, and once she took a fancy to a pair of shoes in a shop window; looking back, it must've been during one of her rebelling-against-the-guilt phases when she was inclined to the odd reckless impulse. Why she had wanted shoes she couldn't say, because all her life she had preferred her bare feet. When she was growing up in Lerwick the only way for bairns to have shoes was to get a note from the Parish Council instructing a shop to supply a pair at their expense, but it was rare for anyone to bother: everyone preferred baries. Now here she was spending five and elevenpence on these shoes, but the saleswoman refused to give her the one in the window and she had to wait another week to get it. Even so, she got both shoes, thanks to the extra work at Sutton's, and she was always fast at picking things up even if she wasn't clever, so she learned about kippering too, and it was Aeneas himself who taught her much to the amazement of the other workers.

'Now I know you know all about gutting herring,' he told her with his neat little smile, 'but kippering is different. We split them along the back so that they can be flattened and hung up for smoking by the strongest part, the shoulder.'

Ina watched him, wondering how anyone could get so much real satisfaction from smoking fish.

'We take the intestines out,' he continued, and it seemed entirely in character, somehow, that he said 'intestines', it fitted with the neatness of the man. 'Neatness' might have been his middle name.

'And then,' he said, leading her to a barrel of fish steeping in a dark brown liquid, 'we put them in salt and dye for about fifteen minutes. We call it BFK dye – brown for kippering,' and he laughed as though he'd made a joke, as he put a hand under her elbow and led her to a table covered with freshly salted and dyed fish. The table had a slope towards the middle for the excess liquid to run off, and lassies stood at either side. 'These,' he said, 'are tintering sticks,' pointing to strips of wood running above the table at eye-level in front of each worker. Ina noticed the sticks were about a metre long and studded at close intervals with nails like hooks. 'And if you watch the ladies you'll see that they hang the fish on the hooks – by the shoulder, as I said – to let the BFK dye drain off.'

Ina wondered why he was giving her a guided tour, why he hadn't just said 'Watch the others and you'll get the hang of it,' then she noticed the other lassies, most of whom she knew, grinning quietly and exchanging glances with each other.

'The ladies all look as though they're heavy smokers,'

Aeneas smiled – another joke, she supposed – 'but they're not, their hands and arms are stained by the dye you see. It's an occupational hazard, I'm afraid, a cross you have to bear, eh ladies?'

The 'ladies' made no reply, but Ina read their sly smiles.

'When we have about eight pairs of drained kippers on each stick it goes in to the smokehouse,' Aeneas said, walking off. 'Over this way, Miss Polson.'

Ina followed but swore to herself that she'd have a word with the 'ladies' when the little man had cleared off.

'As you can see, it's high so that we can get lots of tiers of sticks inside, but it's narrow, and the smoking's done by lighting a fire of oak chips and sawdust and letting it smoulder away for anything up to twelve hours. I actually like that smell, don't you?' he asked brightly.

Ina nodded as the tutorial continued.

'The main problem we face is controlling the temperature,' he sighed, 'that's one of the improvements I hope we can develop in due course. The optimum oil content is about fifteen percent, but I don't have to tell you, Miss Polson, that the fish don't care about our preferences. In November it can be as low as nine percent and in summer as high as twenty-five percent.' His brow furrowed and he shook his head; this was something that mattered greatly to Aeneas Hamilton, she realised, the vagaries of fish and their seasonal oiliness.

'If the heat's too high we get burned offerings instead of kippers, and even a slight draught through the smokehouse can bring the lot crashing down on to the floor.' To his furrowed brow he added a shake of the head this time, then he suddenly brightened up. 'Did you know that we also make red herrings?' he asked, almost excitedly. 'We leave them to soak in brine for weeks and weeks, then we smoke them for weeks and weeks more, that's what gives them their colour. Started out as food for slaves on ships taking them to America, so they tell me, and now they're part of African cuisine. Very strong taste, though,' he said, this time grimacing, 'not at all my cup of tea, Miss Polson, but they're very popular abroad. No accounting for tastes, I suppose.' He stood in silence as if contemplating a deep mystery of the universe before looking up at Ina again. 'If you'd like to look around on your own, do feel free,' he smiled and left her.

If she wanted to look around by herself, Ina thought savagely, heading back to the tintering tables, where she was met by raucous laughter from 'the ladies.'

'My God, Ina Polson!' shouted Maggie, a woman she knew from Lerwick, twisting around to wipe her eyes on her rolled-up sleeve, 'and that wee man has a fancy for you all right! Wait till the folks at home hear you've caught yourself a big fish, even if he is a dry one!'

'Don't be so stupid!' Ina retorted, trying to ignore the laughter. 'He was only showing me round.'

Maggie looked around the other lassies and shouted out 'Hands up any other body here who was given a personal tour by wee Aeneas.'

There was a moment of silence as Ina scanned the room but not one hand went up, then she met Maggie's gaze and the entire workforce of lassies burst out laughing.

'I told you!' Maggie said smugly.

'Rubbish,' Ina replied dismissively and turned to go.

'You mark my words, Ina, don't you let that wee dry fish get you in a corner, that's all we're saying — right lassies? You've brought out the beast in him, Ina, and I'll be buggered if I ever thought there was one in him!'

As she left, Ina tried to walk as slowly as possible to give the impression that the banter had failed to hit its target, but all the same, she was glad she didn't bump in to Aeneas again on her way out.

The part of the herring trade at Sutton's she never liked was canning, though she was fast enough at it. After the fish were canned a spoonful of vinegar would be put in, or some kind of sauce like mustard or tomato. For some reason she couldn't stand the smell of it, even if she did get used to it to some extent.

'All these years covered in fish guts, scales and blood,' Ella would laugh, 'and it's the tomato sauce that does for you!'

'I know, I know,' Ina would laugh. 'I can't understand it myself, but I hate it!' And though she never complained, she noticed that Aeneas didn't ask her to do canning work unless there was no one else to do it.

Then came the war in 1939 and the lassies were sent home or to work wherever they were told by the authorities. It was the end of an era, though they didn't know it then. Ina was told that she would be going to work in the Naval Hospital in Aberdeenshire. She was quite happy about it. As ever, she didn't want to go home. She was over thirty years old, well on her way to being an old maid, and contentedly so. There hadn't even been a near miss, so the gypsy had been as much a waste of money as she had suspected at the time. She had been away from Lerwick longer than she'd ever lived there; she wasn't who she had been then and knew she could never live there again. Over the years, she and Ella had established the pattern of their lives, working their way down the east of the country for however many months the fish kept being landed, taking any odd jobs here and there that would keep them from going home until absolutely necessary, then returning to Lerwick, hopefully for as short time as they could manage. The war had brought that to an end, though, and Ella wasn't just disappointed, she was distraught at the prospect of going home for what could be the rest of her life. And that was when Ina found out her sister's secret and cursed herself for not knowing before. What was it about her that she didn't spot things?

'I don't want to go back to Ronnie,' Ella sobbed, 'and anyway, I can't.'

Ina looked at her, bemused. 'Why not?'

'Because he hits me, that why.'

'He hits you?' Ina asked in a silly tone of voice that annoyed even her, but it had taken her by complete surprise. 'Since when?'

'Since the day we were married,' she said quietly. 'I'd looked at him in the wrong way, so he said, though I couldn't remember it, and the minute we got back to the croft he punched me in the stomach. Some brides get carried over the threshold, I got punched across it.' She looked at Ina and mistook her shock for disbelief. 'Oh, he was always careful,' she said darkly, 'never hit my face, so nobody would ever have cause to mention it. And if I had a few bruises on my arms, well, you get bruised working about a croft, don't you? Usually he went for the body.' As she talked she wrapped her arms around herself protectively. 'He has a mean kick with those boots, I can tell you, would've made his fortune if he'd gone in for the football.' She tried to laugh but broke down in tears again.

Ina's mind was in turmoil. She thought of their father and brothers. They wouldn't let any man hit Ella. 'And have you told Da?' Ina asked.

Ella laughed bitterly. 'What good do you think that would do?'

'But Da and the lads, they'd never let him get away with that!' Ina said, shocked.

'You're helluva daft at times, Ina,' Ella said quietly. 'Of course they'd let him away with it. He's my man, he owns me, he can do what he likes!'

'But have you *told* them?' Ina persisted.

'I don't have to tell them, they know. They're men, Ina. If Ronnie hits me, it must be my fault: that's how they think.'

'Now you're the one being daft!' Ina said. 'Da wouldn't —'

'Och, Ina, you know nothing! Besides, he has one reason, it's not the only reason, but Da and the lads would think it reason enough. I've always refused to have bairns to him. He hits me for that as well.'

'But how do you stop having bairns?' Ina asked innocently. Ella laughed through her tears. 'My God, Ina!' she said, wiping her eyes. 'You really are a bairn yourself, aren't you? You're a woman in your thirties, do you really not know?'

Ina shook her head.

'I won't sleep with him, that's how. That first night he raped me. That's what it was. Though they say a man can't rape his wife, he's entitled after all: the law says so, so does the kirk. I was in agony after he'd hit me, so what he got out of it I'll never know, but he seemed content enough. After that, I refused. I've slept with a kitchen knife under my pillow every night ever since. I said I wouldn't sleep with him till he stopped hitting me'

'And he didn't?'

'Of course he didn't!' Ella said wryly. 'I knew he'd go on hitting me *because* I wouldn't sleep with him, so I had the perfect way of never sleeping with him. I hate him; he's no man. A real man doesn't have to hit a woman. There were times when I was at home that I hoped he'd try it on again so that I could stab him, I hated him so much. I'd have gone to jail happily to see him dead. They could've hanged me and I'd still have thought it was worth it.'

'Was he always like that?' Ina asked. 'Before you married him, like?'

'I was seventeen, Ina, how would I have known what he was like? That's why they marry us off at that age up there: we don't know what life's about so we accept the one we're given.'

Ina thought back to the ends of all those seasons when they eventually had to go home to Lerwick, when they had exhausted all the temporary jobs and had no choice. She was so low herself at the prospect each time, and she knew her sister hadn't been entirely happy either, but she hadn't noticed how deeply Ella felt. Then the start of the next season would arrive and Ina was anxious and happy to go away again, as was Ella, but at the time she thought it was part of the Polson liking for travel, for being away from their own small place and out in the world, even if it was only the fishing world.

Yet all that time Ella was either going back to Ronnie's violence and his frustrations or escaping from them.

And Ina had to be honest, there had always been a tension in the family about Ella; when her name was mentioned there was an unspoken something. Now she realised that tension marked the knowledge of her parents that their daughter wasn't happy, and yes, she had to admit it, the knowledge that she was being beaten by her husband. And what if Magnus Polson had taken Ronnie to task for mistreating his daughter, and Ronnie had said she wasn't fulfilling her wifely duties in the bedroom and thus preventing him from having his own family? It was the truth, after all, not the whole truth, but enough of it, and they would have backed Ronnie, of that she had no doubt. And she thought of herself being in that position, and knew her Da would have done the same, her Da who made her laugh and taught her about the stars; he would have said it was her own fault and let her be beaten, too.

'So what are you going to do?' she asked quietly, her voice still tight with shock.

'I'm staying in Yarmouth,' Ella said. She looked up at Ina. 'I said I couldn't go back, anyway – well, I was telling the truth. I'm expecting.'

Ina just stopped herself from asking, 'Expecting what?'

'But Ronnie will be pleased, then,' she said happily. 'Now that you're having a bairn he'll be happy and he won't hit you any longer.'

'Honesty Christ!' Ella shouted. 'Are you really that stupid, Ina?'

Ina stared at her in puzzlement.

'It's not his!' Ella shouted. 'How could it be his if I never sleep with him? I'm four months gone and I've been away for the last six!'

Ina felt as though she'd been thrown into the deep end of a swimming pool.

'Well whose is it, then?' she asked.

'It's Eddie's, of course!'

Eddie? The only Eddie that Ina knew was the fisherman who was always around, teasing the lassies, the one who'd treated her and Ella to a port and lemon in the White Lion all those years ago. *That* Eddie? And *of course*?

Ella saw the light finally filter through to her sister's eyes. 'That's right, *that* Eddie,' she said. 'Are you really telling me you didn't know?'

Ina shook her head dumbly.

'Well that takes the biscuit,' Ella laughed bitterly. 'Every other body knew, but you didn't. Why does that not surprise me?'

'Everybody knew?'

'Of course! It's been going on for years,' Ella told her. 'You mean nobody told you?'

Ina shook her head.

'Not even a hint?'

She shook her head again, but in the back of her mind she knew hints never got through to her. If anyone wanted Ina to know something, they had to tell it to her straight; she'd always been like that. What was it Dolina used to say about her? 'Ina spends too much time looking to the heavens to have any time for frills and fancies.' It had always irked her that she missed things, but then, she thought, the other herring lassies probably assumed that as she was Ella's sister she would know more than they did, so why would anyone hint to her, far less tell her face-to-face?

She thought back to all those times she had departed alone with her plastic folding telescope for her star-gazing sessions, leaving Ella to read her penny novelettes. Maybe Ella wasn't reading, then – obviously she wasn't. How was Ina supposed to have known? It seemed that Ella had found romance far nearer to home, and her own flesh-and-blood hero. There were herring lassies married to fishermen, and whenever the weather was bad they would walk up and down the river, watching for the first sight of their boats. She had seen Ella there, too, and just assumed she was keeping the others company on their vigil, but Ella had been watching for Eddie's boat, and now here she was, pregnant for the first time at the age of forty. And to Eddie, the fisherman the other lassies warned each other off. 'It would take a brave lassie or a stupid one to take that one on,' that's what they used to say. Which one was her sister, she wondered?

'So what will you do?' she asked Ella again.

'I'm staying here with Eddie,' she said, looking quickly at her sister then looking away again. 'Oh, I know what everybody says about him, that he's a ladies' man and he'll never settle down, but that's all on the outside.' Ella smiled. 'I wouldn't have believed a man could be so gentle, Ina, so kind. My first thought was to get rid of the baby, there's always somebody can help you out, I'm not the first one to get in this state, for God's sake, and I won't be the last, but at my age – you don't have to tell me how stupid I am! Eddie wouldn't let me, though. He wants this baby. He wants us to get married, too; but there's not any chance of that happening. Still, as he says, we'll be as good as, and them that don't like it can just please themselves. I know one thing for certain, we'll be more man and wife than Ronnie and I ever were.'

She was silent for a few moments, then she looked at Ina. 'I was thinking, Ina, that maybe when you go back to Lerwick you'd take Ronnie a letter.'

Ina didn't reply. She would have no difficulty doing that; she'd like to have a few words with him herself for what he'd done to her sister.

'And maybe you'd tell Da and the others?' Ella rushed on, as though the faster she went, the less chance there was of Ina refusing.

Ina looked aghast. Even at her age she didn't know if she could tell Magnus that his married daughter was expecting by another man and wouldn't be coming home again.

Then she took a deep breath and thought again. Ella may have been Ronnie's wife but she wasn't his possession. She was a human being, she was no one's possession, and her Da should've helped her. 'I'll tell them, Ella,' she said. 'Don't you worry about it.'

But Magnus didn't have to be told. The next morning they received news that he had died in Lerwick and, wartime communications being what they were, by the time the sisters heard the news he had already been buried. So Magnus Polson had been saved having to face the scandal that would make his family the talk of Lerwick yet again, but he would also escape his youngest daughter's questions on why he had never tried to help poor Ella.

4

Leaving Ella behind in Yarmouth felt strange after so many years making these journeys with her, and even stranger given the circumstances. Not only was Ella in this predicament, but their father was newly dead, so the family would be grief-stricken and, not knowing what had been happening in Yarmouth, they would be expecting the two sisters to arrive together, as they always had. She had never before heard of a Lerwick woman who had left her husband, far less one who was already pregnant by another man with whom she was now living in sin, but she didn't have to imagine the reaction: it would, she knew, be explosive. The family was in mourning, and added to that they would be deeply ashamed of Ella's behaviour. Whether that was merited or not wasn't the issue; not for the moment, anyhow: the fact was that they would be.

Strangely enough, Ina didn't feel any shame. She had been shocked and embarrassed that she hadn't known something about her own sister that the entire universe seemed to have known for a very long time, or the universe of the herring lassies, at any rate. She wondered if any of the Shetland fishermen might already have found out about Ella and Eddie and have passed it on, then she realised that couldn't have happened. For one thing there would have been some delegation sent to confront the couple if anyone at home had known, and for another the lassies lived in a world of their own. It was a matter of pride that they protected each other as much as they protected themselves, so Ella's secret would have been kept, indeed it had been kept, even from Ina.

She would head for Lerwick for the weekend before reporting to the hospital near Aberdeen for whatever duties she had been assigned to carry out for the duration of the war. Safely tucked in her kist, with her working clothes and the presents bought with her Sutton's money, was the letter Ella had written to Ronnie. Ina hadn't read it, so she had no idea what words her sister had used to convey the enormity of this situation. On the long train journey to Aberdeen her mind constantly revised how she would break the news, then thoughts of her father would intrude, and how there hadn't even been time for a last goodbye. She remembered the stories he had told her about their family in Canada, unwittingly setting the scene for Danny and Isobel's elopement, and the things he had taught Ina about the stars. Together they had watched Halley's Comet in 1910. She had been so young that she could remember only Magnus's excitement; he had talked about it so often and in such detail that his memory had become hers. They had lain in the grass and watched the meteor showers of shooting stars together every year: fast, brilliant white Lyrids in April, blue Lyrids in June, bright, exploding Cygnids in August; no matter how often they saw the annual shows overhead they had been transfixed and elated.

On a previous reluctant trip home she had shown Magnus her cheap telescope, and he had been so captivated by it that she decided on the spot to tell him that she had bought it as a present for him. Once back at the fishing, she had to go through all the saving-up again to buy another, but it had been worth it to see her father's face as he vainly searched the skies for Pluto, the new planet next door to Neptune. That was the year Danny and Isobel had eloped and her brother had been banished from the family, though Danny and Ina kept in touch by letter. Pluto appeared, she would think, and Danny disappeared, wondering if her Da had considered it a fair swap. But he had never mentioned it; only the stars seemed to matter to him. The times when they compared notes on what they could see; she could never see as many stars in Yarmouth or as clearly as he saw them in Shetland. Now those times were over and the gap was, she knew, unfillable; there would be less reason than ever to return to Lerwick at the end of every season now that Magnus had gone.

As ever, as the boat approached Lerwick, she was struck by how little her island home had changed, and yet how much smaller it seemed each time, as though it shrank in direct proportion to the time she was away and the width of her experiences in the outside world. One day, she thought, she might make this journey and find that there was nothing at the end of it – Lerwick and all the Shetland Isles would have shrunk to the size of a handful of pebbles and been washed away by the sea.

There hadn't been time to tell the family when she would be arriving, so Ina had to make her own way to Cheyne Crescent. Not that there was ever a great deal of fuss – arrivals and departures were part of normal, ordinary life – but usually there would be someone to help with the kists, or kist, in this case. As she drew near to Cheyne Crescent she saw her brother, Sandy, and waved. Sandy still worked as a cooper, though he no longer followed the fleet. He had stayed in Lerwick when he married, the year Ina went off to the herring. He ran forward and took the kist from her, at first smiling, then remembering why she had come home this time. She patted his shoulder sadly.

There was no great excitement as Ina entered the house: they were a family in mourning, after all. At first no one mentioned Ella's absence, thinking she had gone to her own home first. Nothing much had changed, as the years had passed there were more nieces and nephews, and as they had grown and married, grandbairns had arrived for Magnus and Dolina. Dolina was sitting by the fire when Ina entered, look-ing up at her daughter with those sad eyes, now even sadder. She seemed so small, so old and so defeated as well. Ina heard the account of Magnus's death that had obviously been gone over time after time so that it could be accepted. He had gone to Staney Hill to bring back a kilshie of peats. He had been feeling off-colour before he set out. Dolina had thought he looked pale and told him to get one of the grandbairns to go instead. He had said no, it would be quicker just to go himself and he could have a rest when he got back and, anyway, it was just a wee bit pain. He'd touched his chest, though Dolina hadn't remembered that fleeting gesture till much later, and as she related this part of the story she touched her chest just as he had.

When Magnus came back he had dropped the peats outside, opened the door and, as Dolina looked up, he had fallen to the floor in front of her. That was it, not a word more had passed his lips, not a look even. The doctor said he had gone at that very moment when he had opened his own front door and seen his wife looking up at him. As her mother recounted the sad tale, the other family members listened intently, though they had doubtless heard it many times. Ina followed the unfolding tale in her mind, looking at the door as she heard how Magnus left, watching it open again, staring at the floor where he had fallen and died. Dolina was dry-eyed; she must've have cried herself out, Ina thought.

Magnus had been buried beside Angus and, even now, as Ina thought of them lying there in the cold earth together, she saw her aged father and the beautiful boy she had never been able to replace in her mother's affections. As a child she saw him in her mind's eye growing and becoming more beautiful, more perfect, but now she suddenly realised that he had stopped growing when she had gone away for the first time at the age of fifteen. That was her last picture of Angus, as a handsome teenager. She couldn't see him growing older, and now he had his father with him. 'Angus will take care of him,' Dolina said, as though she had heard Ina's thoughts, 'and he will take care of Angus. I always felt anxious knowing my boy was lying there alone.' Then she nodded her head contentedly. It was how people made sense of their grief, Ina supposed; they made up in their minds whatever little scenarios would bring them comfort so that they could move on with their lives.

After a while Dolina looked up. 'When is Ella coming at all?' she asked tetchily.

Ina took a deep breath, swallowed, then said in a small voice that Ella was still in Yarmouth.

'I see,' said Dolina, 'you came along first, then.'

'No, mother,' Ina said. 'She won't be coming.'

Dolina looked confused and shocked. 'And her father dead? What is she thinking about? And it's the end of the season, too. What can she be doing that's more important than coming home here to her family at a time like this?'

All eyes were on her, but Ina didn't reply. All the prepared explanations she had rehearsed so carefully on the train and on the boat had disappeared like a morning haar in the heat of the sun.

'And she'll be needed up at the croft, too. Whatever can she be she thinking about?' Dolina demanded again, her eyes and her voice quietly angry as she looked around her family for their agreement.

'She's not coming back here, ever,' Ina said.

There was a sharp intake of breath all round the room and Ina was so surprised at the sound of her own voice that she almost joined in.

'She's found someone,' she rushed on. 'His name's Eddie, he's a fisherman.'

'What are you saying?' Dolina demanded, her voice like a shard of ice. 'What kind of thing is that to say about your own sister?'

Ina felt their stares turn more disapproving, hardening. 'Mother, you have to listen to what I'm going to tell you,' she said with a sigh. 'It's important that you understand.' She looked around the room. 'Ella's never been happy with Ronnie. He beat her, did you know that?'

There was no reply.

'Well, did you?' she asked, her confidence buoyed by the silence that remained unbroken.

'From the day they were married, he's hit her. Every night she's spent on this island ever since, she's slept with a knife under her pillow.'

Still silence, then Dolina said quietly, 'What goes on between a man and a woman is their business, Ina.'

They did know! she thought furiously. 'And she stopped being your daughter the minute she married that . . . that beast?' she demanded, trying to control herself. 'She was seventeen years old!'

'Old enough to be a married woman,' Dolina said severely, wringing her hands. 'And she had done well. There was a croft and a living there for her: many a woman's had less.'

'I don't understand you,' Ina said, getting up and walking around the dark room that had once been her home. 'Do you really believe that when a man marries he can treat his wife worse than he'd be allowed to treat an animal? If you knew she was unhappy, did you never think of asking her why? And did none of you big, strapping men,' she looked around at them, 'never think they should have a word with Ronnie about what was going on?'

Silence.

'Did Da know?' she demanded.

'Don't you be saying things about your father,' Dolina shouted at her, 'and him barely cold in his grave!'

'He was Ella's father as well,' Ina replied angrily. 'I just want to know, did he know what was happening to her?'

'He didn't really know,' said a voice guiltily. 'None of us did.'

She looked up into the eyes of her brother, Sandy, and held his gaze. 'You didn't know?' she asked him directly.

'Not for sure,' Sandy said.

'Well that makes it all right then,' she laughed bitterly. 'As long as you didn't know *for sure*, you didn't have to take your courage in your hands and do anything about it, is that what you mean?'

Sandy looked down wordlessly at the floor.

'Does Ronnie know about her fancy man yet?' Dolina demanded sourly.

'He's not her fancy man; he's the only real man she's ever known.' She looked around the room. 'And that,' she said, 'takes in every one of you.'

'What kind of man would take another man's wife?' Sandy demanded angrily, more in an attempt, she suspected, to deflect blame from himself and the family than to criticise Eddie.

'A better man than any here it seems!' Ina spat back at him. 'The kind of man who won't beat her and kick her; the kind of man who would stop anyone else doing it as well!'

'So who'll tell Ronnie?' Dolina asked. 'The poor man will be devastated. The hussy! A daughter of mine no better than a whore. What he'll think of us, I don't know!'

Ina stopped herself from turning on her mother, reminding herself that she was newly widowed after all.

'Oh, no need to worry about that,' she said with relish, 'I'll tell Ronnie. I wouldn't have anyone else do it!'

She walked to her kist, rummaged around inside, found Ella's letter and turned towards the door.

'Wait,' said Dolina from the corner, 'you'd better take one of the men with you.'

'Men?' Ina said savagely from the doorway, looking every one in the eye. 'I don't see any men here. I'd have to go back to Yarmouth for one of those!'

Ronnie was in the byre when she arrived. He was busy with the animals and didn't see her at first. She stood looking at him. He was good-looking, all the girls had fancied him, she knew that; a tall, well-built, grey-eyed man, his hair more golden than red. He was much taller and heavier than Ella, she mused, shutting her eyes as she pictured him punching her sister. He looked up and smiled. 'Bastard!' she thought viciously. He looked behind her for Ella.

'Is she in the house?' he asked.

'No,' Ina said shortly. 'She's not coming home. She gave me this for you.'

She held out the letter and he wiped his hands down his sides and took it from her.

'What's in it?' he asked, turning it from side to side.

'You'd better read it,' Ina replied, standing in front of him.

He tore the end of the envelope open and stared inside, then he pulled the letter out and began reading, his eyes squinting slightly. Ina kept her eyes on his face, saw the changing expressions, watched his muscles clench and his lips narrow as he read. She could see that Ella had written only a few lines, but Ronnie kept staring at them.

'Is this true?' he asked eventually, more to himself than her. 'It must be a joke!'

'Is she in the habit of laughing with you?' Ina asked coldly. 'She's expecting by this man?'

Ina nodded. His face changed from red to white and back again.

'How long has this been going on?' he asked.

'Does that matter?' Ina asked.

He tore the letter into pieces and threw them down on the hay, pacing about angrily, unable to think of what he should do.

'And you knew?' he demanded, advancing towards her.

'Not at the time,' she said, looking up at him, 'but that was my fault. Everyone else knew.'

'Other people knew? Who is he?' he demanded, his fists clenching as he stomped about. 'I'll kill him! I'll go down there and I'll kill him!'

'Well, you'd better take an army with you,' Ina said tartly. 'He's not a lassie, he'll hit back. And don't think the crew of *Ocean Wanderer* will stand by and let anything happen to him either.'

'What do you mean by that?' he demanded, but she saw by his eyes that he knew perfectly well what she had meant.

'You've been hitting Ella all these years, that's what I mean,' she said calmly, then she looked down at his feet. 'And kicking her as well. She should've stuck that knife in you. If I'd known what you were doing to my sister, I'd have stuck it in you myself.'

'You don't know –' he shouted.

'What? That she refused to sleep with you after you'd punched her then raped her on her wedding night?' Ina said in a loud, calm voice. She had her hands deep in the pockets of her coat, and she felt the little pile of money there that she had screwed up inside an envelope to give to her mother. From the corner of her eye she saw a pitchfork lying against the byre wall, nearer to her than to him; if need be she would grab it to protect herself. Then she changed her mind; she wouldn't protect herself, she'd get him with it. She thought of places to hurt him. His handsome face; between his legs. Yes, that was it, lift the mucky pitchfork and stick its prongs between his legs, and twist them hard! Please, let him try to hit me, *please!*

Ronnie stopped in his tracks and stared at her, his eyes ablaze. 'I don't suppose,' he said tightly, 'she even gave you her barrel money to bring with this letter?'

Ina gasped. 'Now *you are* joking!' she replied, getting angrier by the second. She wanted to goad him into coming at her so that she could hit back, not just for Ella, but for herself, too.

'I'll give you his name and address if you want,' she said. 'Ella tells me he's twice the man you ever were, and in every department, if you know what I mean. Not that she had much to go on with you.'

He stood still three feet from her, his face so suffused with anger that she thought he'd explode. She imagined the scene: big handsome Ronnie's rubber boots standing there in the byre and the rest of him dripping from the walls and ceiling and running into the hay the animals were crapping on. She laughed at the thought.

'I wonder how many people here know that, Ronnie – that you only managed to bed her once and you had to rape her to do that? Wouldn't that make them laugh?'

He took a step towards her and she darted forward and grabbed the pitchfork, holding it menacingly towards him. He stopped.

'Come on, Ronnie, you're not going to take that from a lassie, are you? I'm going to tell everyone, you see if I don't! I'll tell them big Ronnie's wife is having another man's bairn because he can't get it up!'

He moved closer.

Please, another step, she pleaded silently.

'And even if he could, it's not worth the bother. Nothing there to see, so Ella says.'

Suddenly Ronnie slumped to the floor and knelt, crying, in front of her, and Ina felt so disappointed that she almost joined him. She watched him, trying to think of something more she could say to get him in fighting trim again, but her repertoire had been exhausted. She laughed out loud again. All the smutty talk she had heard over the years, the banter she didn't take part in, the conversations full of crude innuendo that she'd so disliked: who could've known that one day it would come pouring from her mouth so effectively? It was true what they said then: nothing in life is ever wasted! Then she turned to leave and, finding the pitchfork still in her hand, threw it against the byre wall and walked out, still laughing.

Back at Cheyne Crescent she found the family all still discussing the situation, but they fell silent as soon as she walked in. She looked around at them.

'If you're thinking of doing anything,' she said, 'I'd think again. Anything daft, I mean, like her brothers going down to Yarmouth or getting some of the local fishermen to see to Eddie. I wouldn't bother. There's not a man in Shetland able

67

for him, and there are a lot of men down there who'd stand by his side. Besides,' she said, dragging her kist to the door, 'you don't want to leave Ella's bairn without a father, do you?'

A babble of shocked words rippled round the room.

'It'll be your kin, too,' she smiled.

'It'll be no kin to anyone here,' Dolina shouted, rising from her chair. 'And neither will she. First your brother shaming us with his carrying-on with that lassie, and now your sister!'

'Danny's your son and Ella's your daughter,' Ina said firmly.

'They're nothing to me,' Dolina replied. 'I wish they'd never been born, the pair of them!' She looked heavenwards, shaking her hands imploringly. 'What did I do to have to suffer this?' she wailed. 'And to think I lost a decent one, too!'

'I don't know how you can be sure about that,' Ina smiled, though her insides were turning. 'If the saintly Angus had lived, he might've been worse than the rest of us put together, Mother.'

'Don't you badmouth your poor dead brother!' Dolina rounded on her.

'Maybe if you'd given the rest of us as much thought as you gave Angus, you'd have had the time to do something to help Ella!' Ina shouted back at her.

'Don't mention her name in this house,' Dolina replied angrily. 'She will never be welcome in this family again!'

'Well in that case,' Ina said contentedly, 'neither will I.' She went to her kist again and took out the jars of sweets she and Ella had bought. 'Here,' she said to Sandy, 'you may as well take these, give them to your bairns.'

'Don't touch them!' Dolina hissed. 'Whatever comes from that direction is tainted.'

Sandy withdrew his hands and Ina put the presents on the table and turned to go. As she did so she put her hand in her pocket and drew out the envelope of barrel money. 'Here, old woman,' she said, throwing it to Dolina, 'I'll bet anything you won't refuse that. But you'd better make the most of it; there won't be another penny from me as long as I live.'

As she pulled her kist out the door, Sandy moved as if to take it from her. She fixed him with a stare. 'Don't,' she said to him menacingly. 'Just don't.'

Down at the harbour the boat was preparing to leave again for Aberdeen. As Ina got on, she was aware of the stares of the locals. They were used to the herring lassies coming home, and knew that with the war most would be home for good this time, yet Ina Polson had just arrived after her father's death and here she was leaving again almost within the hour. Ina held her head high and smiled serenely. She had intended visiting her father's grave, but she hadn't; events had overtaken her. Never mind, he wouldn't know the difference and, as Dolina had said, he was with Angus now, the perfect and beloved Angus. Who could want for more, even in the grave? She would never come back to Shetland, she decided, never. But she was wrong; there would be one more time.

5

Ina had a boring war, that was the truth. The hospital at Newmachar in Aberdeenshire had been an asylum, but it had been converted into a naval hospital and Ina was sent to work in the laundry. She had no contact with the sailor patients — the WREN nurses jealously guarded their professional positions from the untrained — and for five years she washed, dried, starched, ironed and folded sheets, pillowcases and the rest of the paraphernalia needed in a hospital. Granted it was cleaner work than she was used to, and the conditions were as hot as gutting herring had been cold, but even so, her one thought was to get back among the herring lassies. And she knitted: that was her main contribution to the war effort, she was convinced. The Navy delivered large amounts of thick, heavy wool to the WRENS and asked them to knit seaboot socks, but Ina was the only one who could work at speed and knew how to turn a heel, so she was given the job almost exclusively. At least she was warm as she did it. To this day she would watch TV coverage of sea battles during the war and wonder how many of the sailors were wearing Ina Polson socks.

There was no contact with or from Lerwick, but there were letters from Danny and Isobel in Canada as often as the wartime postal service allowed, though Danny was far from his new home, spending the war years protecting naval convoys making their way across the Atlantic. She had a picture of them in her room taken after they arrived in Canada, two beautiful young people, excited and happy, Isobel still with her hair in the long, golden ringlets Ina had so admired when

70

she was a child. Ella kept in touch too; three years on she was the mother of not just one boy, but three. Making up for lost time, Ina thought. Ella had married Eddie shortly after the birth of the second boy while he was on leave, having been conscripted into the Royal Navy for the duration. Not that Ronnie had divorced her: there was no such thing as divorce for people like them in those days. Ella had written in great distress to tell her that Ronnie had hanged himself in the byre where Ina had last seen him. As his legal next-of-kin she had to be informed, and she had the right to whatever he had left behind, but she had wanted nothing. Ella was in a no-win situation, of course: she was no longer welcome in Shetland because of what she had 'done to Ronnie', and if she had claimed her legal share of the croft she would have been further vilified; but, even so, there would be an element in Lerwick that would exchange righteous nods of the head and say that her refusal to do so amounted to a confession of guilt.

There was a tiny piece in one of the Aberdeen papers about Ronnie's suicide. He had been depressed, so it said, after his wife had left him. 'Depressed because people knew,' Ina supplied, 'depressed because he missed her money.' She had no sympathy for him; maybe that was hard, but it was the truth, and there was no use pretending otherwise. She told her sister not to hold herself responsible either, not to blame herself as she had when Ina had been exiled from the family for taking her part. 'I did that, not you,' Ina told her. 'All I had to do was keep my mouth shut and I'd still be the dutiful daughter. I knew what I was doing.' The truth was that she was grateful to have broken away, and if the life she was leading in Aberdeen wasn't the one she wanted, well, there were millions of people across the globe who could say the same.

At the end of the war Ina decided she would make her way back to Yarmouth. There was no point in talking about 'going home' – she had no home – and at least she had Ella in Yarmouth where she had waited till Eddie came home after the war. And someone else, too. Danny had survived the war, and before going back to Canada he had made arrangements to see his sisters. He was waiting for her at the station. It had been more than fifteen years since Ina had last seen him, but she would have known him anywhere because he had turned into a younger version of Magnus. He was older, broader and more assured, if a little weary, but it was still Danny. The last time she had seen him was the year before he and Isobel had made their great escape, and here he was, just turned forty and the father of two sons.

Ella was now a middle-aged mother, far more relaxed than she had been the last time Ina had seen her nearly six years before. She was distracted by her boys but happy, and Eddie, the gorgeous ladies' man, had very quickly grown into his role as husband and father. He even had the beginnings of a paunch, and his hair was thinning, Ina noticed, smiling to herself. Looking at him now it was hard to find the handsome devil who had introduced her to drink all those years ago. Now he sat quietly in the corner, smoking his pipe, while the three Polsons caught up with each other and discussed their individual, self-imposed exiles from Lerwick. The two sisters listened enthralled as Danny described how he had eloped with Isobel.

'When she came off the boat at Aberdeen we caught the next train to London,' he smiled. 'For some reason nobody had thought of us going all the way down there, and by the time her family caught up with us we'd got married by a registrar. You were allowed to get married without going to a kirk in England, you see. I don't think they knew that; I think they expected us to be hiding out in Scotland some-where for three weeks for the banns to be read and all that. Not that they could do anything about it, we were both over the age of consent, but they would've tried anyway. Old Carnegie had that look on his face when he found us, the one when he was winding up to use the tawse on you, remember?'

'I never knew you had such sneakiness in you, Danny!' Ella laughed. 'And not getting married in the kirk, I'll bet that didn't go down too well.'

'I'm sure that's what did for my mother,' he winced, 'but I was prepared for that. Then we went to Canada. I kept telling Isobel that we could just turn up in Nova Scotia and knock on a Polson door and we'd be welcome, but, to tell the truth, I was scared witless!'

'And you found them all right?' Ina asked.

'The place is full of them,' Danny smiled. 'I called the first Andro Polson in the phone book. God knows how many generations he was removed from the first one, but he was so excited to see us. He'd been brought up on the same stories as us, and I suppose he'd always wondered how much truth there was in any of them. He's a nice guy; once we'd calmed him down he took me to see his grandfather – Magnus, would you believe? – and once the family tree had been sorted out it was as if we had known each other all our lives. It was the strangest feeling.' He looked at Ina. 'Remember all those stories Da used to tell us when we were bairns?'

Ina nodded.

'I thought they must be myths. Still, I couldn't think of anything else to do, but to go there and find out for myself. They were all I had to rely on, but they were true. I never got to tell Da that. I wrote, of course, but he never replied, I don't even know if he was allowed to get the letter. I never heard his voice again, either: that still hurts. I used to think of ways I could contact him. I was near at hand sometimes on different boats, and I would've liked to have met up with him somewhere, made my peace with him, but he would never have done it. Mother would've stopped him. I only heard he was dead from Davie. You remember Davie, Ina?'

Again Ina nodded. 'The boy in the boat,' she smiled.

'That was him. He's been a good friend to us. Isobel and

I would never have managed to get away if it hadn't been for him, and he keeps me up to date with what's happening in Lerwick. We called our first boy after him and we called the second Magnus.'

'You didn't think of calling one Angus, then?' Ina teased.

'Dear God, no,' Danny said with feeling. 'I've heard enough of that name to do me for two lifetimes!'

'And you think it was my mother more than Da?' Ella asked.

'Of course it was, Ella! Old Dolina always called the shots. She had complete control of him; you must know that.'

The two sisters exchanged bemused glances.

'You mean you didn't?' Danny laughed. 'I'm not saying she didn't need to, mind. He had his head full of other things: stars, galaxies, planets, fairy stories.'

'That's true,' Ina laughed. 'I never heard him talk about anything else.'

'Couldn't have been easy to be married to a man like Da,' Danny said fondly. 'There she was having a bairn nearly every year, and there he was, lying in the grass getting us to recite the order of the planets from the Sun, and we always did it better than the ten-times table!'

The three of them laughed.

'Do you remember, Ina, when we were going to collect the peat? He was never quiet, he told stories the whole time. And do you remember him telling us off even one time? Well I can tell you, he didn't. He couldn't. Mother always had to do that, she was the one who made the practical decisions. It wasn't her fault either, but it made her, I don't know, harder somehow.'

'Did you feel that, too?' Ella asked, surprised.

'You mean you did?' Ina asked, even more surprised. 'I thought it was just me and Danny she was coldest to, because we were nearest to Angus. He was the one before, I was the one after.'

'I think she was like that with all of us, Ina,' Ella said. 'She got harder after she lost Angus. He was the only one she ever talked about and he never actually lived. Maybe she could only love the dead properly, you know, at a distance.'

They all nodded.

'Poor woman,' Eddie said quietly in the background.

'What do you mean by that?' Ella demanded.

'Well, if she could only love the dead, how could she be loved by the living?' Eddie said.

'I never thought of that, Eddie,' Danny laughed. 'You know, I think this one's all right, Ella. You didn't do so badly after all . . . It couldn't have been easy for Da either, though,' he mused. 'A man like that, with such a lively mind, that imagination, and he was stuck in a rut all of his life. All he ever did was work hard. Think what he could've achieved if he'd been educated.'

'You're the image of him, Danny,' Ina said softly.

'I know!' Danny laughed. 'Sometimes I catch sight of this face in the mirror when I'm shaving and I see him. It's quite eerie, I can tell you.'

'But I can't get over him not doing something about how Ella here was being treated. If he hadn't gone so quickly he'd have been seeing stars close up, I'd have made sure of that,' Ina said ruefully.

'Don't be too hard on him,' her brother said gently. 'He was a man of his time, Ina, a man of his background. I can see Da making sure he didn't know, if you see what I mean. He was a gentle soul. He couldn't have faced up to anything so harsh.'

'That just means he was weak. It's no defence,' Ina protested.

'No,' Danny replied, 'you're right, it's no defence, but it is a reason. We had a Da who couldn't handle the hard side of life, he had to rely on his wife to do that for him, but we were also blessed with a Da who taught us to think for ourselves and to see outside that life, weren't we?'

Ina and Ella looked at each other and smiled. 'You were

75

always good at pouring oil on troubled water, Danny,' Ella smiled. 'Da would've been proud of the way you've turned out, son.'

'You mean if I wasn't an outcast?' Danny chuckled.

'We're all outcasts,' Ina laughed. 'We're the three Polson reprobates!'

'Only three out of eight,' Danny mused. 'The old man didn't do too badly out of his brood, did he?' Going over Danny's thoughts on their father later, Ina could see that he was right about the relationship between their parents, but she still couldn't quite shake off a feeling of angry disappointment over what she saw as his neglect of Ella. A man of his time and of his background; a man of his personality. Her head accepted it, but her heart didn't – or maybe it was the other way round.

Just before the meeting of Polsons broke up, Ella said excitedly, 'I knew there was something I had to tell you, Ina, you'll never guess who I bumped into the other day?'

Ina shrugged; if she would 'never guess' there was no point in trying.

'Mrs Brown!' Ella said, slapping the table in front of her.

'She's still alive then?' Ina asked.

'Of course she's still alive! I met her at the butcher's, trying to get an extra sausage off her ration book, just like the rest of us,' Ella smiled wryly. 'You'd think we'd earned the odd sausage after all these years, wouldn't you?'

Ina and Danny looked at Eddie sitting by the fireside in his slippers and exchanged amused glances. 'Some might say you've already got the oddest sausage of the lot,' Ina muttered, and Danny laughed.

'Don't you go running my Eddie down,' Ella scolded, smiling despite herself. 'He's a gorgeous big man, is Eddie, a handsome brute.'

Ina and Danny looked again at Eddie then both of them laughed out loud.

'Anyway,' Ella continued, glancing archly at them, 'I told

her we'd pay her a visit when you came down, so you can judge for yourself if she's still alive.'

'Och, Ella, why did you do that? She won't even remember who I am, she probably didn't remember who you were, come to that.'

'She asked for you by name,' Ella stated smugly.

'I don't believe you!' Ina replied.

'She *did*,' Ella insisted indignantly. 'Sure as I'm sitting here.'

So the next afternoon the two sisters set off for King Street.

'Isn't it funny?' Ina mused. 'I feel as if my feet have a life of their own, they just turned down the street of their own accord.'

When they knocked on the door they heard the familiar pattern of Mrs Brown bustling through the hallway and the little noises she made turning the lock, Ina even recognised the creaking of the door as it opened. And there she was, tinier than Ina remembered, but wearing exactly the same outfit as every other time she had seen her all those years ago. The wrinkled little face almost imploded when she saw her visitors and tears sprang to her bright blue eyes as she rushed to embrace them both at once.

'My girls, my girls!' she cried, ushering them inside, and it was in the midst of that triple hug that Ina thought she saw the perfectly coiffed hairstyle, well, move, slightly.

Once through the parlour door, a place they had never been inside in their days of fish scales and guts, though sometimes a head would be permitted inside if they were looking for their landlady, they were bade sit down and plied with tea and scones. Ina was touched by the little woman's generosity, wartime rationing would be in force for years yet, so the feast she was providing them with must have taken up a lot of her allowance of things like butter and sugar. As she listened to their news her mouth still worked furiously, as though she were trying out words before she said them, but she made the appropriate sounds of surprise over Ella's growing family, with a delighted 'My, you never wasted much time, did you?'

Then, looking at Ina she made the usual inquiry. 'And what about you, Ina? No young man in your life yet?'

Ina shook her head.

'Well, he'll come along,' Mrs Brown said firmly. 'You're quite right to take your time.'

Ina and Ella glanced at each other. Taking her time might be something of an understatement given the fact that she was pushing forty years of age.

'I never married, you know,' Mrs Brown whispered over her teacup and saucer. 'I just put on my mother's ring when she died and called myself "Mrs." Isn't that terrible?' she giggled, shaking her head at her own naughtiness. 'Not that I didn't want to, of course, I always planned to have a big, big family, took it for granted, maybe that's why it never happened.'

She sighed.

'I'm sure you had your chances,' Ella said kindly.

Mrs Brown looked up. 'Do you know, Ella,' she said thoughtfully, 'I never did.' She chortled to herself. 'Not one, never even been kissed, shows you what a let off some man had!'

'I find that hard to believe,' Ella insisted. 'Surely the men around here must've been really stupid if that was the case, they couldn't have known what they were missing.'

'Maybe they did,' Mrs Brown said, still chortling. 'Maybe they did!'

Ina said nothing.

'My mother always took in boarders,' she explained, 'and when she died I just kept it going. I'd been helping her all the years I could remember, so it was the natural thing to do. I never had children of my own, that's why I was so fond of all my girls, you were like my own. When you all went your separate ways during the War I didn't know what to do with myself, I'd spent my life looking after people and then they were all gone,' she said sadly.

Then she looked up and flashed them a cheerful smile.

'Still, now that it's over we'll soon be back to normal, won't we?'

As they were shown out, Mrs Brown gliding them to the front door, she hugged them again and wiped her eyes.

'Now I want you both back here as soon as the herring picks up,' she said, 'and all the others, you mind and tell them I'll be waiting for them.'

Ella and Ina waved to the tiny figure till they rounded the corner, then walked on in silence for a few minutes.

'You know,' Ina said quietly, 'I may be wrong, but I think Mrs Brown does wear a wig after all.'

'Do you?' Ella smiled, slipping her arm through Ina's as they walked along. 'What makes you think that?'

'Well I'm almost sure I saw it move back there.'

'Really?' said Ella, looking at the ground.

'And when you think about it, did you ever see as much as a single hair out of place, ever?'

Ella laughed out load. 'You may be right, Ina,' she said.

Neither said a word for a few paces, then Ina turned to her sister. 'You knew!' she accused her.

Ella nodded, still laughing. '*Everybody* knew!' she giggled. 'Everybody except you, of course!'

'Everybody?'

Ella nodded.

'Why did no one ever tell me?' Ina asked incredulously.

'Because we had so much fun with you going on about it.'

'You were all laughing at me?'

'Of course!'

'My own sister!' Ina said, shaking her head and smiling wryly. 'And Edie and all those lassies I worked with every day! All laughing at me!'

'It was just like you, Ina,' Ella said, wiping her eyes. 'You never noticed anything unless somebody sent you a telegram with instructions!'

Ina thought for a moment then nodded her head. 'You're

right,' she smiled. 'Do you think there's something wrong with me?'

'Of course there's not!' Ella retorted.

'Sometimes I wonder, though,' Ina smiled, then they walked on in silence once again.

'It's not going to happen, you know,' Ella said quietly.

'What isn't?' Ina asked.

'The herring fishing,' Ella replied sadly. 'It won't pick up again, so they say, or at least not the way it was. Hard to believe, but they say the good old days have gone for ever and soon there won't be an industry left.'

'Who's "they"?' Ina demanded.

'Well Eddie says everybody's saying so. He was looking for a job now that the war's over and the other fishermen were saying the herring fishing will just keep fading, they say it'll soon be a thing of the past.'

'Och, who wants to believe your Eddie?' Ina said, nudging her sister with her elbow. 'And the rest of them gossip like old women as well, worse than old women, you know what fishermen are like, always looking on the gloomy side. Did you ever know one that was cheerful?'

'Well Eddie always was,' Ella replied defensively.

Ina threw her head back and laughed. 'He was never cheerful, Ella,' she giggled, 'he was just daft, that's all!'

'You cheeky—' Ella replied, trying to look affronted.

Not too many years later Ina would remember that conversation and how she had dismissed the thought of there being no more boats delivering their catches at Bloomfields or any other curers and how she had dismissed the notion out of hand. It had always been, she had thought, therefore, it always would be, because she wanted life to take up again where it had left off. Like a be-wigged Mrs Brown and a great many people who wanted the same thing after surviving those six years, she had been wrong and Eddie, daft as he was, and all those gloomy fishermen had been right.

★ ★ ★

There was no large-scale resumption of the herring trade, so in 1946 Ina got a job with Erie Resistors, an electronic components factory in Yarmouth. She couldn't believe how much money she was being paid. The herring lassies had staged frequent strategic strikes for more wages before the war, and by always taking action when there was a lot of fish to be gutted, they had succeeded in getting what they wanted, more or less. Now she was working considerably fewer hours doing a great deal less work, and she was coming out with four times the money. She even asked the foreman if he'd made a mistake. But it wasn't enough to keep her there; like many people she wanted to recapture the life she had before the war, even if there was a sneaking suspicion in the back of her mind that it had gone for good, that the world had moved on and there could be no going back.

On a whim one day she went to Sutton's, the kippering firm that had kept her and Ella from going home at the end of so many seasons, just to see if there was anyone there she knew from years past, and the first person she saw was Aeneas Hamilton. She watched him bustling about for a few moments before he saw her. He was still the same; he still wore a tan checked three-piece suit, collar and tie, cap and highly polished brown shoes. The entire world had changed and somehow Aeneas Hamilton, like Mrs Brown, had managed to stay exactly as he was when she had last seen him six years ago. She was still smiling when he looked up and saw her, returning her smile. There were times in her life that she now knew held defining moments, though there had been nothing to highlight them at the time. No drums had beat, no cymbals clashed; yet when you cast your mind back you couldn't believe that they hadn't. Was that it, she wondered? Had the path her life would take really rested on finding a particle of that warmer world she had known before the war? Had her future rested on Aeneas Hamilton remembering to polish his brown shoes that morning?

Aeneas had been pleased to see her and they had gone for

a drink; two lemonades: he was no more a drinker than she was. He talked of his plans, of how he had been saving for years for the chance to buy his own smokery. It struck her that his world wasn't wide, he was content with the small corner he had, and though her own horizons were broader, after the turmoil of the last years there was something comforting about being with someone who knew who he was, where he was and where he was going. He also offered her a job back at Sutton's, which she gratefully accepted, even though it meant canning herring and putting up with the smell of the sauces that had made her feel sick, and the wages were lower than she was now used to. Money no longer mattered. She had no responsibilities apart from herself. She had taken her barrel money home to her mother until she was a grown woman in her early thirties, but those days, along with so much, were now gone. The only settled thing in her mind was to save her money to visit Danny and Isobel in Canada, and she could still do that with what she made at Sutton's.

Ina continued to see Aeneas outside work, but there was no great romance. He was simply someone she had known in a previous, happier existence. When Ella laughed at the thought of the two of them together, though, she felt annoyed in a way she couldn't understand, so she joined in rather than give her sister any reason to seriously wonder. Then one morning he had asked her if she'd like to come to the pub at lunchtime as he had some news. He had put in an offer for a smokery in the fishing village of Acarsaid, the home of *Ocean Wanderer*, the boat Eddie had left to be with Ella. It had been accepted, he told her calmly, and asked if she'd like to come with him. Ina saw no reason why not: the prospect of going somewhere, anywhere, appealed to her, and he was obviously offering her a better job, maybe even asking her to be his manager. 'Good,' he said. 'We'll get married before we go up there.'

There had been no nervous speech, no declaration of

undying love, and certainly no proposal on bended knee. It was more a statement of practicalities, and she had no idea till later why she had simply agreed, except that, equally, she had no strong reason – no reason at all – to refuse. This was another pivotal moment to be analysed at a later date. Why had she married him? There were so many reasons, some she wouldn't understand till she was an old woman, an old widow. There were the obvious ones: they had a meeting of minds rather than any romantic notions; they worked well together and they got on. Neither of them was given to emotional outbursts, to emotional anything, come to that; in general they were both calm people, though Ina was occasionally prone to trying things to see what happened – the impromptu visit to the White Lion all those years ago was one, her last trip home was another. And so, arguably, was her marriage to Aeneas – in part, at any rate.

Ina didn't have high expectations of marriage. She was forty years old, for one thing, far too old to be kidding herself; and for another, over the years she had seen what became of those who had. She thought back on the married herring lassies who went away year after year for months at a time from their husbands without their hearts breaking. Given their longings, she had often wondered why they never seemed to miss their men. Even Ella, who had been banished from home and family because of the shameful circumstances of her love for Eddie, had settled now for a very ordinary, unexciting life. He had been a dashing figure, so Ina was always told, and even if she could never quite see him like that, she knew he had been a handsome man who played the field and liked his freedom. But it hadn't taken him long to settle down to a domestic life where he was looked after by his wife. Whatever sparkle there had ever been about Eddie had dimmed long ago. Not that Ella complained. She would look at him asleep by the fire sometimes and say affectionately, 'Look at him, it's like having another bairn,' as she continued to find romance in her penny novelettes.

Marriage, it seemed to Ina, had less to do with passion and romance than it had to do with a whole set of circumstances that came together at a crucial time in folks' lives. People simply paired off when it suited them, when they had reached a phase in their lives when they needed to settle down and when the timing was mutual. Marriage was nothing more than a set of compromises that enabled them to live together in some degree of harmony. Nothing wrong with that, she reasoned, except that most people didn't seem to understand it, though she suspected that men understood it sooner and better than women, who seemed determined to and were encouraged all their lives to regard the whole thing as magical. Even men who ran after every female who crossed their paths eventually stopped running, not because they had met the one true love of their lives, but because it was time, it suited them to stop. If it all depended on passionate love, then why did so many people meet what they insisted was their only possible partner in life near at hand? Wouldn't anything so life-shattering and affirming be just as likely to be found at the other end of the world, rather than at the bottom of the road or in the same workplace, or did she just think that because she had never experienced the heady love other women professed? It seemed to her that her chances of contentment with Aeneas Hamilton were as good or as bad as with anyone else. It was all a lottery when you looked at it calmly, but he was a man who wanted to better himself, who had ambitions. Even if his dreams were more pedestrian than travelling the Milky Way, or the world for that matter, he was a reliable, commonsense hard worker who would provide, and she could think of nothing to say against him. And the look of shock on Ella's face when she told her she was marrying Aeneas Hamilton did nothing to dissuade her and a lot to amuse her. She didn't know where this liking for upsetting the odd applecart came from, but there was no denying it was part of her personality.

6

When the Hamiltons arrived in Arcarsaid it was a working fishing village. Its reincarnation as a tourist spot lay in wait some years up ahead, a welcome safety net happily in place for the days when the fishing was in decline. Ina was pregnant, and it was difficult to tell which of them was more surprised by that. It certainly hadn't been in the plans, and took some getting used to, but at least Ella got her own back by laughing till she cried.

'You'll have three by the hand the next time I see you!' she shouted, as the train pulled out from Yarmouth; but that wasn't in the plans either, and Ina was determined the plans would not be deviated from again. She'd make sure all the gypsy's predictions came true if it was the last thing she did.

The Acarsaid smokery had been owned by an old man who had faced upgrading or replacing the existing wooden buildings. As he had no one to take the business over from him, he had decided to sell instead. Aeneas had already paid a visit to the village long before he had mentioned it to Ida, which was no more than she would have expected from him. Aeneas was a tidy man – he liked everything shipshape, as they said, and made sure there were no loose ends in his life – so the imminent arrival of his bairn threw him. He didn't want bairns, he hadn't thought for a minute that Ina could have them, but there it was and he'd have to make the best of it. That was like him, too; if he met an obstacle he had the ability to know whether it was one he could do something about, and if he couldn't, he coped with it. It would be a boy, that's what he had decided, Ina knew that without asking him, a son to take over the business one day. The plan had been altered but not abandoned, and Aeneas moved on inside the newly drawn boundaries.

He had ambitions for the business, but not huge ones; that wasn't his way. The Acarsaid fishing fleet consisted of mainly smaller boats that went after white fish and the herring that could be caught nearby. The boats didn't follow the herring all the way down the coast for months; they stayed out for a few days, landed their catches in their own harbour, and sold them to agents who sent the fish on the way to the cities by lorry immediately. There was enough there to keep the smokery busy: herring for kippers and other fish for smoking, too, with locally caught salmon and trout gradually being added to the menu. It was a thriving business, but one compact enough to remain within Aeneas's control; he wanted success, but he didn't want an international conglomerate to rise from his efforts. He wasn't a man who gambled in any shape or form: he had his rules and he stuck to them.

Aeneas and Ina bought a house up the Brae, as they called the hill going through the town, and that's where Margo was born. Ina was a late prima gravida – a late first-time mother – but large families were the norm, and women in those days had bairns in their forties, so Ina's pregnancy was routine up to a point. It was harder – she knew to expect that, she was older and tired more quickly – but the midwife came armed with her forceps and Margo was born after two days of labour; for the rest of her life Margo carried a series of scars under her hairline where the instrument that had dragged her out of the womb had dug into her flesh. So Aeneas didn't get the son he had decided upon when he knew he was to be a father, but a daughter who was the image of Dolina Polson: dark-haired with deep blue eyes. Not that Aeneas knew this, of course. He had never seen Dolina, and that suited him and his wife; neatness above all else, he wanted no outside influences.

From the first time he set eyes on his daughter, Aeneas adored her. Ina remembered the moment for the rest of her life, the look of utter adoration in his eyes and the stab of fear she felt when she saw it. The child looked like Dolina, but that look, that immediate and, she knew instinctively, exclusive attachment between father and daughter – well, that *was* Dolina, and Margo became the love of his life. If there had been any chance of Ina and Aeneas being a true partnership it was lost at that moment. He had enough room and love in his life for just one person: his Margo. Ina would smile wryly; second best again. Then she thought of the gypsy's promise that she wouldn't have many bairns and smiled even more wryly; there had been no chance of it after Margo appeared. Any passion Aeneas had, which admittedly hadn't been a great deal, had thereafter been transformed and diverted towards his strikingly beautiful daughter.

Not that Ina minded greatly: she had lived without sex for most of her life, and couldn't see what the fuss was about once she had discovered it. If Aeneas didn't intend to make demands, she wouldn't be complaining. It was the first time she truly understood the other herring lassies and their longing for romance, especially the married ones. Once she had wondered how they could spend those months away from the objects of their desires, seemingly content with their substitute love stories, but now she saw it. It was romantic love they craved, a romantic love they didn't get from their men, anyway. In all probability they read their penny novelettes when they were at home, too, because the same gap existed in their lives when they were with their men – perhaps especially then. The sex, she realised, they could do without far more easily than they could live without romance, even if it was fictional.

In all other aspects Aeneas remained the same: a dapper little man standing just over five feet tall, with sandy hair and brown eyes. He was not handsome, but always clean and neat – that was a description everyone would give of Aeneas even long after he was dead, 'neat'. But his daughter added a new dimension to his life. He probably had never thought himself capable of such overwhelming feelings, or prey to them, but for the rest of his life Margo would transcend everything else. There would be no rules for her except that she would get whatever she wanted, whatever she needed and whatever he could possibly provide for her, as long as he had her near. And that was a great pity, because more than anyone Ina had ever encountered, Margo needed a set of rules imposed with a firm hand.

Ina could tell from the start that Margo wasn't like other bairns. Probably she wouldn't have spotted it so early or so clearly if she hadn't experienced something like it before, but to Ina it was so obvious that she couldn't understand why no one else commented on it. The child would look at you with Dolina Polson's eyes. She would survey you in a detached way; she didn't admit you into her life or ask to be admitted into yours. Not even her poor, besotted father overcame that, though his every breath was devoted to breaching the barrier without ever admitting that it was there. After all, to have done so would have been to bow to the possibility that his Margo was less than perfect.

The ever-honest and practical Ina couldn't help noticing every facet of the undeniably beautiful child she had brought into the world, though, and she saw that Margo didn't behave like other bairns in so many ways. Even as a very small child, if she fell she didn't cry and run to her mother, and if Ina ran to her she found herself shrugged off. To expose her emotions seemed to Margo like a weakness, a lack of dignity – she preferred to sort things out for herself. The only time she came near to another human being was when she wanted something – from Aeneas, usually, because she could always be sure he would give it, and even then the approach was carefully worked out in advance so that she didn't get too close, it only looked that way. Aeneas loved being manipulated by his daughter, he loved being the doting father, but it seemed to Ina that Margo tailored the extent of daughterly affection exactly to get what she wanted. She was always in total control. She employed the same tactics with other people, but with Aeneas most of all, yet somehow she knew that they didn't work with her mother, and as Margo couldn't control the relationship between herself and Ina she had decided to keep her mother at a distance. Neither of them ever acknowledged this arrangement, though both understood it, and it was a source of great sadness to only one: Ina.

7

If anyone had felt close enough to Margo Hamilton to ask about her childhood, and if she had been the kind of person who discussed such things, she would have replied that she had spent it waiting. She had no idea what she was waiting for, but she felt that something was about to happen; something had to happen. Life couldn't just be like this, she might have said. There had to be more than Acarsaid, something bigger; something different and better. All through her childhood and teenage years she had been confident that whatever she was waiting for would come to her, or else what was the point?

Margo had always been aware that she was different from other people, even if she really thought that it was they that were different, not her. At school all the bairns were stupid, like everyone else in this tiny place: they were little people who spent their entire lives getting caught up in trivia, in things that didn't matter, like small-talk and having pals. Margo had no close friends because she chose not to, though there were transient companions who were let go now and then when she had no further use for them or their friendship; she thought that was what friendships were about until those she had cast aside reacted as though she had hurt them. Not that she understood hurt, either; it was a word her mother used to describe the feelings of other bairns she had dropped. It was something they said about her, she knew, 'That Margo Hamilton, she picks you and drops you again whenever she feels like it', but she didn't understand why this should hurt them, only that it did. She didn't mean it, she would think coolly. It was as if she had been born with no innate understanding of the rules of human engagement, and had to learn them, one at a time. But she could rarely be bothered.

The emotions of others left her feeling uncomfortable, and she was always keen to get away from them. She had quickly learned how to deal with her father, though. He was richer than other fathers, she worked that out when she was quite young, and he would give her whatever she desired, though she had to jump through several tiresome hoops to get it. In order to part him from whatever he had that she wanted, Margo had to deliver sweet words and smiles and often a hug or two: things that did not come naturally and made her shiver with discomfort at times. So she perfected an act that she would bring out and perform when necessary. She could see the disapproval in her mother's eyes, but it didn't matter as long as she got what she wanted. And pretty soon, too, she came to understand that Aeneas was regarded as an important man in Acarsaid, and that was something else she could use to her advantage. As far as she could work out, his position in the village was due to the fact that he was wealthy, and if you had money the rules were different: you could more or less do whatever you wanted. She was clever like that, she could see the bones of most situations pretty quickly and how to deal with them, and she noticed that she got away with things other bairns didn't, simply because of who her father was, and that in turn was because he was rich. As she had never understood rules, this was a great help to Margo; as far as she was concerned, whatever rules were, they only applied to other people. Not that she set out to be difficult, it was just that she couldn't see the boundaries of behaviour and so didn't know when she had overstepped them.

It was a situation that had worried Ina from the day her daughter had been born. She hadn't been the kind that formed close friendships herself, but that hadn't stopped her mixing in and getting on with other people. She thought back on her days at the herring, and how much she had enjoyed being with the other lassies, even if she was never one to exchange her deepest thoughts and secrets. Margo, though, was far more extreme than she had been. It wasn't that Margo didn't notice; it was that she didn't care what other people got up to. Their lives held no interest for her except where they might touch on her own, and she took great care to ensure that that didn't happen too often. Ina had some warmth, Margo had none; that was the worrying truth of it. Ina had become a mother long after she had accepted that she never would, accepted it calmly and without regret, too; but, now that she had, she felt the same concern as any woman did when she had a bairn. She wanted her daughter to be happy, to have good friends and a good life, and instead she had Margo, who existed without seeming to have any capacity for joy or excitement. What Ina had no way of knowing was that Margo was waiting. Ina tried to share her concerns with Aeneas, but what she saw as a problem he regarded as proof of his daughter's perfection. Every time he went on business trips to Glasgow he returned with boxes full of clothes and shoes for Margo, all of them exquisite and expensive, and Ina thought that there had to be something not quite normal about any father knowing his daughter's exact sizes. She looked at the taffeta and velvet dresses with their lace trims, and the dainty patent shoes – things other bairns would only wear for special occasions but Margo wore every day – and she asked him if perhaps he thought they were spoiling her. She meant 'you', but 'we' sounded less judgemental.

'We're only looking after her, Ina,' Aeneas had chided her. 'We have the money to do that properly, why would we make her wear rags?'

'But Aeneas,' Ina replied gently, 'all these nice things make her stand out from the other bairns.'

Aeneas beamed.

'What I mean is,' Ina persisted, 'that other folk can't afford these kinds of things and the bairns might get jealous and take it out on Margo.'

'Tell me if they do,' he said angrily. 'No one will treat my Margo badly!'

'No, no, Aeneas,' Ina sighed, 'you're not understanding me. Look, it's hard enough for her to make friends being how she is.'

Aeneas stared at her in bewilderment.

'She's different, Aeneas,' Ina tried again. 'Margo doesn't join in. Maybe that's because we treat her as though she's meant to be different.'

Aeneas beamed with understanding. 'Of course she's different, and no shame in that. She's better behaved,' he smiled. 'We've brought her up that way, Ina.'

'But she thinks how she lives – all these fine clothes, all the toys and treats – is the way life should be,' Ina said. 'It wasn't like that for me, or for you, Aeneas; we had to work to get where we are now. You don't want her thinking it will always be like this, do you?'

'Of course I do!' Aeneas boomed. 'That's why we worked so hard, to give our daughter nothing but the best.'

Ina recalled that they hadn't planned Margo, hadn't wanted bairns, in fact, yet now Aeneas seemed convinced that all their planning had been for Margo from the start.

'If we raise her knowing that she should have the best of everything, she won't accept any less. She'll make sure she always has the best, won't she?'

Ina nodded as though her doubts had been laid to rest, but though she had lost the argument, she knew she was right.

When Margo was about seven years old, Ina had a phone call from Lerwick. It was her brother, Sandy, to tell her that Dolina was dying. Sandy had tracked Ina down, apparently, through Danny's friend, Davie, and was phoning from the minister's manse. All those years, she thought, when he could have done the same and hadn't.

'And has she asked to see me?' Ina asked.

'No,' Sandy replied, embarrassed. 'I just thought you might think the time was right. . . .' his voice trailed off.

'Even though my mother obviously doesn't,' Ina commented. 'And Danny and Ella?' she asked.

'I haven't told them,' he said, 'I thought they were too far away for it to make any difference.'

True, Ina mused. 'Well, thanks for letting me know, Sandy,' she said, 'but I don't think I'll be rushing over. I have responsibilities here and my man and bairn to take care of.'

There was a pause. 'It's a pity,' she said tartly, 'that we don't have another parent. Then we could be sure that we might talk to each other again someday. Goodbye.'

Once off the phone, though, she began a conversation with herself. It had been no more than Sandy would've expected. Ina Polson had always been known to stand her ground, and she was still angry with him and the others that they had let Dolina control them, never once trying to contact the three outcasts until now, when Dolina was in no fit state to keep them in order, her order. Then something else took over that she would look back on through all the decades later: pride. She'd show them, she decided. She would go back to Lerwick, taking her daughter in all her finery. There was no possibility of Aeneas going, too, though he wavered when he realised Ina was determined to take his daughter away and nothing he could say would change her mind. The thought of being without his adored Margo for even a few days would leave him bereft, but Ina reminded him sharply that he often went off on business trips for a few days at a time and this would be no different.

From Aberdeen they took the boat to Lerwick, a journey that seemed both familiar and strangely alien to Ina after all those years, and when they arrived at Lerwick she took her daughter not to any member of her family, but to the Grand Hotel. Dolina was dead, she learned, so all she could do was attend her mother's funeral. It was winter, there was snow on the ground, but she was comfortable in her fur coat. Beside her stood her extraordinary child, dressed in blue pantaloons like jodhpurs, with little frills of material buttoned down over her shoes and held by a strip of elastic under the soles. Margo wore a matching coat with black fur collar, a black fur hat and, suspended around her neck on a cord, a blue muff trimmed with the same black fur at each end, to keep the Shetland cold from reaching her hands.

In the kirk Ina and Margo sat at the back, staying well away from the rest of the family and mourners, well aware that their eyes were on her considerably more than their minds were on the event taking place, she and Margo were stealing Dolina's thunder. They all looked much older than she had expected somehow, then she reminded herself that they had worked hard all their lives; that unlike her they had never reached a time when they could live well. At the end of the service she and Margo walked out last, after all the Polsons had left, to emphasise that they were not officially part of the funeral, and instead of heading for Cheyne Crescent they turned towards the Grand once again. Her brother, Sandy, approached her and said they would be pleased if she would join the rest of the family to await the return of the men after they had buried Dolina beside Angus and Magnus.

Ina shook her head. 'We're booked on the next boat,' she said, pulling on her fur-lined leather gloves. 'I just came to pay my respects. She was my mother, after all,' she said firmly.

Sandy looked at Margo, who stared calmly back at him. 'Everyone's saying how like my mother your wee one is,' he smiled. 'She's more like her than any of us — what a shame she never saw her.' He knew immediately that he'd said the wrong thing, and the look on his face showed clearly that he knew he couldn't recall it.

'And whose fault was that, if not her own?' Ina asked coolly, and with that she took Margo's hand and walked the short distance to the Grand to collect their luggage.

When the boat left for Aberdeen again, Ina didn't look back. That had been the last time she had been on Shetland; the last time she had ever seen or heard from the Lerwick branch of her family. What on earth had she been thinking, she wondered afterwards? Showing off in all her finery that she had a comfortable life, certainly, but why? Was she still trying to prove herself to her mother as she lay in her coffin? It made no sense, but it was the only explanation she could come up with. She had never been as good as Angus, never been clever as he would have been, but maybe she was trying to show Dolina that she'd turned out all right despite that. And there was the rest of the family to impress.

The number of times in the years that followed that her mind had dissected that episode! She had tried to show them that, though they had all sided with Dolina and turned their backs on her, she had survived – more than survived, prospered; though she knew they would have seen it differently. They would have talked after she had gone of how she had used the occasion of her mother's funeral to flaunt her wealth. She couldn't blame them, because in a way that was what she had done. She had been angry with them because they had done as Dolina had said without thinking for themselves. They had cast her and Danny and Ella out without one voice being raised in opposition, not even Sandy's. But she knew he felt bad about it, and another voice in her head would argue that she couldn't judge them, she hadn't had to live with Dolina day in, day out, so who was she to say how easy it would've been to stand up to her? Not that it mattered. These days when she argued with herself from her fireside chair, her warm prison, it was too late to go back and try to put it all right by explaining her side while they explained theirs, because they existed only in the wandering memory of an old woman. They were all gone; she had outlived them all.

8

It was hard to say if the geography of Acarsaid was a curse or a blessing. The village was, as the locals said themselves before anyone else could, a dead end, the last stop on the road map to the far northwest. To reach points further north you either had to hire a boat and go by sea, or travel back the way you had come, drive halfway across the country and approach them from other routes. Not that this was any great hardship, as the scenery was so eye-catching, even after the new road had straightened out most of the bends, swirls and blind corners. They were still there, of course, though as time passed only the oldest villagers – or those who had lived there longest, which wasn't quite the same thing – remembered using them.

When Ina and Aeneas Hamilton arrived in the village in the late 1940s, the Brae, the steep hill that neatly dissected the village, was still the main road to and from the harbour. Ina had reason to remember it; being heavily pregnant for the first time at the age of forty, and having no car at that time, the only way to her home at the top of the Brae was to walk. The drivers of the fish lorries taking the catch to the cities in those days dreaded it almost as much as she had, and said that later generations of drivers taking the new road didn't know how lucky they were. As the juices from the fish flesh and salt water – the bree – dripped from the lorries, and mixed with the melting ice, the steep road became treacherous. 'A pig of a thing it was,' the old drivers would tell the younger ones. 'There was aye a race to get up first, because once the water and the bree was running down the Brae, anything trying to get up slid about like bairns sledging in the snow.'

Not, of course, that they saw much snow in Acarsaid, which was something of a sore point with generations of bairns: being so near to the sea and having a toe in Gulf Stream meant the snow melted as it landed – but you knew what they meant. In years gone by there had been some, so these same older villagers would insist, one or two mistakes by nature that had covered the whole area in snow two or three feet deep, but no self-respecting child ever believed them. One of the few things that made the Nicolson bairns feel special was that their grandmother, old Ina Hamilton, had regularly seen snow in her native Shetland. When their friends didn't believe them, they would be escorted to the home they and their mother shared with Granny Ina, to hear it for themselves.

'Every winter the snow was so deep that we couldn't see over it,' she would tell them.

'*Every* winter?' a small, hushed voice was sure to ask.

'Aye, and it would turn to ice so that we could play on sledges for weeks.'

'For *weeks?*' another voice would ask in awe.

Granny Ina would nod. 'Everybody had great big sledges, big enough to take whole families, and we'd polish up the iron runners till you could see your face in them, so that they'd go faster down the hills – and the hills were that steep, mind. That was the worst part, of course, having to pull them back up again for another go. Once my brother was coming down a hill so fast that he couldn't stop and he went through the legs of a horse and out the other side! We stayed out till three or four in the morning playing in the snow, till our hands were so cold we couldn't feel them. Everybody did it. Funny how you could be that cold and barely feel it.'

The Acarsaid bairns would nod respectfully, but they didn't really believe old Mrs Hamilton. Either she was spinning a yarn or she was talking about an exotic, mystical land that only existed in her mind and now in theirs, with the kind of snow they could only dream about in their village. They would have swapped their unique 'last' tag any day for snow like that. Margo Nicolson would listen to the tales as she worked about the house, a wry smile on her lips. The old one was an incomer here, just as Aeneas had been. It didn't matter how long you'd lived in the village, if you hadn't drawn your first breath there, you would forever be an incomer.

For Margo it was different. She had been born in this house four months after her incomer parents had moved up from Yarmouth, so Margo was a native. It was always said to her by the villagers as though she should be proud of it, but she never had been. They were stupid little people and she had longed all her life to get away from them, but circumstances had taken care of that, damn them to hell. Yet the funny thing was that old Ina, though she would never truly belong, loved Acarsaid and loved all the people. Since her legs had stopped working she had sat there by the fire, her feet forever slipping out of the slippers everyone thought she should wear. She was spending the last years of her life reading her books on astronomy – with difficulty despite her glasses and magnifying glass; and talking to her visitors – though she couldn't hear much of what was said; or watching her TV programmes – though she could hardly hear them even with the hearing aid and the TV volume turned up full. She didn't seem to understand that she was trapped here, as trapped as Margo herself was, or else she didn't mind, or not as much as Margo did.

If only she hadn't married Quintin Nicolson. That was the stick Margo beat herself with every day of her life. If she hadn't married him, she wouldn't have been here, trapped by her mother's infirmities. She had planned the marriage as her escape route, but it had been the mistake that sealed her fate and anchored her to this detested place forever. If only she had waited a few years, her father would've been dead and she would've been free anyway; instead of which when that time came she was a widow with five bairns and another on the way. Her own fault, of course, it had always been her failing that she thought she was smarter than everyone else, something the doting Aeneas had told her with great pride many times. But it had been a failing, there was no doubt about that: look at the life it had condemned her to, and among people she despised. It had been her father's fault first of all, because he had held on to her with such a firm grip of smothering affection that she had to devise a plan to loosen it, but it had all gone wrong, and here she was, listening to her old mother talking about snow to bairns who thought she was mad anyway. Bairns who thought they were something special, she smiled grimly to herself as she scrubbed the sink viciously, because they lived in the village that was the last one on the map. God damn whoever had thought that one up, she thought. Without it the entire place might've slipped in to the ocean and never surfaced again, and even if she went with it, she would at least be out of it for good. The last village! The end of the bloody universe, more like!

Even if it hadn't exactly been the saving of Acarsaid, no one could deny that being the last village on the map had become a peculiarity that drew tourists, especially once the terrors of the old approach road had been dealt with in the sacred name of progress. Once it spiralled ever upwards through the hills, plunging down into the hamlet of Keppaig before sweeping on up the coast to Acarsaid. Now, though, the adrenalin rush of meeting another vehicle coming in the opposite direction round the next corner on the single-track road had given way to a pleasant drive on an almost straight dual carriageway. To the utter bemusement of the locals, though, one or two small roundabouts had been included in the construction. They didn't bother much with them. One had been built in the centre of a slight bend in the road that didn't actually connect to anything. It was a sure sign, they muttered darkly, that any day now some far-away pen-pusher intended building a stretch of six-lane superhighway there, in the middle of nowhere, even though parts of the road were so narrow that passing places were needed. 'We'll be having traffic lights any day now, too,' the more suspicious would mutter darkly, 'mark my words. And what's more, we'll be expected to obey them or go to jail.'

The new road bypassed Keppaig completely, leaving it marooned on the right-hand side, separated from the sea on the left by a strip of tarmac and white road markings. From there, instead of meandering along the old coastal path, the new three-mile route had been blasted through hills of solid rock that had once cushioned the southern aspect of Acarsaid from the sea, so that approaching it in modern times meant driving straight through what had once been the lower reaches of a mountain. On the right stood what was left of the green hills, with houses nestling beyond, while on the left the road finally met up again with the coastal path and widened it, with tantalising glimpses of the pounding surf through the jagged remnants where once the mountain had become a hill, before sloping down and becoming a cliff that had held back the waves for many centuries.

Follow the road to the right and you would pass the curing sheds where Aeneas Hamilton's smokery had stood a long time ago. After many years of lying derelict, the remaining smokery building was now used as a museum of fisheries. As an added bonus you could still smell the distinctive aroma of smouldering oak flakes and fish about the place to give it authenticity. Beyond that, on the right, beside the railway station, stood the Railway Hotel, the only one in town. The tourists liked to stay there because it was so near to the harbour, and the kind of tourists who made their way to Acarsaid usually had romantic notions about the fishing; that, after all, was why they came. Then suddenly you were in the heart of Acarsaid, the fabled 'Last Village on the Map'. The dramatic approach, new road or not, taking tourists to the end of the trail, enabled them to think of Acarsaid as a kind of Brigadoon – and it was in its way, mainly because the villagers colluded in the illusion.

During the summer months the place was so busy that you could hardly move in the centre, but the real Acarsaid somehow purred along beneath the surface, like a sound too high or low for outsiders to hear, or a language they couldn't understand. To the poor souls who were forced to live in cities for all but a couple of weeks a year, it was indeed a bit like a Highland Disneyland, with pleasant locals always happy to give directions in their soft, lilting accents. And providing every opportunity to enhance the fantasy was the working harbour with fishing boats going to sea and coming back in again to unload their catches, a scene that couldn't help looking picturesque. The overall impression was that this happy atmosphere was the permanent way of life here. It was a harmless enough deception and, because they could tell the difference between reality and fantasy, the people of Acarsaid went along with it. After all, it did their village no harm and a lot of financial good.

Mind you, the notions of some tourists soon wore off after a day, and certainly after a night, as the noise of a working fleet going to and coming back from sea knocked the romance out of their heads. This coincided with a quick rethink about the hotel, too, as what they had determinedly thought of as quaintness was suddenly revealed as dilapidation. The service was appalling, too, when they came to think of it. Add to that the noise of the younger fishermen racing around in souped-up Vauxhall Novas half the night, and it was amazing how the scales seemed to fall from even the most determinedly romantic eyes, and after just a single sleepless night, too.

The more realistic dreamers among Acarsaid's admirers knew that it was better by far not to stay in the centre of the village. Instead, from the safe distance of one of the many B&Bs on the outskirts, or up the Brae on the now unused road, the illusion could be preserved without too much effort. But the Station Hotel had at one time really been something, they would tell each other, all red chintz and gold flocked wallpaper, the kitchen dominated by a chef who wouldn't have been out of place in the Café Royal in Paris. That was in the glory days, of course, the 1960s and 1970s, when fishing paid, when the fish came out of the water not just silver, but gold-plated; days now long gone.

Having passed the few shops in the village and, on the right, the now largely unused Brae running straight up from the harbour; the road followed a long, lazy curve to the left and climbed high above the bay to the plateau called Mac-Ewan's Row, and even the most enthusiastic tourist had seen all there was to see of Acarsaid. Where the road rose above the village and looked down on the harbour and the fishing boats was where the houses of the richer residents stood; then, well, then nothing, because MacEwan's Row was where it came to its famous sudden halt. On the plus side this did give the place a tourist trade, a second string to its fishing bow, with every other sign including the word 'last': the last petrol pump, last shop, last chance to part with your money. It made the tourists think that they belonged somehow, that they'd bought an ounce of genuine Acarsaid essence.

Those who came back year after year felt that they knew it and its people, felt that they belonged. They didn't, of course. Even if they did hail the shopkeepers by name every time they returned, or 'came home', as they liked to put it, they would inevitably remain outsiders because they didn't share the daily ups and downs of the place. They didn't live through the winters as well as the summers, knew nothing of the generations of tragedies and the hand-to-mouth existences that were part and parcel of being a fishing community – though of course that was hardly their fault. Whether the tourists knew it or not, their attachment to Acarsaid was superficial; but the villagers were kindly, welcoming people in the main, and no one ever resented the fact that the visitors danced to a tune that only they could hear.

If there was a downside it was that the accident of geography which made the tourists buy everything they could bearing some 'last' legend also added to the traffic and bustle, so that in summer it took longer for the locals to get where they were going. The younger fishermen were always complaining that they couldn't find a parking space in their own village, while the older ones reminded them that they were lucky to have cars to park; in their day you worked hard at sea then walked home, after stopping in at the Inn, naturally, when your boat docked. The younger ones, like younger ones anywhere, would shake their heads and smile quietly at each other, but everyone in Acarsaid still knew everyone else, so at least there was no verbal abuse of the old ones; for that your mother would still give you a slap about the ear in these parts.

And if your boat was tied up at the picturesque little harbour and you were doing something, sorting a net, maybe, or hosing down the deck after the catch had gone, the tourists were always hanging about asking damn fool questions. Not that you really objected, it just made you feel a bit daft, answering them as the other crews looked on, laughing at you behind their blank faces, just as you did when it was their turn to be questioned. In truth, it wasn't so much the questioning that you tried to avoid as the looks and silent laughter of the others, and the ribbing that you knew would follow. As soon as the tourists appeared, festooned with cameras, their smart casual clothes in ice-cream colours contrasting sharply with the blacks, greys and navy blues of the fishermen, a voice somewhere would mutter, 'Aye, aye, here they come!'

The fishermen would try to look too busy to be interrupted, or at least less approachable than the man on the next boat. Not that it really worked, but it was worth a try. 'Is that a net?' a stranger would ask, snapping away as you stood there with one in your hands, checking it for tears, or, 'Are you a fisherman?', and the scales covering every part of you and tripping over the top of your wellies. 'Aye, aye, but you'll likely find your picture in one of they fancy magazines,' one would say quietly to the hapless interviewee in the Inn later, 'but I never knew you were such an expert. I just wish I knew as much about seafaring as you do yourself!' Heads would nod in solemn agreement with each other as pints were sipped and eyes exchanged amused glances over the rims of glasses. 'And tell me,' another would ask seriously, 'that round affair sticking out the floor inside the wee house thing on top of your boatie there, would that be what they call the wheel, then?' and they'd all laugh out loud, relieved that it hadn't been them this time, and knowing full well it could be next.

Sorley Mor handled the tourists best, which was just as well, because they usually made straight for his boat. At thirty-four metres and, in the herring and mackerel seasons, carrying up to ten men, *Ocean Wanderer* was the biggest boat in the harbour, easily dwarfing the others, which were mostly thirteen- and fourteen-metre shellfish boats with crews of three or four men. As the industry had gradually declined since the heydays of the 1960s and 1970s, most of the smaller boats had increasingly concentrated on fishing for prawns, lobsters, crabs and scallops, many with crews that had never worked in the deeper ocean, but they still knew better than to believe any of Sorley Mor's exotic stories. The tourists were easier victims, though, and the skipper would spin them yarns about huge whales, catches that nearly tipped the boat over, storms so severe that he never thought he'd see harbour again. The other fishermen, checking ropes and nets and washing down decks on their own boats, listened and laughed quietly as they caught each other's eyes.

When the tourists went away, happy that they'd been given a glimpse into the hardy but romantic life of a deep-sea fisherman, the others would shout out to Sorley Mor, 'Ach, you told that one better last week!' or, 'You missed the one where you saved the crew from yon pack of hammerhead sharks up by the Minch! You're slipping, Sorley Mor!', and Sorley Mor would take off his Dylan cap, bow deeply to all sides as though their catcalls were applause, and make his way through the harbour to the Inn, the tall, thin figure of Gannet by his side, or more usually, a step or two ahead, smiling graciously to his tormentors. When he was sober Gannet would whisper that Sorley Mor had walked one step behind him all his life, that wherever they went he always arrived first, because the skipper took so long to run the gauntlet of wisecracks and throw a few back.

'Is that a fish you've been catching then, Duncan?' he would call as he passed a boat unloading. 'My, my. A whole fish, eh? You've done well the day. You'll have to try and remember where you got that one and maybe you can get another tomorrow!'

'And no thanks to you, Sorley Mor!' Duncan would shout back from the deck of *Southern Star*. 'There you were, up to your ears in fish, and not a word to a friend!'

'Ach, Duncan,' Sorely Mor would return, all hurt innocence, 'you're not suggesting that I'd be selfish, are you?' A ripple of laughter would run around the harbour. Brothers under the skin they might be, but no fisherman would ever let another know when he was in the middle of a shoal. 'When you called me my radio kept breaking up – is that not true, Gannet? I tried to get hold of you time and time again to give you our position, almost in tears of remorse I was – wasn't I, Gannet? It must've been them atmospherics that was to blame!'

A few steps on, Lachie Macdonald, skipper of the *Barbara Jean*, would call out from the deck of his boat. 'My, but that's a helluva bright jersey you're wearing, Sorley Mor. You look like a tourist, man!'

'Ach now, Lachie, don't let Chrissie hear you saying that!' Sorley Mor would lie, his voice full of mock hurt. 'I don't mind for myself, you understand, but Chrissie knitted this for me herself, knitted it with love and devotion, so she did. She'd be cut to the quick to hear you making fun of it.' Then he'd turn around as he passed, if he hadn't meant to all along, 'And those nice green wellies I saw you with last week, Lachie, man,' he'd say. 'I was wondering where a man could buy a pair?'

'I've got no green –'

'They go well with that pink shirt you had on the other day, and I for one don't believe there's any truth in a word they say, Lachie. I'll always stick up for you, you can be sure of that.'

'What d'you mean?'

'Well, when they say you're light on your feet,' Sorley Mor would reply kindly. 'I know fine that they're just admiring yon quick way you jump about the deck. In your green wellies, too.'

When Sorley Mor married Chrissie, being the most successful skipper in Acarsaid, he had a house built up on the plateau where the road ran out, which was when it had become known as MacEwan's Row. Most of the houses in the village belonged to the MacEwan clan; as everyone knew, Acarsaid could just as well have been called MacEwanville. They were all related to each other, but it wasn't always easy to work out how closely, because they were descended from the larger families of long ago, when birth control depended on how long the men were at sea. There was that other kind, of course: post-birth control, the men lost at sea. Many a big family had been whittled down by that. And even those who weren't called MacEwan any longer, the women who had married and taken other names and their families, they were still MacEwans anyway. MacEwan blood, as everyone knew, was stronger than any other variety, so it was a dangerous business to speak ill of any of the clan.

Not that they always agreed with each other – they were as likely as any other large family to be riven by disputes and feuds – but no one who wasn't a MacEwan would ever get away with bad-mouthing anyone who was. There was always a Sorley, of course, just as there always had been. The name had lain in wait for the first son of the current Sorley Mor for generations. 'Summer Wanderer', that was what Sorley meant, more or less, which was why every boat had been called *Ocean Wanderer*, and as each senior Sorley died his son assumed the mantle of Sorley Mor, Big Sorley. At the same moment *his* son became Sorley Og, Young Sorley, regardless of how old or young they were. There was something of 'the king is dead, long live the king' about it, but the system had worked for as long as anyone could remember, and so no one had ever thought about it, far less questioned it.

There were no other Sorleys, there being a kind of unspoken contract that only the first family, the one that fell heir to the *Ocean Wanderer,* should carry the name, but there were so many MacEwans that ways had to be found to avoid confusion. There was MacEwan Sandy Bay, for instance, who took on the name of his house in nearby Keppaig, or the English version at any rate, to make life easier for the tourists who rented it during the summer months. MacEwan Sandy Bay was also the driver of the few trains that had escaped the Beeching axe in the 1960s, though his enthusiasm had waned somewhat since the end of the steam age. These days, he would say dismissively, he just drove 'a big metal box with wheels on', though he still remembered to sound the horn as he passed the local cemetery, to greet his parents, who had taken up residence there long ago. The tourists thought he was greeting them and waved back, giving them another story to tell their friends to prove how accepted they were in the area.

As many others did, MacEwan Sandy Bay kept a few sheep, a hangover from the days of his crofter forefathers that he could never quite shake off, and of course they provided him with a government subsidy. The necessary skills in looking after them had waned over the generations, though; you always knew, for instance, when shearing time was nigh, because the normally brainless sheep tried to hitchhike out of town, or so the locals said. MacEwan Sandy Bay didn't much like shearing sheep and he didn't have enough to employ professional shearing teams, so he did it himself, and he did it badly, giving the locals a stick to beat him with. A lost sheep was said to have spotted MacEwan Sandy Bay sharpening his shears and have run away, and a dead sheep by the side of the road had simply gone one further and committed suicide by jumping off the hill. He didn't have any reason to feel ashamed, his friends would tell him kindly, any one of them would be happy to do it for him; after all, shearing a few sheep was such a simple task. If you knew how, that was.

MacEwan Sandy Bay ignored all the taunts with exaggerated dignity, but he needed a dram or two to fortify himself each time his sheep needed to be sheared. No one was quite sure if over-fortification was to blame for the odd nick the sheep got, or if MacEwan Sandy Bay was just a bad shearer made worse by a couple of drams, but what was certain was that the sheep liked the business considerably less than he did. MacEwan Sandy Bay's sheep needed no single dab of colour to identify their owner; they carried so many brown antiseptic stains on their carcasses that they looked like a separate breed. Occasionally a couple from another flock would wander into his, only to end up decorated in the same manner, much to the annoyance of the true owner, who knew he would have to fend off taunts of 'I see you have Sandy Bay doing your shearing for you these days,' until some other diversion came along.

Across from MacEwan Sandy Bay was Gannet's house, or as Chrissie MacEwan had dubbed it, his official residence; his unofficial residence, the one where he could usually be found when ashore, being her house on MacEwan's Row. The little whitewashed cottage on the machair by the sea in Keppaig had been left to Gannet by his uncle, who had inherited it from Gannet's grandfather, and once it had been separated from Sandy Bay by a field. When Gannet's uncle had lived there, Keppaig inhabitants who did not wish to argue with their nearest and dearest over a visit to the local pub would 'go for a walk along the shore' instead, knowing – as did their nearest and dearest – that they would get no further than the cottage. The tradition had continued on the few, the very few occasions when Gannet had slept there, until the new road put an end to the skive by cutting straight across the field. That left the cottage to stand alone, looking even more isolated than Keppaig itself and, as Chrissie MacEwan never tired of pointing out, usually empty as well, since Gannet had never married.

'And why the hell would he bother getting married?' she would demand of no one in particular, looking the usually silent Gannet up and down as he gazed back at her amiably. 'Sure, he gets looked after perfectly well here. The only service I don't provide is sleeping with the man!'

'Ach, Chrissie,' Sorley Mor would protest with fake disapproval, 'we don't need any coarse talk, now.'

'Crap,' Chrissie would reply flatly. 'Half of Acarsaid thinks I do anyway, and the other half pretends that they think I do. I know perfectly well that they gossip about us when they're bored. There's nothing like the prospect of illicit, sweaty sex to get their juices running.' She stood back, looked Gannet up and down again and shook her head. 'Look at the creature,' she said, 'super-stud himself! You can tell that he's an unstoppable sex machine. Is it any wonder I can't resist him?'

'Ach, Chrissie,' Sorley Og would wince theatrically, covering his tender, sensitive ears with his hands to protect them.

From Gannet there was never any reaction; he had heard the same remarks made for as many years as he could remember, and nothing had ever changed.

9

On the old road to Acarsaid, just past Mary, Star of the Sea Roman Catholic Church and its chapel house at the top of the Brae, lived MacEwan Black Rock. He was Sorley Mor's cousin, son of his father's brother who, like Sorley Mor's father, had died young. MacEwan Black Rock was now the local carpenter and undertaker. He lived with his widowed mother, Thomasina, or Auntie Tam, as she was known, and his two spinster sisters and brother, a bachelor like himself, in the family home. The sisters suffered from religious mania, or rather the local priest, Father Mick Houlihan, suffered from their mania. The eldest was Bernadette Agnes Theresa who, thanks to a little clever wordplay on her initials, was otherwise known as Batty, while the youngest of the family, Madeleine Anne Dolores, rejoiced in the nickname of Maddy, though if either sister ever saw the joke they never showed it.

Even in her early sixties, Batty, the eldest, regarded herself as a virginal flower waiting to be plucked, so she had never stopped dressing to attract Mr Right. Her hair was henna-rinsed, but badly, so that it stood above her increasingly wrinkled face and her thick, upswept, diamanté-studded glasses like a red warning flare. And not for Batty the comfortable clothes most women regarded as an advantage of getting on in years: she had somehow managed to lay hands on a constant supply of the kind of padded bra that had been popular in the 1950s among Hollywood 'sweater girls', an era Batty had always identified with and found difficult to move beyond on account of its undeniable glamour. As other women of her six decades had long since surrendered their pertness to gravity, the round-stitched, rigid, conical cups of Batty's garments of torture ensured that her breasts remained in all their volcano-shaped glory, hoisted up and strapped into position just under each collarbone. Those of a robust disposition would occasionally wonder aloud what happened when the tortured breasts were set free at night, a thought usually banished with a slight shudder.

Batty's dress sense had never changed, only the colour schemes: she sported a high-necked sweater, tightly worn, all the better to appreciate the twin peaks it strained over, a broad, tight, shiny black belt with a large buckle, and one of many skirts she had worn during the rock 'n' roll era. These were of a very full design and had been intended to be worn with numerous net underskirts, so that as a girl spun round while dancing to Bill Haley and his Comets, Eddie Cochran and the Big Bopper, the skirt would reveal more than her parents would have wished but, because of the underskirts, look feminine at the same time. Then the 1960s had come along and Batty had made one of her few concessions to the age by drastically shortening her skirts so that they ended inadvisably and disturbingly on the wrong side of mid-thigh. Doing away with the length also meant losing the weight of the material that kept the skirts down, and in their minuscule incarnation they flounced and flew about in an alarming way that she was sure enhanced her allure. The effect was completed with black tights and very high black stiletto court shoes but, as had often been mentioned with another shudder, thanks to her occasional concession to fashions other than those of the 1950s, she at least spared the populace the sight of stockings and suspenders.

To complete the picture Batty had remained true to the make-up of 1950s Hollywood: dramatic black eyebrows, mascara so stiff that the lashes threatened to fracture with each blink of the eye, ruby-red lipstick, lashings of Max Factor pan-stick covered with face powder and rouged cheeks, all as precisely applied as the ravages of age would allow on her complexion. It was hardly surprising that Batty rarely failed to draw attention, even from those who saw her on a daily basis. Being pure of soul, however, she interpreted the looks of horror and astonishment as gazes of admiration, as tributes to her undoubted beauty and sex appeal, though she had to admit that that part of her allure was something over which she had no control: it was God-given, obviously, even if thus far there had been no takers. Whenever she noticed a look of bemusement she would pat her head, smile coquettishly while firing a glance in reply from the corner of her eye, and blush, giving the impression that, though she knew she was irresistibly attractive, this was both a great natural attribute and a great burden at the same time.

Her sister, Maddy, was entirely the opposite, in that she had been a younger version of her mother all her life. She had worn variations on the basic uniform for as long as anyone could remember: dark, pleated skirt, lace-trimmed blouse with Peter Pan collar, cardigan, single string of fake pearls and hair in a bun, even if it had once been known as a French Roll. Maddy had been one of nature's maiden ladies since birth, as understated as her sister was overstated. No hint of Max Factor pan-stick had ever touched her features, no block of mascara had ever been worked into a frenzy with a little brush and spittle then applied like black cement to her lashes, no rouge had ever graced her cheeks.

The one thing they did share, however, was religion. Visitors were expected to cross themselves and genuflect as they entered the Black Rock house, making full use of the holy water conveniently situated at the front door, to cross themselves and genuflect whenever they passed a holy picture or statue within the house – and there were many of both – and cross themselves and genuflect as they left the house once more. There were other complicated rituals while inside, involving more crossing and kneeling, as well as bowing of the head when the name of some deceased member of the family was mentioned; the same motions had to be gone through on hearing the Lord's name or those of the many saints who were regularly referred to in conversation. Prayers were, of course, said before as much as a glass of water could be consumed. The sisters and their antics ensured that few came to call without good and urgent reason, but Father Mick was at a distinct disadvantage. If the sisters weren't chasing after him to bless some newly acquired religious medal, picture or rosary, they were reminding him of his duty to visit their mother regularly to hear her confession and give her the sacraments.

'I'm there every few days. They hold me hostage till someone else comes to the door and I take the chance to bolt for freedom while the door's open,' he'd complain to Sorley Mor, demanding that he do something about his relatives. 'I mean, what in hell can an old woman like that have to confess, tell me that? They're your family, Sorley Mor, take pity on a man of God and crack the whip with them!'

'What do you think I am?' Sorley Mor demanded. 'Ringmaster of the whole MacEwan circus?'

'You know damned well you are!' the priest replied accusingly.

'Language,' Sorley Mor said in a hushed voice. It was a ploy he'd been using against his wife, Chrissie, for years and, though it had never worked with her, he still thought it might with the priest.

'Language be buggered!' protested Father Mick, proving him wrong. 'By the time I escape from Black Rock my head's spinning so much with all the crossing and kneeling that I can barely walk straight.'

'Away with you, Father Mick,' Sorley Mor replied calmly. 'It's the falling-down stuff does that to you. Everybody knows that.'

Batty and Maddy's younger brother, Archie, a tall, thin chap with a shock of wiry red hair and an even redder complexion, was Acarsaid's only roadman. His various duties entailed clearing drains, sweeping the seaweed and pebbles off the road after storms – and stones and mud when heavy rain had caused minor landslides – as well as patching the odd pothole. It was common knowledge that you could pass Archie, otherwise known as Haffa, leaning on his shovel as you drove past on the road to far-off Inverness, and come back three days later to find him in exactly the same position on exactly the same piece of road. He was, in his cousin Sorley Mor's words 'a professional and highly qualified shovel-leaner', though he constantly protested that he had just been taking a rest when so-and-so happened to pass and came to a false conclusion.

'You know fine, Sorley Mor,' Haffa would complain, 'that it's my left knee.'

'Your left knee be damned,' Sorley Mor replied. 'It's a shovel! We all know a shovel when we see one, Haffa, you can't fool us, man.'

'That's why I occasionally have to lean on my shovel,' Haffa explained patiently, 'because I hurt my knee in the line of duty years ago and I need to rest it.'

'First I've heard of it,' Sorley Mor replied.

'That's because you never listen,' said his cousin peevishly. 'I hurt it, then the years of standing in ditches full of water –'

'You stand in ditches of water over your knee?' demanded Sorley Mor incredulously. 'Well I've never seen that.'

'You've never looked,' said Haffa. 'As far as you're concerned, Sorley Mor, the only job in the world is the one fishermen do.'

'True, true,' Sorley Mor said, nodding to Gannet.

'But other people work as well, and it's possible to get injured in ways that don't involve catching fish. Well, that's what happened to me, and if I was the type to sue I could be rolling in money by now, but I'm just a decent, hard-working roadman.'

'And fully paid-up shovel-leaner,' Sorley Mor added.

Haffa gave up. There was no reasoning with Sorley Mor when he was in that mood and, come to think of it, he always was. Not only did he have to stand above knee-deep in water-filled ditches, but he also had to use the shovel occasionally for another part of his duties. Haffa was also the local gravedigger. This auxiliary occupation had earned him the nickname Digger for a time, until an unfortunate occurrence in his youth. Digger had had a heavy night in the Inn and next day felt particularly unwell and in just the right state of fragility for a spot of serious and uninterrupted shovel-leaning. As luck would have it, though, an elderly local man had died that morning and Digger was called upon to dig a grave. To make matters considerably worse he was faced with making room for the burial by first removing an older coffin from the grave and digging a deeper hole before replacing it, thereby making room for the latest dearly departed to be buried on top.

Feeling somewhat the worse for wear, and necessity being the mother of invention, Digger had come up with a solution that he promised himself would be a one-off. The coffin he had to remove was very old; therefore, he reckoned, there would be little left inside, so to save time and effort he hit on the brilliant idea of collapsing it in on itself and heaving it over the wall that ran along the back of the cemetery. For now, he promised, till later. Behind the wall was the scrub of the hillside and nothing else, so no one ever went there because there was nothing to do or see. He would, he told himself, rectify the situation at a later date by reburying the flattened coffin in the plot that, after the forthcoming burial, would be full anyway and would never be reopened. So what would be the harm and, more importantly, who would know?

But in his youth Digger had a few such heavy nights at the Inn, and not only did he keep putting off the reburying of that first old coffin, but he resorted to the same shortcut more times than he chose to remember. It all came to a head the day a dog was spotted running through the village carrying a human skull in its mouth, and when followed went immediately back for more. The results of Digger's handiwork were soon discovered behind the wall. Digger was penitent and probably more shocked than the other villagers by the pile of ancient bones he had consigned to their second resting place; in his mind he had decided that he had only heaved one or two old boxes over the wall. 'He's not a proper digger at all,' said one wag. 'He's damned well only half a digger!' and thereafter Digger was renamed Half a Digger, a name that had become corrupted over the years to Haffa.

Haffa continued as the local gravedigger, though. For a start no one else wanted the job, and besides, he and his brother, MacEwan Black Rock, the carpenter and undertaker, made an undeniably good team in the task of burying the dead. They worked hand-in-hand, so to speak, and it would take years for another gravedigger to build up such a seamless partnership with Black Rock. The only remnant of the hangover lapses of his youth were his nickname and Sorley Mor's occasional demand that, when his time came, Haffa should dig him a hole decently deep enough to constitute value for money or face Chrissie's wrath – and no sane man, Sorley Mor told his cousin, wanted to do that.

The eldest son, Black Rock himself, was a lesser version of Sorley Mor in every way. Smaller in height and build, he had dark hair, though not as dark as his cousin's, the same blue eyes only less so, and mainly he had so little conversation that he simply nodded or shook his head when the need arose. He was, as even Gannet had been moved to observe, 'a bit like the skipper with the sound turned off'; until that was, he had something specific to say, when he would indulge in so many niceties before getting to the point that people would run off screaming rather than listen to the end. The four Black Rocks were separated from each other by a year, and they were all eccentric.

Their mother, Auntie Tam, on the other hand, was perfectly normal and respectable, though it was said that MacEwan Black Rock's second-sight had been inherited from his mother's father, who had also been a carpenter-undertaker in her native Barra. Once, when he had been about five years old, MacEwan Black Rock had been taken to see a neighbour who was at last on the road to recovery after a long illness, and the boy had looked at her in bed and asked who the baby was. 'What baby?' his mother asked. 'The one lying beside her,' he had replied, only there was no baby there. 'And what's that tapping?' he demanded; only there was no tapping. Almost a year to the day later the neighbour had died in childbirth with her baby, and when MacEwan Black Rock had been taken to pay his last respects, he had looked at the child in the coffin beside the neighbour and said, 'There it is. That's the baby that was in bed with her.'

After that he always heard the noise of a hammer tapping nails into wood if someone had died or was about to die, as long it was no one of his own blood, and these days he started making a coffin as soon as he heard it and before being told there had been a death. No one in those parts questioned it, they had seen it often enough to know that he simply heard something they didn't; they saw nothing supernaturally spookie in it. 'I heard MacEwan Black Rock tapping away as I passed by,' they'd say conversationally to each other. 'I wonder who it will be?', and sure enough in due course Haffa would be seen digging in the cemetery high above the village.

10

There were many other MacEwans in Acarsaid: MacEwan
My Haven, a trio of them at High Trees, Green Trees and
Monkey Puzzle, and, of course, MacEwan Clinker Dell, who
considered himself a bit of a wag, even if no one else did.
However many MacEwans there were in the vicinity, though,
it was traditionally accepted that there could be only one
Sorley Mor and Sorley Og at a time, and thus far fate had
fallen in with convention to make sure there always was. The
present Sorley Mor, teller of tall tales to innocent tourists, had
carried the name for a long time, after his father had died in
his forties, at least breathing his last in his own bed in his own
house, whereas *his* father had been lost at sea. So it was that
Sorley Og had become Sorley Mor a quarter of a century ago
when he had been in his early twenties. But it sat easily on
him from the start. He was the most respected man in the
village, and being the senior living Sorley was only one reason
that he was called Sorley Mor; it was a measure of his standing,
too, because he was a big man in every respect, apart from
height, of course. He would do anyone a good turn without
waiting to be asked, even those who might have done him a
bad turn in the past, everyone knew that (apart from tipping
them off when he was catching serious amounts of fish, of
course, only a fool would do that), not only in his home
village but in further away ports, too. He was, as the villagers
said with proprietorial pride 'always spoken well of'.

For him being the skipper meant more than owning a boat
and sitting in the big swivel chair in the wheelhouse. It meant
doing the job properly. He was safety conscious: the accident

that had killed his friend, Quintin Nicolson, had seen to that. It had been bad luck, unavoidable, a random occurrence, nothing anyone could have done about it; all these things were said whenever the terrible tale of Quintin's death was recounted, but Sorley Mor had taken the view that if simple bad luck could kill a man, then you had to eliminate every known risk to keep bad luck at bay. Aboard the *Wanderer* he enforced strict discipline; the sea was not to be treated lightly, he would say. Regardless of how long they had been fishing or how many generations of their families had been fishermen, the sea wasn't interested in family histories and it owed them nothing, and he would point to a framed tract on the wall of his house on MacEwan's Row, as well as the wheelhouse of the *Wanderer*.

The Sea

I don't want your manmade ships defiling my undying beauty,
But if you must, then the effort must be of your best;
Nothing else will serve.
If you build a ship there must be no error,
Or I will find it out and will punish.
Of the men who serve there must be no error,
Or I will find it out and will punish.

Anyone with a sloppy attitude would not have been invited to work on the *Wanderer,* and he made sure that safety requirements were met by both the boat and his crew; even though he already knew they were the best available without the certificates, he made sure every man had them. Drink was never a problem on the *Wanderer*: Sorley Mor had never allowed even the smell of it on board, a rule that was never broken, however merry a time he and the men had in the Inn when they came ashore. Every piece of equipment was regularly inspected, and at sea the *Wanderer*'s two-hourly look-outs were exactly that – they stayed awake on watch and they had the knowledge and experience to know what they were looking for. When Sorley Mor had first started fishing at the age of fifteen there were few men who carried life insurance because the big companies loaded the premiums against them, citing their hazardous occupation. As the men never knew how much they would take home, or in some cases how long they would be employed, many did without. Without making any announcement about it, Sorley Mor, being the man he was, arranged accident and life insurance each year for his crew through the local fishermen's association. A responsible skipper might have done the same and deducted it from the wages of his crew, but Sorley Mor chose instead to absorb it into the running costs of the boat rather than ask his crew to pay for their own insurance. These were some of the reasons why he was acknowledged as the best skipper, and why his men stayed with him over the years – though they never mentioned the insurance arrangement, because they knew he would have found that embarrassing; after all, it was his feeling that he wasn't doing anyone any favours, he was only doing what he knew to be right.

But Sorley Mor was more than a good skipper; he had the kind of personality that lit up company. He was full of humour, always ready with a wisecrack or a tale, and, truth to tell, when he was away fishing, the village seemed quieter without him. In conversations about the place gossip would be exchanged, opinions aired, then at some point someone would be sure to ask when *Ocean Wanderer* was due in. When she arrived and the catch had been sent to its various destinations, he and Gannet would make their way to the Inn before going home, as fishermen had done for generations. As they entered a chorus would shout out gleefully, 'The Wanderer has returned!' It was a silly thing to do, but over the years it had become a tradition, and then it had taken on all the connotations of a superstition, and no one would risk stopping it. Not that anyone believed any of the old tales any longer, of course, and especially not Sorley Mor himself, but on the other hand, it did no harm to touch every base, did it? And over the years Sorley Mor had tried every way to beat them at their own game, coming in by the back door, sending Gannet in on his own, even bursting in and shouting it out first himself, but the others had always found out what he was up to and lay in wait anyway, and in his heart he knew there was no way of avoiding that welcoming cliché – nor did he really wish to.

He was the very man to ridicule the hundreds of fishing superstitions, like never turning a boat in harbour against the sun, or always turning it sun-ways when first leaving shore. There were endless beliefs and all of them had adherents, even if they didn't like to admit it. When going to collect a new boat it was lucky to start the journey when the tide was flowing, and unlucky if any unforeseen hitch meant returning without her. The making of a new fishing line had to begin on the outgoing tide and be finished without interruption, and meeting a red-haired woman or one who looked like a witch were bad enough portents of doom for a fisherman to turn and go back home instead of to sea. Some words were such bad luck that they couldn't be said; rats were called 'long tails', for instance, pigs were 'curly tails', and salmon were 'red fish'. Above all, whistling aboard a boat was forbidden, because it was sure to whistle up a wind.

Most of the reasons behind the superstitions and the forbidden words were lost in time, but if any of them were inadvertently uttered on board, there were still those who would shout 'Cauld iron!' before grabbing the nearest piece of metal. In modern times they did it for a laugh, they said, but there was still an underlying relief that someone *had* said the words of absolution, if truth were told. Not Sorley Mor, though; superstitions were all nonsense, he would say, ways for bad fishermen to blame something else. His great delight was to visit a wheelhouse where the clock was on the left and the barometer on the right. 'I've never seen that before,' he would say, whistling quietly to himself, 'they're usually the other way about. But no matter, I'm sure you know best,' knowing full well that, as soon as he left, the skipper would swap the positions of the clock and barometer. Then he would go to the next boat and say the opposite, just for the fun of it.

The other fishermen got their own back in the Inn, though: baiting Sorley Mor had become as much a preoccupation with them as baiting them had with Sorley Mor. The opening gambit was always about Eric, the *Wanderer*'s Glaswegian engineer, a mere warm-up for another attempt at wrong-footing the skipper. The hope was that if they got him to open fire about Eric he might find it harder to defend himself against their accusations of being secretly superstitious, especially as by the time they got round to that topic the skipper would have thrown enough down his throat to nudge his thought processes off-balance.

'So you still haven't persuaded that big man to join us, then?' a voice would ask mildly.

'Now, now, lads,' Sorley Mor would counter, 'I'm sorry to hear that tone in your voice, mocking a man who is big enough to admit to his failings.'

'Eric's definitely big enough, Sorley Mor,' another voice would add. 'What we're still wondering after all these years is if he's man enough.'

'Would you listen to that?' Sorley Mor would say to Gannet, shocked to the core. 'I'll tell you this now, if you were to say such a thing in front of Eric himself you might never draw another breath!'

'I suppose,' another would join in, 'there's nothing wrong with a man dancing to his own tune right enough.'

Sorley Mor would sip his pint in quiet contemplation for a moment before replying, a moment that would fool only someone who didn't know the skipper, and here everyone did. 'In my book,' he would say in a measured tone, 'it says a lot for Eric that he avoids the drink when it does him nothing but harm. There's a few of you here could benefit from his example.'

'Aye, aye,' someone else would remark, 'I'll say that about the big man, he's never been tempted to take a drink ever since he joined the crew of the *Wanderer*. Never a lapse in all that time. You have to admire the man.'

'True, true, Colin,' Sorley Mor would reply solemnly. 'My, but it's good to find a sympathetic, intelligent soul like yourself in this den of thieves.'

'Must've been hard for him,' Colin would continue quietly, 'never being tempted off the wagon, never falling into step with the rest of the crew.'

'Now that's a funny way to put it, Colin,' Sorley Mor would reply amiably after another sip, 'but I see what you mean all the same.'

'Big Eric always walks a straight line, not like the way the rest of you stagger out of the Inn, that slow, slow, quick, quick slow way,' the tormentor would continue.

From Sorley Mor there came not a squeak by way of reply.

'And are you not superstitious about having a sober man aboard, then, Skipper?'

'Now, you know perfectly well that I have *only* sober men on board the *Wanderer,* and I'm also the sanest man in this port,' Sorley Mor would reply, quietly and deliberately sipping his pint. 'I am a man of the world and a man of science. I believe in none of your old wives' tales, as well you know!'

Amused glances would be exchanged around the bar, then someone would remind Sorley Mor that he did believe in one superstition at least, 'the man in the black coat'.

'There you go again,' he'd say smugly. 'Minister, man. Priest. Look, the sky's still where it should be! My, but you're like a bunch of bairns telling scary stories to see who'll cry first!'

Well, call them what you will, they'd say, but wasn't it true, and they all knew it was, that he wouldn't let one set foot on his boat? Furthermore, wasn't it the God's honest truth that when a man in a black coat, usually Father Mick, the local Catholic priest, was rumoured to be in the vicinity,

Sorley Mor had been known to dash down to his boat and to stand, arms crossed, blocking the way, just in case the religious fellow tried to hop aboard?

'Now that has nothing to do with bad luck,' Sorley Mor would say, sipping his pint and determinedly ignoring the catcalls. 'That's to do with Father Mick himself. You couldn't let him on your boat, you know that fine, because he's never sober, and he's not altogether a bad wee man, you wouldn't want him to fall overboard, now would you?'

At this the Inn would erupt in jeers, which Sorley Mor would ignore with exaggerated dignity.

'And if you lost Father Mick,' he'd continue seriously, 'you'd be sure to be held responsible by Rome. The Pope himself would likely sue you for every penny you had.'

'Well I've never seen *any* man in a black coat on your boat,' MacEwan Sandy Bay would say slyly amid the laughter.

'Ach, you must've been looking in the other direction all your life!' Sorley Mor would reply, his clear blue eyes staring straight ahead, two pools of total innocence. 'Sure Gannet here has seen them himself, we've had enough ministers and the like aboard over the years to start a whole new religion all of our own!' At that a huge shout of laughter would go around the Inn, as Sorley Mor sipped on, smiling to himself.

'And I'm surprised at you, Sandy Bay,' he would say, glancing at him, his blue eyes almost brimming over with hurt, 'attacking a kinsman from behind. Aye, betrayal within the family is a hard cross for a man to bear, right enough. And what's more, would you ever allow a minister to sit beside you in your engine?'

'I don't think one's ever asked, Sorley Mor,' replied the train driver, laughing.

'Aye, well, there you go then!' Sorley Mor said triumphantly. 'A likely story if ever I heard one. And what are you doing in here anyway? Don't you have any sheep to shear?'

'And so, Sorley Mor,' someone else would suggest quietly,

'you're saying you'd be happy to let one, apart from Father Mick, on the boat?'

Sorley Mor would take another sip of his pint, trying to convey an air of calm logic. 'Put it this way,' he'd say. Sip. 'That's something I'd have to decide at the time.' Sip. 'Depending on the cut of the man himself, you understand, and whether he was sober.' At that another huge snort of derisive laughter would run around the company. 'Now,' Sorley Mor would demand, looking around as severely as he could and shaking his finger at them, 'the question you have to ask yourselves is this, boys: how many *sober* men of the cloth have you seen?'

All around him the Inn would shake with laughter, some of it Sorley Mor's own.

'No, boys, I'm telling you.' Sip. 'Take my advice, steer well clear of religious men, they're a risk you can never take.'

Whatever his views on letting him on board his boat, it was the priest's name and telephone number that Sorley Mor gave in case of an emergency at sea. If something happened to a boat, the emergency beacon would activate and one of the coastguard stations would pick up the signal, identify the boat and call the emergency contact. Some skippers left the name of the local agent, Dougie Nicolson, with his home and office numbers, others wanted the Seaman's Mission informed, but some wanted their wives to be contacted first. Nine times out of ten activated beacons proved to be false alarms and a wife would say wearily over the phone that the bugger wasn't even at sea; he was sleeping by the fireside after coming home from the Inn.

'I've given them your number,' Sorley Mor told Father Mick one day, as they bounced about in his ancient Land Rover on the way to the Inn.

'Well that's helluva nice of you!' said the little priest sarcastically. 'And will you slow down? You didn't think of asking me first?'

'No,' said Sorley Mor, screeching around a corner. 'Sure,

why would I do that? Would you have refused, and you a man of the church?'

'I'm a man of enough responsibilities, that's what I am,' Father Mick grumbled. 'I have your mad cousins at Black Rock to contend with night and day for a start!'

'Ach, away with you,' Sorley Mor laughed, changing gears so clumsily that Gannet groaned in the back. 'Sure, what do you do with your time anyway? Say a few masses, drink too much communion wine, visit poor sick bodies that would rather be left alone, and listen to loads of codswallop that you call confession.'

'I'll have you know, Sorley Mor,' said the priest, 'that there's quite a bit of serious sin in this village.'

'They make it up to keep you amused!' Sorley Mor retorted. 'If they've got serious sin they go to confession in some other port. You know every voice in this place and they don't want you staring at them with your wee beady eyes as they're buying their papers from Hamish Dubh.'

'I resent that,' Father Mick said primly. 'So. If someone calls and says you've disappeared, what am I expected to do? Row out and save you?'

'My God, if I was depending on you saving me I'd have a long wait,' said Sorley Mor. 'Did you hear that, Gannet? Is the man not a comedian?'

Gannet chuckled quietly.

'You see?' Sorley Mor laughed loudly. 'Even Gannet there thinks that's a mad idea. No, no, you just tell Chrissie and the families of the rest of the crew.'

'But you know fine well that Chrissie won't let me in the house. You won't let me on the *Wanderer* and she won't let me in the house.'

'Ach, now, you see? You'll believe anything! Did you hear that, Gannet? I won't let you on the boat for very good reasons, you know that fine, and Chrissie lets you in the house fine, she just shouts at you a bit, that's all.'

'That's the same thing.'

'How is it?' Sorley Mor demanded in a bemused tone.

'There's no way I'm going in if I'm to be shouted at. She's a powerful woman, your Chrissie. She terrifies me. When she comes at me I feel I'm about to be beaten up.'

'She's an angel,' Sorley Mor laughed. 'What's wrong with you, man? A sweet, gentle wee angel is what she is!'

'We'll leave that to one side for the minute,' Father Mick said, exchanging a doubting look with Gannet. 'But *why* does she shout at me? That's what I don't understand.'

'She says you lead me astray, you get me mixed up in all sorts of capers, and that when I go down to the Inn for a quiet game of dominoes, you get me drunk, that's what she says.'

'Who told her such a damnable lie?'

'It was maybe Gannet, here,' said Sorley Mor in a vague voice, 'I'm not sure. But I know that I backed him up. Is that not the way it was, Gannet?'

Gannet, stone-cold sober, simply smiled, nodded and muttered noncommittally.

'Besides, what are you complaining about? If she beats you up, that's so many bruises towards canonisation. You'll be suffering for your faith, after all.'

What Sorley Mor had was character, he had a presence, and he would've been noticed wherever he was and whatever he did for a living; but the good folk of his home port didn't think in those terms, because he was who he was, and he was theirs. What they would say, though, was that they wondered where his good nature had come from, because it certainly didn't come from his father. It has been said so often that it had become a mantra, but Sorley Mor's father had no heart at all, unless you called a lump of granite swinging on a rope a heart, yet funnily enough he had died young of a heart attack. The old ones would nod to each other; now there was irony for you.

His father came from the last generation of fishermen who

could, as the saying was, 'read the sea'; though technology was already making inroads even then, he just had to look out at the waves to tell where the herring were. Some of it was commonsense, like watching for porpoises and other rorquals, the kind of creatures that hunted for herring by herding them and keeping the shoal bunched while they feasted on the fringes or took turns diving into the pack. Concentrations of gannets diving vertically were signs that herring were about, or sometimes the sighting of a basking shark – a plankton feeder like the herring – would be enough to give away the position of a shoal; or a whale would break the surface through the middle as it fed on 'the silver darlings'. For fishermen of the old man's era there were other signs now lost to his son and his peers, signs they only talked about when yarning to each other. Sorley Mor's father found herring by looking out for streams of bubbles breaking the surface and oily patches, he recognised the 'black lump' of a shoal in dull, wintry weather, or a red sheen on the water in bright winter sunlight. He knew big shoals, 'fields' or 'parks', were to be found by the green phosphorescence of late summer or autumn – '*losgadh*' it was in the Gaelic, 'burning' in English – and he could hear the noise of a big 'play' of herring breaking the surface of the water from miles away, skills honed to instincts that had been lost over the years, lost to Sorley Mor except in stories about his father.

So he had been well respected as a fisherman, the old Sorley Mor, but he was never as well liked as his son, who was popular even as a boy, and so it would continue throughout his life. He had something it was hard to put a finger on, people would say if asked, unaware that they had smiled instinctively at the mention of his name before relating some anecdote about him. If pushed to list his qualities they would undoubtedly have shrugged their shoulders and looked bemused before telling you that he was honest and fair, a decent man who had a generous nature and hadn't an enemy in the world, all of which was true, but that description could easily have been used for other men in the village who weren't thought of in quite the same way as Sorley Mor. In a less macho culture, in a less reserved community, Sorley Mor would've been described as well loved, but that kind of language would have embarrassed the undemonstrative folk of Acarsaid. It would've struck them as insincere and flowery. So instead Sorley Mor was talked of as well liked, which meant the same thing anyway.

What they had no means of knowing, because they had never been without him in their midst, was that Sorley Mor would've caught the attention of strangers even if the other fishermen didn't encourage them in his direction. He had an unconscious magnetism, or perhaps what the young ones called an aura or a vibe; but whatever it was that drew people to him, it had little to do with his physical appearance. He was only about medium height, certainly no taller than five feet six inches, though he had the strong muscles of a man once used to working with his entire body before advancing technology had taken away much of the physical aspect of the fishing, a strength and bearing that caught the eye. And it was true that he was a handsome man all his life; like all the men in his family his hair had started to turn grey at an early age, though there was little showing from under the washed-out Dylan cap he'd bought from Hamish Dubh in the village store sometime in the 1960s. He took the cap off only when attending weddings or funeral, times when he deemed himself to be officially off-duty, and then a startlingly pale patch of forehead was exposed just below his hairline, a band of skin that had been protected by the cap peak from the wind and sun that had bronzed his features over the years, emphasising the blue of his eyes. Even as he approached his sixtieth year he was a good-looking man, but there was indefinable something more, that something special from within Sorley Mor, even if no one could quite say what that might be.

II

When young Rose Nicolson thought of Sorley Mor she always pictured his eyes, his laughing blue eyes, and smiled. Like the five other Nicolson bairns she had gone to school with Sorley Mor's bairns, but he had been even more of a constant in her life than in the lives of anyone else in the village. It was partly because her own father, Quintin, had died in an accident at sea on a previous *Ocean Wanderer*, just before she was born, she knew that. She had grown up without him and, having no memories of him to take comfort from, she had decided at a very early age that, if she could have chosen a father, it would've been Sorley Mor. And besides, they were entwined, entangled: the MacEwans, the Nicolsons and her mother's family, the Hamiltons, shared a common history. In old stories the names of Sorley Mor, Quintin and Gannet were always mentioned in the same breath, and more than that, it was said that Sorley Mor was the man her mother, Margo, could've had, only she had chosen to marry Quintin Nicolson. So to the young, fatherless Rose, Sorley Mor *could've* been her father. Even if that was stretching it a bit, what were dreams, after all, but stretched reality? Just like his own bairns she would wait by the harbour when *Ocean Wanderer* was on its way in, and her heart would jump as she spotted the familiar figure waving from the wheelhouse. He was waving to his own bairns, she knew that, but in her heart she hoped that he was waving to her too.

Sometimes she would hang around after the catch had been landed and sent on its way in the lorries, and Sorley Mor and Gannet would be checking one more thing on the boat before heading for the Inn then home to Chrissie and the bairns, and he would look up and spot her watching him. He'd smile and wink at her, encouraging her to come closer. Then he would produce a piece of 'treasure', a shard of pottery or a peculiarly shaped piece of metal, things dredged up with the catch that he knew would interest her. There would be that feeling of giddy, breathless excitement that, while he was working out at sea, Sorley Mor had thought about her; with the boat pitching and tossing on the waves, he had still made time to look through the nets and pick out 'treasures' to bring back to her. Then, with Gannet smiling silently by his side, he would engage her in conversation like an adult. 'And how are things up by, then, Rose?' he would ask. 'How's life with yourself?' She would tell him about school, about some fight or other with a brother or sister, childish things, and Sorley Mor would nod seriously before saying, 'That reminds me of the time . . .', a preamble to telling her stories of the old days, stories about her father. That was what she had wanted, of course; she had wanted Quintin brought to life for her. Maybe that was where her fascination with past lives came from, the need to know the father she could never know. At the time she always thought she had tricked Sorley Mor into talking about his friend, recounting their schooldays, their jokes and laughter. She had been in her twenties before she realized that he had known of her need all along, and his gentle kindness had made her love him even more.

Now, lost in her thoughts by the big window of her grand house, she wondered if that had been part of what had attracted her to his son. Had she married Sorley Og because she loved him, or to make his father as near to being *her* father as she could, or was there maybe something more to it than even that? She remembered coming back that summer three years ago and seeing them together, working on the boat, Gannet, Big Sorley and Young Sorley. It had struck her that Sorley Og looked so like his father when he had been younger, the image of the man who brought her back 'treasures' from the deep and told her stories when she was a child, his blue eyes smiling and his black hair already showing flecks of grey, though he was only in his late twenties. She had known him all her life, but that moment was fixed in her mind, captured for ever in a delicious, languid slow-motion. Sorley Mor had waved to her, and his son, slowly looking round to see who it was, had met her eyes, and she was lost. It all seemed so long ago. Had all that happened in three short years?

Standing in the living room of the house on MacEwan's Row, where the road north ended, Rose occasionally changed her focus to stare at her reflection in the glass, hardly recognising the dark-haired woman she saw there, the one who had always been regarded as cool and calm and the only one in the Nicolson family who had inherited Quintin's sallow complexion and large, oval, brown eyes. It had been a cruel twist of fate; all the others resembled their mother, Margo, but only Rose looked strongly like their father, and yet her father hadn't lived to see her. When she was a child she would hear the villagers as she passed by, 'My, but Quintin couldn't have denied that wee one'; she hadn't understood at the time what that meant.

She looked around the room. She hadn't wanted this huge place, though she had never said it out loud; Sorley Og had wanted it. He had wanted it because he had been hurt by her family's opposition to their marriage. It was a defensive thing; he wanted to show them that he would treat her like the princess they thought she was by giving her a castle to live in. If she was a princess living in a castle, then she hadn't done too badly in marrying a simple fisherman, that's what Sorley Og had reasoned. Though no one could ever call the MacEwans simple fishermen, she knew what was in his mind without ever having to be told. He didn't understand the reaction of the Nicolsons, so he had been stung into making grand gestures, and her family didn't understand either that they had hurt him; they didn't really understand things like that. He was Sorley Og MacEwan, son of Sorley Mor, and

133

everyone knew how laidback and confident the MacEwans were. They had money to go with their history and position in the fishing industry; there wasn't a port that didn't know and respect them; nothing could ever penetrate the MacEwan sense of themselves. Only something had, and despite her attempts to make him see that nothing mattered except the two of them, Sorley Og couldn't get over the fact that the Nicolsons, people he'd known all his life, whose family had known his for generations, objected to him as a husband for their Rose.

The engagement ring he had bought her, therefore, had to be bigger than she had wanted or needed, and it sat on her finger, a sparkling and painful symbol of his confusion. The wedding had been the same. Rose's ideal would've been to get married quietly, but Sorley Og had insisted on Father Mick doing the full honours with as much pomp and ceremony as he could muster, and Father Mick had even been prevailed upon to remain sober, so that he wasn't like Father Mick at all. And there had to be every innovation that America could dream up, from tulle bags of toasted almonds, matchboxes with their names in silver, and a three-man band from a video company filming the smallest details. The wedding cake was the biggest and most ornate ever seen, but the icing on the entire occasion had been the arrival of an open carriage with two white horses to take the bride to church, though God alone knew where he'd got them from or how much it had cost to bring them all the way to a Highland fishing village. Rose had sat in the coach in all her unnecessary finery, trying not to meet the eyes of other villagers en route and hoping that if they noted her burning cheeks they would think she was just excited, when all the time she was wilting with embarrassment, her brother Dougie sitting beside her in silence, apart from a self-conscious whistling under his breath. 'Don't,' she joked, squeezing his arm, 'you'll whistle up the wind,' and Dougie smiled.

As he waited to receive her and Dougie at the door of the

church, Father Michael Houlihan had a pronounced look of resigned disapproval on his little gargoyle face. He stood barely five feet tall and had a big nose, long earlobes, thick lips and a furrow splitting his chin marginally deeper than those across his forehead. Despite a nature built for fun and more fun, Father Mick looked like an undersized Apache Chief on good days, according to some, and a gargoyle on normal to bad days. He had landed in Acarsaid many years ago as a punishment and, by one of those quirks of fate, he and the villagers had suited each other, so there he had remained. The problem that had led to his banishment was rooted in Father Mick's short fuse. He was a man prepared to go that extra mile for anyone, a man with a wide and generous interpretation of the ways in which his God could be praised and in what locations. The local Inn, he reasoned, was as good a place as any, meeting with his fellow man to give thanks for fellowship and the bounties of fermented nature, but if he should feel in the slightest put-upon, taken for a fool or for granted, he tended to lash out in some way. All those years spent in Acarsaid had probably mellowed him slightly, in that perhaps he lashed out physically only in the direst circumstances, but when he was a young man he had often resorted to violence first.

The pivotal moment had come when he was a priest in training and he and his fellow wannabe men of the cloth had been banished to a retreat at a monastery as part of their preparation for the wider world. It was a dull, miserable place, and the twin-bedded cell he had been given was, like all the others, lit only by candle. He was partnered with another rookie who, he reckoned, did not pull his weight; the kind of individual you would meet in any area of life who perfects an affable, hail-fellow-well-met air to cover the fact that he is a waster who leeches off others. Mick had done the decent thing several times and covered up for his cellmate, but this was taken not for the kindness it was, but as a sign of weakness and stupidity on Mick's part that was further encroached on as time went on.

Mick was a man who liked his sleep, and the worst offence anyone could commit was to deprive him of even a few minutes of his legal amount without good reason. No matter how often he complained, however, the other chap was always late in taking over from him at vigils. After it happened on what was to prove to be the last occasion, Mick's diminishing levels of fellow feeling and goodwill were stretching dangerously thin, and when his fellow novice failed to turn up until well after the arranged time of 4 a.m., to take over for the next four hours, they ran out completely. The nearly Father Mick had pounded his way angrily to their cell and prepared to exact retribution. In the darkness he looked at the lump in the bed, still wallowing peacefully in sleep, and the red mist had intensified.

'Right, you lazy, good-for-nothing bastard!' he yelled, and taking a good run from the door he delivered a ferocious kick at where he calculated the sleeping figure's nether regions would be. 'Get your fat arse out of that bed and take over!'

It was just unfortunate, and not Father Mick's fault in any way, that the sleeping arrangements had been changed while he had been struggling to keep awake on his four-hour stint in the monastery chapel. No one had told him that he and his roommate had been moved out, and the cell, reputed to be the best one, had been commandeered by the archbishop of Edinburgh, who had arrived unexpectedly. As Mick's foot found its mark, the figure leapt from the bed, howling in pain and shock, and hopped about the dark cell.

'You don't like that, do you?' demanded Mick, as though there were some who might. 'Well, here's another one!' and being unable to see the figure clearly enough for identification purposes, he delivered another direct hit to the lazy arse's arse. 'Well,' said Mick, warming to his theme, 'I don't like having to cover up for you all the time, you fucking waste of space!' and he continued kicking the yelling figure all round the room.

It was only when the commotion brought others running

136

with enough candles to illuminate the proceedings that Mick realised his mistake. Though technically he hadn't been to blame, Mick knew he would suffer. He wouldn't be kicked out – the church was too desperate for priests for that – but the archbishop, a man known to hold considerable grudges, would make sure that Mick's path to the Vatican and the triple crown was barred for eternity.

'If you ever had any ambitions concerning Rome,' the leader of the flock said maliciously after Mick's ordination some time later, 'you can forget them. After this passing-out parade we're sending you to the hinterland to live among the mad teuchters, you ugly wee shite. See how you like that!'

As it happened Mick had liked it, so he was quite content. Though his short fuse never really grew much longer, it became marginally less physical with the passing years. On the day of Rose and Sorley Og's wedding, some three decades later and long after the archbishop had been consigned to pushing up the daisies, he looked even more disgruntled than usual, like an angry gargoyle.

'I know, Father Mick, I know,' Rose whispered. She tried to push him gently down the aisle in front of her as she took Dougie's arm, but Father Mick, determined to have his say, stayed in step beside her so that they walked down the aisle as a threesome, two of whom were in deep conversation throughout. Standing at the side of the altar waiting to take her bouquet was her bridesmaid, Tess, the new schoolteacher and current lady in the life of the local doctor and best man, Gavin Johnstone, who stood across from her with the groom. Tess was a bright, bubbly blonde from Glasgow, ogled by all the attached men in Acarsaid and pursued by all the unattached. Rose didn't know Tess all that well but, given their disapproval of her marrying Sorley Og, Rose had decided not to ask any of her sisters to do the honours. Tess was handy and willing to help out, and at least Rose could count on the best man and the bridesmaid getting on; that was one worry ticked off the list. She wished she could say the same about

Father Mick, who was now listing every misdemeanour committed by the groom since the day he was born as they walked down the aisle in their unique arrangement.

'Don't say anything, please,' she sighed. 'Let's just get it over with.'

Father Mick shook his head as he walked slowly on. 'If ever a man needed a drop of the falling-down stuff to keep him going, it's this man, here!' he muttered out of the corner of his mouth. 'What else has he got planned, do you know? Am I likely to be faced with a troupe of acrobats doing somersaults off the altar as I start the service, or maybe a trapeze act? If I'm to be grabbed and forced to do a back flip through the air I'd rather be prepared for it, that's all I'm asking.'

'I wouldn't rule it out,' replied the blushing bride. 'It would be safe not to rule anything out, Father Mick.'

'Do you know he forced me to use an electric shaver this morning? Said he wasn't having me standing there with a toilet roll arranged about my face.'

Rose laughed despite herself; Father Mick had more than one nickname, and he was often called Mick the Nick, because he couldn't shave without cutting himself at least four or five times. 'Dear God,' she whispered. 'He never did, Father.'

'God?' the small priest hissed back. '*GOD*, is it? Bugger God, a helluva lot of help he's been in all this. It's me you should be thinking about!'

'Sshh, Father! Everyone'll hear you.'

'Well bugger me, why shouldn't they? I christened that boy, patted his head every time I saw him, they all know that, and he stands there and *watches* me shaving to make sure I don't use a real razor. I said I wouldn't shave at all if that was his attitude, and he had the damned cheek to say I look like a tinker when I need a shave, and he wasn't having his wedding pictures spoiled by a tinker!'

'Aye, well, Father Mick, you can see his point. A tinker in the photos might be going a bit over the top.' She smiled at him from under her veil. 'After all, he wants this whole thing to be quiet and tasteful, doesn't he?'

But Father Mick wasn't prepared to have his mood lifted by kindly sarcasm. 'He all but turned me upside down to get into the cleft in my chin, so he did! And anyway, who the hell said I wanted to be in his wedding pictures in the first place? I just do the necessary then go off for a snort of the falling-down stuff. I don't appear in photographs.'

'Calm down. You know what he's like, Father Mick, he wants everyone in the photos, even my mother, for God's sake,' Rose whispered, laughing; Sorley Og was probably right, in certain lights Father Mick could look more like a tinker than an apache or a gargoyle, but then he'd always looked like that; he wouldn't be Father Mick if he looked any other way.

'And it'll do no good, I'll tell you that now, I'll be black again in a couple of hours!'

'He'll have thought of that, Father,' she whispered. 'If I know Sorley Og he's probably got the electric razor in his pocket now to give you another going over in the vestry afterwards.'

'Oh, Holy Mother of God,' Father Mick moaned. 'I never thought of that, but I bet you're right at that.'

At that moment the bridal threesome reached the groom standing before the altar with his best man. The little priest shook his head disapprovingly, gave Sorley Og a long, foul look, then, instead of the more traditional, 'We are gathered here today,' the first words the congregation heard, words recorded clearly forever on the video of the big day, were, 'A tinker, is it? Well, if a tinker I am, boy, I'm content to stay a tinker!'

'Ach, Father Mick,' Sorley Og replied sadly in that slow, mocking tone Rose knew so well. 'Didn't you promise me you wouldn't touch a drop till after the service?'

Throughout the service Father Mick added his own unique touches. 'We are gathered here today to witness the joining–

139

together in marriage of this . . . this . . . *MacEwan*,' he said with feeling, then bestowing a sickly sweet smile on the bride, he said softly, 'to this lovely Rose.' When the time came for Rose to affirm that she did indeed take Sorley Roderick MacEwan as her lawfully wedded husband, Father Mick looked at Sorley Og with deep distaste, added a theatrical pause, and asked again, 'You're sure, now, Rose?'

The final touch of nonsense came when Sorley Og was told he could kiss his bride, which he did with some aplomb, then he hugged Father Mick and kissed him on the cheek too. The ensuing row continued all the way to the vestry and back, every word not only clearly audible to the congregation, but also recorded for posterity.

'I suppose you think that was funny?' demanded Father Mick.

'Ach, away with you man,' Sorley Og replied casually. 'Have you no sense of occasion? Now pipe down.'

'Pipe down, is it? Sure am I not even the boss in my own chapel? What right have you to be kissing me in front of everybody?'

'You're lucky anybody wants to kiss that ugly thing you call a face,' Sorley Og replied. 'Sure everybody knows your own mother couldn't tell if you were upside down in your crib. You only became a priest because nothing of woman born could ever bring itself to have anything to do with you. That's probably the first kiss you've ever had in your life, and I'm willing to bet anything it'll be the last, too.'

'I've a good mind to declare this marriage null and void,' Father Mick announced, throwing his arms about, the wide sleeves of his white vestments flying up so that he looked like a particularly irritated seagull having trouble getting off the ground.

The noise of the argument receded as the bridal party disappeared to sign the marriage register, only to grow in intensity as they came once again into view, like a radio being turned up in order that something important should not be missed. The happy couple passed her family and Rose stopped and kissed Granny Ina, but her gaze didn't linger too long on the rest of them. On the other side, in the sea of MacEwans, were the groom's immediate family including his sisters on a rare visit from their homes in Australia, New Zealand and Canada specially to see him marry Rose. Chrissie wore a neat outfit in deep pink with a glorious confection of a hat perched on her head, shaped like a small, pink, ornate choc-olate box, with a large ribbon bow on top and a veil that came down to her nose. Rose smiled; her new mother-in-law wasn't one for high fashion: the hat, she knew, would soon be discarded.

There was Gannet, ever present beside Chrissie and Sorley Mor and their daughters, then the current crew of *Ocean Wanderer* interspersed with the villagers. There were the two engineers with their wives, Stevie and Jean, who had come all the way from Fife, and Eric and Marilyn from Glasgow. Eric towered above everybody else, his year-round tan freshly reapplied for the occasion, and his hair, dyed an improbable jet black, caught up in a small ponytail. At his side stood his wife, Marilyn, who was just as well preserved, with her face beautifully painted; to them the wedding was a kind of per-formance, she supposed. Then small, motherly Molly Stewart stood alongside her husband, Stamp, the diminutive ship's cook, his green and black checked bunnet, his flat cap, still glued to his head, nodding and smiling as she met his gaze. She noticed with surprise that his eyes were shining with tears, then remembered that he had been on board the day her father had been killed, and she knew what he was thinking. She fought an impulse to stop and hug him, then a few steps further on regretted that she hadn't. The bunnet looked slightly odd with his best suit, Rose thought as they passed, but there again, he would have looked even odder without it, she imagined. Among the long-serving, core crew of the *Wanderer* were the men who made up the relief crew, those who stepped in when one of the permanent crew couldn't make it for some reason, or were added during the busy herring and mackerel seasons. Everywhere she looked were MacEwans of one variety or another; all of them, like the rest of the congregation, familiar people among whom she and Sorley Og had grown up.

'This church does not approve of divorce, Rose,' Father Mick said emotionally as Rose smiled happily back at him, 'but as far as I can see you have grounds the Pope himself could not refuse. You have made a terrible mistake here today and no one would blame you if you wanted out of it. I urge you to think seriously about annulment before it's too late.'

'Ach, be quiet,' said Sorley Og dismissively, as they continued the long walk back down the aisle with Father Mick still in deep and agitated conversation with the bride.

Past old Alex and Davie Kerr, the brothers who had worked with Sorley Mor and with his father before him, and Alex's son, gorgeous Pete, the nearest Acarsaid came to having a playboy – all golden hair, stunning smile and baby-blue eyes. Beside him sat the pretty but decidedly homely Alison Watt, who, rumour had it, would soon be coming down the aisle herself on Pete's arm, though he probably didn't know it yet. Rose smiled at them and then at her new husband and the belligerent figure of Father Mick on the other side. She had come up the aisle as a threesome, and here she was going back down again as one.

'You give religion a bad name with your carrying-on,' said Sorley Og said to the still-protesting priest. 'Here.' From his pocket he produced a half-bottle of the priest's favourite tipple, Islay Mist Whisky, and handed it to him. 'It's the withdrawal symptoms you're having, Father. Have a nip and you'll be as right as rain again.'

Later, at the reception, there had been the usual speeches and, on the secure grounds that he and the groom's father were inseparable, Gannet decided to deliver an unplanned word or two of his own. As Rose had suspected, Chrissie's hat had been the first thing to go; it was now sitting slightly askew on top of Gannet's pointed bald head. The only thing about Gannet that had changed over the years was that the tiny halo of dark hair around the expanse of pink, freckled scalp had become white. Chrissie said his eyebrows had become bushier as well as white, and his large ears 'furrier. His father and grandfather were just the same as they got older,' she'd say. 'Like baboons that had been shaved in bits for a joke. Gormless baboons, they were too, just like this one.'

Gannet rose to his feet and spoke entirely without notes and from the heart, and as he'd had a dram or two his heart was full to brimming over, so his speech, both articulate and affectionate, was in danger of reducing a happy audience to tears. Hearing the odd sentimental sniffle from around the room, Rose stole a look at her mother, Margo, sitting nearby; there wasn't the slightest hint of emotion, and not for the first time she wondered what made her tick. Gannet finished his oration by throwing his arms around the bride and telling her he had never seen one more beautiful. 'I knew your father well,' he said in his deep, attractive, inebriated voice, 'and I look at you today, Rose, as I have almost every day of your life, and I see him. I would say that it is a tragedy he is not here to see you wed to Sorley Og, the son of our dearest friend, but I know that he *is* here. Quintin is with us today as he always is, and he's smiling on the two of you.'

'Ach, sit down, you great fool,' whispered Chrissie Mac-Ewan severely, 'or I'll come over there and kick you where it hurts.'

'Chrissie!' Sorley Mor said, his voice pained. 'Do you have no soul, woman?'

'I don't have a good bottle of whisky softening my brain, if that's what you mean!' the mother of the groom muttered dismissively.

Gannet, who had heard similar putdowns from Chrissie for as long as he could remember, took no notice, but threw his lanky arms around Rose and Sorley Og and hugged them close. 'Sorley Og,' he said, 'you have married the best of lassies, and you, Rose, have married the best of men.'

'Quite right, Gannet,' called Stamp from across the room. 'I couldn't have put it better myself, man. That's it in a . . . in a . . . lump!' He had 'nutshell' in mind, but it didn't matter; everyone knew what he meant. Stamp had summed up the occasion in his own style, but also to perfection.

After the reception they were bound by air for a honeymoon in France. Sorley Og was none too sure about air travel, but he was considerably surer of flying in a metal box that he didn't trust than of setting foot on a cross-Channel ferry: that way, he said, he would return in a wooden box. Before they left, though, the newly married couple had made their way to the cemetery, where Rose laid her bridal bouquet on her father's grave. Instead of changing into her more manageable going-away outfit she had stayed in her white finery; Quintin wouldn't see her, she knew that was just fanciful, but she still felt as though he could.

So their wedding had been just like their fine house: a bit off-beat, a touch overdone, reflecting Sorley Og's need to win over the Nicolsons and his hurt at being slighted. The opulence of the structure on MacEwan's Row provided the villagers with a great deal of gentle amusement, and they quickly dubbed it 'MacEwan's Castle'. Sorley Mor would describe the latest innovation to them in Hamish's shop or the Inn, shaking his head slightly and smiling affectionately at his son's folly. Early on, when he and Chrissie had come from their home next door to inspect the ever-changing plans and the start of the building work, Rose had asked Sorley Mor if he could have a word with his son, try to persuade him to scale things down perhaps. He put his arm around her and hugged her close.

'You'll not stop him lass,' he'd said quietly. 'Best let him go his way. You wait, though; he'll grow up one day. The MacEwans always do.' He winked at her as he used to down at the harbour when she was small, and she smiled.

144

'Huh!' Chrissie said beside him. 'Would you listen to the man?'

Sorley Mor looked at his wife, an expression of genuine puzzlement on his face. 'What do you mean by that, Chrissie MacEwan?'

'I mean,' she said slowly, 'that you were no better when it came to building our house.'

'*Me?*' Sorley Mor replied. 'Why, it's a perfectly simple house, woman.'

'And every room is the size of a barn,' Chrissie said, stabbing a finger accusingly at his chest. 'We could've fitted the whole family into one bedroom and still not been able to find each other!'

'Ach, but that was just because boats are so cramped,' Sorley Mor responded, sounding almost convincing. 'You don't know what it's like to be at sea for weeks on end, woman –'

'Oh, God, here we go! Another lecture from the old man of the sea on the hard life he's had. I'm not one of your tourists, Sorley Mor, and stop calling me "woman"! It was to do with you showing everybody what a big man you were –'

'"Were"?' Sorley Mor interrupted, a hand clutching at his heart, his eyes wide with feigned hurt. 'What a big man I *were,* Chrissie MacEwan?'

'A big man,' Chrissie continued, 'who needed a big house, that's what it was all about, but as I've said to you every day since, you should try keeping it clean!' Chrissie stared at him, a tiny woman with tightly curled blond hair that no hairdresser could straighten out for more than half a day, sharp grey eyes and an air of bustle about her. If Sorley Mor was known to be relaxed, his wife had never been known to be still. Chrissie was always on her way to do something, or having completed that task, on her way to do something else, and usually clad in the kind of wraparound pinny that her own mother would have worn. She was the wife of Sorley Mor, a man of some standing, but she was just Chrissie when it came down to it;

put her in fancy clothes and you would be looking at Chrissie MacEwan dressed up and looking uncomfortable. She'd still be who she was, and if she had ever had any worries about her lack of sophistication, she had left them behind her long ago. She stood in front of Sorley Mor, staring up in to his face, their noses only inches apart, her hands on her hips, and he suddenly put his arms around her, bent her backwards and kissed her full on the lips.

'Will you stop it, you silly sod!' Chrissie shouted, frantically slapping any part of her husband she could reach, but he was nuzzling her neck and hugging her closer the more she struggled, until her feet were completely off the ground. Eventually he let her go and she stood trying to smooth her unsmoothable hair, red-faced and breathless. 'You have no shame,' she said.

'Can I help it if you're irresistible, woman?' Sorley Mor demanded pathetically. 'There's just something about that old pinny! Don't think I don't know you only wear it to drive me into a frenzy; I'm only a man, after all!' With that he made to grab her again and she ran through the bare bones of what would be Rose's house, chased by the skipper. Chrissie's shrieks and laughter rang out as she and Sorley Mor, both in their fifties, behaved like teenagers, and Rose thought of the times her mother talked disparagingly of how the MacEwans always drew attention to themselves; this was undoubtedly an example of what she meant. But, she thought, her mother was wrong, there was real joy between them, and if she and Sorley Og were still like that after all those years – well, she'd be more than happy, that was all.

And MacEwan's Castle was a beautiful house, no doubt about that. It had every modern innovation. The floors throughout were stone-tiled and heated from underneath. There were four bedrooms in the long, low-lying castle, each with its own en-suite bathroom and fitted wardrobes, so that there was nothing out of place; it had, after all, been designed for, and mostly by, a fisherman, someone who understood the need to have everything stowed safely and tidily away. But this was a house, it was meant to be a home, Rose would think, knowing all the time that it was neither: it was Sorley Og's statement to his reluctant in-laws. The sparkling, hi-tech fitted kitchen led to a splendid dining room that they never used, and in the centre a big, beautiful rosewood table stood day after day, but no one ever sat on any of its eight chairs. Rose was just as lost in the enormous sitting room he had insisted on. Crossing to the big window facing out to sea seemed to take forever; she never quite got over the notion that she was walking onto a stage and that any moment a spotlight might illuminate her and oblige her to do a few numbers and a quick tap-dance. That was what it was for, anyway, to showcase Rose Nicolson MacEwan.

'It's so, so *perfect!*' Rose had exclaimed, when it was finally finished, trying not to catch his eye, and Sorley Og had smiled back delightedly. 'But will we ever use it all, Sorley?'

'Of course we will!' he had replied, smiling broadly. 'We'll fill this house with bairns; there won't be room for all of them. One day you'll be complaining that we didn't make it bigger, you'll see.'

And just in case the number of bairns should run well into double figures, there was a floored loft, ready for conversion into anything they might want in the future.

Her sister and her family lived a few hundred yards away in a perfectly good kit-built house: they were the two most recently built houses, one a home, one a – well – the Mac-Ewan statement; and they would be the last to be built because there was no more space. Sorley Og had insisted on having an architect to design it, then he had gone over every inch of the drawing and increased dimensions here, changed measurements there, till the architect said, not altogether in jest, that Sorley Og should've designed his own house and cut out the middle man. In effect that's what he'd done any-way, Sorley had treated the architect's finished drawings merely as a guide to hang his ideas on.

147

Everything had to be of the highest standard, the furniture, the fixtures and fittings, and anything he found fault with had to be replaced immediately. Rose had stood back, hoping that his hurt would blow itself out and she would magically be left with a home of manageable proportions, because the reality was that he was building a house she would live in more than he ever would, given that he would spend a lot of his time at sea. She didn't say this, of course, because that's not what it was about. The house on the hill wasn't a functional home for a family, big or small, it was never intended to be. And it was all so unnecessary, that was the silliest thing about it. The Nicolsons didn't disapprove of Sorley Og himself, but of their Rose marrying a fisherman, *any* fisherman. She had explained this often enough, but somehow Sorley Og didn't quite believe it; a reflection, she knew, of the softer side below the invincible MacEwan facade.

12

The fathers of Sorley Og and Rose had been friends all their days, and probably their grandfathers too. There were three of them, Sorley Mor MacEwan, Quintin Nicolson and Ian Ross, known all his life as Gannet, because there was nothing he wouldn't and didn't eat. They were always together, even as bairns, but for many years now there had only been Sorley Mor and Gannet. Even so, as the older villagers would tell you, the wound left by Quintin's death had never healed, there was still a space beside the other two that would never be filled; and to those who remembered them as a trio, the image of Quintin would never fade. All the years that Rose had known Sorley Mor, though, there had only been him and Gannet. She had never seen the three of them together, so the two of them – Gannet always a step ahead – seemed entirely normal to her.

Gannet, Quintin and Sorley Mor had started their lives as fishermen on the same day aboard an earlier *Ocean Wanderer*, skippered by Sorley's father. When they first went to sea they had all been fifteen years old, but Gannet, because he was the younger by a few months, had been appointed ship's cook; that was the tradition. He proved worse at the job than anyone in living memory or even myth, though, serving the crew delicacies like kippers with custard that even the hungriest fisherman refused to eat. Gannet, though, as everyone knew, refused nothing: just like a gannet. He had been Gannet for so long, in fact, that it took a great deal of deliberation for anyone to come up with his real name.

Everyone looked at the three of them as they walked through the village, everyone talked to them, though mainly to Sorley Mor. He was the extrovert, the talker of the trio, and always lagging behind, engaged in some verbal joust, even then. Quintin was dark, quiet and amiable by nature, but he liked to laugh, so the conversations were between him and Sorely Mor, whereas the thin, lanky Gannet didn't really talk much; well, not when he was sober anyway. When he was sober he talked in whispers if it was necessary to talk at all, but he was prodigiously well read and wherever he went he always carried a pile of books or magazines – the *National Geographic* was his favourite. Then, when he'd had a few, he couldn't shut up. All through her life Rose could remember him visiting Granny Ina when he'd had a few and the two of them talking for hours about books they had read, about solar eclipses and the workings of the human mind, the subjects that fascinated both of them, and sometimes they would sing together, though unlike the Gannet, her grandmother never touched a drop. He spoke in a beautiful deep voice with an eloquence that stirred the blood. In his cups Gannet became an orator, a philosopher who could wring tears from a glass eye with his almost artistic conversations and detailed observations on a whole range of topics. He memorised everything he saw, heard or read, including, it was said, the words of every song ever written, and when he'd had those few he would sing them in a pure, glorious voice that brought a lump to the throat of listeners, though they couldn't ever explain why. On the whole, though, he just whispered.

These were the things Rose would think about as she sat staring out of her huge window: the characters in the village, the history of the place, and the part her family had played, the part both sides of her family still played in Acarsaid. There was a warmth in belonging, in being part of the fabric of the place, though at times it could be claustrophobic, too. The incomers felt it mainly, those romantic souls who felt drawn to a culture where they would never belong, but who kept trying anyway, and others, like herself, who had experienced the outside world and come back, for whatever reason.

The window took up almost the entire surface area of the sitting room wall. It had been put in to give a clear view across the sea to the islands and beyond, to where the sky merged with the ocean, and you could see the boats heading for harbour, tiny dark shapes against the brightness during the day, or little clusters of twinkling light by night. On this day, though, Rose wasn't watching for *Ocean Wanderer* or any other boat, she was just standing there, gazing out without seeing, thinking, trying to make sense of her life – if, that was, there was sense to be found in it, and she was far from sure about that.

All the times Sorley Og had been away fishing she would look out over the water from this window and wonder where he was at that very moment, what he was thinking, how the trip was going, and what the weather was like out where he was. When he called from the boat to say he was heading for harbour she would sit here sometimes for hours, scanning the horizon with binoculars for first sight of the boat. That was what the window was for, after all; the beauty of the view was a secondary consideration.

Further down the road she knew that her older sister, Sally, would be doing the same, waiting and watching by *her* big window, though it was nowhere near as big as the one Sorley Og had to have. Sally would be watching for first sight of *Ivy Ann,* bringing her husband, Alan Guthrie, home. Alan was originally from Glasgow, but he had left home as soon as his time as an engineer was up and he had his tradesman's papers, to roam the world, or so he thought. By the 1970s he was in his early twenties and working in the oil industry; he had been on a shore break in Aberdeen when fate had trawled him and brought him to Acarsaid. The oil industry wasn't as exciting as he had hoped. In fact, it was probably bound by more rules, regulations and routine than the life he had left behind to look for excitement, a fact that Alan was reflecting on that night in a pub by the harbour, when the skipper of an Acarsaid fishing boat had come in, looking for an engineer.

The *Ivy Ann* had called in to Aberdeen for emergency repairs a few days before, and the engineer, an Aberdeen man, had taken the opportunity to go on the skite in his native town, eventually being thrown out of the pub he'd been drinking in. After throwing the obligatory amount of abuse at the bar staff he had left somewhat unsteadily, vowing never to return, a threat he carried out by tripping and falling into the harbour, where his drowned body was recovered the next day. Was there anyone, the skipper wanted to know, who could take on the job until the end of the trip in a week's time? Alan Guthrie, unattached, fed up with the boring predictability of two weeks on an oil rig followed by another two drinking his leave away, was ready for any opportunity for change that came along, so on the spur of the moment he volunteered. He had never been to sea before, except on the rigs, and he enjoyed that first trip taking the boat back to Acarsaid enough to make him sign on for another, then just one more before he left to roam the world. In Acarsaid he met Sally Nicolson, and that, as they say, was that.

Qualified engineers were a breed thin on the ground in a small harbour like Acarsaid, and when Sorley Mor had taken delivery of the current *Ocean Wanderer* in 1976, he needed not just one but two engineers, because of the size of the boat. Naturally he had asked Alan if he was interested, because Alan was known to be a good, steady worker, and, now that he was married to a local lassie, he was anchored; if he was not quite a native Acarsaid man, he was as near as anyone not of the blood could get. It had taken Alan a great deal of soul-searching to stay with *Ivy Ann* rather than join the crew of *Ocean Wanderer*, because Sorley Mor, even at the age of thirty-seven, was a fine skipper, and everyone wanted to work with him. He had no complaints with his own skipper, though, and the work suited him; the smaller *Ivy Ann* mainly concentrated on shellfish, so the journeys were no more than a few days at a time, whereas a big boat like *Ocean Wanderer* could be away for weeks at a time. Reluctantly turning the offer down, he told Sorley Mor that he might have a solution: his cousin, Eric, might be interested, he said. Eric had been an engineer in the Merchant Navy for years, but Alan knew for a fact that he was fed up of going on long trips.

'What age would the man be about?' Sorley asked.

'A wee bit older than me,' Alan said. 'About thirty, I'd say. A good guy, straight as a die.'

'And he comes from Glasgow, too?'

'Oh, aye,' Alan said. 'Different part, mind you. I come from Maryhill, Eric comes from the Southside.'

'And that matters, does it?'

Alan thought for a moment then shook his head. 'Only if you're in Glasgow. Would you like to meet him? You'll like him, he's dead easy to get on with.'

'Very well, Alan,' said Sorley Mor grandly, 'conduct the candidate to the boardroom for his official interview.'

And so, in due course, Alan accompanied his cousin to the Inn for the usual 'official interview', a friendly grilling by Sorley Mor and Gannet over a drink or three.

'Now, Dan,' Gannet said to the barman, 'don't give the skipper here anything to eat, you know that your food gives him the boak. How in hell you can cook like that, and you the brother of Stamp, I will never understand.'

'Well at least I can read and write,' Dan offered lamely in his own defence.

'Aye, betting lines is one thing, Dan, but it's obvious you can't read cooking instructions,' Gannet replied. 'Can you not get Stamp to give you a few lessons?'

'He certainly will not!' said Sorley Mor. 'Stamp belongs to the crew of the *Wanderer*, I pay his wages, so I own his cooking. I won't have him passing on his secrets to a common barman, even if it is his brother! Now, Dan, don't you go listening to Gannet here, he's had a few. Just you refresh our glasses and bring me one of your delicious Ploughman efforts like the good man you are.'

'As opposed to a common barman?' Dan asked wearily.

'Ach,' said Sorley Mor, 'was that you said that, Gannet? No, no, Dan, your Ploughman efforts are probably your best attempts at food. Just you bring me one here, if you please, and don't spare the pickle!'

'You'll be sorry,' said Gannet. 'You always are.'

The door opened and Alan came in. Sorley Mor and Gannet shouted out a greeting then, shocked into silence, stared at the man following him. Eric Guthrie had to stoop to avoid hitting his head on the ceiling beams. He was the biggest man either of them had ever seen. He stood six feet six in the socks covering his size thirteen feet, which were then encased in gigantic boots that looked as though they could be used as lifeboats in an emergency. Sorley Mor gulped and looked at Gannet, who immediately swallowed another half of whisky to avoid having to make any immediate comment as Alan drew near with his cousin. And Eric Guthrie wasn't just tall, he was *big*. He wore American-style, bib-and-brace, denim overalls over a tartan shirt with the sleeves rolled up – probably, Sorley Mor was to say later, because the cuffs wouldn't stretch around his wrists. Atop his head in what seemed like the far distance, a baseball cap tried valiantly to contain a head of thick, curly black hair, which met up with a full beard that covered much of his face and was of just as lavish proportions. He looked, in fact, like a particularly suspicious, short-tempered hillbilly, or the nearest to it that had ever been seen in those parts. His eyes were visible in the shade of his baseball cap only because they burned with an unusually fierce intensity that suggested strongly that this was not a man to cross, and they seemed to stare right through the two old sea dogs at the bar. Sorley Mor was aware that a quiet hush had fallen on the Inn, so it wasn't just him and Gannet who had noticed something unusual.

'This is my cousin, Eric,' Alan smiled.

Eric stuck out a huge hand. As he watched Sorley Mor's hand disappear somewhere inside the proffered paw, Gannet decided that he would risk no more than a brief wave and

'Hello, there'. Eric stared steadily and without any great friendliness at them in a way that made them uncomfortable, so they tried to affect nonchalance, as Alan stood beaming from one to the other, seemingly unaware of the impression his cousin was creating.

'So, Alan tells me you're interested in working in the fishing?' Sorley Mor smiled, making a great show of being so relaxed that he could conduct the interview and eat Dan's Ploughman effort at the same time.

''Sri' anuff,' replied the big man shortly in a big voice, still staring at them solemnly.

'And you're with the Merchant Navy at the moment?'

'Aye.'

Sorley Mor tried to dismiss the notion that however short and to the point his answers were, the Inn vibrated every time Eric spoke. He cleared his throat. 'Had enough of the voyages, then, is it?'

'Aye.'

Sorley Mor looked helplessly at Gannet who looked away. 'And you know something of the fishing, then?'

'Aye.'

'And you think you could handle the engines, do you?'

'An engine's an engine.'

'She's a big boat,' Sorley Mor said, not altogether without pride.

'Worked oan bigger.' And still the stare didn't waver.

Gannet having determined to abandon his skipper, Sorley Mor searched his mind for something that would open up a deeper, wider, more convivial conversation. 'Would you like something to eat?'

Eric glanced at the skipper's meal and wisely declined with a shake of his head.

'A drink, maybe? Let me buy you a dram.'

'Naw. Don't drink.'

'So how do you manage to stay alive?' Sorley Mor asked, desperately laughing at his weak attempt at humour.

'Ah suck stanes,' the big man replied humourlessly, his eyes boring into Sorley Mor.

'Aye, well. And you have your papers and everything?'

'Aye.' Eric dug into the pocket across his breast and pulled out an envelope packed with papers testifying to his excellence and experience as a ship's engineer and handed it to Sorley Mor, who was so put off his stride that he gave them only the briefest of looks.

'So when can you start, then, Eric?'

'The noo, if ye waant,' he said, taking the envelope back and stuffing it into his breast pocket again.

Once outside and on the road to MacEwan's Row, Gannet berated Sorley Mor. 'By God, man, but you let him away easy.'

'Don't you talk to me about letting him away easy! You barely looked at him, never mind talked to him! Come to that, I could barely make out more than two words he said,' said Sorley Mor. 'Could you, Gannet?'

'Well, he didn't say more than two words,' replied Gannet. 'Which one of them did you actually understand then?'

'Well, maybe it's not fair to judge him on a few grunts, right enough,' the skipper said wisely. 'He is a Glasgow man after all, and they can be hellish difficult to understand at the best of times. I'm sure I remember it was a good two years before I understood young Alan when he came here at first. Whatever he said I'd just smile and say, "The same to yourself, Alan." Was years before he started to speak properly like us, and I realised he'd been asking if I wanted a dram, and by that time he was so fed up asking and getting no real reply that he'd stopped asking altogether. But with that big man it was more the way he said it and, my God, that look in his eye!'

'And have you ever seen anything so big?' Gannet asked. 'Can you imagine running in to him in the dark?'

'Aye, well, that was my thinking, Gannet,' Sorley Mor lied. 'I was thinking to myself that we'd never be in trouble with a man like that at hand.'

156

Gannet laughed out loud.

'No, no, hear me out,' reasoned Sorley Mor. 'And will you stop a minute till I catch my breath, man?'

'You're getting out of condition!' Gannet accused him.

'I am not!' Sorley Mor puffed. 'What you don't take into consideration, Gannet, is that it's hard for normal people to climb hills and talk at the same time.'

'What do you mean by "normal people"?'

'People not like you, that's what I mean. You go about not talking unless you've had a skin-full, which I'll grant you is often enough, while the rest of us have to talk all the time. It's not that you have more puff than the rest of us, you just don't use all the puff that you have at your disposal.' He sat on a large boulder by the side of the road. 'And those bar lunches of Dan's!' he said, rubbing his chest and belching loudly. 'My God, but the man has nothing in common with Stamp at all, has he, apart from his name? He can't cook to save himself!'

'I tried to tell you,' said Gannet smugly.

'Oh, aye, be Holy Joe,' Sorley Mor said, wincing slightly, 'that's a big help.'

'I don't know why you insist on eating at the Inn,' Gannet continued in the same tone of voice.

'You see, there you go again, Gannet. You ask these wee questions knowing full well that I'll have to go into all sorts of detail to answer them. I eat there because that's where I am when I'm hungry. Or would you rather I ran all the way home to Chrissie for a bite to eat, then ran all the way back to the Inn again? Now, as I was saying. About the big fellow there. We've been in a couple of tight corners over the years, in different ports, like, we've run into the odd troublemaker, is that not true?'

Gannet nodded. There had indeed been a few incidents in their younger days they might not want Chrissie to ever hear about, though privately he was sure she had anyway and had stored them up to use as ammunition at some later date.

'There was that time you were making remarks about yon big fellow off that Russian klondiker when we'd stopped in Shetland for a few days,' he said.

'Now, Gannet,' said Sorley Mor severely, 'you know that's not true. He *thought* I was making remarks about him, but I wasn't.'

'Aye you were, Skipper,' said Gannet. 'You said his beard looked daft, as if somebody's had grabbed it and cut across the bottom with a pair of scissors, then you fell about laughing fit to burst, you know the way you do when you've had more than enough and everything seems helluva funny to you.'

'He didn't understand English, Gannet, that was the real problem, if you remember. I simply said it was interesting, not "daft". That's just one of those lies certain people tell to make it all sound funnier than it was.'

'He didn't think it was funny,' Gannet scoffed. 'As I remember it we had to leg it back to the boat with a big crowd of drunken Russians after us. If they'd known what boat we were off we wouldn't have stood a chance. And what's more, they must've been in a worse state than us not to find us, with you laughing like that, and shouting at them in the dark that their mothers took in washing.'

'Now, Gannet, I don't remember it like that at all —'

'And worse than that about their mothers, too. I was shocked at you, Skipper, I was that. Chrissie would've given you a hiding if she'd heard the things you were saying about their mothers; in fact she still might. It was lucky their English wasn't very good, or as you say —'

Sorley Mor held a hand up to fend off further disclosures. 'Not that we've ever caused trouble, ourselves,' he butted in self-righteously, stressing every word, 'but as you say yourself, we've been caught up in the odd thing.'

Even though Gannet knew this was stretching it a bit, he nodded all the same, curious to know what Sorley Mor would come up with.

'Well, I was thinking, there would be no trouble, none of those wee misunderstandings if we had a man like that beside us, now would there? I can just see us marching down some harbour with that big bear of a man bringing up the rear, and him staring like that and everybody watching. Ach, I'm telling you, no one would dare cross us in any port in the land!'

'But Sorley Mor,' Gannet said patiently, 'it wouldn't be just the opposition that would be scared to cross him. He put the fear of death into me the minute I saw him! That look of his! Did you see a smile once cross his lips? How are *we* going to handle him aboard the *Wanderer*?'

'Ach, now I think you're maybe overreacting there,' Sorley Mor said persuasively. 'You know what you're like when you've had a couple, now, Gannet.'

'You were shaking in your boots, man!'

'I was not!'

'Aye you were. If I hadn't been there to brace you you'd have slipped off your stool.'

'Now that's a damnable lie, Gannet! And furthermore, I'm sure it's treason as well.'

'How the hell do you work that out?'

'Well I'm your skipper, and if it's not treason it's definitely mutiny, I'm sure of that.'

As they approached the house Chrissie opened the door. 'What's the noise about?' she asked, glancing suspiciously from one to the other.

Gannet and Sorley Mor exchanged looks. 'Oh, just pleased with ourselves, that's all we are, Chrissie,' Sorley Mor smiled at his wife. 'Having a bit of a crack, like. We've got ourselves another engineer and we were just saying what a fine fellow he is. Were we not, Gannet?'

There was a slight pause.

'Aye,' Gannet replied. 'That's what we were saying, right enough.'

'And I suppose you've been eating Dan's garbage again?' Chrissie asked. 'What have I told you about that? Sure, even

Gannet there doesn't eat it, and if you gave him a spoon he'd munch his way through a dustbin. Am I wasting my breath, or what?'

'Now, Chrissie, I've had a delicate digestion all my life,' the skipper said. 'It has nothing whatever to do with Dan's food, it's just a sign of a sensitive nature.'

'Sensitive,' Chrissie snorted, rolling her eyes. 'There's no point in talking to you. The Milk of Magnesia is on the table by your chair.'

Sorley Mor pulled a face as he looked at the bottle.

'I've just been saying the same thing myself, Chrissie,' Gannet said righteously. 'He never learns.'

'Ach, be quiet, you,' Chrissie said, waving him away with her hand as he passed her anyway. 'Sure, when have you ever been a good influence on him?'

13

Eric and the latest *Ocean Wanderer* had arrived in Acarsaid at more or less the same time in 1976, and they were both still there over twenty years later. In due course Sorley Mor and Gannet would realise that he had kept a little something hidden during his 'official interview', his real reason for wanting out of long voyages with the Merchant Navy; but even if his off-duty passion had been known at the time, he was still a fine engineer. He was introduced to the rest of the crew the next day, most of whom had been with Sorley Mor since his earliest days as a skipper. Brothers Alex and Davie Kerr were still deckies at that time; they'd worked with Sorley Mor's father and, when they retired in due course, Alex's son, Pete, Acarsaid's playboy, would take his place, with Sorley Og joining the crew as Davie left. Stevie Smith was the other engineer, a Fifer in his twenties, and Donald Stewart was the cook, a little man of, he insisted, over five feet tall, though no one ever measured him to make sure. Donald was around the same age as Sorley Mor and Gannet; in 1976 they were each of them a few months before or after the age of thirty-seven years. Donald was a slight man with calm, grey eyes set in a complexion criss-crossed with lines that would deepen and increase with the years. No one knew for sure if he had hair, because since his teens he had worn a checked bunnet, or flat cap, waking or sleeping, and unlike his skipper he even wore it when off duty. Rumour had it that he wore it in the bath, too, though no one felt strongly enough to check the accuracy of that either.

He had earned the job of ship's cook permanently when

Gannet's subsequent efforts proved that his earlier forays into the world of preparing simple meals had been his best efforts. His memorable kippers-and-custard breakfasts were followed by many others, all equally gut-wrenching. Lumpy semolina was not, it was discovered, an acceptable substitute for mashed tatties, and he never did master the basic fact that water had to be boiling for even the best-intentioned egg to progress from raw to semi-raw. And they couldn't even accuse him of doing it deliberately to get out of the galley, of serving up horrors that he wouldn't eat himself, because he did eat them – and with relish.

The custom aboard fishing vessels had always been that the youngest man on board worked his way up from cook, earning perhaps a quarter of one share of the catch after the boat's running costs had been paid. Then, over the years, he would become a deckie and earn a half share. But Stamp proved to have a talent that no one had suspected. Though Donald had gone to school, as his brother, Dan, the barman at the Inn, had mentioned, the world of words was an enduring mystery to him. Normal, routine conversations presented him with no difficulties as long as he spoke plainly and simply, which he did, giving the impression that this was a man of precise speech. Comparisons, similes and turns of phrase would, however, remain a minefield to Donald. Tell him the ball was in his court, for instance, and he would look around for a ball to kick; say something was six of one and half a dozen of the other and he would lie down with a headache. Those who had known him all his life knew how his mind worked, and had developed a sixth sense that enabled them to understand his attempts to repeat these phrases. In fact, instead of Donald's use of language improving over the years, his 'Stamp-isms' as they were known, became widespread within the crew, with Sorley Mor in particular incorporating his very individual sayings into his normal speech without being aware that he was doing so.

Though Donald got by in talking, his main problem in life

was that he had never mastered the finer points of reading and writing. As a child the nearest he ever got to writing his surname, Stewart, was 'Stamp', so Stamp he remained for the rest of his life. Let him near food of any kind, though, and he became a culinary artist. As he couldn't read he didn't consult recipe books, and he never measured anything, but he had a natural instinct for which ingredients went together and in what proportions. There seemed, to him, a very basic and straightforward logic about such matters. His Welsh Rarebit on toast was a delight – not so much a snack as a flavoursome soufflé that literally melted in the mouth – and that was before he hit on the idea of finely grating just the right amount of onion into the mixture to further tickle the taste-buds. His steak and kidney pudding, steamed for five hours in a pot of simmering water while the biggest of swells tossed the boat about, was full of moist, meaty flavour cosseted inside suet so light that to call it a pudding was almost an insult. His meals were legendary, and he couldn't explain where his talent came from, it was just something he 'knew'. Chrissie, like all the women in Acarsaid, suspected that Stamp had taken secret courses in cordon bleu cooking at the Paris Ritz, and had once swallowed her pride and asked him for one of his recipes. Stamp shrugged his shoulders; he had no recipes.

'You must have recipes,' Chrissie said suspiciously.

Stamp shrugged again. 'I just throw things together,' he grinned.

'But you must know how much to throw together?' she cajoled, convinced now that he just didn't want to give away his secrets, and she wasn't above pulling rank. 'C'mon now, Stamp, I'm the skipper's wife. You can tell me, and I swear I won't tell anyone else.'

Stamp looked back at her from under his bunnet with friendly grey eyes. 'I would tell you if I knew,' he said help-lessly, 'but I don't. Honest, Chrissie.'

'Did your mother teach you?' she persisted. 'Is that how you learned?'

Stamp shook his head. 'Never cooked in my life till Sorley Mor told me I was cook,' he smiled self-consciously. 'It all seemed to come natural, like. I just think of things.'

So though his share in the catch increased with the years, Stamp remained cook: a situation that suited everyone.

'This is Donald Stewart,' Sorley Mor had said to Eric that first day in 1976, then suddenly realising the possible implications of Stamp's magic fingers being mangled in Eric's great mitt, he placed himself between them, reached up and put a restraining hand on the big man's shoulder in what he hoped would pass for a friendly gesture. 'You'll maybe remember the barman in the Inn,' he said, 'well that's Donald's brother, Donald.'

Eric looked suspiciously from one to the other. 'Naw,' he said, 'there's only wanna brothers can be called Donald, surely, Skipper?' He pointed towards Stamp. 'He's Donald, i'n't he?'

'Well, aye, he is, but so's his brother. They're both called Donald,' Sorley Mor smiled a little tightly.

'Canny be,' Eric laughed quietly. 'That's daft!'

'Well now,' said Stamp just as quietly but much more firmly, 'the skipper's right, you know. Me and my brother are both called Donald.'

Eric now stared again in his solemn way from Sorley Mor to Stamp and back, then he broke into a grin. 'See yous teuchters,' he laughed. 'Ye're tryin' tae make an arse o' me! Dae ye think Ah came up the Clyde in a banana boat? Ah might come fae Glesca, but Ah'm no' saft in the heid.'

The tiny Stamp looked up at him like, as Sorley Mor related to Chrissie afterwards, 'Samson and Delilah'. He meant David and Goliath – he had known Stamp all his life and sometimes it showed – but Chrissie understood.

'I can assure you, my friend,' said Stamp in a very calm, precise and decidedly unfriendly tone, the lilt of the West Highland accent soft and gentle against the big engineer's harsh Glasgow tones, 'that no one is trying to make an arse of you.' He pulled himself up to his tallest and craned his neck

164

to return Eric's frank stare, 'And no one here is suggesting your head is soft either, but I am called Donald and so is my brother.'

Sorley Mor looked desperately at Gannet, trying to work out in his mind if they should both attempt to restrain Eric together, or if he could telepathically instruct Gannet to launch himself into the fray alone, while he looked around for a hawser that might hold him after Gannet had subdued him.

There was a long, silent moment, then, 'Nae offence, wee man,' said Eric apologetically. 'It's just that Ah've no' come across that afore. Where Ah come fae we a' hiv different names, that's a'.'

'It's quite logical,' said Stamp with great dignity. 'Both grandfathers were called Donald. As the eldest son, my brother was named for my father's father, as happens in these parts, and when I arrived I was called after my mother's father. That's how we . . . "teuchters" . . . do things, you understand.'

Once again everyone present held their breath.

'Ah'm helluva sorry,' Eric said contritely. 'It's just me an' ma big mooth, Donald, son.'

'That's quite all right,' Stamp replied condescendingly.

'Ah can see noo that it isnae really daft, but dis it no' cause a bit of bother, like? When yer Maw shouted "Donald" when ye wur weans, did ye no' get mixed up?'

'Not at all,' Stamp replied, without absolute logic. 'I can understand an outsider might be thinking that, but my brother has always been called Dan and I've been called Stamp since I was at school, so there's never been any confusion whatever.'

Eric soundlessly mouthed 'Dan? Stamp?' then shook his head slightly. 'Naw,' he said to himself under his breath, 'Ah don't think Ah'll bother askin'.'

It was yet another case, as Sorley Mor told his wife later, of Samson beating Delilah.

It didn't take long for the difficulties surrounding Eric to appear. That he was teetotal could have been a difficult one to overcome — no one had ever heard of a fisherman who didn't drink, after all, and his masculinity could well have been called into question if the crew were to return to port, go through the welcoming ritual at the Inn and then request a mineral water for the big engineer. It would, as Sorley Mor knew, reflect not only on Eric, but on the entire crew, and especially on himself as skipper. At first he had tried very gently to find out why this sorry state of affairs had come about, and was staggered when Eric replied that he simply didn't like alcohol; so staggered, in fact, that in the skipper's desperation other possibilities began to suggest themselves. Then he hit on it, the perfect plan of action.

'We won't actually say he's an alcoholic, Gannet,' Sorley Mor explained. 'No, no, we don't have to actually say it. All we have to do is hint at it.'

'Hint at it?' muttered Gannet.

'Aye, sneaky like. We say, "I wouldn't offer Eric there anything with alcohol in it," and give them a look.'

'A look?'

'A look, Gannet. One of them looks that suggests they shouldn't take the matter further. A kind of a wink.'

'A look that's a wink?'

'Now stop being difficult, Gannet, you know damned fine well what I mean,' said Sorley Mor. 'One of those looks that might come across as a wink. Holy Jesus, it's simple enough, man! We just let them understand that Eric has a problem with the drink, infer that with a bit in him he can become, well, dangerous, and with the size of him, who'd be daft enough to ask him about it?'

Gannet nodded uncertainly, knowing perfectly well that his opinion was of no importance, that the skipper had made up his mind.

'We say the odd thing like, "Ach, the last time he had a drop, well . . .," and we leave it there. Then we say, "It would be better all round if nobody offered him drink, that's all I'm at liberty to say." And we advise them not to raise the matter with Eric himself. We give a wee shake of the head and we say, "He's a big man, he can do a lot of damage, we've seen it ourselves," and I look at you and you nod. Now you can do that, surely? "If I were you," we say, "I'd just regard it as his private business and leave it alone." You see? Problem solved.'

The next problem wasn't so easily solved. It happened during Eric's third trip and a week from port. Sorley Mor had gone down to the engine room to see how his new engineer was doing, and found the big man singing to himself while dancing up and down with considerable grace, his hands on his hips. The skipper stopped in his tracks, turned briskly and headed back for the wheelhouse in an agitated state.

'What's the matter, Skipper?' Gannet had muttered. 'Have you seen a ghost or what?'

'I wish I had, Gannet, and that's the truth!' said Sorley Mor, shutting the door and sitting down in his big rotating chair. 'To be perfectly truthful,' he said, rubbing his chin anxiously, 'I'm not sure what I saw. It's Eric.'

'Aye?'

'Aye.'

There was a long silence during which Sorley Mor fidgeted and moved about in his chair.

'Gannet,' he said eventually, 'go you down to the engine room and tell me what you see there.'

Gannet shrugged and left the wheelhouse, only to return a few minutes later.

'Well?' asked the Skipper.

'I saw Eric,' Gannet replied, and attempted to settle down with the latest *National Geographic* magazine, to read the secrets of life among the Amish.

'What the hell do you mean, you saw Eric?' Sorley Mor demanded excitedly. 'And will you put that damned magazine down!'

Gannet looked up at him and shrugged again, in a bemused way this time.

'Was Eric doing anything?'

'Like what?' asked Gannet.

Sorley Mor walked around the wheelhouse loudly damning and blasting everything and everyone for a few minutes. 'I swear to God, Gannet,' he shouted, 'I wish you were drunk all the time so that we could get a few words out of you! Did you see what Eric was doing, man?'

'He was dancing,' said Gannet.

'*Dancing,*' the skipper moaned.

'Singing a bit, too,' Gannet supplied after a moment's thought. 'My, but he's light on his feet for such a big man.'

'*Light on his feet,* Gannet! What in hell are we going to do?'

Gannet shrugged silently; he'd already spoken more in this sober conversation than anyone had a right to expect, while the skipper wandered around the wheelhouse, talking to himself and occasionally moaning.

'I know,' said Sorley Mor eventually. 'He'd never hit a wee fellow like Stamp. Go you and tell Stamp his skipper would like him to go down to the engine room and ask Eric why he's dancing.'

'And singing,' said Gannet.

'Aye, aye, and the singing too,' Sorley Mor said impatiently. 'But if he's really dancing then the singing doesn't matter a damn, Gannet; after all, there's plenty of normal men who sing, even stone-cold sober. It doesn't necessarily mean there's anything wrong with them.'

Ten minutes later the diminutive figure of Stamp appeared in the wheelhouse. 'Well, Skipper?' he asked.

'What's wrong with everyone?' Sorley Mor demanded. '*Well?* Is Eric dancing in the engine room?'

'And singing,' Gannet supplied.

'Will you stop with the bloody buggery singing!' Sorley Mor shouted. 'Is he dancing, Stamp?'

'Aye, Skipper,' Stamp replied pleasantly.

Sorley Mor glared at Gannet and at Stamp, then he threw his arms skywards and strode around. 'Of course,' he shouted, 'nothing could be more natural! I've got a six-foot-six grizzly bear in my engine room, a teetotal grizzly bear, and he's dancing, and everyone else on the *Wanderer* is quite calm about it!' He turned and looked threateningly from Stamp to Gannet; Stamp smiled calmly and Gannet stared back in his bemused fashion. '*Why* is he dancing?' the skipper demanded. 'Have either one of you ever known a dancing engineer before? Is it me that's mad?'

Stamp laughed and scratched his head under the edge of his bunnet. 'Come to think of it,' he said, 'seeing as you put it like that, I have to admit that no, I never have. It's just his hobby, Skipper. Did he not tell you?'

Sorley Mor shook his head, looking dazed.

'Come you down to the engine room with me,' said the little cook kindly, leading the way. 'He'll tell you himself.'

Sorley Mor followed as though he, as well as the boat, was on auto-pilot, and when he looked into the engine room Eric was still dancing – and singing. As the little group watched, Eric removed his right hand from his hip and executed an overblown salute. Sorley Mor gasped and covered his eyes. 'Dear God,' he whispered.

'Eh, um, Eric,' Stamp said above the noise of the engines. 'We're sorry to interrupt you.'

Eric stopped mid-step and bestowed a look of deep affection on Stamp. 'Whit kin Ah dae fur ye, wee man?' he asked.

Gannet looked at Sorley Mor and Sorley Mor looked back and shrugged. 'Not a word,' he whispered, 'not a damned word did I understand.'

'Sorry to bother you when you're busy, Eric, but the skipper here was wondering about your dancing,' Stamp said diplomatically.

Eric stared back; where he came from in Glasgow diplomacy was a positive disadvantage. 'Whit?' he asked.

169

'For some reason he doesn't seem to know about the dancing,' Stamp said, smiling encouragingly.

'Aw! Right! It wis the Military Two-Step,' Eric supplied helpfully. 'Ah've been makin' an arse o' it, let masel' go a' tae hell, so Ah hiv. Jist been daein' a bitta practisin'. Ah'm tryin' tae sherpen it up, know?' He turned his attention from a horrified Sorley Mor to Stamp. 'Ah don't know, Stamp, son,' he said conversationally, 'bit Ah think it's gaun' right doon the lavvy. Ah'm shite at it, so Ah um, an' wi' the European's comin' up tae,' he shook his large head despondently. 'Mibbe Ah should jist pit the kybosh oan it noo, the hale thing's mingin', so it is.'

'No, no,' said Stamp, 'I'm sure it's something simple, Eric. From what I can see, you're starting the salute half a beat or so before that final step, that's all it is. You've got it out of sync, as you say, and you're worrying yourself about it. It's just a confidence thing, it'll come back.'

'Ye reckon?' Eric asked uncertainly.

'Aye, aye, I'm sure it'll fall into place in no time. Look.'

To Sorley Mor's amazement Stamp, the Stamp he had known all his life, put a hand out and gently pushed Eric to one side and proceeded to perform the Military Two-Step.

'This is how you're doing it. See?' said Stamp. 'Now watch this foot as I do the salute.'

Sorley Mor gulped.

'It's wrong, see?' Stamp then retraced his steps and repeated the movement, and even Sorley Mor spotted the difference. 'Now it works. It's just that split second that can throw the whole thing off. You're thinking about it too much. I think you should give it a rest.'

'Mibbe yer right,' Eric said. 'Mibbe we kin practise in the mess later if ye've goat time?'

'Aye, we'll do that,' Stamp said kindly. 'But I promise you, you're worrying about nothing. It'll all fall into place.'

Sorley Mor turned and wordlessly motioned upwards with his thumb to Gannet and Stamp, who followed him into the wheelhouse, where he stood, holding his hands out, palms upwards. 'What?' he asked.

'What what, Skipper?' asked Stamp.

'What damned everything!'

'So you really didn't know about the dancing, then?' Stamp laughed quietly.

'Stamp, do I look as though I knew about the dancing, then?' he shouted. He looked at Gannet. 'Did you know about the dancing?'

Gannet looked up from where he had already settled back down with the Amish and shook his head.

'And you're not, well, surprised? Curious?'

Gannet shrugged his shoulders this time.

'As God is my witness,' shouted Sorley Mor, shaking his hand skywards, 'you are not normal, Gannet!'

Gannet smiled in reply.

Sorley Mor looked at Stamp again. 'Why is he dancing? Just tell me in idiot's terms, that'll do.'

'Sit down, Skipper,' Stamp said kindly, putting out a hand and guiding Sorley Mor to his chair. 'You're getting yourself all worked up for nothing here, man. Eric is a ballroom dancer, him and his wife, they do the Old Time. That's why he wanted away from the Merchant Navy. It was interfering with the competitions.'

Sorely Mor started at him in silence.

'They go all over the world,' Stamp supplied helpfully. 'You've likely seen them on the TV in that "Come Dancing" and never known it.'

'*On TV!*' Sorley Mor moaned.

'Aye, they're on all the time, and they're in the dancing magazines as well. The big man looks fine in his tails and white dickie, and he's that light on his feet you'd hardly notice the size of those great big patent pumps. It's amazing, really.'

'*Light on his feet,*' Sorley Mor groaned again; the phrase was haunting him. '*Patent pumps!*' Then he gathered himself together. 'How long have you known about this?' he demanded.

'Ach, ages, Skipper,' Stamp replied amiably. 'Sure, I wouldn't have believed it was that interesting. Relaxing, too. You should try it yourself.'

'And he's got you doing it?' Sorley Mor asked, aghast.

'Ach, not to his standard,' Stamp laughed gently, 'no, no, Skipper. Eric's been kind enough to say I'm a natural, but I'm sure all I've done is pick up the rudiments. I don't have his talent. He needed somebody to help him out while we're at sea and I found that I picked it up, just like the cooking. I wish I'd discovered it years ago, so I do. He's got me and Molly dancing around the kitchen happy as sandbags.'

Sorley Mor spent much of that trip in silence, trying to ignore the occasional bursts of singing and dancing from the mess and the engine room. At one point, against his better judgement, he had looked into the engine room and found Eric, blissfully unaware of his skipper's presence, dancing with one enormous paw on his left hip, while he waved an oily rag with great delicacy with his right paw. He found that once he knew what was going on he couldn't avoid it, the awful reality of his dancing engineer jumped out and ambushed him at every opportunity, so that he would have given anything to have turned the clock back to that innocent, ignorant time, those halcyon days when all he had to worry him was the fact that Eric was teetotal. Once ashore he propelled Gannet towards the house at MacEwan's Row, there being no way he would risk being overheard in conversation in the Inn. Chrissie stared at them as they walked in.

'Somebody sick?' she asked.

'No, woman,' Sorley Mor replied solemnly. 'Just get us a bottle of whisky and a couple of glasses and disappear about your housework. Gannet and I have things to discuss and I need a few in him for that.'

'Tell you what,' Chrissie replied, 'just you whistle and I'll dance for you!'

Sorley Mor looked at her sharply, but Chrissie had already turned and left the room.

In the eyes of Sorley Mor the situation was serious. He had an engineer who looked tough and dangerous, a big Glasgow man at that, and everyone knew they were the most dangerous of all, or should be. On finding out that the big, dangerous Glaswegian didn't drink, he had managed to convey the impression that Eric had been forced to give up the booze because he did terrible things when under the influence, and Eric, looking as he did like a grizzly bear, reinforced that notion among the other crews. Sorley Mor still didn't understand much of what Eric said, but that was a problem that time would overcome as Eric mixed more with civilised people like himself and learned how to talk properly, much as his cousin, Alan, had before him. He was also a good engineer, there was no doubt about that, but how was his ballroom dancing to be covered up? He closed his eyes as the last terrible picture seared in to his mind of Eric, hand on hip, hopping gracefully from one foot to the other while waving an oily rag about; no skipper should be expected to come face-to-face with such a thing in the engine room of his own boat. The big man had even got Stamp involved. After that first shocking encounter he had walked into the galley to find Stamp in his usual bunnet, stirring one of his delicious concoctions as it simmered gently on the stove. His other hand was raised to hold Eric's hand, and the big engineer was dancing delicately around on tiptoes in a semi-circle of tiny steps. It had been too much; he had eaten in the wheelhouse that night.

'You were there with me that day in the Inn,' he said to Gannet. 'Did you hear him saying he wanted to leave the Merchant Navy because he wanted more time to dance?'

Gannet shook his head, smiling as he refilled his glass. 'If you remember, Skipper,' he said, 'neither one of us could understand a word he said. He could've explained it all in detail for all we knew and we'd still have been none the wiser.

173

Anyway, you can't sack him for not telling you he liked to trot about the dance floor, can you?'

'No, no, we can't get rid of him on those grounds,' Sorley Mor replied sadly. 'But I'll tell you this, it's a question every man taking on an engineer should be warned to ask in future – are you, or have you ever been, a teetotal ballroom dancer?'

Gannet laughed out loud.

'What's so funny? If we'd only thought to ask that very same question we wouldn't be in this position today,' Sorley Mor said with feeling.

'*You*, Skipper,' Gannet laughed, 'not we. And if he's to be sacked you're the one who'll have to do it. Count me out.'

'He's a bloody good engineer anyway,' said Sorley Mor quietly, 'he's reliable and easy to live with, on the whole that is. We don't have any grounds to sack him –'

'There you go again with that "we" business . . .'

'– apart from the dancing.'

There was silence only broken by the clinking of glasses.

'But how will *we* be able to face the rest of them?' Sorley Mor asked deliberately. 'How will *we* live it down if they find out? A teetotaller who dances like a nancy-boy! Oh God, why did this have to happen to us?'

'You could have a word with him,' said Gannet.

'There you go again with that "you",' accused the skipper sarcastically. 'This will affect you as well, Gannet, you know.'

'Ach, not as much as it'll affect you,' Gannet laughed, almost choking on his drink. 'They'll make your life hell!'

'And all you can think of is having a word with him?' Sorley Mor demanded angrily. 'And what would you have me say? "Look here, Eric, would you mind giving up the dancing and start drinking?" That's your best suggestion? I wouldn't fancy our chances if he turned nasty, would you?'

'Well, you could get Stamp to talk to him with you,' said Gannet. 'They seem to get on well for some reason. After all, the big man's provided you with the only all-cooking,

174

all-dancing Stamp in captivity!' and with that he fell backwards, laughing loudly.

'Well, I'm sure you didn't mean that in a constructive
way,' Sorley Mor said severely, refilling Gannet's glass, 'but
that might be the only way out.'

And so the difficulties had been explained to Stamp. The
catcalls from the other fishermen, the sniggering as they
walked down harbours, both home and away, the name calling; it was all too much to bear. Stamp reassured Sorley Mor
that when Eric and his good lady wife, Marilyn, appeared on
TV the big man shaved off the whiskers, trimmed his hair
and had the rest gelled flat. Unless you knew it was him,
Stamp explained, you wouldn't know it was him, and how
many fishermen did Sorley Mor know who regularly watched
'Come Dancing' or bought a dancing magazine? The other
thing to remember was that Eric's home had remained in
Glasgow and, as he didn't drink, he tended to take off as
soon as they hit port, so the chances of him mentioning his
interesting pastime to other crews were low.

'I think you're worrying about something that won't happen,' said Stamp. 'No one will ever find out, it's just a fig-leaf
of your imagination, Skipper.'

Stamp was, of course, being kind to his skipper, and Sorley
Mor, in his desperation, allowed himself to be consoled. He
would contain the problem, he decided; he would swear anyone who knew of Eric's dancing to secrecy. Stamp and Gannet
nodded solemnly, knowing there wasn't enough secrecy in
the universe to cover this information. The entire crew had
to keep the secret, as had their families, and Eric's cousin,
Alan, and his family. Above all, Chrissie must never know of
it because, as Sorley Mor often remarked of his 'tiny wee
angel', she had been known to fight dirty. At this Gannet
smiled. He had realised from the start that if anyone had found
out instantly it would be Chrissie, and she wouldn't give
herself away all at once. She'd let the damage be done in
drip-drip fashion over years to get the best out of it. The first

thing was to summon Eric to a meeting around the mess table at the end of the next trip. Eric had his bag in his hand, ready to throw it into his car and drive to Glasgow to get ready for the European Old Time Dancing Championships in beautiful Blackpool.

'The thing is,' Stamp said to Eric, 'that as you know perfectly well, my friend, there are many people in the world who are not as cultured as you or me.'

Across the table Eric nodded solemnly. 'Yur no' wrang there, Stamp, son,' he said sadly. 'Summa the numpties Ah met in the Merchant Navy widda shocked ye. They used tae laugh at ma dancin'. Said Ah was a big poof, so they did.'

'Tragic, tragic,' commiserated Stamp, shaking his head in disbelief.

'Ah don't mind tellin' ye,' Eric said, a tiny hint of emotion creeping in to his voice, 'Ah was near tae tears at times, Ah was that hurt.'

Sorley Mor gulped and closed his eyes. The thought of a teetotal, dancing engineer was bad enough, but one who also cried! Eric caught his expression and misunderstood. 'Ah know, Skipper,' he said wearily. 'Terrible, intit? That wan human bein' could dae that tae another.' He sighed heavily. 'The cruel things that huv been said tae me, ye widnae believe it!'

'Well that's our concern exactly,' Stamp said. 'We know you must've suffered for your art, Eric. Geniuses like yourself often do; it's the way of the world.'

Sorley Mor had a feeling that he had woken up in a parallel universe. That the poor *Ocean Wanderer* should live to hear such language!

'And we have to admit that fishermen are, on the whole, much rougher sorts than Merchant Seamen. Is that not right?' He looked at Sorley Mor and Gannet, who both nodded their heads in agreement.

'The worst of the lot!' said Sorley Mor with feeling. 'Demons and devils they are!'

'So to save you from all that,' Stamp continued, 'seeing as you have a fresh start with us, we think we should keep the whole thing between ourselves. We don't mention the dancing to anyone, we don't give the ignoramuses the chance to mock.'

Eric looked down at the table in silence.

'Not that you have anything to be ashamed of, Eric, or we of you, don't think that,' Stamp told him. 'There's no one prouder than us to have a man of such artistry as part of our crew. Is that not right, Skipper?'

Beside him Sorley Mor nodded glumly; a dumb lie. It crossed his mind that he would henceforth have to join those who went to confession in other ports, there was no way he could tell Father Mick any of this either. Oh well, in for a penny, in for a pound, he supposed.

'We just won't have your life made a misery, Eric,' Sorley Mor said seriously, 'and if some of these uncouth fellows find out they'll never leave it alone. We'd defend you; you know that. On this boat it's one for all and all for one. Is that not right, Gannet?'

Gannet nodded wordlessly, and once again the skipper wished he had relaxed his ban on alcohol aboard the *Wanderer*. He could have done with a touch of Gannet's eloquence at this juncture. Sorley Mor searched his mind for something else to reinforce his heartfelt empathy with his engineer. 'After all,' he said, wondering what in hell he was talking about, 'aboard the *Wanderer* it's always been a case of birds of a feather sticking together!'

Beside him he sensed Gannet laughing inwardly and had an urge to lift the tomato sauce bottle off the table and slap it across his sober pink head.

'Ah understand,' Eric sighed. He suddenly put his huge hands across the table and grasped his skipper's. 'Ah jist waant ye tae know,' he said, his voice breaking and tears filling his eyes, 'that Ah love youse guys!'

Sorley Mor stared at him, transfixed with horror and shock,

his mind racing with unspeakable thoughts of what could happen next. Then Eric got up from the table with his bag, wiped his nose on his sleeve and sniffed loudly.

'Stamp, son,' he said, trying to regain his composure. 'Ye wur right about the Two-Step, by the way. Ah jist stoapped thinkin' aboot it an' it a' fell intae place, jist like ye said.' He sighed heavily and blinked. 'Ah'll never leave this boat,' he said emotionally. 'This is where Ah was meant tae be! Who'd huv thoaght Ah'd find ma soulmates wi' a buncha teuchters?'

'Aye, that's right, Eric,' said Stamp kindly. 'As the Skipper here said, on the *Wanderer* we're just like a . . . a . . . a bunch of feathers tied together!'

Eric sniffed even more loudly and, unable to control his emotions, almost ran out of the mess.

'Well, Skipper,' Stamp said smugly, 'I think that went well, don't you?'

And so Eric's dancing had been kept under wraps, as far as Sorley Mor had been concerned at any rate. Then one day the big engineer made an announcement. 'Ahm gie'n up the Auld Time,' he said over a meal in the mess one night, and Sorley Mor's heart leapt with happiness.

'You are, are you, Eric?' Stamp asked in his quiet, gentle way. 'My, but that's a big step, is it not?'

'Aye,' Eric sighed, then he reached for a large brown paper package at his feet and put it on the table. 'Ah've aye hid a fancy fur Latin American!' he said, eyes ablaze. From the packet he drew out a long, scarlet, shiny garment and spread it out. 'This,' he said, 'is ma catsuit.'

Sorley Mor stared in horror as the said catsuit was opened up to reveal a pattern of sequins spread about its surface.

'Only thing is,' said Eric, 'it needs mair sequins, it's too dull like this.' He then picked up a plastic bag and spilled on to the table a myriad of sparkling discs of every colour. 'It's helluva time-consumin',' he said to Stamp. 'Mibbe ye could help me, Stamp, son?'

'But of course, Eric,' the little man said kindly, 'but you'll have to tell me more about the Latin American.'

'Oh, it's dead fast,' said Eric excitedly. 'The wey tae look at it is that the man's a bullfighter an' the wumman's his cape.' He leapt to his feet, grabbed a tea towel and did a few graceful passes at an imaginery bull on the high seas. 'See?' he said. 'Ye treat the wumman like that, so ye dae!'

'Interesting,' said Stamp, 'and you'd need pretty fancy foot-work I'd imagine?'

'Oh aye, ye need to be quick oan yer feet a'right.'

'As well as light,' moaned Sorley Mor to Gannet. 'Eh, Eric, I hope you don't mind me asking what is a personal question?'

'Fire away, Skipper.'

'Well,' said the Skipper, 'that suit thing looks pretty close-fitting.'

'It is,' said Eric. 'It's supposed tae be tight.'

'Aye, well, what I was wondering was how it contains all your bits?'

Eric threw his head back and roared with laughter. 'Ye get special drawers!' he laughed. 'Look.' From the paper package he brought out a pair of elasticated pants.

'They look like corsets,' Sorley Mor whispered in horror.

'Aye, Ah suppose they dae.' Eric laughed again.

'Do they not, em, cut off the blood supply to important regions?'

Eric's huge head went back once again and he howled with laughter. 'Ye're an awfy man, Skipper!' he roared. 'Naw, they jist haud ye in, like, gie ye a flatter outline, merr stream-lined, like, nae bulges sticking oot. D'ye waant me tae show ye?' The big man stood up and moved to unfasten his overalls, and Sorley Mor realised that he was about to treat the crew to a practical comparison between the bulging Eric and the streamlined Eric. It was more than the skipper could bear.

'No, no, it's all right Eric,' he smiled weakly, 'I was only wondering, that was all. I'll take your word for it that it will do you no damage,' and with that he headed for the wheelhouse to ruminate on the ways of the world. Now his non-drinking engineer would no longer be doing silly dances and funny salutes wearing a tailed coat, white dicky and shiny shoes, he'd be wearing a corset and a shiny catsuit covered in sequins instead – sequins, moreover, that the ship's cook, Stamp, would help him to sew on while they were at sea. What could be more normal? How could any other fisherman find that even faintly amusing compared with the silly dances with the salutes? He just had to keep telling himself that this was progress, this was better all round, and one day he might begin to believe it.

14

As Rose and Sally waited and watched for their men coming home, they were no different from past generations of fishermen's wives, except that from their vantage points high on MacEwan's Row they could at least see them. These days there were radios and mobile phones, but when the sisters were bairns there had been few means of keeping in touch, and in the low-lying village the boats often weren't visible till they came round the point. Everyone had a vague notion of when a boat should return, though, and the bairns used to sit by the harbour, waiting for a glimpse of a father, brother or uncle, sometimes all three on the same boat, while the women stayed at home and got on with their work, afraid of tempting fate. Only when a boat was actually overdue and there had been no sightings by other crews, when fate had already struck, would women wait by the harbour in those days, just as their mother, Margo, must've waited all those years ago, though she never talked about it. The latest technology had transformed much of the fishing industry and made vast changes to the working lives of the men, but it did nothing to allay the deepest fears of their wives. It was something that would never change, that waiting spell, and the relief when he opened the door remained undiminished, no matter how many years your man had been going to sea and coming home safely again.

Fishermen tended to marry within their own communities, or took wives from other fishing communities. Either way, they convinced themselves that the women didn't dwell on what could be happening out at sea, didn't think of the danger. They were brought up in the industry; they coped with it: so the men reasoned. The notion that they spent their time in fear and worry while their men were away was one that outsiders invented; fishermen's wives were cut from harder-wearing cloth. That was the way the fishermen coped, by believing that their wives didn't worry while they were at sea. Rose knew this wasn't true, though. Of course they worried. Oh, you didn't walk about the house all night crying, 'Ochone! Ochone!', you got on with things, but it was there in the back of your mind all the time. Sometimes you dreamed about it; it was often the first thing you thought of when you woke in the morning. And what was that rush of happiness when you set eyes on him again but proof of your worry, even if you only said quietly, 'So, you're back, then?'

Coming from a fishing community did help, though not in the way the men rationalized it. These days she understood the silent contract between fishermen and their wives not to acknowledge the dangers, least of all between themselves. The men had to go to sea without the worry of an anxious, fearful wife at home, so being a fisherman's wife meant learning not to let that fear show, not to let it rule your life. From the point of view of the men it therefore made sense to choose a wife from a family who had lived within that silent pact for generations, one who understood it almost instinctively and would get on with raising your family without you, even if that meant permanently. Some wives listened avidly to every weather forecast; others made a point of not listening to any: both were signs of their fears. There was a tacit agreement that you never let your man go to sea without any arguments you might have had being settled, and if there was bad news at home while he was away, a child ill or a relative dead, you didn't say a word till he was home again; what could he do from hundred of miles away except worry? In those circumstances a trouble shared was a trouble doubled. Not that you seriously thought something would happen to any of the men in your family, of course. If you thought that, you'd never let them go out of the door.

Rose often wondered what thoughts her mother must have had, though she knew better than to ask, which was just as well, because she would've been shocked at the answer. Every time he went to sea, Margo had hoped Quintin wouldn't come back. He had been the biggest mistake of her life; he had ruined her life, in fact. She had spent her all her years waiting for something, convinced that she would only be in this place until whatever she was waiting for arrived, but it never did. There was that one time when she was seven years old, when old Ina had taken her to her grandmother's funeral in Lerwick – though she didn't know where she was or why at the time. They were going somewhere: that was all she knew. Even at that young age, when they arrived in Aberdeen it seemed to Margo that this was the end of waiting and the start of what she had been waiting for. It was a huge place, with cars and buses and people and streets everywhere; it was the kind of place where she felt she belonged. Then they had got on a boat then off again, at a place that was as small as Acarsaid. There they stayed at a place that looked like a castle. Rose remembered feeling horrified and confused, and people looking at her. Her mother had spoken briefly and stiffly to a man, then they had got on the boat again.

Margo had been anxious about this, but when they arrived back in Aberdeen she had relaxed; she was where she wanted to be. But Ina had taken her straight home to Acarsaid. Her father had been waiting for them and threw his arms around her, squeezing her till she could hardly breathe. She hated people touching her, hated anything holding her tightly – a neckline or a necklace touching her throat, even her dark pigtails too tightly bound caused her to panic – and she had tried to push Aeneas away, gasping as she did so. He hadn't noticed, or if he did he thought she was just excited to be back, he was too involved in the reunion and the presents he had bought to welcome her home after two days, and when she noticed how moist his eyes were she almost felt sick.

It was how Margo had always felt about emotion; even though over the years she had come to understand that other people didn't feel the same way, it hadn't made her feel any less uncomfortable. Emotion crushed you, it held you tight, it squeezed the breath out of you – at least it did her. She had never felt any emotion for Quintin; she had just thought how smart she was for picking on him. In the 1950s and in that community the man ruled the family – though to be truthful not much had changed as one century had given way to another. Didn't matter how stupid he might be or how smart the woman, the man was boss, and her father was more boss than anyone. Aeneas Hamilton controlled her with his money. He had snared her early, giving her a life of luxury that she thought was the norm. He had even refused to let her go to university, which to her was no more than a means of escape from Acarsaid and from him, because he knew, quite rightly, that if she succeeded in getting away she would never come back. Every time she built herself up to go, he stopped her. He had bought her the first car in the village, gave her a job with just enough money to stop her saving up enough to leave with; he had brought her up with an appetite for the best of everything so that she didn't know anything else existed.

Aeneas had had it in mind that she would eventually marry the then Sorley Og MacEwan, the son of the richest family in Acarsaid, because as there was no way he would ever leave his home, that would mean neither would she. Margo had been determined to look around for an alternative. Sorley Og was too strong a character. She knew he was wedded to this place and nothing but death would end that union. But there was Quintin Nicolson: shy, easy-going Quintin Nicolson, who blushed every time she even glanced in his direction. There was no way to pass from the ownership of her father except to the ownership of some other man and, she decided, it would suit her purposes if he should be a man she could control. So she had picked Quintin, picked *on* Quintin. If she became his property she could get him to leave Acarsaid, to take her in to the world outside, and once away she would be free to move on without him. It was a master plan and she had believed it would happen just because she had always had everything her own way all through her life.

What a shambles she had made of that! And all because her father had brought her up to believe that she could have whatever she wanted, that everything would work out as she decided. Maybe if she had had more to do with men she wouldn't have made such a silly mistake, but Margo had always kept her distance from them. Quintin, she discovered, might have been quiet and shy, but he turned out to be solid as a rock; he knew his own mind and he was stubborn. It had taken her a while to understand that she couldn't move him. At first she had just thought, give it time; Margo Hamilton always got her own way. She would have to put up with him in bed a bit longer, the worst, most constricting feeling she could ever imagine, lying there with him on top of her, squeezing the breath out of her, suffocating and invading her; after the first time she had rushed to the bathroom and vomited, and every time after that she had gritted her teeth and concentrated on keeping breathing, surviving, until he was finished.

It would soon be over, this time and for good, Margo told herself, and it would all be worth it, because once she got him to take her away from here she wouldn't have to see him, or the village ever again; wouldn't have to put up with this violation ever again. Then, two months after they had married, she discovered that she was pregnant. She felt like killing herself. Trapped. That's how she felt then, trapped. Six years later, when he died in an accident at sea, the only emotion she had been consumed by was rage. Why hadn't he died sooner? There she was, pregnant with number six; why hadn't he died before number one was conceived? And she knew there was no one she could tell. Everyone loved Quintin, and she was expected to play the tragic widow, but she cursed him, and them, every day of her life. One thing was for sure, though: never again would she lie under any man. Her body, like her life, was now her own – or would be when the bairns had grown. Maybe she could leave them with her mother and father when this last one was born. The old woman had more time for them than she did, anyway.

Margo and Quintin's daughter, Rose, had never thought about the village or her life there until she had left Acarsaid; like all bairns she had just absorbed whatever underpinnings supported adult life without really thinking about them: that would come later. She had left Acarsaid at the age of eighteen and had been surprised at how much she'd missed the place while she was away, and at how clearly the distance brought it into focus. Till then she hadn't been aware of the various currents bubbling away underneath village life, so it had been like standing back from a painting and suddenly seeing colours and depths that hadn't been visible close up. Like all the other youngsters she had been anxious to leave the familiar boredom of home, to become part of the bright, exciting world beyond, to walk down a street where no one knew her name, where there were pavements on both sides of the street, even! Yet her university years, much to her embarrassment, had been marred by homesickness.

When it was really bad, Rose would lie in bed and conjure up every detail of life in Acarsaid. In her head she would watch the fishing boats unloading at the harbour and hear the banter of returning fishermen above the clamour, as they teased each other about over-fishing their quotas and exchanged insults with Sorley Mor. She would follow people she had known all her life going about their business, stopping in at Hamish Dubh's store at the bottom of the Brae to complain about his prices, a ritual everyone observed; and she would listen to the conversations of the women as they put out washing or issued threats to errant bairns about what would happen to them when their fathers got home. It was like having her own private film show in her mind, that she could rewind, pause and fast-forward in time as well as place, to whatever incident, whichever character she decided to see again.

Rose had gone to St Andrew's University on the east coast of Scotland at the age of eighteen to do archaeology, intending to go on after that and specialize in marine archaeology. But she had only completed the first part of the plan. She had always been fascinated by the stories of lost galleons lying at the bottom of the sea, and by stories of pirates. It wasn't so much that she wanted to find fabulous treasures, casks of golden doubloons and precious stones, as that she was excited by the idea of connecting with past lives, of piecing together what people were like and how they lived long ago, of bringing things from the sea that had been lost for centuries, giving life again to those they had belonged to. If she went on to do her second course at university, she would become one of a very select band of females working on wrecks all over the world, collecting artefacts from sunken ships from any time in history, understanding and explaining the past. She would join expeditions to find Bluebeard's flagship, lost somewhere in the Caribbean; she would search off Egypt for Cleopatra's Palace, rumoured to be lying fathoms deep just off the coast, and she would hunt for the *Esperanza*, sunk off the Philippines in the 17th century on its way to Mexico when carrying a 500-million-dollar cargo of gold, silver, coins and Chinese tableware. She lived in fear of someone else finding her dreams before she could. So that had been the plan, until she saw Sorley Og on the deck of *Ocean Wanderer* that day. It was the first thing she looked for every time she came home, the sight of the boat tied up at the harbour, with the figure of Sorley Mor standing on deck, usually with Gannet somewhere nearby. On that day Sorley Mor's son had been standing beside him, though, truth to tell, Gannet could've been there too without her noticing, because the sight of the two Sorleys was all that registered.

And yet Sorley Og had always been there. She remembered him at the village school, an amiable boy a few years older than herself, who didn't much care for learning, didn't see much point in it. The teacher, Miss Nairn, had come from Glasgow to teach the heathens (that was how she had thought of it); a small, skinny creature who had heroically risen from a poor family to become a teacher and thereafter hated her roots and anyone who reminded her of them. The people she had lived among were all lazy and stupid, she would tell the Acarsaid bairns; they hadn't wanted to learn, preferring instead to wallow in their ignorance, but none of her pupils would ever be allowed to do that. Then her gaze would fall on Sorley Og, staring out to sea or up to the sky and, her mean eyes narrowing to slits, she would sneak up on the boy as quietly as she could in the hope of making him jump. The fact that he never did jump, but instead turned to greet her with his slow, friendly smile, reduced her to a screaming heap every time. What, she would screech, was he looking at, a boy like him? Castles in the air? He had no imagination, how dare he conjure up illusions in the clouds, *a boy like him*, who was destined to be a fisherman, a *lowly* fisherman just like his forebears, who had as much brainpower as he had imagination!

The judgement was a measure of how little the school-teacher understood of the community that had given her a living. Had there been a hierarchy in Acarsaid, then the Mac-Ewans would have been at the top, and Sorley Og, far from being 'a boy like him', would have been the equivalent of the heir to the throne. The tirades never bothered him, though; his dignity remained intact and he kept smiling his easy smile. He wasn't making castles in the air, he would tell the enraged Miss Nairn, he was looking at the sky to gauge the weather, because his father was still at sea. And Miss Nairn was right, he would tell her, almost congratulating her on her insight, he *would* indeed become a fisherman, it was all he had ever wanted to be, just like his father, and his father before him, and his. He had no time for school, he would tell her kindly; she should just get on with teaching the others and not bother about him. After all, his mother had taught him to read, write and add up long before he'd started school, and what more could there possibly be to learn in a classroom? Miss Nairn would produce her leather belt and strap him in a frenzy till weals stood out on his hands and up his forearms, but the lazy smile on Sorley Og's face barely dimmed. Even then, Rose, one of the smart ones, would hold her breath and wonder if Sorley Og's performance was deliberate, or if he was fully aware that the damage to Miss Nairn's leaping blood pressure and life expectancy far outweighed whatever pain she was inflicting on him.

His best pal was Gavin, the son of the local doctor, who, like Rose, was also a smart one. They made an odd pair, Sorley Og and Gavin: one easy-going, full of laughter and practical knowledge, and the other a determined scholar who would one day become a doctor and take over his GP father's practice in the village. Perhaps that was the bond between them, Rose often thought, they were both determined, or pre-determined, to succeed their fathers. The friendship had endured, though, even when Gavin went down to Glasgow University and Sorley Og to sea. When they met up again down the years they effortlessly picked up where they had left off. He wasn't stupid, Sorley Og, he just wasn't academically minded. He needed to be outdoors, to work with his hands, to have his own space and freedom, but he had a quick intelligence and a dogged approach to anything that interested him; as his mother said, the house was littered with clocks as his father's boatshed was with old engines that he had taken apart, 'to see how they worked.' He did the same with minds. Nowadays Rose knew that he'd been fully aware of what he had been doing to Miss Nairn way back then, just as he was now. If there was one thing Sorley Og was good at apart from fishing, it was finding where people's weak spots were located. Rose MacEwan, née Nicolson, smiled. Ask anyone, friend and stranger alike, and they'd tell you that he had the sunniest and gentlest nature imaginable, but she knew that her Sorley could also be a vicious swine if you gave him reason! But these days, too, she knew that other side to him, the gentle side that was easily hurt, the side her family had hit full square.

15

The village store at the bottom of the Brae always stayed open when the fleet was due in, but even if Hamish had closed the door, you only had to think of tapping lightly and he'd come downstairs to sell you whatever you needed. Hamish Dubh he was called, Black Hamish, a tall, exceptionally thin man, and dark, that was how he was inevitably described, in English or in Gaelic. No one could ever say for sure what colour his eyes were, only that they were deeply set and dark. It became one of two trick questions they asked each other in pubs or at ceilidhs. First of all they'd ask, 'What's Gannet's real name?', and when someone eventually came up with Ian Ross they'd all laugh, because Gannet *was* Gannet, it suited him perfectly, while Ian Ross suited someone else entirely. Then the second question: 'So what colour would you say Hamish Dubh's eyes are, then?', and the other person would look blank and say 'Damn me! Would you believe that? I've known the man all my life and I haven't a clue! Not a clue! But they're dark, that I *do* know for sure!'

Hamish's complexion was wrinkled, darkly wrinkled, and his hair, which had remained the same for as long as anyone could remember, was, well, dark. His daytime wear never varied: dark trousers and a cream shirt that had first seen the light of day countless years ago as white, with a green and black striped tie. The tight knot of the tie hung loosely from the crumpled collar of the shirt, which in turn hung just as loosely from the scrawny neck underneath. Over it all was a sleeveless Fair Isle pullover of depressingly dark hues. There was a time, in the 1970s, when to the delight of the village,

Hamish's pullover had become unexpectedly fashionable, and everyone who came into the shop commented wittily on his up-to-the-minute tank top. Hamish would smile back at them, nodding quietly, and muttering some reply in his dark voice, but when fashion moved on Hamish's attire stayed where it was and always had been.

He'd been in the Acarsaid shop all the years that Rose could remember, all the years anyone could remember, come to that. No one could recall Hamish looking any different. Occasionally someone would come across old photos of the village and pass them round, identifying fishing boats and crews from years gone by or Aeneas Hamilton and the workers at the smokery, and there would be Hamish Dubh smiling quietly in the background, looking just as he always had. Though others had aged, put on weight, gone grey, even gone to meet their Maker, Hamish Dubh remained as he was. Sorley Mor would run his fingers through his own grey locks and look at Hamish. 'By God,' the skipper would say amiably to him, 'but you must have a painting in the attic, Hamish Dubh, except of course that you have no attic and, anyway, it's difficult to think of a painting looking uglier than you do yourself.'

But it was his night attire that became even more legendary than Hamish himself. Tap on the store door at night and he would appear with his upper half clad in the same clothes that he wore every day of every year, but below the waist, forever being hitched up about his bony hips at the very last minute, he wore ancient brown-and-white striped pyjama bottoms, held at the waist by a fraying white cord and, on his feet, dark, checked slippers, his toes easing through the worn, disintegrating fabric, the rubber soles warped and twisted. There was a horror about those pyjama trousers that haunted generations of villagers, similar to the one about Batty Black Rock's freed breasts: that one day the cord would finally fail to hold, or that Hamish would miscalculate the last-minute hitch that kept them aloft. In those awful circumstances God alone knew what would then be revealed and, it was earnestly hoped, God would keep it to himself as well. The ever-present fear expressed itself in constant entreaties to Hamish that he should invest in a new pair of pyjama trousers, preferably with an elasticated waist, a belt or braces – or preferably all three.

'Would you look at him!' Sorley Mor would say loudly to Gannet. 'Can you not buy another pair of trousers, Hamish Dubh? For God's sake, man, you must've made enough the way you've been skinning us down the years to afford something better than them old things!'

'Now nobody ever made a penny profit out of you, Sorley Mor, or out of any MacEwan for that matter,' Hamish would smile back his quiet, friendly smile. 'The same name and the same money has been handed down through the ages. Sure, everybody knows that "Every penny is a prisoner" is inscribed under your clan crest. There's not much wanders far from *your* pocket!'

Sorley Mor would take off the Dylan cap he had bought from Hamish Dubh. 'Away with you, Hamish, man!' he'd say in amazement, brandishing it about for all to see. 'I bought this from you not forty years ago, and look at the old thing! Blue it was then, though you'd hardly know it to look at the pale thing it is now, and look you at how it's fraying about the peak. Two shillings it cost me, as God and Gannet here are my witnesses, two whole shillings, and look at the state of it!' He'd slap the cap back on his head. 'And you say you can't make enough from poor misguided Highland people like me to buy yourself a decent pair of breeks! Well, I just hope you don't confess sins that size to Father Mick. I just hope you have the decency to go elsewhere for absolution and not destroy the wee man's faith in humanity, that's all I'll say!'

It was odd how rituals began, Rose thought, those little things that all young lovers think they are the only ones ever to have thought of. For her and Sorley Og it was that, at the end of every trip, Sorley Og would go in to Hamish Dubh's store and buy her an ice cream. She had no idea how it had started, but it had become their 'thing'. Silly and soppy it might be, but it meant something precious to them, for all that. It was always one of those big affairs on a stick that he bought, pointlessly covered in chocolate that cracked and fell off in big sheets as her teeth bit into it; always too much, she said, to eat all at once. Rose would cut it in two, putting one half on a saucer in the freezer, feeling his eyes on her, laughing at her.

'I know what you're thinking!' she'd say, trying not to sound too defensive.

'You do, do you?' he'd smile back slowly.

'You're going to say, "You always do that. I don't know why you insist on having a big one when you could have two wee ones instead."'

'I am, am I?' he teased gently.

'You are.'

'Sure, don't I know that size is important to you?' he'd say innocently, and if her mother, Margo, and Granny Ina were there he'd smile sweetly at them. He was admired by the other in-laws for the way he played his mother-in-law like an old fiddle; sometimes it was all they could do not to laugh out loud at the subtle cheek he gave her.

'Aye, I was daft enough not to realize that was all there was to you, Sorley Og, your big notions of yourself!' Rose would reply in a tart stage whisper, her eyes glowing, then she'd raise her voice again. 'And I'll say what I always say, that I can have the other half with a spoon later, when you're not here.'

Sorley shook his head. 'If you got two wee ones you could still have one later, when I'm not here.'

'There you go!' she'd reply accusingly, and the two of them would laugh about – well, about nothing really.

Margo would struggle to contain herself, sitting stiffly in the big house she could never come to terms with, any more than she could Sorley Og marrying her clever daughter. Rose would be the one who would escape this place, she had decided long ago, Rose would justify her own miserable existence caught in the Acarsaid trap – and now a fisherman had caught her, too.

'You understand nothing, son,' she would say. She always tacked 'son' on at the end in an attempt to make her intervention sound friendlier than it was, because his constant cheerfulness and joking got on her nerves as much as the size of the house. Why did they need this great fancy place with its fitted this and fitted that? Sally and Alan's house down the way wasn't like this. It was a perfectly functional house, all that was needed, nothing like this great palace Sorley Og MacEwan had insisted on building. All show it was, just like him, everything overdone, and for what? To impress the little minds of this place? She hadn't wanted Rose to marry him, but then she wasn't alone on that.

'I don't know what you see in him!' Margo had wailed when the news was first announced. 'He takes nothing seriously!'

'Have you never been in love?' Rose had protested.

'*Love?* What's the matter with you, lassie?' Margo had thrown at her daughter viciously. 'You're too old to believe in that nonsense! You're educated, for God's sake! Love? You know fine well that there's no such thing! So that's what you want to do, throw away all your chances and become a fisher-wife, all because of this "love" of yours? For God's sake give yourself a shake and grow up!'

Margo threw the word 'fisher-wife' at Rose like an insult, though it was what her own grandmother, Dolina Polson, had been. Granny Ina's mother had baited the nets that her husband and sons had used to catch fish, then gutted and salted the fish when they were brought home; sold them too, sometimes, and even helped drag the boat up onto the shore. It was part of keeping her family fed and alive. There was nothing to be ashamed of in that, but Margo obviously looked down on it. Granny Ina listened to the encounter without saying anything. She had long ago abandoned any hope of moderating her daughter's views, let alone fully understanding how her mind worked, and even when Rose went to her later for support, the old woman was reluctant to take sides.

'She said there wasn't such a thing as love, did you hear her, Granny Ina?' Rose asked. 'How could she say that? Didn't she love my father?'

Ina looked at the hurt brown eyes staring at her and wondered what to say. 'I don't know, Rose, I can't answer that question. Maybe not even your mother can,' she replied quietly. 'How does anybody know how other bodies really feel? How can we know what love means from one body to the next, come to that?'

'You must know if you loved granddad!' Rose said, shocked.

'Aye, but is what I call love what you call love, lass? That's what I mean.'

Ina knew that she was dodging the question. Had she loved Aeneas? Now there was a puzzle. There had been none of the passion that she'd read about in the herring lassies' penny novelettes, that was for sure, but did that really exist, Ina had often wondered, or did what you understood as love change from one set of circumstances to the next, from one generation to the next, for that matter? Aeneas had been a good man, solid and steady. She remembered feeling that from the start, that he was a man you could trust, a man who would provide. In her terms, given where she came from, with her experiences of life, that could be love, she supposed. They got on well enough. There had never been a cross word between them – apart, maybe, from the odd remark she might make about how he spoiled their daughter. If Ina had had her way, Margo would have been encouraged to leave Acarsaid when she was young, that was the truth. Margo had too strong a personality for a little village; she had needed to get out into the big wide world. If she had come back later, well then, at least she would not have done so from ignorance, but knowing that other places existed.

Ina knew what it was to have a restless spirit, and she knew Margo had inherited it from her, but Aeneas clung to his daughter, giving her whatever would keep her at home. He had been devastated when she married Quintin, and so had Ina in her way. That was no reflection on Quintin, either: he would have been better suited with someone else and so would Margo; that was all. There had been nothing Ina or anyone else could do about it, though: the surest way to make Margo do something was to tell her not to. Maybe you had to be a woman to understand another woman; maybe you had to have had Dolina as your mother to understand Margo.

Ina had thought it over a lot, what caused what and why. As far as she could make out, it was as if two people with a dormant gene had married and in the resulting child the gene had become active, causing an illness, a condition. She and Aeneas had produced a child with a serious malfunction in her character, one that stopped her feeling for anyone – relative, friend or foe – in a normal way. She seemed devoid of the human sensibilities that enable people to get along together and make relationships. And poor Margo also had a strong personality like her grandmother's, only it had been backed up by Aeneas's money and position, so that her flaws were magnified, while those around her allowed her to get away with more. Aeneas hadn't intended it that way any more than Ina had herself. They had wanted their daughter to have a better life than they had had, but they had not meant to indulge her flaws. Neither Ina nor Aeneas were emotional people. She supposed they could be judged anti-social in the way they shied away from close friendships; and maybe what they had each needed was a partner who was the opposite.

Ina knew she had strands of her mother's outlook; she had worked that out long ago. Her brothers and sisters also carried similar strands to a greater or lesser degree. All those years as a child growing up, trying to be good, trying to win her mother's love away from the stillborn Angus, or at least get her share, and decades after Dolina's death she had come to the conclusion that she had got it all wrong. The conversation she, Danny and Ella had shared before her brother had returned to Canada had probably come as near as anyone ever would to solving the enigma that was Dolina Polson. Dolina was a woman uncomfortable with closeness, and she had used Angus as a ploy to keep a distance between herself and everyone else, even her own bairns. It was easier to concentrate your feelings on one object, better still if that object had no capacity to form a real relationship, and Dolina had settled on someone who didn't and had never really existed. There could be no interaction between her and her lost son, no real emotion between her and Angus, so he became a device for avoiding it with her real, living, breathing family. Ina hadn't failed her mother, neither had Danny, Ella nor any of the others. Dolina had failed them. But Ina had married a man like her mother, a man who had sunk whatever feelings he had into his daughter, just as Dolina had in Angus. Aeneas was equally safe, because Margo had no emotion to give back.

And why had Ina married Aeneas? If there was any one reason it was that she had been angry with her father; that was why. There she was, in her thirties, and she had still worshipped Magnus like a wee bairn, but the discovery that her hero had turned a blind eye as Ella had been battered by her husband, had bruised Ina, too. Then Magnus had died, so that she had never had the opportunity to have it out with him, to demand an explanation, and no chance either to get to know him afterwards as an adult, to see him as the man he was instead of the fallen hero he had become in her estimation. If she had married at all, and she was far from sure she should have, Ina knew she should've picked a man like Magnus, who entertained her and made her laugh; she should have chosen a man like Gannet, she had often thought with a smile. Had he passed her a generation before, he would've been the man for Ina Polson. But how could Ina explain any of this to Rose, who looked so like Quintin and yet had inherited the tender, romantic heart of Ella?

'Look, lass,' she told her granddaughter kindly, 'only you know what you feel for Sorley Og and if it's enough. For me there were no bolts of lightning, and I would say the same for your mother, though I can't be sure about that and neither can you. You know what she's like and you know something of why, but you can't judge her, you've never stood in her shoes. Just accept her as she is.'

Margo's simmering anger was, Ina told Rose – as she had many times over the years – caused partly by bitterness at being left a widow with six bairns under the age of six all those years ago. She suspected too that Margo knew she wouldn't have been in that position if she hadn't married Quintin, if she'd married Sorley Mor instead, though Ina had never been convinced that Sorley Mor had been seriously interested.

'So why did she marry Daddy if she didn't love him?' Rose asked.

Granny Ina shook her head. 'How would I know? Because everybody else said she shouldn't, maybe,' the old woman smiled in response.

Not that there was anything wrong with Quintin, of course, but he was so different from her, so quiet and reserved with women. He was a nice man but he had no money, and money was something Margo had always been used to having. Though Quintin and Sorley Mor had been friends, they weren't in the least alike; the MacEwans had always been boat-owners, whereas Quintin had never aspired to do anything more than work for others. He was an unassuming, content man, happy to work here and there. He enjoyed having a few laughs with Sorley Mor and Gannet, but he was completely devoid of ambition, and why should he have it if it wasn't in his nature? Everyone knew that Quintin would never have any interest in owning his own boat, for instance.

As long as he had enough to live on and his beer money, he thought life was pretty much OK.

'He was a nice man, your daddy,' Granny Ina said kindly, 'and my, but you're his image, Rose. It's a great sadness that he never lived to see you, but maybe he should never have married and had bairns at all.'

Rose accepted this as code for 'feckless'.

'It was your mother pushed him into marriage, I've told you this before, Rose. He would've been quite content as a bachelor all his days, young Quintin. It was always my opinion that Gannet should have married and Quintin should have been the bachelor. He would've been quite happy like that, having a couple of drinks at the Inn with Sorley Mor and the lads, if only she'd left him alone.'

'So she chose him over Sorley Mor to be perverse?' Rose asked. 'Just because she always did the opposite of what was expected of her? That's a terrible reason to marry anyone!'

Granny Ina laughed. 'The truth is, Rose, that your mother and I were never close enough for me to ask her. She was always one for her own counsel, even as a child. I remember the last time I went to Lerwick, when she was young. I'd taken her to show off to my family, if the truth be told, and I always felt she was angry when we came back, though I couldn't work out why. It's hard to explain, but right from the start there was this bit of her that no one could reach. I used to think I should've tried harder with her, but I don't think she would ever have let anyone in, not even me. Maybe that was my fault, I don't know, but my mother was very like that too. I've often thought that was why her father gave her so much; he was trying to buy a way into her thoughts, into her affection.'

'But people still talk about her,' Rose said. 'They say she was a real character when she was young.'

Ina laughed quietly. 'As I recall it she was a bit of a character,' she said. 'But the funny thing was that I was never sure she realised it. It was almost as though she behaved as she was and didn't understand that other people didn't do the things she did. For all we know she maybe thought *they* were the odd ones.'

'And yet they say Sorley Mor was interested in her, and he's such a lovely man,' Rose smiled.

'Well, you know what Sorley Mor is like now, and he was just the same then. He was the one who drew your eye; maybe it was just natural that other people might expect them to make a match of it. Certainly your grandfather wanted them to marry, but your grandfather thought in terms of money and position – love was never part of it for him. For all we know neither one of *them* thought they would make a match, though, and when she married your father I can't remember Sorley Mor showing any great feeling either way. You know what small places are like for myths and stories: maybe there never was anything in it but gossip.' She laughed. 'Not that there was any shortage of other lassies ready to take Sorley Mor on, handsome devil that he was, but Chrissie was the only one I ever saw him with. She worked in your grandfather's smokery, so I saw her every day, and Sorley Mor would be there looking for her every day that the *Wanderer* was in harbour. Then they married.' Ina looked at her grand-daughter. 'Now, Rose, if you want to know whether or not love exists, it strikes me that you could do worse than look at Sorley Mor and Chrissie. If that's what you want, then I can't see you doing any better than Sorley Og. All I'm saying is that you have to be clear about what you want, and, if you are – well, nothing anyone else thinks or says matters, not even me.'

As she was growing up, Rose had often looked at them, trying to imagine her mother in Chrissie MacEwan's place, but she couldn't. Sorley and Chrissie were supremely happy together; as everyone knew, they were a perfect match, that was the general opinion, with Chrissie cutting Sorley Mor down to size whenever she could and Sorley Mor chasing her around as she shrieked and giggled, like two young lovers who just happened to be in their fifties. They embarrassed their bairns, or so their bairns often said – not that Chrissie and Sorley Mor bothered about that. When she was a child, Rose would get so caught up in their laughing and larking about that she laughed out loud herself, and she would wish it could be like that at her house. To her romantic young heart it was as though they were meant for each other, and maybe they were. It seemed that every boy in the village had had a crush on the outrageous Margo Hamilton in those days, hard as that was to believe looking at her now. Maybe Sorley had grown out of his crush, if he ever had one, and found the love of his life in Chrissie.

Though Rose hadn't known her father, she had grown up with him all around her; everyone, it seemed, remembered Quintin Nicolson as though they had spoken to him yesterday. Somehow she had always sensed that this wasn't entirely because of his scintillating personality, but more to do with how he'd died, the awfulness of it, and the fact that those who died young never grew old. She wished she knew more about him, but he had been the only son of elderly parents who had originally come from from the Isle of Barra, and he had outlived both of them, though Granny Ina would some-times tell her stories about him. Mostly, though, she concen-trated on the old photos that she and her brothers and sisters looked at when Margo wasn't around. Rose would spend hours gazing at his gently smiling face, trying to get to know him so that she could at least grieve for him. He was her father, he had died tragically young, but how could she really grieve if she hadn't known him, hadn't seen him, hadn't even been alive when he had, despite the fact that he was her father? For some reason she had always wished she could hear his voice, because without being able to recreate the tone, the expression, the actual sound, it would always be as if he had been mute. It was the only thing no one could give her, the sound of his voice, and she would concentrate on his image as hard as she could, almost as though she was conjuring up a spell to enable the gentle, smiling man to talk to her from the grave: funny the things a child could dream up.

Back then she used to think he was smiling out of those old photos at her alone, just as she did when Sorely Mor came into harbour, waving to his waiting bairns. She liked to think that she and her father were sharing a secret bond too, but looking back she knew better. She was the only one who couldn't claim to remember him, though she sensed that the memories her brothers and sisters claimed to have were just that, claims, because they had been too young when he died to form strong memories of him, especially as he had spent so much time at sea. They had done what all bairns in those circumstances did, what she had done as she gazed at his photos: tried to establish some kind of relationship with the father they would never know. A fantasy father was better than none at all.

Even when she was very young she had been aware of the strong resemblance between them. Looking at those photographs she knew that she was the female version of Quintin, no one had to tell her. She stared at them so long that she could've sworn the images had actually moved and, sometimes, guiltily, she would examine her father's outline, scrutinising the head that the winch had ripped off. Yet there it was on his shoulders, exactly where a head should be, attached to him, part of him; it was hard to imagine the force needed to pull him apart like that. He had just slipped and fallen into the winch gear as the catch was being lifted; it had been as simple and quick as that.

The whole village had felt the shock of Quintin's death. Acarsaid was a small place where everyone knew each other and lives were inextricably linked by the fishing, so even one death at sea left a scar. You could tell by the way they never talked of it that the rest of the crew who had been on the boat with him that day, Sorley and Gannet among them, had never been able to forget it. Even when she was small Rose had been aware that those men looked at Quintin's bairns in a certain way, and especially at her, because she looked so like him. Even if you hadn't known them all your life and hadn't known they had been on the boat and watched helplessly as he died that terrible death, she thought, you would guess by the way they looked at you. Sorley Mor, Gannet and Stamp as young men, and the others, the older men who had been on board, now retired from the fishing, they had never really recovered from it; you couldn't help but pity them.

She thought of the rest of the crew having to cope with the horror of her father's accident out at sea, of their panic at being isolated on that huge expanse of water, unable to help him, then having to untangle him before making that long journey back to their home port. The rescue services had been too far away to be of any use, though Quintin had been beyond anyone's help, and the crew had to bring him back to his family, shocked and distressed themselves and knowing there was nothing they could do to disguise the awful facts of his death. Quintin was well liked, he didn't deserve to die like that, no one deserved to die in that brutal way. But accidents happened all the time on boats: men with fingers missing, with whole limbs gone, were a common sight in fishing villages. The kind of accident that had killed Quintin, horrifying though it was, was not too unusual.

The newspaper and TV people took little notice of individual tragedies. They thought only in numbers; a boat being lost with its entire crew was news, but the mutilation or death of one man rarely merited a mention, regardless of the grief of his family and community. Maybe, Rose thought, gazing out of the window, that was no bad thing. At least her mother had been spared the waiting packs of jackals at the door, baying for pictures of her and her fatherless bairns, demanding nothing less than copious public tears to go with the transient lies that would appear on an inside page. For those left behind the lies weren't transient, of course. If you weren't part of a fishing community you might read what the jackals had printed and then forget it in a moment, but those left behind never did. It became part of their grief and intensified their pain forever. Those who had been scarred by the media's attentions could quote the offending words decades later, by which time the writers would be elsewhere, door-stepping some other hapless, grief-stricken family. Another day, another tragedy. But as Quintin had been the only one to die on the boat that day, Margo had at least been spared their attentions.

Rose remembered looking at her mother in those old photos, too, and feeling sad at the stark difference between that young woman and her mother. She had never known the pretty, dark-haired woman Margo had once been, any more than she had known her father, but she didn't have to in order to feel pity for both of them. She knew her mother's personality had changed when Quintin died, because Granny Ina had told her, and shortly afterwards Aeneas Hamilton had died too. After that, Rose decided, Margo must have decided to protect herself from further loss by disliking outsiders, by making them feel like intruders.

Margo didn't want anyone taking all she had left, her bairns; but her tight grip of them had persisted even when they were adults, with every boyfriend and girlfriend being given a hard time that didn't get any easier when they officially joined the family. No one escaped her wrath. You could have known Margo Nicolson all your life, you might even have got on with her, but only at a distance, as long as you didn't get close to her family and threaten to lure them away from her into marriage. The grandbairns these interlopers gave her were accepted, but not the outsider parents who had helped pro-duce them; they might have been found under a gooseberry bush, or cloned, for all the credit she gave their in-law parents. Give her her due, she tried to cover up her animosity, but it was always there, just beneath the surface, biding its time. The unwanted, unwelcome in-laws would repeat her remarks to each other, 'Wait till you hear what Margo said to me the other day!' they'd say with glee, setting up the latest acid drop, laughing like conspirators or, more likely, survivors of a shipwreck, huddled together on the same wave-tossed raft.

Margo was so quick to jump on them that a barbed remark could suddenly burst from the undercurrent and ambush them, seemingly from nowhere. Wedding albums would be produced, each one showing Margo, her dark hair slightly greyer with each marriage, but still styled in a Connie Francis bouffant, as it had been in her own wedding pictures. She wore a different outfit for each occasion, her left arm through the handles of her handbag, her gloved hands clasped tightly in front of her, and in each posed photo she had that same agonized expression, silently appealing through the lens of the camera to the world beyond. 'Please!' her tortured blue eyes transmitted, as she stood slightly apart from the rest of the group. 'I'm here because I have to be, but I'm not part of this, I don't approve and I refuse to pretend otherwise. Feel my pain! See my suffering!'

Comparing those photos with the ones before she was widowed you wouldn't believe they were of the same woman. For Margo hadn't always been like that. She had been quite a character in her day, so everyone told her youngest daughter. Margo had been the first woman in the village of Acarsaid to hold a driving licence and have a car, a black baby Austin that tore around the twisting, single track roads much faster than it should have, though no one would ever have dared tell her so. She had a quick mind and an even quicker tongue and she was game for anything; a lassie of some feistiness, that's what the old people said, Margo would accept any challenge. Say she couldn't and she'd drink the men under the table; bet her a pound that she couldn't run in her bouffant skirts and peerie heels and she'd take off like the wind round the harbour and be back in no time. And she was good fun, too, even if some of her pranks were a bit much. She had a liking for practical jokes and was renowned for setting fire to people's newspapers while they were reading them; then she would laugh so much at their reactions that she could barely stand. And there was the time she encountered some Danish fishermen in the Inn and insisted, through various bits of sign language, that they should yodel for the assembled company. The Danes had signed back that they couldn't yodel, that she had the wrong nationality altogether for yodelling, but Margo proved them wrong. 'I bet you'll yodel if I grab you by the knackers!' she'd said. Even without the use of her very graphic mime, the Danes had instantly understood, and Margo had been right, they could indeed yodel. And much as the villagers frowned on a woman saying those kinds of words, they couldn't help laughing; somehow there were special rules for Margo Hamilton. She was quite a lassie, they'd say, giggling behind their hands as they passed the latest story from one to another; you couldn't help liking her, even if they all agreed that they wouldn't be too keen on her marrying their sons or brothers, because she would be handful for any man.

But hearing these stories repeated troubled Ina. She knew that Margo didn't play practical jokes, she was cruel to people, she had no empathy, no fellow-feeling, and the only reason the villagers laughed instead of disapproved was because of her father's standing in the area. And his money, too, was a big influence on how the villagers regarded Margo's casual humiliations of other people.

For a lassie of Rose's age it was hard to believe, but finding a man was still the main pre-occupation of young women in the 1950s and 1960s. It was an expectation thrust on them by their parents till it became a duty. Teenagers may well have been invented then and a sexual revolution taking place across the land, but not in Acarsaid. In Acarsaid the old values held true and lassies were expected to be safely married by the end of their teens or held to have been passed over, but there were damn few men would've wanted to cope with Margo, even though her father was rich, and fewer still who could. Say what you liked about her, she could sing and dance at

ceilidhs with the best of them, and was often far more boister-
ous, but, they'd say with heavy emphasis, nodding approv-
ingly, everyone knew she always went home alone. Aye, a
real character, Margo, but no floozy, that's what the old ones
all said with approval. She kept herself to herself, if you knew
what they meant, not like these days; yet more seeds, perhaps,
of the fiercely insular figure tragedy would one day make her.

Listening to the old stories, Rose had felt it hard to reconcile
the different character strands of the Margo Hamilton who
would one day be her mother: game for anything, a feisty
lassie, gregarious to the point of sometimes being outrageous;
descriptions Rose would never have applied to her. She had
always been ready for a laugh back then, and there seemed
nothing she wouldn't tackle for the hell of it. In those days,
as the older villagers were forever saying, the Brae from the
harbour rose steeply, causing problems for the fish lorries
leaving for the city markets with the latest catch. The first
lorry carrying the boxes of gutted fish would get up the Brae
easily enough, but as it climbed the bree, the combined juices
from the fish flesh, salt water and melting ice, would flood
out of the back, making the road slippery for the next lorry.
More bree would be added with each successive lorry, till it
became like a skating rink. Hearing the drivers complaining
one day Margo had said she didn't know what they were
moaning about, that any decent driver could get up the Brae.
'So *you* try it, then. Bet you a pound you can't do it!' one of
the men had challenged her, and Margo had climbed into the
cab in her fancy dress, crammed the net underskirts under her
as she sat in the driver's seat, placed her stiletto-shod feet on
the pedals and driven the lorry effortlessly to the top at the
first go, then returned to demand her pound. After that any
driver who couldn't handle the Brae went to Margo to take
his lorry up, and Margo Hamilton always charged a pound:
not that she needed the money, but it was the principle of
the thing. To the drivers' minds it wasn't like being beaten
by a lassie, because Margo was no ordinary lassie.

Rose would look at the old Brae and doubt the stories. It was so steep that surely nothing could climb it, let alone a fleet of heavily laden lorries, but the old folk insisted that it was all true; they had seen it with their own eyes. Though it had long ago been by-passed, and the struggles to negotiate it were nothing more than distant memories, that era lived on in old village tales, and the bright, gutsy lassie Margo had once been was the same. In later years the older villagers would shake their heads as she passed and say, 'You wouldn't believe what she was like as a lassie.'

Rose was wrong about Sorley Og; he understood perfectly about the ice cream he bought in Hamish Dubh's at the end of every trip. He had always understood. Each half lying in its saucer in the freezer was a hostage to fortune. It connected to a time when he'd come home safely, and so promised that he'd come home safely again, in a way that two smaller, individual ones somehow couldn't. Even though he'd called to tell her he was on his way home, Rose would wait, scanning the horizon with binoculars, till she spotted his boat heading for harbour. Only then would she take the remaining ice cream from the freezer, scrape off the covering layer of new frost with a spoon, and eat it, balancing the saucer on a tea towel to stop her fingers from sticking to the frozen surface. Only when she could see *Ocean Wanderer* with her own eyes and knew that the promise had been kept, would the ice cream be consumed, then home he'd come with another hostage from Hamish Dubh's store to replace it.

She'd never told him this part of this ritual because she knew she didn't have to; she knew he already knew. It was really no different, she thought, from the model of the boat that Sorley Og never finished. The times he could've finished it, the times he should've finished it, then he would find something else to do that meant he couldn't do any more work on it until the next time he came home. It still stood on a small table in the corner of the living room, surrounded by bits of wood, knives, brushes and various tins of paint, though painting would actually be the very last task after Sorley Og had finished the building. The real *Wanderer* had been a bright turquoise blue for years, but recently it had been repainted in green and white, so naturally Sorley Og had lined up tins of green and white, ready and waiting for the moment when the model was finished.

'Look, why don't you finish it first?' Rose had teased him. 'By the time you do the real boat will have changed colour another ten times, and you'll be left with all these pots of paint that you'll never use.'

'A woman would never understand,' Sorley Og replied. 'Back to your kitchen, woman!'

'So, explain it, *man*,' she laughed. 'Use very short words and I'll try to concentrate really hard, I promise.'

Sorley Og's face assumed an expression she knew so well from his father, the one Chrissie called 'his old man of the sea face'. 'The model would know,' he said grandly. 'Oh, you can laugh –'

'Don't worry, I will!'

'But if I didn't have the right colours ready for her, she would know, and she wouldn't turn out right.'

Rose threw him an incredulous look and shook her head. 'Just getting her to turn out at all would be something!'

'You have no respect for the master of the house,' Sorley Og said sternly. 'Y'know, in some parts of the world I'd just have to say "I divorce thee" three times and you'd be returned from whence you came. You realise that, don't you?'

'Don't think I'd have to be dragged kicking and screaming,' Rose snorted, 'and I wouldn't want your rotten old never-to-be-finished wreck as part of the divorce settlement either! You're not fooling me, Sorley Og. I know fine it will never be finished, don't think for a minute that I don't, and I know why.'

'Away with you!' he said, turning back to his work. 'You're married to a perfectionist, that's the problem. I can only do perfect work and, if it's slow, well, that's the price you pay for perfection.'

Rose threw a cushion at him, knowing full well that, however long he was at sea. the model would be waiting for him, unfinished, when he came home. It was every bit as much a hostage to fortune as the half ice creams she kept in the freezer, and they both knew it. As was the cairn she had started at the front of MacEwan's Castle. She wasn't quite sure if Sorley Og had worked that out yet, but she thought he probably had. One stone for every week they'd been married, and one for every trip he had returned safely from. Now that *was* sheer superstition, there was no getting away from it. Rose MacEwan might have spent years away from Acarsaid, and have a university degree she had no use for, but underneath she was still a lassie from a fishing village after all.

16

When Sorley Og first mentioned selling *Ocean Wanderer*, Rose knew that it wasn't a whim. He had had something on his mind for months, and she knew him well enough to know that he'd come out with it when he had thought it through and come to his decision. Normally the boat was away for anything up to four weeks at a time, back home for two days, then off again, but it was March and with the end of the mackerel and herring seasons the crew would be at home for the next three months. In June they would be off again in search of sand eels for pet food, but the lull gave them time to attend to all those minor repairs that Sorley Mor insisted be logged, when the boat was repainted and checked for damage that could not be seen by the naked eye. She knew Sorley Og had been mulling something over, but when he voiced his thoughts it was still a momentous, if low-key announcement. Not only was the boat going, but it wouldn't be replaced; the MacEwans were getting out of the fishing.

A decade before the very thought would have caused fatal seizures in and around Acarsaid. To those who had lived and worked beside them for generations the MacEwans *were* the fishing, but these days everyone knew there was no longer a living to be made. It had been bad enough in the mid-1960s, when herring fishing had been banned to allow stocks of 'the silver darlings' to recover from years of over-fishing, driving skippers out of business, crews – and curers, too – out of jobs. It had been the end of Aeneas Hamilton's livelihood; with no herring being landed at the once thriving port, he was forced to buy what fish he could from other ports to keep the smokery in work. It wasn't economical, but he hoped it would be a short-term measure – only it wasn't, of course. When stocks had recovered and the ban had been lifted, years had passed and the public had lost the fish-eating habit; a whole generation of consumers had discovered the delights of beef-burgers, pizzas, chicken nuggets and other convenience foods. It had coincided, too, with a wider change in society, with more women going out to work and spending less time cooking, so convenience had become their priority, preferably anything that would heat up in the microwave in minutes without preparation.

Traditionally fish had always been cheap, but now it was regarded as too expensive, when the true cost, as with coal, was in the lives of the men who harvested it. Aeneas had stuck with his business to the very end, unable to comprehend that it was over, that now the fish had returned he no longer had a market to supply, or to face the fact that the situation was permanent, so that he was left with a smokery that no one wanted to buy because they had no use for it. He had gone from being a wealthy man with a thriving business to nothing, and all through no fault of his own. Ina watched him withering in front of her eyes and was unable to do anything to help him. He had worked hard all his life in an industry he knew well but, like countless others, he had been unable to conceive of a time when the fishing wouldn't be there. If there was a downturn it would surely be followed by an upturn, that was what he thought, what they had all thought once. Finally Aeneas had to stop working because there was no work, and soon after he had just died.

Right until the end he had still got up every morning at the same time and put on his three-piece tweed suit and his brown shoes that he polished every night before going to bed, but then he found that there was nothing to do and nowhere to go. Work had been his life: he had never taken a holiday, and he had no hobbies. He was the type of man, Ina knew, who would go on forever as long as he had his work to do.

It gave him both status and purpose, and without it he became a shadow of himself. Over the years Ina had adjusted to his workaholic ways. She was too old now to sob that her husband didn't love her. She had made her own life, quietly making up for the education she had missed out on, reading books and furthering her already wide knowledge of astronomy. Aeneas had nothing. They had never shared the same interests, and now she realised a huge gulf had opened up between them and it was too vast and too late for it to be bridged. At the same time, Margo, the daughter he adored, had been left a widow with five bairns and another on the way, and Aeneas could do nothing to help her. It was who he was and what he did: he provided, especially for his Margo. He felt a failure in every way, and there was no way of persuading him otherwise because only his own opinion mattered.

Ina watched him sink lower and lower. One morning he had sat in his favourite chair to read his newspaper and, when she came in minutes later, the paper was on the floor and Aeneas was unconscious. Old Dr Johnstone had shrugged his shoulders and asked Ina if she wanted Aeneas kept at home or taken to hospital. In those days there was no cottage hospital – that wouldn't come till old Dr Johnstone's son, Gavin, was the Acarsaid GP. Dr Johnstone meant Raigmore General in Inverness, many miles away from the village. She knew from his voice that it would make no difference to the outcome which bed Aeneas lay in, so he might as well lie in his own. 'You can talk to him, Ina,' Dr Johnstone suggested kindly. 'Hearing's the last thing to go. It'll make him calmer if you talk to him.'

It took Aeneas three days and nights to die, and all the time she sat beside him, listening to his breathing. That last day, with the ticking of the clock sounding so ominously in the background, she talked to him about Yarmouth, wondering if he really could hear her, or if Dr Johnstone had just been giving her something to do to make her feel better, offering words of comfort for her, not for him; but still, she supposed, there might be a chance. She wondered if she should do something more for him – hold his hand, perhaps; but they had never been that kind of couple and it would have been false. In their everyday life such a show of affection would have embarrassed both of them, she decided, and all she could do for him was sit there talking about the old days and hope he could hear her voice. Then she noticed a new pattern to his breathing: one moment it would be loud and heavy, then the next so low and quiet that she thought each time he had gone. When the doctor looked in she asked about it, and he told her it was a sign that his brain was finally dying and meant the end wouldn't be long, and in the early hours of the third night he stopped breathing completely.

It had been a neat and tidy death, Ina thought, with no fuss; a death that suited the man and the life he had led. 'CVA', it said on the death certificate. It stood for Cerebral Vascular Accident or, in layman's terms, a stroke, but everyone in Acarsaid knew Aeneas had simply given up and died, and if he hadn't had a stroke he would have died of something – anything – else. If ever there was a broken man, that man was Aeneas Hamilton. Not that he was the first or the last to be driven out of business by the dictat of the here-today, gone-tomorrow politicians. They were advised by career bureaucrats, who sat behind desks looking at figures on pieces of paper and, without the slightest understanding or knowledge of the fishing, made decisions for which they would never be held accountable. Meanwhile whole communities lay in ruins. That was the way of the fishing world.

It wasn't just because it was becoming harder and harder to make a living out of the fishing that the MacEwans decided to get out of the industry, though; they had been successful for years and were hardly on their uppers. In fact, far more valuable than the boat was the licence allowing *Ocean Wanderer* to fish. A worthless piece of paper when it had first been granted years ago, it would now fetch millions of pounds.

The real reason for giving up the sea was because Sorley Og wanted to be at home more. He wanted to be with his wife and, when they had bairns, he wanted to be there as they grew up.

Sorley Mor had rarely been at home when his son was small. He was more like a visitor, and Sorley Og had desperately wanted a father. It was the way of life in a community like Acarsaid; there was no cruelty intended, and it was no reflection on Chrissie's care of all her bairns, but Sorley Og was the only boy in a family with three sisters, and it seemed to him that he had spent his life waiting for his father to come home, then trying to hide his grief at the inevitable next parting. They say like attracts like, and Sorley Og had often thought that maybe there was something of that in why he and Rose had ended up together: they both had missing fathers.

Rose had never known her father, but Sorley Og sometimes wondered if that might be preferable to having one you loved who was forever leaving you at home. Maybe, too, that was something that might not have affected another youngster so badly. He had never heard anyone else voice feelings like his, but it had affected Sorley Og, and he was determined that it wouldn't happen to his bairns. And that was another thing: he sometimes wondered if he and Rose would ever have bairns, given that he was so rarely at home, as absences grew longer for less reward. These days he had his skipper's ticket and had more or less taken over command of *Ocean Wanderer*, giving Sorley Mor the chance to stay at home more, though he and Gannet would still go to sea every second or third trip. So, how to tell Sorley Mor that the end of an era had come, that was the problem.

Rose had been surprised but not shocked at her husband's decision. She had known he would talk about what was on his mind when he was ready. They were sitting close together, contented, something on TV slipping effortlessly past their eyes.

'I was thinking,' he said quietly, 'that it was maybe time to give up the fishing.'

For a moment Rose didn't reply; she knew that the partings were getting harder rather than easier as time went on. 'You don't have to do it for me,' she had told him.

'So you don't want me at home, then?'

'You know I do,' she laughed, 'but I married a fisherman, Sorley, that's what I'm saying. I knew what I was taking on.'

'Well, you knew more than me,' he laughed. 'I never gave the future a second thought till you trapped me into marriage.' He grinned at her. 'So, when Sorley Mor's looking for someone to blame, I'll point my finger at you, Rose Nicolson!'

'MacEwan,' Rose corrected quietly. 'Rose MacEwan.'

He put his arms around her. 'When I was a wee boy I was scared all the time,' he said.

'About what?'

'About whether or not I'd see my father again,' he replied.

'Really?' she asked, pulling back from him to look up into his eyes. 'I didn't know that.'

Sorley Og laughed gently. 'Every day of my life I was prepared for the worst. I'd watch the boat coming into harbour and I'd relax, but as soon as she left I was scared again.'

'You never showed it.'

'Well, you learn not to, don't you? It's part of life.' He was silent a long time. 'I always wanted to be close to him,' he said.

'But you are, Sorley!'

He laughed. 'I didn't mean that to sound as pathetic as it did,' he said. 'I meant I'd grown up knowing him through other people's stories,' he said quietly. 'Everyone has a Sorley Mor tale, you know what he's like, and they always assumed that I must have as many that they hadn't heard, but I hadn't. He was never at home long enough. He would come off the boat with the others, dog-tired after working twenty-two hours a day for five days, with little to eat while they were fishing because there wasn't time. He'd wave to us from the wheelhouse, come ashore, and even then it was difficult to get him alone because everyone wanted to talk to him. Then they'd all head for the Inn and get drunk – not that it took much when they were so tired and had nothing in their stomachs. Gannet would drag him home, Chrissie would shout at Sorley Mor and slap Gannet, they'd sleep it off, and, before you knew it, they were back at sea.'

'I used to talk to him down at the harbour as he was mending nets,' Rose smiled.

'Did you?'

She nodded. 'He used to bring me pieces of treasure,' she laughed.

'Treasure?'

'Bits of pots and things that he'd brought up in the nets. I used to think I was so special to him!'

'Well, isn't that something? He never mentioned that. Good for the old man,' Sorley Og smiled. 'Doesn't that say a lot for him? You learn something new about the man every day.'

'It was because of my father, I think,' Rose said.

'I'm sure it was,' Sorley Og said, 'but what a good man he was to take the trouble, do you not think so?'

'Of course. I adored him then and I do now. But I know what you mean, Sorley. I only know my father through the eyes of other people. I used to take his photos out of the bureau when my mother wasn't around and look at them, and I'd have given anything to hear his voice, to hear him saying my name, I suppose. When your father's dead, no one can tell you what his voice sounded like.'

'I never thought of that,' he said, pulling her closer. 'It must've been hard growing up in a place where everybody kept talking about him, yet you'd never seen him and knew you never would. I remember hearing about him all the years I was growing up, too.'

'Everybody spoke about him except my mother,' Rose grinned wryly.

218

'Really?'

Rose shook her head. 'Not a word. Never.'

'Did you ever ask?'

'No! We knew not to. Don't know how we knew, but we did. We talked to each other, but I don't think the others really remembered him: they were too young when he died. Granny Ina used to tell us a bit about him, and Sorley Mor used to tell me stories too.' She hesitated for a moment. 'You know those stories about my mother and your father?' she said. 'Do you think there was anything in them?'

Sorley Og laughed. 'Hard to imagine, isn't it? I find it difficult enough to think of him and my mother being young lovers, but him and Margo?' He shook his head. 'Well, I find that damned near impossible!'

'Me too. They're so different,' Rose said thoughtfully. 'I hate to say it about my own mother, but she's so cold. They say she was full of life as a girl, but that's just as hard to imagine. I don't think I've ever heard any warmth in her voice, never mind in her expression. I think back and all I hear is that bitter tone. Maybe that's why I've always wanted to hear his voice, in the hope that it would be warmer than my mother's, the missing link that could never be filled, I suppose.'

'Well, that's one thing we'll never have to wonder about Sorley Mor!' his son laughed. 'He never stops talking. He's like one of those people who can sing and draw breath at the same time: he's unstoppable. The times when we've been at sea together have been the best, getting to know him as a man, but I'd have liked to have known him when I was young, without the anxiety that he might not come back. I don't want my bairns saying that about me.'

'Our bairns,' Rose said quietly.

When Sorley Og and Rose went next door, Sorley Mor was snoozing upright on the couch by the fire. There was a huge stone fireplace reaching to the ceiling, with the hearth sitting on a raised platform of marble, where Sorley Mor's feet rested. It was an enormous sitting room; Chrissie had been right, Rose thought, smiling. The furniture looked as though it had started out desperately trying to cover gaps, then, having given up the ghost, had simply settled for arranging itself in individual little groups here and there. It looked like doll's house furniture. Ideally, oversized tables and chairs would have been needed to suit the grand scale of the rooms. Though he would never admit it, Sorley Mor had acknowledged the fact that the house was too big by creating his own space by the fire. It was a bit like having a study, only without walls or a door.

'He's too nosey for walls,' Chrissie would scowl, 'and he wouldn't be able to rest not knowing what was going on outside a door.'

When anyone came into the house looking for Sorley Mor they would turn automatically to where he was to be found when ashore and not in the Inn, sitting in 'his' space on the couch in the corner of the room nearest to the fire, with his back to the window so that he only had to turn his head to keep an eye on what was happening in the harbour and the rest of the village. Beside this sat a small table where 'his' books and magazines lay, and on the edge 'his' coffee cup sat; no matter how untidy it might be, nothing on the table was ever disturbed or, as Chrissie said, 'World War Three would break out.' On the wall in 'his' space was another copy of the framed quote, 'The Sea', that he had picked up many years before and that he had in the *Wanderer*'s wheelhouse as well; Chrissie called it 'sentimental crap', but Sorley Mor loved it.

Looking round Sorley Mor and Chrissie's house, Rose was always struck by the similarities to the one their son had built. Though MacEwan's Castle was new and had every modern innovation and design feature, basically it was big, just as Chrissie had said, like this one. It was as if Sorley Mor had looked at the plans for an ordinary bungalow, then ordered it to be built three or four times normal scale; in his way,

Sorley Og had done the same. She recognised, too, Sorley Mor's table; in their house was another that was never tidied up, with the unfinished model of *Ocean Wanderer* sitting on top, all its bits and pieces, paints and glues in disarray around it.

Chrissie had a tea towel in her hands, drying dishes; she had never come to terms with the dishwasher in the corner of her kitchen. What was the point in it, she would ask, when it took so much longer to do what she did in minutes?

'If you're looking for sense,' she told Sorley Og and Rose, 'you won't get it.' She glanced towards her husband. 'That one's just back from the Inn. I thought I'd see more of him these days, but he's always holding court at that bloody Inn.'

'That is a lie, woman,' said the snoozing figure by the fire. 'I'm perfectly sober. I was playing dominoes with Father Mick, if you must know. Dominoes is a skill requiring complete concentration. One does not get blootered when one is at the dominoes, woman, especially not when Father Mick is involved. He cheats.'

'I hope you didn't bring him home with you?' Chrissie demanded.

Sorley Mor threw his arms wide, his eyes still tightly shut. 'Do you see him here, woman? How could I bring him home when you've banned him?'

'So where is he? You were in no fit state to drive him back up the Brae, that's for sure.'

'He's asleep in the back of the Land Rover.'

'And where's the Land Rover?'

'Outside the Inn.'

'And you've just left him there?' Chrissie demanded. 'Lying in the back, drunk?'

'We covered him with a tarpaulin,' Sorley Mor replied wearily. 'And anyway, what grounds do you have for saying he's drunk?'

'Don't talk daft!' Chrissie said, flicking him with the tea towel she had in her hands. 'Of course he is!'

'Why is he banned?' Sorley Og asked.

'He's not banned,' Rose said. 'Not exactly. I just think he should do the decent thing and receive the ear-bashing he deserves over –' she leaned close to her husband and said into his ear '– shall we say, several unfortunate escapades.'

Sorley Mor moved not a muscle.

Chrissie straightened up. 'Naturally, being a man, he's too much of a coward to show his face. When he sees me in the distance down in the village he takes off up the Brae to claim sanctuary in his chapel house. You should see him take off, his wee legs going like pistons!' Chrissie laughed.

'Your mother is a sadistic trollop,' Sorley Mor told his son solemnly. 'She has this peculiar idea that Father Mick leads me astray, so she's torturing the poor man.'

'That's not true either!' Chrissie said.

'Which bit?' Sorley Mor asked innocently, a sly smile playing over his lips.

Chrissie reached over, lifted his Dylan cap and slapped his head.

'I think that proves my point,' said Sorley Mor, eyes still firmly shut.

'They're as bad as each other, that's the problem,' said Chrissie. 'The minute the three of them get together, all common sense goes out the window. Like that damned helicopter nonsense.'

'It was a perfectly feasible proposition,' Sorley Mor interrupted, in a superior tone.

'Only for an idiot,' Chrissie replied, 'or in this case, three idiots.'

'What happened?' Sorley Og asked.

'Didn't you hear about that?' Chrissie asked. 'Must've happened while you were at sea, but didn't I tell you, Rose?'

Rose shook her head.

'Well, Laurel and Hardy went down to the Inn –'

'Gannet and I went for a stroll about the village,' Sorley Mor corrected her.

'As I was saying, Laurel and Hardy *went to the Inn*, and

222

they collected Hooligan on the way, Father Mick being crucial to their ability to stroll about the village, as we all know.'

'Your mother's also unduly sarcastic. Did I mention that?' said Sorley Mor.

'The first thing I know is a phone call from a firm in Inverness that hires helicopters. Could I confirm that Sorley Mor MacEwan lived here and was he all right?' I asked what they meant. 'Was he suffering from any mental problems?' You knew they had to be strangers when they would ask a thing like that. Seems this one here, egged on by Father Mick, had hatched this plan to hire a helicopter to take them to some wee lochan up the hill where he and Gannet used to catch trout when they were lads. The helicopter people thought he sounded odd on the phone, so they'd asked for a back-up number and got this one. Apparently there are deranged souls who hire helicopters then jump out and commit suicide, and the people in Inverness were worried their caller fitted the bill. I told them he sounded odd because he was drunk and trying to sound sober, as were the other two, just stupid men, that was all. That was the end of the plan, of course.'

'As I said,' said Sorley Mor, 'a perfectly feasible proposition. Father Mick had never seen the lochan and wouldn't believe how big the trout were until he saw them with his own eyes. I reasoned that he wasn't fit enough to get up the hill, so we decided to hire a 'copter. I can't see what all the fuss was about.'

'You see?' said Chrissie. 'They're impossible to control when they get together. One sparks off the other, and there's no sensible woman waiting at home to slap Father Mick.'

Sorley Mor sighed as though he had the weight of the world on his shoulders.

'Look at him,' Chrissie said. 'Great gormless lump. And he's been eating Dan's food again. Doubled up with indigestion when I opened the door. We should buy shares in Milk of Magnesia.'

'Nonsense,' said Sorley Mor in a dignified voice. 'Besides, Gannet's in a far worse state than me.'

'You mean that long waste of space who carried *you* home? That reprobate who's snoring in the porch?'

'Conservatory,' Sorley Mor corrected her primly, and tutted. 'I took the woman out of a wooden hut all those years ago and gave her a decent way of life, gave her some culture, but she still can't drag her mind with her. *Conservatory, woman.*'

'Ach, shut up, you great idiot!' Chrissie retorted, heading back towards the kitchen.

Rose went over to the porch and looked through the closed glass door.

'For God's sake don't open it, Rose,' Chrissie said. 'Listen to him! The noise he makes snoring would destroy your eardrums.' She crossed the room to where Rose was standing and the two of them looked through together. Inside the porch was a long table, and on top lay Gannet, fast asleep, his hands clasped across his stomach. 'Sleeps there whenever he has a few,' Chrissie said. 'Falls off a couple of times, remembers nothing about it afterwards. I often think if we could get MacEwan Black Rock and Haffa on the job quick we could have the bugger boxed and buried before he had a chance to wake up,' she said, shaking her head. 'I don't know why he keeps that house in Keppaig. He's never bloody there, he's always here!'

'Tut tut,' muttered Sorley Mor, 'language, woman,'

'If you want language,' said Chrissie, advancing on him, 'I'll give you bloody language!'

The skipper didn't move, but he raised one eyelid just to be sure. 'Gannet is my faithful retainer,' Sorley Mor protested with dignity. 'Where else would he be but asleep on my table in my conservatory? He is my bodyguard,' he said grandly, then closed his eye again.

'He's your fellow drunk,' Chrissie replied. She looked around, then her eyes fell on the local newspaper. Quickly she rolled it up and slapped him over the head with it. 'And he always will be!' she said.

Sorley Mor, eyes still shut, didn't flinch. 'You just can't get the staff these days,' he said resignedly. 'You have to put up with violence from foul-mouthed harridans like this one.' Then he reached out just as quickly and, catching Chrissie off-guard, he grabbed her round the waist and pulled her down across his knee where the two of them wrestled and shrieked. There were loud, smacking kissing noises from Sorley Mor and giggles of protest from Chrissie.

Sorley Og looked at Rose and laughed, shaking his head at his parents. 'Is this not embarrassing? Can you imagine what it's been like growing up and having to see this kind of thing every time your father's in port?' he asked, smiling all the same.

Rose thought it would have been wonderful to have both a mother and a father, especially like these two, but she said nothing. Not only hadn't Quintin been there, but there had never been the slightest feeling of him around her house, the grieving widow not wishing, it seemed, to keep any aspect of him alive. His name was mentioned frequently and with affection in the village, but never at home, except when Margo wasn't around and the bairns felt safe in asking Granny Ina about him. The old woman would repeat to them the tales she had been telling them for years, tales they had heard so often that they could have repeated them word for word, hoping that perhaps some little extra nugget of information might reveal itself *this* time. The photos of him in the old bureau were only taken out by the bairns, who would gaze at them quietly, secretly, whispering comments to each other, before guiltily replacing them in their dark home before Margo walked in on them.

As far as Rose was aware, Margo never visited her husband's grave in the cemetery up on the hill at the far end of the village, or, if she did, she kept it from them. Rose had always assumed that the memories were so painful for Margo that she had decided the best way forward was not to look to the past. She had never been to her father's grave, either. In the atmosphere Margo created at home it was a notion that had never occurred to her; nor had it, as far as she knew, occurred to her brothers and sisters either. It was Chrissie who had prompted that first visit. In the run-up to the wedding the year before, she had said, 'I suppose you'll be wanting to put your bouquet on your daddy's grave, Rose.'

It wasn't a question, more an assumption, and Rose had simply nodded, trying to cover the fact that she hadn't thought of it.

'Aye,' said Chrissie kindly, as though it was the most natural thing in the world, 'seeing as he won't be there.'

Rose hadn't mentioned that visit to Margo, though, nor the others she had made since, and she couldn't explain why not, not even to herself. Somehow she sensed that her mother wouldn't approve of a gesture that seemed perfectly natural to others, and not for the first time it made her wonder what kind of person her mother was.

Back in Chrissie and Sorley Mor's house, Rose and Sorley Og waited a moment as the giggling and protests continued. 'Father,' Sorley Og asked, sighing heavily, 'are you up to some serious talk or would you like us to leave you alone?'

Chrissie jumped up and breathlessly went through the straightening routine Rose had come to know: smoothing her hair, making sure her pinny was over her knees, protesting that the man was always making a fool of himself and of her, that he had no shame.

'Father, I'm thinking it's time to give up the fishing,' Sorley Og announced calmly.

There were no thunderclaps as Sorley Mor looked up. 'Aye, well,' the skipper said just as calmly, 'that sounds like serious business right enough. Better wake Gannet and get him in here.'

'You'll do no such thing,' Chrissie said. 'He'll still have a bit in him, he'll talk to us, and worse than that, he'll sing at us!'

'This is my house, woman,' said Sorley Mor. 'I'll say who sits round my fireside.' He tried to grab Chrissie again, but she body-swerved him.

'It's *my* house, Sorley Mor,' she retorted. She held up a hand to stifle any argument. 'Bought and paid for with my sweat over the years, bought and paid for by being sold into marriage with a MacEwan –'

'*A* MacEwan? Sorely demanded. '*A* MacEwan? *The* MacEwan, woman, and don't you forget it!'

'– and I'll lock that long streak in the porch –'

'*Conservatory!*'

'– if I have to.'

Sorley Mor proved to be considerably less under the influence than Chrissie had thought, and if he was even as surprised as Rose had been by his son's decision, he didn't show it.

'It's getting harder all the time since they cut the quotas again,' he told his son solemnly. 'I know that. I heard that *Westering Home* had to throw back about ninety-eight per cent of its catch the other day because they were immature haddock.' He shook his head.

By law immature fish caught in the nets had to be thrown overboard, even though they were dead, and the fishermen's protests that killing immature fish would lead to fewer mature fish to be caught in the future had fallen on deaf ears.

'They sit there in their pinstripe suits and play chess with us, they always have. I used to leave on a Sunday and sometimes be back in harbour on a Thursday, the hold loaded to the gunnels. I came home because we couldn't have carried any more. Now men with smaller boats are spending ten days at sea and, if they're lucky, coming home with enough to cover costs. I know that, Sorley Og.'

'And these days the lads have to ignore the weather and go to sea when every instinct tells them not to,' said a voice in the porch.

227

'Oh God, he's awake,' moaned Chrissie. 'And he's talking so he's still drunk. Go back to sleep, Gannet, you're having a dream.'

Gannet entered the room, stretching his long limbs, yawning, and, as Chrissie had predicted, talking.

'Boats are going down and men lost because they have to go to sea in bad weather.' He sat on the marble fire surround, shivering slightly from having just woken. 'The problem is that we're not farmers,' he said. 'Have I not always said that, Sorley Mor?'

'You have indeed, Gannet,' said Sorley Mor, 'and right you were every time, too.'

'There are no gentlemen fishermen sitting in that big pile down by the Thames,' said Gannet, 'braying like donkeys, but there are plenty of gentlemen farmers and landowners. That's our trouble, we have no political muscle.'

'You're right, you're right,' nodded Sorley Mor. 'There has never been a fisherman in any government. We're too busy working.'

'And fishermen have too much pride to become politicians,' Gannet said firmly.

'Look at the two of them,' Chrissie said, 'chests puffing out there fit to burst their shirt buttons.'

'They get money for producing too much, money for not producing enough, money for not planting crops in their own fields when they can't sell them anyway,' Sorley Mor said.

'Money for poisoning the food chain,' Gannet added, 'by feeding bits of other animals to grass-eating beasts. Just say you're a farmer and that gives you a right to be one and be supported with public money, whether it's economical or not; and damn the rest of us, steelworkers, shipbuilders, car-makers or fishermen.'

'Aye, Gannet,' said Sorley Mor, 'you've never said a truer word. Farmers get all the money, while we get no respect and damned all consideration! Remember the women from Peterhead? They had to raise the money to bring their men

228

home when the *Sapphire* sank after that Blair fellow refused to pay for it, and him and his pals down there spending our money like it's water. That crony of his, that great ugly fellow – what d'you call him? – spent more on wallpaper and nonsense than would've paid for the *Sapphire* operation ten times over!'

'The Lord Chancellor,' Gannet supplied with a distasteful expression.

'Lord Chancer, more like!' Sorley Mor snorted.

'Fishing communities just don't matter, that's the truth of it,' said Gannet. 'We are of no importance to those people.'

'That's it, Gannet, that's it,' said Sorely Mor. 'Our big mistake was in not selling our boats and buying land, then waiting for the subsidies to roll in.'

'You know, I was reading something the other day –' said Gannet, in philosophical mood.

'Oh, dear God, no,' Chrissie muttered. She looked at Rose and Sorley Og. 'If you had any plans for the next fortnight, cancel them,' she said, looking skywards. 'He's been reading again, there's no escape, trust me.'

'– and it seems that in the last five years seventy-one Scottish fishing vessels and forty-six men have been lost, and I was thinking, if it wasn't for us taking safety and survival so seriously, there would be more men than that lost. Do you not think so, Skipper?'

'I do indeed, Gannet,' said Sorley Mor, his voice taking on a heroic tone. 'And the lads of the emergency services, we can't ever forget them, the finest body of men –'

'Outside fishermen,' Gannet supplied, standing up and raising an imaginary glass.

'Outside fishermen, as you say, Gannet. Both undervalued and the salt of the earth, but do we care? Unbowed we are by it, Gannet, integrity intact! One day they'll look back and feel black-hearted shame for having such a low opinion of fine men such as ourselves.' Sorley Mor got to his feet and raised an empty hand too.

'I couldn't have put it better, Skipper,' said Gannet.

'Ach, you could, you could, Gannet, but it's a measure of the man you are that you'll give another credit. And it's a credit you are, too, to our fellow fishermen.'

Chrissie mimed playing a violin. 'How many years have I been listening to this?' she demanded.

'But it's true, woman!' Sorley Mor replied.

'I know it's true, but all you've ever done is talk. It's taken Sorley Og here to do anything about it. *My* son.'

For a moment there was silence.

'But what will you do?' Sorley Mor asked.

'Well, financially we'll all be fine: the licence is worth a lot now. It will probably go abroad. None of us will starve, but I don't think I could sit at home twiddling my thumbs,' Sorley Og replied. 'I was thinking I could set myself up as an agent, buying and selling prawns.'

Sorley Mor nodded. 'Poacher turned gamekeeper?' he smiled.

'I'm sorry, Father, that I have to be the one to finish things. If you want to keep the boat and hire a skipper and crew, I'll go along with that. It's your boat after all,' his son told him uncertainly. 'But I've made the decision for Rose and myself. My days at sea are coming to an end.'

'No, no, lad, that thought hadn't even crossed my mind,' Sorley Mor replied, looking genuinely surprised. 'I went to sea to make a living, not to keep any tradition going. Your great-great-grandfather was a crofter, he didn't want to go to the fishing, he only went when the croft failed and it was the only way to provide for his family. To hell with tradition, lad, but if there are no MacEwans on board the *Wanderer*, then I'd rather sell her too, cut the tie altogether. Do you not agree, Gannet?'

Beside him Gannet nodded, staring into the fire. Another silent moment passed.

'No, it wasn't that. I was just thinking, maybe I should've given up the fishing before this myself. The old woman here's right,' Sorley Mor glanced at Chrissie, 'for the first time in her life.'

Chrissie, sitting on the couch beside him, arms crossed, returned his glance with a sharp one of her own through narrowed eyes.

'I could see how things were going for many a year now. I liked the life, though, maybe I was just being selfish.'

Sorley Og looked at him. 'How do you make that out?' he demanded.

'Well, I was never here, was I? When you and your sisters were growing up I was at sea. Your mother had to bring you up alone.'

Chrissie, wordlessly and without looking at him, slipped her hand over his.

Rose watched Sorley Og closely as he shrugged his shoulders. 'That was your work,' he said. 'It's the same with all fishing families, always has been.'

'Aye, but still, I saw more of Gannet here than I did of my wife and bairns.'

'I'll give you that one,' said Chrissie, glaring at Gannet. 'You pulled the short straw there. At least I got peace from him when you were at sea.'

'Gannet never married; maybe he was more decent than I was,' said Sorley Mor, ignoring the interruption.

'No, I won't have that, Sorley Mor,' exclaimed Gannet, rising unsteadily to his feet and throwing his long arms about. 'There's never been a man alive more decent than yourself!'

'Holy Mary, Mother of God,' Chrissie mocked. 'Listen to this couple of old drunks: their very own mutual admiration society!'

'There's no need to take anyone's name in vain, Chrissie,' Sorley Mor said in a pained voice.

'Bollocks!' Chrissie responded cheerfully.

'Ach, would you listen to the terrible coarseness of the woman? Just you shut your ears to her, Gannet.'

Gannet looked unfazed as he sat down on the marble plinth

again. 'The fact is, I never met anybody I wanted to marry,' he grinned quietly, 'and I've always envied those who did.'

'Away with you,' Chrissie said dismissively. 'Don't bother trying for sympathy. There were plenty of lassies about. The trouble was that you could never talk to them when you were sober, and when you were drunk they couldn't get a word in edgewise, that's the truth.' Around the fireside everyone laughed gently, looking at Gannet.

'And besides,' Chrissie jabbed his arm with a finger and tried to sound angry, 'what do you need with a family when you've always had this one at your beck and call, you great skinny thing? I'll tell you this, when I got married all those years ago, I certainly never heard anyone asking, "Will you take these *men*", but that's how it turned out!'

'Ach, I don't know,' Gannet teased her, rubbing his arm. 'If I'd had a family of my own they might have been nice to me: that would've been a change, at any rate.'

'Only if they didn't know you,' Chrissie replied tartly.

Sorley Mor stared into the fire. 'I loved it all, those bright clear mornings when you could see to the other end of the world, and the quiet, and the sun on the sea. I even loved the dangerous stuff,' he said quietly.

'Are you still on about that?' Chrissie asked.

He looked up at Gannet. 'Do you remember that time off Shetland, Gannet?'

'There were a few times off Shetland, Skipper,' he smiled, 'and a few times *on* Shetland, as I recall.'

'That time when we hit a northeasterly, just blew up from nowhere, and we had the nets down. I said, "Never mind, lads, a northeasterly always blows itself out by dark", and dark at that time of year was about three in the afternoon.'

'Aye, I remember that one all right,' Gannet smiled. 'Seas of forty feet. We could only get the nets in when we were going downhill, and the skipper here's telling the crew that everything would be fine. Then we heard on the six o'clock forecast that it was building up to hit Force Ten!'

'All the lads were crammed in the new wheelhouse – we'd just had it fitted, d'you remember, Gannet? – and it wasn't quite finished, and we picked up a mayday from another boat and found we were the nearest to her. Well, the electrics went, but we had the radar. Remember?'

'Only the radar packed up!' Gannet laughed.

Chrissie looked at Rose and shook her head. 'You can see how that might be funny, can't you?' she asked, and Rose laughed back in reply.

'I couldn't see a damned thing,' chuckled Sorley Mor, 'but these huge seas and the driving snow, like a thick curtain in front of us. The only way I knew where we were was by the feel of the sea. I knew if we caught the mother wave – what is it the Shetlanders call it, Gannet?'

'The *moderdai*,' said Gannet. 'They say it's like your mother; it leads you to safety. If you catch it it'll take you to shore, no matter which way the wind's blowing.'

'Aye, that's the one. Your grandfather taught me that, Sorley,' Sorley Mor said to his son. 'He knew all about that kind of thing. He could look about him at the cloud forma-tions, the colour of the sky, even the calls of certain birds, and tell you what the weather was going to do without bother-ing with the forecast. He would look up at a heavy motion on the water and say, "There's a bound, better turn for port before the storm hits us," and he could tell by the wee ripples and squalls between the waves that a southerly was on the way. The call of the great northern diver meant a southerly, too, and he'd haul the gear and head for home. He was never wrong either.'

'They were all the same, that generation,' said Gannet solemnly. 'They could read the sea: they had to. We've lost all that; we're so bound up with technology these days that we don't need any sea knowledge. These modern boats are equipped for bad weather and they're more efficient, I'll grant you that, but these days the skipper here doesn't need to set foot on the deck; he doesn't even need to leave the

233

wheelhouse. He can sit in his slippers, flicking switches, pressing buttons, and playing at turning circles in his big swivel chair for the whole trip if he wants to.'

'Only some, Gannet,' Sorley Mor responded tautly, 'there are still leaders of men among us, myself for one.'

'And none better, Skipper!' Gannet exclaimed loudly, attempting to stand up without falling over. He put out his hand and shook Sorley Mor's warmly. 'You are the finest skipper on the high seas and a gentleman to boot. I would lay down my life for you!'

'Have you ever heard such . . . ?' Chrissie rolled her eyes, words failing her. 'Sit down, you,' she said, pushing Gannet, 'and behave yourself, or I'll kick your arse till it turns blue.'

'Och, Chrissie,' Sorley Mor groaned. 'Do you have to use the language?'

'I didn't have the language till I got in tow with you,' Chrissie replied. 'Marriage to you drove me to it − you and that,' she looked at Gannet, 'that great lump.'

'So what happened off Shetland, then?' Sorley Og reminded them.

'Well, once we'd caught this wave I knew we were OK,' said his father.

'Aye, but the wind was still howling and tossing us about,' Gannet grinned, 'and we couldn't see a thing through the snow.'

'Then Gannet here spots a tiny wee light and says, "Look, a space ship!"'

The others looked on as Gannet and Sorley Mor laughed and slapped each other joyfully, lost in their memory.

'I suppose it's one of those stories where you had to be there,' Chrissie said wearily.

'So we made for the wee light in the distance, and the next thing this damned great bow appeared right in front of us. It was the boat that had sent out the mayday, a French trawler. She was taking in water and all she had on was this tiny wee light − in those seas, too! I barely managed to turn the boat away before she hit us, must've been feet in it!'

'Inches, Skipper,' Gannet insisted emotionally. 'No more than inches! You saved every life aboard that day. You are a true hero.' Once again he stuck out a hand to shake the skipper's, and this time Chrissie slapped it hard.

'I tell you, Gannet, I was glad I had a change of trousers that night, I fair needed them!'

'We all did,' Gannet chuckled. 'I can still see it clear as day: the big, black shape of her coming at us through that thick snow, and hearing this great gasp of air as we all breathed in at the same time.'

The two of them held their sides and laughed, then Sorley Mor wiped his eyes. 'But you know,' he said, quietly again, 'even though I was frightened, I enjoyed it, too: the feeling of having the lives of the crew in my hands and getting through it.'

Gannet put a hand out and slapped Sorley Mor's knee. 'There are some who can handle the heat of battle, Skipper,' he said admiringly, 'and you were the best of them, you *are* the best of them.'

'Oh, God give me strength,' Chrissie muttered. 'You'll get used to this, Rose,' she told her daughter-in-law. 'It's men's talk only. It's called being surplus to requirements or, in this case, not wanted on voyage.'

'But I could never have managed without you, Gannet,' Sorley Mor replied. 'You were the best first mate, the best friend, a man could ever have.'

'We shall now,' Chrissie announced primly, holding an imaginary microphone in her hand, 'have a drunken rendition of "Dear Old Pals",' and with that she began to sing raucously.

Sorley Mor and Gannet ignored her completely. 'That's what I mean, you see,' Sorley Mor said. 'I liked the life and the companionship, but was it fair on my family?'

'Well,' said Chrissie resignedly, 'I can see you're deter-mined to be melancholy. Carry on.'

He looked at his son. 'I used to come into harbour and

see you all waiting there for me,' he said. 'All those wee faces watching and lighting up when they saw me. To tell the truth, lad, I felt guilty every time; yet I still went back. I knew I was missing so much, but so were you, and you hadn't a choice.'

'Can somebody tell me what good all this pathetic soul-searching is doing?' Chrissie demanded in exasperation. 'You were a rotten husband and a worse father – will that do you? Does that make you feel better, you bloody old play-actor?'

'I'm just saying I wish I'd seen more of my bairns,' Sorley Mor protested. 'Can a man not say that sitting by his own fireside without this hard woman butting in?'

'You are not,' his wife said. 'You're trying to show us all what a sensitive, caring kind of a bugger you are. But we're not buying it, I'll tell you that, so you might as well button it!'

'Never mind, father,' Sorley Og laughed. 'At least you'll know all your grandbairns.'

Sorley Mor looked from his son to Rose. 'You mean. . . ?'

'No, not yet,' Rose laughed. 'But it's part of the plan, don't worry!'

'Young Pete told me the other day that his Alison is expecting,' said Sorley Mor, 'and they only got married six months ago. Here's you two been married a year and those two have beaten you to it. We can't have the fair name of MacEwan running out, now.'

'Aye, like your family is the only MacEwan that counts,' scoffed his wife. 'The village is polluted with them.'

'They're not all of the true, noble bloodline, woman,' said Sorley Mor grandly. 'They are sub-strains. We are the only true MacEwans, as well you know.'

'There are times I think he believes the nonsense he comes out with,' said Chrissie. 'That's how daft the man is.'

'Aye, Pete was fair excited,' said Sorley Og. 'Smiled the whole trip after he got the news. You'd have thought it was the first baby ever to be born.'

'Funny when you think of him running around all those years, sowing wild oats and trying to avoid them taking root,' Gannet laughed.

'Aye, well, you've all been in that position, I'm sure,' said Chrissie, 'but we don't want any details here, thank you.' She turned to her daughter-in-law. 'I only hope you do better than I did, Rose,' Chrissie said. 'I hope when it's your turn you have the sense to have a son first.'

'And what do you mean by that?' her husband demanded.

'Don't be like me, that's my advice,' Chrissie said, ignoring Sorley Mor. 'A bairn a year till I finally managed the son and heir.'

'That is a damnable lie!' Sorley Mor exclaimed.

'No it's not, *you're* the liar!'

'We wanted all our bairns. Three fine daughters I gave you, Chrissie MacEwan, and then a son.'

'Ach, come off it,' Chrissie retorted. 'If Sorley Og had arrived first, we'd probably have stopped there, and you know it.'

'Are you suggesting that I don't love my daughters?'

'I'm *saying* you wanted a son more than anything, you old fraud, and I'd have been kept barefoot and pregnant for however many years it took to give you one. Is it any wonder our lassies took off for the far corners of the earth instead of staying here, when they knew they were only the warm-ups for the main turn – another Sorley?'

'Well,' said Sorley Mor in a shocked voice. 'We have obviously been at cross-purposes all our married life, that's all I can say.'

'I wish it was!' said Chrissie.

'Did you ever hear the likes of it, Gannet?'

Gannet smiled lazily and said nothing.

'It was always my impression that we had four bairns because we wanted four bairns, Chrissie MacEwan. Now I find out that you've been harbouring this resentment all these years.'

'And if Sorley Og had been another daughter?'

Sorley Mor cleared his throat. 'Then I would've loved her every bit as much as the others,' he said unconvincingly.

'And you would've stopped there? You wouldn't have wanted to keep trying for a son?'

'Well, we have no way of knowing that, do we?' Sorley Mor said, trying to sound as though he had given the matter some real thought as Chrissie laughed at him. 'I mean, had we been in that position we might have looked again at the situation, but there again, maybe we wouldn't have. How will we ever know? It is one of life's great imponderables, Chrissie MacEwan, and that's the way it will have to stay.'

'Bullshit!' said Chrissie. 'I know perfectly well, Sorley Mor, and so do you. Rose — have a son first time round, that's my advice.'

As the young couple left, Sorley Mor, Chrissie and Gannet saw them to the door. It was the kind of bright, crisp evening when winter fades into spring, the boats in the harbour below moving gently in the swell. Rose and Chrissie were talking quietly to one side as the men talked about boats.

'What do you think the lads will do?' Sorley Mor asked, not altogether expecting an answer. 'I wonder how they'll take it?'

'Well, Stamp is ages with us, Skipper,' Gannet said. 'I'd imagine he'll either retire as well, or help Dan to make some edible food.'

'Aye, that's a thought.'

'And God alone knows what Eric might turn his hand to,' Sorley Mor said, as the others laughed in response.

'He's been talking about starting his own dancing school,' Sorley Og said. 'He and Marilyn are getting a bit fed up with criss-crossing the world for competitions. And, as he says himself, they're not as supple as they used to be.'

'Well at least we've kept *that* secret all these years.'

'Do you think we have, Skipper?' Gannet asked, smiling.

'Of course we have! I made up my mind early on that if anyone asked me outright I'd deny it completely, threaten to let the big man loose on them for saying such scandalous things about him. Luckily none of them ever did, though I must admit that once or twice I wondered if one or two of them might have been hinting. But Stamp was right, all those years ago; it was nothing but a fig-leaf. Oh yes, we did a fine job there, all right. Not the snifter of a suspicion among them!'

At that a silent, amused look passed between Gannet and Sorley Og.

'Pete won't have trouble finding another job,' Sorley Og said. 'He's a good worker and a decent lad, they'll be queuing up to get him. Stevie, too: no engineer is ever out of work long. And the relief crew, they're all good men.'

'Aye, that's true,' said Sorley Mor, his hands deep in his pockets, all eyes fixed on the gleaming green-and-white boat that dwarfed all the others. 'So she'll be the last *Wanderer* then?'

'Aye, father,' his son said sadly.

'So be it, then,' he said brightly. 'Goodnight all.'

Chrissie reached out and hugged Rose. 'Thank God,' she whispered. 'Thank God. Now we'll be able to sleep at night knowing that they're safe.'

Rose looked at her. 'You too?'

'All of us, Rose, all of us,' Chrissie replied quietly. 'And that fool of a man as well. Every time Sorley Og goes to sea without him he paces about, watching the sky, tapping the barometer, listening to every forecast. Now he knows what it's been like all these years.' Then she looked at Gannet and Sorley Mor. 'Look at us,' she said, pushing them towards the house in front of her. 'It's been like this not only all my married life, but before it, too. I used to believe the best man went back to his own house after the wedding, not that he joined the happy couple. And baby makes three! Get inside the pair of you!'

As they walked the short distance home to MacEwan's Castle, Rose linked her arm through Sorley Og's. 'That was kind of you,' she said.

'What?'

'Letting him off the hook. You could've agreed with him when he said he knew he'd been selfish staying at sea because he liked the life.'

'And what good would that have done?' Sorley Og asked gently.

'None at all, but there's many wouldn't have understood that.' She stood on tiptoe to deliver a kiss to his cheek. 'You're a good man, Sorley Og.'

'So is he,' he smiled. 'So is he.'

Before they went into their own home, Sorley Og stopped again and looked down at the harbour. 'It's funny to think of her as the last *Wanderer*,' he said softly, 'of any boat being the last *Wanderer*, come to that.'

'Well,' Rose said, 'at least that model you've been building all these years might finally get finished!'

Sorley glanced at the cairn she had been building this last year. 'Aye, and maybe you'll stop putting stones on that thing,' he replied.

'You know!' Rose said accusingly, slapping him on the shoulder.

'Of course I know. I'm a MacEwan, I know everything, woman!' he laughed, mimicking his father, then he swept her up in a bear-hug. 'We're going to have a good life, Rose,' he said contentedly. 'We could go on holiday. I mean a real holiday, not a week here or there.'

'Well, we'll have to choose carefully,' Rose said, looking up at him, her expression mock serious. 'You won't go on a boat and you're scared of flying. Now what does that leave us?'

'Tell the truth, Rose MacEwan.' Sorley Og laughed self-consciously. 'I won't go across the English Channel, and you know my perfectly valid reasons for that.'

'And you're not scared of flying, then?'

'Well, I don't understand how planes stay up there. It's a technological doubt rather than a fear,' he said defensively, then he laughed. 'It's a man's thing; you wouldn't understand. Women don't have the brains to think about things like that. It's not a fear as such.'

'Liar!' Rose accused him, and he pulled a face at her.

'To be serious for a moment, Mrs MacEwan,' he said pompously and she giggled. 'I'd like to go some place where there's lots of snow. I've never seen really heavy snow. Do you remember when we were kids and Dougie used to take us to your house to hear your grandmother's stories about the snow? Well, I never believed her.'

Rose pushed him playfully. 'Are you saying Granny Ina is a liar?' she demanded.

Sorley Og laughed. 'None of us ever believed her – didn't you know that? We just thought she was a mad old Shetlander, but her fairy stories were still worth hearing!'

'You swine!

Sorley Og laughed. 'And who knows,' he said thoughtfully, 'maybe your family will approve of me once I'm not a fisherman any more. I always liked your brother Dougie, you know, but I've never felt at ease with him since the day we told them we were getting married. Even when we're talking business, when we're haggling over prices for our catch, there's this barrier where there wasn't before.'

Rose felt tears stinging at the corners of her eyes. It wasn't right and it wasn't fair. He had made her happy, yet her family still disapproved and he was still affected by that.

'I feel like I've lost a friend,' Sorley Og said sadly. 'I miss Dougie.'

'Well,' she said, her voice too high with false brightness, 'you gained a wife!'

'Mmm,' said her husband, 'and I'm still not sure I got the best out of the deal . . .'

She tried to pull away from him but he pulled her still

closer. 'Maybe after we get out of the business I'll have both,' he said into her hair.

She was on the point of telling him what Chrissie had said about his father worrying about him, as he had once worried about Sorley Mor, but just then a voice rose from the house behind them, singing 'The Silver Darlings' in a pure, beautiful tone. They looked in the direction of the singing and laughed. Chrissie hadn't been entirely right about Sorley Mor, but she had been spot on about 'baby'. Gannet did indeed still have a bit in him.

17

Whenever Margo Nicolson thought about her son-in-law she simmered with dislike and resentment. Not only was he another unwelcome in-law who had stolen one of her chicks from the nest, but he had stolen Rose, in whom so many family hopes had been invested. Worse still, unlike the others who never openly challenged her, she had the feeling that he was forever mocking her. Though she couldn't quite put her finger on anything specific, the suspicion spiced their encounters.

'He thinks he knows everything that one,' Margo would shout to her mother, 'but he understands nothing, does he?'

Granny Ina would smile and nod, and turn off her hearing aid, the better not to hear her with, though she was aware that she was hearing less these days and what she did hear didn't always make much sense. They all talked such nonsense, the lot of them, thinking they were the first to say whatever it was, and she'd worked out long ago that they were quite happy as long as she smiled and nodded when they bellowed at her. Her daughter would say to the others, 'I think the batteries are going, but she's happy enough thinking her own thoughts,' and she'd smile patronisingly. In all the years Granny Ina had been staying out of family conflict in this way, Margo had never noticed, so if anyone knew nothing, the prime candidate was Margo herself. But Granny Ina felt guilty about Margo. Even given her early widowhood, Ina had always felt her daughter's bitterness must also somehow be her fault – partly, at least; she was her mother, after all, and guilt about bairns is and always will be a mother's lot. Though she couldn't quite understand what she'd done to produce this determinedly unhappy woman, or how she could've evolved from the girl she had been.

After Quintin's death, followed by Aeneas's, Margo and the bairns had moved in with Granny Ina. Having been widowed herself so recently, Ina was glad of the company, and of the feeling of being of use again by helping her daughter care for her family. Aeneas had left a little money, but things were tight until the ground the smokery stood on was finally sold. The business itself was worth nothing; the business itself did not exist. There were always rumours about what the owner would do with it, that he would demolish what was there and build a factory or a garage, but nothing happened to the little group of buildings and sheds that had been Aeneas's pride and joy, except that they grew more derelict over the years. Eventually what Aeneas had built was spruced up and the old smokery had become a museum, not that it mattered to Ina.

Once she and her family had moved in with her mother, Margo took odd jobs about the village. Thanks to Aeneas's efforts she was qualified for very little that would bring her a living. A smattering of knowledge about how to keep books was all she had to offer apart from the housewifery she had learned while being a wife and mother. She decided that if she had to be a cleaner she would do it when there was no one about so that she didn't have to be engaged in conversation; she had never been good at conversation, it bored her. So she cleaned the school when the bairns and staff had gone home, and the surgery after hours, times and places where she didn't come in to contact with people. The bairns did what they could until they were old enough to look for adult jobs. They managed, but once they were all under the same roof Granny Ina could see at first hand how little love and affection her daughter gave the bairns. Margo looked after their physical needs, their clothes were always washed and pressed, food was always on the table on time, but in other ways – the ways Ina thought counted more – she was as distant a mother as she had been a daughter.

At first Ina expected this to be an understandable but passing effect of the shock of losing her husband, but if anything Margo's attitude became more entrenched as time went on. There was little laughter and no joy that Ina could see, no real bond between mother and bairns, and she saw them trying to get close to her in little ways that provoked vivid memories of her own relationship, or lack of it, with Dolina. It had been her father, Magnus, who had brought laughter and affection, she remembered, realising that the older she got the more she missed him, but the Nicolson family had no one like that; it was a wonder the bairns had all turned out as well as they did. The death of a decent man like Quintin had been a tragedy, to be sure, but the lives of every fishing family were marked by the loss of menfolk, and most women managed to get on with their lives. Although they never forgot, they moved on, however reluctantly, whereas Margo seemed to hold the entire human race responsible for her misery. But then, as Ina was the first to admit, she had never fully understood her daughter and could only guess at what was going on in her mind.

From Margo's standpoint it was different, of course. She was seething with resentment, angry at Quintin for not dying sooner, before she had produced these bairns. When he had been killed it was Ina who got the phone call. It was thought that it would be easier on Margo if her mother broke the news. Margo knew that at the time and it had made her smile wryly; given that her reactions had always shocked people, her reaction to Quintin's death would have blown them off their feet. She had been ironing clothes when Ina came in and made her sit down. She remembered watching the scene from the outside, and knew that this was the conventional way bad news was handled. She had wanted to say, 'Look, whatever it is, just tell me,' but knew she had to go through the motions, even if she didn't understand them.

'It's Quintin,' Ina said quietly.

'What is?' Margo asked blankly.

'There's been an accident at sea,' Ina explained. 'I'm sorry, lass, but he's been killed.'

Her first thought was to ask if Ina was sure, not because she wanted it otherwise, but just that, to be sure. Then she felt deep relief. Her whole body sagged with it, then she wanted to jump up and down and shout with joy. He wouldn't be coming back; she was free; it was over. Then she thought of the bairns and felt anger because he had died too late for her to be free. Even if he had gone three or four months ago, she wouldn't have this one in her belly. To everyone viewing the scene from the outside she was going through the stages any widow would be expected to go through, especially a young one with tiny bairns, only Margo knew it had nothing to do with that.

She had to follow form, go down to the harbour as the boat came in, the eyes of the place on her, all of them tear-filled except her own – shock again, they'd said, sympathetically. Then she'd gone home to explain to the bairns, though none of them were old enough to understand and, as their father wasn't home very often, it would make little impact on them anyway. It was the villagers who imposed Quintin's death on them, treating them as tragic orphans, or half orphans.

In the years ahead Margo had set about organising the practicalities of their lives, making sure they would have jobs outside the fishing. Everyone understood, or thought they did, that she didn't want any of her bairns to go into an industry that had claimed their father; the thought of losing another loved one was too much for her. Nonsense, of course. She didn't think any of them had the slightest spark of ambition or imagination in them, but if they had she wanted them to be able to aim for more than the fishing, to be able to escape one day. They heard no tales of Quintin from her as they grew up; for one thing she didn't know him well

246

enough to tell any, but she knew the mythologists of the village would more than make up for that. There was nothing she could do to stop their father becoming a hero to them, even if in reality he had been a boring wee man. And she wouldn't marry again, she knew that without a doubt. She had made her one huge mistake and wouldn't be repeating it; she was free of wifedom forever. No doubt that would be interpreted in Acarsaid as devotion to Quintin, but that was a product of their small minds and it didn't bother her what they thought: it never had. And who knew? One day, with the bairns taken care of, maybe there would still be time to escape.

And so the two widows settled into their life together, with Margo taking the practical role while Ina supplied the affection and the dreams. She told them stories of her childhood and older tales her father had told her, of Uncle Andro, who generations ago had fled to Canada after escaping a press-gang and had gone from Shetland, a windswept land with no trees, to Nova Scotia, where they blotted out the sky; of her brother Danny, who had run away to Canada with Isobel, her father in hot pursuit, and of his stories of his new life there. Uncle Andro's descendants in Nova Scotia had welcomed the young couple, as they would – Ina told them – any of the young Nicolsons, and helped Danny find work in the fishing.

Later, after the war, Danny and Isobel had settled in Toronto. and Danny had worked at the harbour where great big ships docked, bigger even than *Ocean Wanderer*. There was a road there called Yonge Street and it was forty miles long, the longest street in the world, he said, though Ina had no way of knowing if he was maybe exaggerating, and you could travel through Toronto and pass through different parts – the Chinese part, the Greek, the Turkish – all of them looking like real countries in miniature, all within one city. He sent pictures of himself and Isobel, each one showing that in some indefinable way he was becoming more and more North American – and you should never call a Canadian an

American, he said, it was like calling a Shetlander 'Scotch'. Isobel, on the other hand, and much to Ina's amusement, had kept the same hairstyle she had had all her life, so that over the years her face became more and more aged, disintegrating and collapsing under a sea of girlish golden ringlets. And it was a shame, because Isobel had such a lovely old face and the ringlets made her look foolish. Ina would look at each picture and wonder what Danny saw when he looked at his wife — what Isobel saw when she looked in the mirror, for that matter.

In time Danny had sent tapes that the Nicolson bairns could listen to with their grandmother, and they could hear him talking in his Canadian accent for themselves, confirming that Danny was real and not just a story, like the snow in Lerwick. She taught them all to knit, even the boys, and how to identify the constellations, and about her own father who had passed his passion for the stars to her, but she couldn't tell them very much about their own father. Quintin was the one person they wanted to know more about; they hungered for morsels of information that would bring him closer to them and bring him to life in their minds. Feeling for them, she mentioned it tactfully to her daughter, but Margo had shrugged and asked, 'What is there to tell? He was a fisherman; he died at sea. It happens. That's all there is. If they want fairy stories about him, I'm sure the whole of Acarsaid will oblige.'

So over the years Ina watched the absent Quintin take on the heroic status in the eyes of her grandbairns that Angus had in her mother's — and for the same reasons. From the villagers it was inevitable that they heard only good things about the father they never knew, who, just like Angus, hadn't lived in their lives and so would never do anything to make them think less of him, as Ina had come to think less of Magnus. Only now she missed him and would have given anything for five minutes of his company. Swings and roundabouts, she thought: the world just goes round and round.

★   ★   ★

Despite all the years Ina had lived in Scotland, she still looked differently at anyone whose name began with 'Mac'. Not that she looked down on them – that would be silly but, how could she put it?, she noticed them, that was it: there was still a division in her mind between people and Mac people. She had absorbed the prejudice with her mother's milk, she supposed; funny how the things learned in childhood stayed with you, even when you knew better and no longer had any need of them. There were times, as she sat by the fire, when she could hear the voices of her family in Lerwick so clearly that they could have been in the room with her. She would turn to answer them and find there was no one there, yet she had heard them so clearly, even long after they were all dead. Maybe that's what ghosts were, the backward dreams of old folk.

People came to see her and she was glad of the company, but the older she got the more she retreated back into an age none of them could remember. Back and forth she went over events she thought she might have changed had she behaved differently, done something other than she had, sitting by the fire in her own world. Margo was her main concern, and her fear that her daughter's unhappiness was her fault, but deep down she knew she was wrong: Margo would've been Margo no matter what Ina had done. Or was she using that as an excuse? Maybe what you made of circumstances depended on what kind of personality you had; she was sure she had read that in one of her books, or heard it from someone. Gannet, that's who it was. It was New Year and he'd had a few, so he was telling people things he had found out when he was sober. They had all told him to go away, if not quite in those words. Ina would always listen to Gannet, but being more or less confined to her fireside armchair by old age and legs that refused to work as she wanted, she had been a captive audience, anyway. And Sorley Mor was laughing in that way of his where he collapsed in the middle and his legs refused to work too. 'We could make a pair!' she'd shouted to him, and laughed with him; she had never known a man to be so disabled by laughter and, even if you didn't understand what he was laughing at, you couldn't help joining in with him. Not that she'd minded, whatever it was: he was a good man, Sorley Mor, and she'd got almost as much of a soft spot for him as she had for Gannet.

He'd read it in one of his books, Gannet had told her that New Year, and wondered if she agreed that the human mind was a wondrous thing. Not that he was at all sure that personality came from the mind, of course. No, now that he came to think about it, he'd better find another book to explain it, but so far he had learned that personality couldn't be changed and that was a solid fact. You were stuck, Gannet said, with the one you had, so maybe it wasn't the skipper's fault that he laughed so much, or his own that he didn't talk when he was sober: did Granny Ina think that was possible?

Ina had thought of Margo when she heard that; trust Gannet to bring her something to think about. She always smiled when she thought of Gannet. Rose had asked her if she had loved Aeneas, and she had done her best to answer her truthfully. Aeneas had been a good, solid, responsible man, a man Ina admired and appreciated; but that Gannet, he was something else: a good man gone to waste was what he was. Had she known what she was doing all those years ago, understood that she was spiting her father by marrying Aeneas, taking someone who was the opposite to Magnus to snub a dead man, she would've thought some more and waited for a man who amused her and made her laugh, a man like Magnus himself, a man like Gannet.

Life was like that, she had decided ages ago: it didn't let you see things clearly until you were too old for it to make any difference; you only ever saw your mistakes in retrospect. And it must be the same for her daughter, she thought. Aeneas had given Margo everything. He adored her so much that he bound her to him so that she never learned how to make her own decisions, thereby setting her up for the disastrous route her life would take. Margo had done her best by her bairns during the bad times. She had cared for them in her distant way as though her family was a project. She had pushed them into better lives and objected in her bad-natured way when they 'betrayed' her by leaving her to marry and set up families of their own. But the only reason they were able to do that, Ina knew, was because she herself had done her best to give them the love their mother either didn't feel or couldn't show. It was at Ina's knee that they had heard stories, learned to look outwards to different horizons, and so it was to her they brought the hopes and fears that they knew their mother wouldn't want to hear and wouldn't understand anyway. Ina knew that they often wondered why their mother was the way she was, and she wished she had all the answers, but she didn't, that was the truth, and she wondered if Margo did or ever would.

18

Margo Nicolson hadn't been alone in her disapproval of her daughter marrying Sorley Og. It wouldn't have been so bad if she had been; after all, she had disapproved of all her bairns' partners: everyone knew that. It seemed, though, that the entire family disapproved, and their opposition caught Rose unawares, despite being the smart, educated one. And that was at the heart of the objections, apparently – her education. Margo hadn't wanted any of her sons to become fishermen, so she had used her influence and strong personality to steer them into other occupations. Andy worked in the bank, Martin was a plumber with his own business, and Dougie was now the local manager of Crawford's, the fishing agent. On behalf of Crawford's Dougie bought the entire catches of the Acarsaid boats when they were landed, paying the skippers immediately so that they in turn could pay their crews' wages and for the upkeep of their boats, without waiting for the buyers to pay up. For this Crawford's took ten per cent of the price negotiated, an arrangement that seemed fair to all, given that it could sometimes take three weeks for the money to come in. As each boat was a family business, Dougie was in effect in charge of running the businesses of men he'd known all his life, without ever having gone to sea himself. The job suited him, though; Dougie was intensely logical and methodical, and also thought highly of all of the fishermen in Acarsaid, would defend them against anyone, was as close as a brother to most of them. So it shocked Rose when he of all people reacted angrily to the news that his youngest sister was about to marry one. He stood there, a mild man normally, angrier than she had ever seen him.

'You're ruining your life,' he'd said, white-faced with anger. 'You can't marry Sorley Og!'

'You've always liked him,' Rose had replied, stung and confused. 'What's wrong with him?'

'There's nothing wrong with Sorley Og,' he'd replied angrily, as though she was the one objecting to him. 'He's just not for you.'

'Why? I don't understand, Dougie.'

'Sorley Og is one of the finest men I know, but you weren't meant to marry him – to marry any fisherman, come to that.'

'Alan's a fisherman, I don't recall this reaction when Sally married him.' She shrugged, staring at her brother helplessly, as though he were speaking a foreign language.

'Sally's different, Sally's not bright,' he said, pacing up and down, hardly able to contain his rage. 'Being married to Alan suits her, but you were meant for better things.'

'Better things? You've just said Sorley Og's one of the finest men you know!'

'Listen to me, Rose. We all worked bloody hard in this family to make sure you got to university. You wanted to see foreign lands, have adventures, you were going to have a life away from Acarsaid, and you are clever enough to do it. For as long as I can remember every spare penny has gone to giving you that chance. We all gave up any dreams we had ourselves to make sure you got out of here because you were the brightest. Sally is fine married to Alan, Sheena's fine married to her schoolteacher, they'll both spend their lives here, but maybe if they'd got the chances we gave you – ach, I don't know why I'm bothering! Just don't expect me to be happy that you're throwing it back in our faces, that's all, and that's what you're doing by marrying a fisherman.'

'I didn't ask you to do that,' Rose replied, close to tears. 'I just want to live my life, Dougie, my own life!'

Rose had then turned to Sally for support, and was even more hurt to find that her sister wasn't on her side either.

'What have you got in common with Sorley Og?' Sally asked when she heard the news.

'What do you mean by that?' Rose asked, genuinely taken aback. 'Are you listening to yourself? What have we got in common? We were born and brought up in the same village, went to school together, our families have known each other for generations, for God's sake! Whereas your Alan comes from Glasgow, you didn't even meet him till just before you got married, he doesn't come from a fishing community – do you want me to go on?'

'Leave me and Alan out of it,' Sally said. 'This isn't about us.'

'Oh, I see, you can point out what you think is wrong about me and Sorley Og, but you and Alan are some sort of special case?' Rose demanded.

'We're different. We'd have got on regardless of where we grew up. We think the same way,' Sally retorted.

'And you're saying Sorley Og and I don't?' Rose demanded. 'What do you know about us? When did you become the great authority on other people's relationships?'

'I'm only saying I don't think you're suited and that you're making a mistake,' her sister insisted.

'Then mind your own bloody business, Sally, you know nothing worth knowing!'

The row wasn't over when it was over either, it stayed between them from that moment on. In times to come when they watched from their windows for the men's boats steaming towards harbour at the end of trips, and though their homes were within walking distance on MacEwan's Row, they never knocked on each other's door; it was never the same any more. Rose knew Alan felt bad about it, Rose and Sally had always been the closest to each other. He liked Sorley Og, too, everybody did, and he thought the Nicolsons were wrong in trying to force their expectations on Rose. But Alan wasn't a Nicolson, and this was a Nicolson feud, and he had known the family long enough to understand that his opinion didn't count and expressing it would only cause trouble between him and Sally. They were a strange bunch, he had often thought. They made fun of their mother for regarding in-laws as outsiders, but they all did it to some extent – except Rose, funnily enough: probably because she was the only one who had lived away from Acarsaid and had had some experience of the outside world. She wasn't their wee Rose any longer. That was what none of them seemed able to grasp: she had grown up and was her own woman.

And by contrast the MacEwans had reacted with such joy when they heard the news that Rose was ashamed of her own family. Everyone said it was the nearest to tears anyone had seen Sorley Mor in the whole of his life. Before they went to tell his parents, Sorley Og had one instruction for Rose.

'Now that you're to become one of the family,' he said, 'the old man will probably tell you about Eric.'

'What about Eric?' she asked.

'About the dancing.'

'Everybody knows about the dancing!' Rose laughed.

'Aye, but Sorley Mor has persuaded himself all these years that he's managed to keep it a secret.'

'You're kidding!'

'I'm not. He had to tell my mother eventually, spent weeks trying to pluck up his courage, and she had to almost faint with shock, though she knew about it ages ago. So just act as surprised as she did, that's all.'

'So I have to faint, do I?'

'He'd appreciate that,' Sorley Og smiled. 'But a sharp intake of breath would probably do.'

When Sorley Mor heard that Rose was marrying his son he hugged her as tightly as he dared, the muscles of his arms trembling as he tried not to squeeze the life out of her. His hands, coarse and rough from a lifetime at sea, repeatedly stroked her hair, snagging a strand here or there, but Rose didn't care. To be held in Sorley Mor's arms was something she had wanted for as long as she could remember; once she had been Quintin's child, and now she was at last Sorley Mor's.

Standing at the big window in the dark these years later she sighed. Was that what it had all been about after all?

She pretended that she hadn't understood her family's feelings, but she had, that was the problem, and once she had been told, and told so brutally by Dougie, the big brother she had admired and relied on all her life, she felt ashamed. No one had ever sat her down and explained that, because she was clever, the rest of the family would be sacrificing their lives and dreams to make sure she got a university education. They hadn't said to her that she would carry all their ambitions, that they had invested in her future and that she had to repay them by living the life they wanted her to live. The thing was unfair, obscene! Sally and Alan were happy, and the family had been happy, too, when they had married, she remembered that clearly – apart from Margo, of course, who was never happy when an interloper took one of her own. Rose hadn't realised then that the family regarded marriage to a fisherman to be all Sally was good for, the best she could hope for, given that she wasn't as clever as Rose. How could anyone defend that position?

And yet, she must've known that all their hopes rested on her. Wasn't there a feeling somewhere deep inside that she had pushed to the back, quietly accepting without openly acknowledging it? She came from a family with little money, and a big family at that. Quintin's death had coincided with the dip in the industry that had led to the closure of the Hamilton smokery, and though as a child Rose had known there was little to spare, she had known nothing different. Looking back, she remembered all the jobs her brothers and sisters had done to bring in money: painting sea shells and selling them to the tourists; collecting wood into bundles and selling them as kindlers; delivering milk and newspapers; doing odd jobs for Hamish Dubh at the store. And all the while Rose had been doing homework. She had accepted it as the perk of being the youngest, but hadn't there been a suspicion in her mind that there had to be more to it than that? There was a collective family pride that she was doing well at school and that she harboured an ambition to go to university. No one had laughed and told her it wasn't on, as she knew had happened to other clever bairns; her family had been supportive throughout. Even when she said she wanted to study something as peculiar as Marine Archaeology, when most chose the safe path of becoming teachers so that they could earn as soon as possible, there hadn't been as much as a smirk from the Nicolsons.

When she was away at university she had never been seriously strapped for cash. Not that she asked for it unless she had to – she had done all the usual underpaid jobs that all students took to make ends meet – but there was never the slightest hint that the others might be doing without to give to her, they had never cast it up at her. And all the time they were. She felt sick – mainly, she suspected because she *must've* known all along and chosen not to see it. In the light of all that she could understand Dougie's anger, but only up to a point. Was she supposed to live a life dictated by her family to make up for their generosity, their ambitions for her? Had she ever asked them for that? She just wanted to be happy, what was wrong with that? The thought of exploring ancient wrecks, of roaming the world discovering lost, long-forgotten ships, of finding things that had disappeared hundreds of years ago and piecing together what had befallen the ships and their crews: that had fired her imagination. But all that had changed; she had changed. The balance of her life had shifted. Her life was now Sorley Og and standing at the big window watching for the sight of *Ocean Wanderer* heading for port. Now here she was, more than three years later, still standing there.

19

When the phone rang in the chapel house that Saturday, Father Mick was lying down on a couch in his living room, a glass of the falling-down stuff clutched in his hand. He had been up since 6 a.m., had said three masses and visited six houses to hear the pointless confessions of several parishioners who were too frail to make it to the chapel, including Auntie Tam at Black Rock. Black Rock always exhausted him; in his more weary moments he often wondered if the sisters Batty and Maddy were making a fool of him, if it was perhaps their only diversion in life to have him running around 'like a blue-arsed fly', blessing their collection of religious bits and bobs. Sometimes he was almost sure that he had blessed them many times before, and only stopped himself mentioning this in case the two eccentric sisters burst into fits of laughter at driving him over the edge. He would come home, pour himself a snifter or two, and try not to go over in his mind precisely what he had blessed, because if they were making a fool of him for a laugh, that would be exactly what they wanted him to do.

There was a time when he had – he was ashamed to admit it to himself – kept a notebook in which he entered descriptions of every Black Rock statue, medal, rosary and picture he had muttered over, then he thought it would look bad if he should be found dead one morning with the notebook clutched to his bosom. People would think he was mad and the tale would be told for generations. He closed his eyes and conjured up conversations in the Inn in years to come. 'Do you mind that priest?' they'd say to each other, laughing.

'The one that kept a note of things he'd blessed up at Black Rock? My, but they fair ran him ragged!' and they'd laugh even more. So he had put the notebook in the fire: that way it would never be discovered. But even after it had gone up in smoke, he still found it difficult not to keep a mental note. For that reason and no other, he told himself, he indulged in a dram after visits, to keep his mind befuzzled enough to remain in control by remembering as little as possible. On this night, however, his luck was right out. He was clutching his fourth snifter when the phone rang. Picking it up he found Black Rock himself on the other end.

'Hello, Father,' said the eldest son pleasantly, 'and how are things with yourself?'

'Fine, Black Rock,' replied Father Mick, despite himself desperately itemising everything he had blessed at the house earlier in the day, 'just fine. And how are things with you?'

'Ach, fine, fine.'

'How's work? Kept busy?'

'Aye, aye, busy enough,' said Black Rock slowly. 'Had a helluva time making a set of stairs there for Sandy Bay. I tell you, Father, doing work for relatives isn't easy.'

'Oh?' said the priest, wondering how a MacEwan could avoid working for relatives in and around Acarsaid.

'But at least the weather wasn't wet. I got to do them outside.'

'Must have been cold, though, Black Rock.'

'Aye, but dry, Father, and that makes all the difference. I always say you can put up with the cold as long as it doesn't rain. Aye, aye, it's not so bad as long as it's not wet, so it is.'

Father Mick could feel himself being sucked into one of Black Rock's mind-numbing conversations and tried to divert it. 'So why was Sandy Bay after new stairs, then?'

'He was for having an extension built, two more bedrooms on top. I thought you knew.'

'His greed will be his downfall, Black Rock,' said Father Mick. 'He's only doing it to squeeze in more holidaymakers, and what does he want with more money? Sure he's never married, and he's got more than enough pieces of gold will do him for two lifetimes as it is.'

'Well, who knows, Father?' said Black Rock philosophically. 'I always say you don't know anybody as well as you think you do.'

'True, true,' said Father Mick.

'I always say we're doing well if we know ourselves.'

Father Mick closed his eyes and tried not to sob; he had been hearing the fruits of Black Rock's deeper thoughts for more decades than he cared to think about, and they were always the same.

'For all we know the man might have plans we know nothing about. Who's to say?'

'Indeed, indeed, Black Rock. And you managed to finish the stairs, then, did you?'

'I did indeed, Father, took a lot of time to get them right but it was a fine job, if I do say so myself, and now the bugger's complaining about the price!'

'Aye, well, that's Sandy Bay for you,' Father Mick said. 'It's always money with him, and he can't take it with him.' Immediately he bit his lip. They'd been over that. What a mistake! Black Rock couldn't pass up the chance, but if there really was a God –

'Very true, Father,' said Black Rock. 'As I always say –'

There is *no* God!

'– we bring nothing into this world, and we take nothing out.'

Black Rock was right: he *did* always say exactly that. *Always.* Their paths crossed frequently, not least because they were both involved in the dying business to varying degrees, and Father Mick had heard this homily so many times that he thought he might scream next time, and this might well be it. He drank down the whisky in his glass with one gulp, then tried to pull the small table closer with his foot to get at the bottle he had just replaced on it. Instead the table fell over on to the floor, the whisky, thankfully with the top securely in place, rolling out of reach.

'What was that, Father?' Black Rock asked in his measured tones.

'I think it was someone at the door, Black Rock,' he lied. 'I'm sorry, but it sounds urgent, so I'll have to be going now, unless there's anything else. . . ?'

'It was just the same when I made those new doors for him, if you remember, Father. No one does crafsmanship like that these days, and him being family I used only the best of wood and took my time over them. He fought me over every penny then, too. I ended up making them at a loss because I was so embarrassed for the man, showing himself up by going on like that.'

'That says a lot for you, Black Rock,' said Father Mick. 'I think I hear whoever it is at the window now. Did you call about anything important, or . . . ?'

'There was one thing, Father.'

'And what would that be, Black Rock?'

'My mother's just died, Father. Dr Gavin's just gone and I was wondering if you might have time to come up and give her the Last Rites?'

When Sorley Og more or less took over as skipper of the *Ocean Wanderer*, it gave his father the choice of whether to stay at home or go to sea, so he and Gannet settled into a routine of going when they felt like it. This left them at home more often and in a position to experience the day-to-day events of MacEwan family life that Chrissie had been dealing with since she married the skipper. Throughout his sea-going years he had missed births, marriages and deaths, none of which he objected to missing on the whole; Chrissie was, in his own words, 'a fine wee second lieutenent', even if she did use overly colourful language at times. He was at home, however, the night his old Auntie Tam died, the news being broken to him by Father Mick over the phone.

'It's that bugger of a priest for you,' Chrissie shouted down the receiver, to make sure Father Mick heard every word, before handing it to her husband, or trying to.

'Ask him what he wants,' said Sorley Mor, motioning it away with his hands and looking at it with distaste. Sorley Mor didn't like telephones. He said he was always conscious that he was talking into a lump of plastic, to which observation Chrissie always retorted, 'So?'

'Ask him yourself,' Chrissie shouted down the receiver again. 'Sure, why would you expect me to talk to a reprobate like him, anyway?' Then she lifted the entire phone and threw it into the skipper's lap as he sat in his corner.

'For God's sake, Chrissie,' he protested, 'you could've damaged some vital function there!'

'Only if there was one to damage,' Chrissie replied sarcastically.

'Chrissie!' Sorley Mor said severely. 'I know you're only joking when you cast aspersions like that, but I've told you before, some people might think you're being serious.' Then he spoke sweetly into the phone. 'Hello? Hello? Is there anybody there, please?'

'Listen to him,' Chrissie said to herself. 'One knock for "yes", two for "no"!'

'Of course there's somebody there,' said Father Mick. 'Why the hell would the phone ring unless there was somebody there?'

'Ach, you never know,' said Sorley Mor mysteriously. 'Stranger things have happened.'

'Like what?' the priest demanded.

'That's why you're taking up my time, is it?' Sorley Mor asked. 'To ask damn fool questions like that?'

Father Mick sighed heavily down the phone. 'Sorley Mor, has no one told you yet that your Auntie Tam up at Black Rock has died?'

'Is that so?' said Sorley Mor kindly. 'Ach well, poor old Auntie Tam. Mind you, she was a good age. I gave up counting after she passed ninety, didn't see the point. She wouldn't have wanted to hang around much longer, anyway. She's been threatening to go every day since old Black Rock himself went, and that must be more than thirty years now. Well, thank you for telling me, Father Mick, goodbye.'

'Wait a minute,' the priest shrieked at the other end, 'I'm not finished yet!'

'Well, what more is there to say?' Sorley Mor asked. 'If she's dead, she's dead.'

'I need you to run me up there.'

'Run yourself up there!'

'I can't. I've had a few and that new policeman they've sent up from Inverness is still at the stage where he takes things seriously. He's been watching me for weeks now, trying to catch me out. I got so fed up with him following me about that I decided to do the same to him the other day. Spotted him in Keppaig on his way here, so I followed him, right on his bumper all the way, up to the police office. He got out of his wee car, walked back to mine and said "Can I help you with something, Father?" and I said "No, I'm just seeing how *you* like being tailed around everywhere, that's all." I swear to God, if someone doesn't come up with something we can blackmail him with soon I'll have a breakdown with the stress of it all. Great ugly thing he is, too. He must have a brother who wears a dress or something of the kind, somebody should be finding out!'

'Bugger the new policeman –' Sorley Mor replied.

'My sentiments exactly,' Father Mick replied with feeling.

'– but are you saying you're too drunk to see to your duties, man?' Sorley Mor continued in a shocked tone.

'Well, how was I to know the old woman was about to go?' Father Mick demanded. 'I saw her just a few hours back and she seemed, well, not in good form exactly, but in as good form as she ever is: breathing and that. As you say yourself, she's been promising every day was her last for years now, how was I to know she meant it this time? And nobody reported Black Rock himself tapping away, and surely if any-one should've known it should've been him?'

'Aye, well, what you're asking is a great inconvenience,' Sorley Mor lied loftily, 'and I must say, it's a sad day when a man of the cloth is too drunk to visit a fallen member of his flock and bring a little comfort to the bereaved like myself at a time like this.'

'Is a man not allowed a drop of the falling-down stuff?' Father Mick asked plaintively. 'It's Saturday night; is a man supposed to be on duty twenty-four hours every day in case some old dear pops her clogs? Does that seem reasonable or fair to you?'

'Is that any way to be talking to a man in mourning, Father? "Popped her clogs"? I find that most upsetting, I have to tell you.'

'Ach, be quiet, Sorley Mor, it's not a tourist you're talking to here, it's *me*.'

Chrissie had been listening to the one side of the conversation she could hear and, unable to bear it any longer, she grabbed the receiver back.

'If there's one thing worse than talking to a drunk man, it's a drunk man talking to another drunk man,' she said, pushing Sorley Mor back in his chair. 'Listen, Cardinal Hooligan,' she said, 'from what I've heard, old Auntie Tam at Black Rock has died and you're too pissed to drive yourself a couple of hundred yards to her house, is that right?'

'To a T, Chrissie. I might quibble with the terminology, but we'll let that pass for now. Otherwise, to a T as usual. My, but I'm always saying to Sorley Mor himself, he's a lucky man for having married a woman with such a firm grasp of the –'

'Cut the crap! What makes you think he's any more sober than you are?' she demanded.

'Oh, I never thought of that.'

'Aye, well, that's what drink does to the brain. Leave it a minute and I'll see if Rose is in, and she can drive us all up in the Land Rover.'

'You've done it again, Chrissie MacEwan! I'm always saying to Sorley Mor, "Sorley Mor, you couldn't have married a more capable –"'

'Ach, bugger off!' Chrissie said, and hung up.

And so, with her husband at sea, Rose became embroiled in her first MacEwan event. Winter should have been over, but it was a cold night and the roads were icy, especially up the Brae, which no longer mattered in terms of traffic and so wasn't a priority in terms of gritting. Sorley Mor sat beside Rose, giving unwanted advice on her driving and attempting to change gears for her, with Chrissie squashed between him and the door, slapping his hands every time he did so. Gannet, who had been asleep on the big table in the porch as usual, had been roused and was singing gently to himself in the back of the Land Rover; when he was well-enough oiled he had taken to singing every song with 'Rose' in the title whenever he saw Rose, so he was swaying about in the back, singing 'The Rose of Tralee'. When they stopped at the chapel house up the Brae, Father Mick tried to get in the front and was firmly rebuffed by Chrissie.

'Do you think you're going to sit on my knee?' she asked. 'Get in the back with Pavarotti there.'

'Wait now,' said Sorley Mor. 'Have you got all your stage props? It's bad enough having to come out on a cold night like this without having to come back again because you've forgotten a candle or something.'

Father Mick went through his jacket pockets, a determinedly businesslike expression on his little gargoyle face. He found his purple silk stole – the little strip of fringed material that looked more like a tie – in the left pocket, and placed it in the right one. 'Oil,' he muttered to himself, 'Where the hell have I put the oil?'

'It's in your hand, Father,' Rose said helpfully.

'And the wee book thing,' said Gannet, breaking off from his song, 'the one that has the words in it. Have you got that?'

265

Father Mick rummaged in an inside pocket and brought out a half-bottle of Islay Mist.

'But you can be bloody sure he's got *that*,' said Chrissie dryly.

'Now Chrissie,' said the priest, 'I always carry it on these occasions. It can help the bereaved to have a wee nip, and it can help me even more. You have no idea the emotional stress I'm under at times like this. I can get so upset that I'm in tears sometimes.'

'Not to mention legless,' said Chrissie dismissively. 'Ach, just climb aboard. If you've forgotten anything you can just make it up as you go along, as you usually do.'

They were met at the door of Black Rock by Batty, dressed in her usual manner with the colour-scheme tastefully changed to black, or as tasteful as her get-up ever got. They had to go through the normal amount of genuflections and Signs of the Cross with Holy Water. Chrissie caught Rose's eye and shook her head as Batty knelt in front of them, exposing an indelicate amount of sagging, black-knicker-clad rear-end, and an inadvisable expanse of elderly thigh, even if it was covered with black tights. 'I swear to God, if those shanks were hanging up in a butcher's shop you'd report him to the Sanitary Inspectors,' Chrissie whispered to Rose. 'Just keep your eyes closed and go along with it. Believe me, it takes less time than refusing. She does it for you if you refuse.' Then they were shown into the sitting room that was always kept locked, except for special occasions. Sorley Mor muttered that the last time he had been in there was when his uncle had died many years before. In the middle of the room, on top of an Irish coffin table, lay Auntie Tam, already in her coffin.

'So you did know, then?' Sorley Mor asked Black Rock quietly. 'Father Mick here said no one had heard you tapping away.'

'No, I never know when it's family,' Black Rock said in a perfectly normal voice, 'but I knew this day would come sometime soon, so I've had the coffin ready and waiting for her for years now.'

Chrissie looked away and put her hand to her mouth to stifle a giggle. She met Rose's eyes and started her off, too, and Rose dug a packet of tissues out of her bag and handed one to her mother-in-law.

'What a weird bunch the MacEwans are, Rose,' Chrissie said, wiping her eyes. 'Here's your box, what's your hurry? I wonder if old Auntie Tam knew it had been lying there waiting for her all that time?'

Batty, seeing Chrissie dabbing at her eyes, put an arm around her shoulders. 'Don't take it so hard, Chrissie,' she said.

Chrissie, finding herself inches away from the conical breasts, was overcome afresh. 'Maybe we should leave Father Mick here to get on with his business,' she said, directing a meaningful glance in the priest's direction. Then she grabbed Sorley Mor and Gannet by the elbows and ushered them out of the room. 'This is immediate family only,' she said.

They headed for the kitchen, leaving Father Mick with Black Rock, Haffa, Batty and Maddy, then Chrissie and Rose held on to each other and laughed till they cried.

'He had her coffin ready for her, just waiting for the off!' Chrissie squealed.

'Ach, now Chrissie,' said Sorley Mor, 'there's no need to be laughing.'

'He must've measured her up one time while she was asleep,' smiled Gannet.

Chrissie and Rose looked at each other and started laughing again.

'Think if she'd woken up while he was doing it,' giggled Chrissie. 'What would he have said?'

'Now Chrissie, show some respect,' said Sorley Mor.

'I wonder if he consulted her on design and decoration?' Chrissie said, tears streaming down her face as she held her sides. 'Maybe he slipped a coffin catalogue in with the Christmas ones and asked her to pick her favourite!'

'Ach, now Chrissie,' Sorley Mor repeated, with similar effect to the last time.

Chrissie and Rose were lost, totally unable to control themselves.

Gannet watched them, smiling gently to himself. 'Aren't women grand?' he asked admiringly. 'Nothing gets them down. They can even have a laugh in the midst of death. I think that's grand. I think it must be something to do with the fact that the key of life is within them, they can laugh at it because they understand mysterious things about life and death that men never will.'

Chrissie and Rose looked at Gannet then at each other, and collapsed laughing once again, as Gannet smiled even more affectionately at them.

Just then Batty burst into the kitchen. 'Mother's a saint, a saint!' she screeched.

'Aye, she was a nice woman,' Sorley Mor said in a suitably sad voice.

'No, no, she's a saint now,' Batty repeated, crossing herself with a rosary held in her hands. 'Father Mick anointed her on her left hand: that's the hand nuns get anointed on. It means she's a saint!'

Everyone in the room looked at each other in turn, then Chrissie and Rose hid their faces in fresh tissues again.

'Don't be sad!' shouted Batty. 'Mother's not gone; she's become a saint. Come and see her; she even looks different!'

They followed the excited Batty to the sitting room once more, where Maddy, Haffa and Black Rock were waiting with Father Mick, who was placing his various bits and pieces back in his pockets.

'Looks just the same to me,' Chrissie whispered to Rose. 'What about you?'

'Just the same,' Rose agreed. 'In her coffin, dead.'

At that Chrissie shook with laughter, tears flowing over

the now sodden tissue she held over her mouth and nose. She reached out to Rose, waving a hand in request for a fresh tissue.

'Ach Chrissie,' said Batty kindly. 'I always knew you were fond of her. You don't show it much, but you have a tender heart.'

Just as Chrissie thought she might have to sit down, Haffa jumped to his feet and put the radio on. It was Saturday, and on Saturdays Bobby MacLeod and his accordion band played Scottish country dance music on the BBC. As the first notes came through, Haffa started to dance round the coffin in a lively if disjointed way. 'Look,' he shouted, kicking his legs high. 'Look at me! I'm dancing!'

'Maybe you shouldn't,' said Sorley Mor uncertainly.

'But my knee,' yelled Haffa, twirling on his toes like a ballet dancer, 'my knee's cured! Mother's cured my knee now that she's a saint. It's a miracle! That knee has been the bane of my life for years, sure, you know that, and now Saint Mother's cured it!'

At that his sisters fell to the floor and started reciting Hail Marys in a frenzy, as Haffa contined to dance around his mother's coffin. Black Rock, with nothing better to do, sat down in an armchair in the corner of the room and started singing along with Bobby MacLeod.

'Well,' whispered Chrissie, turning to Rose, 'at least he'll be able to dig his mother's grave deep enough, now that she's miraculously cured his knee. He won't have to throw his father over the dyke to make room for her!'

'For God's sake say something,' Sorley Mor ordered Father Mick.

'What the hell good do you see that doing?' the priest asked.

'Did you tell them their mother was a saint now?'

'Of course I didn't!'

'Well you must've told them that nonsense about nuns being anointed on the left hand, and what the hell's the connection between nuns and saints anyhow?' demanded an exasperated Sorley Mor.

'No, I did not,' said Father Mick furiously. 'Why do you assume this has to be my fault? They told me that's how it happened, and I didn't see any reason to start debating theology with them, that was all,' said Father Mick. 'I just grabbed the nearest hand and slapped the oil on and Batty said, "That's the hand nuns get anointed on, isn't it, Father?" and I sort of muttered something back that she took as a yes.'

'But is it?' Gannet asked. 'I don't remember ever hearing that.'

'Well,' said the priest defensively, 'any hand is the hand nuns get anointed on, so strictly speaking it wasn't *un*true as opposed to true, if you see what I mean. And if it brings them a little comfort in their hour of need,' he continued, in a pious voice.

'Ach, be quiet with that rubbish, now. Look at the state of them,' Sorley Mor said, as they watched the four surviving Black Rocks singing, dancing and praying around their mother's ready-made coffin.

'Well, it was a throwaway mutter, how was I to know they'd make such a big thing out of it? You can't blame me because your relatives are all insane.'

'Well you'll have to tell them you've made a mistake,' Sorley Mor protested, 'or we'll never hear the end of it.'

'No fear!' said Father Mick. 'Besides, it wouldn't do any good. It's in their minds now, nothing will shift it.'

By this time Chrissie and Rose had given up and were standing back, their faces hidden in tissues, in that peculiar stage of mirth that looked like grief, unable to glance at the bizarre tableau before them without being overcome by another wave of tears.

'Good job it wasn't Batty with the bad knee,' Chrissie whispered.

'Why?' Rose asked breathlessly.

'Well, if she was the one dancing around she could have

270

someone's eye out with those breasts – probably both eyes, when you come to think of it!'

Rose wondered if they would get control of themselves ever again, and then that thought set off another bout of laughter.

'The only one who looks normal is the corpse,' Chrissie whispered. 'Gannet's got that daft look on his face, Sorley Mor and Father Mick are fighting, Black Rock's singing, Bobby MacLeod's playing the accordion, Haffa's dancing in circles, and Batty and Maddy are on their knees praying!'

'And we're laughing!' Rose sobbed, thereby sending Chrissie off again.

As they were leaving an hour or so later, fully composed as long as they didn't make eye contact with each other, Chrissie looked at the road.

'It's colder now,' she remarked. 'Look at the frost on the road. Rose, you take it easy on the way back, now. Don't you listen to a word any of them say about how they'd go faster.'

'Don't worry about that,' smiled Batty serenely as Rose turned the key in the ignition. 'Nothing can harm you now.'

'Why?' asked Chrissie before she could stop herself.

'Saint Mother will look after you now,' replied Batty, crossing herself, joining her hands and looking heavenwards, her face shining with faith and fervour.

Rose started the Land Rover, drove down the road till they were out of sight of Black Rock, then she had to pull over to the side until she and Chrissie stopped laughing.

'My God, Chrissie MacEwan,' said Sorley Mor reproachfully, 'but I never thought I'd see the day when you'd laugh at the death of one of my family.'

'Shut up!' squeaked Chrissie, throwing her head back and laughing freely for the first time. 'My, but that feels good.'

On the other side of Sorley Mor, Rose was giggling, her head on her arms across the steering wheel, unable to move.

'And look what you've done to this pure lassie here,' said Sorley Mor. 'You've corrupted her, woman.'

'Will you women for God's sake pull yourselves together!' yelled Father Mick tetchily.

'It's all right for you, you're inside. Gannet and I are freezing our ba . . . , our socks off in the back here.'

'Your socks, aye,' said Chrissie, 'at least we can be sure you have *them*.'

'Ach, Chrissie,' complained Sorley Mor.

'"My Love Is Like A Red, Red Rose",' warbled Gannet.

It soon became clear that Sandy Bay was doing more to his house in Keppaig than putting in two more bedrooms with his cousin providing new stairs to connect them to the lower part of the house. Other things were noticed and discussed.

'I saw him with my own eyes,' Sorley Mor told Chrissie, following her from big room to big room as she worked about the house. 'In Hamish Dubh's he was, buying a plastic vegetable rack if you please!'

'Maybe he needed one,' Chrissie replied, pushing him out of the way.

'What on earth would he be wanting with such a thing?' asked Sorley Mor.

'To put vegetables in it?' Chrissie grinned.

'Ach, away with you, woman. This is Sandy Bay we're talking about! And not just any old vegetable rack either, had to be a red one, and when Hamish Dubh didn't have one he asked him to order it. Now,' he slapped the back of a chair as he passed, 'what do you think of that?'

Chrissie looked up at him and shrugged. 'Why the hell would I know and why the hell would I care?' she asked. 'You know something, Sorley Mor? You've become awful keen on gossip since you cut down on trips away.'

'I have nothing of the sort.'

'Unless, of course, and this is something I've long suspected,' the lot of you spend all your time at sea gossiping away like sweetie wives.'

'You'll not get at me like that, Chrissie MacEwan. I've been married to you far too long to be suckered by that kind of nonsense.'

'Suit yourself,' Chrissie smiled, 'but all that leaves is that you've turned into an old sweetie wife since you stopped going away as much.'

'All I said, woman, damn and blast –!'

'Language, Sorley Mor.'

'All I said was that Sandy Bay is taking an awful sudden interest in interior decoration, that was all. We are talking here about a mean sort of a man, a man who has always slept in his own chicken house during the summer when he has holidaymakers in the big house, rather than pay for a decent room somewhere, and now he's going about spending money on plastic vegetable racks, and red ones at that.'

'Vegetable racks, is that all the evidence you're presenting?' Chrissie asked with a knowing smile.

'What do you know?' he asked suspiciously.

'Who said I know anything?'

'Chrissie!'

As with other occasions when his verbal skills had failed to produce the desired effect, Sorley Mor tried to make a sudden grab at his wife, which Chrissie evaded. She ran through the house, her husband chasing after her.

'I only know,' she said breathlessly, stopping and putting a hand up to call it quits, 'that he's been buying other things and he's been going away to Inverness when he thought no one noticed and coming back with boxes.'

'Boxes of what?'

'That's all I know, but if you're asking the opinion of an expert –' she wheezed.

'I am, I am,' he nodded seriously.

'All the signs point to him having a woman.'

'Don't be daft,' Sorley Mor laughed out loud. 'Sandy Bay's

273

never had a woman! Sure, who'd have him? Huh. Next you'll be saying Gannet has a woman!'

'I'm only giving my opinion,' Chrissie shrugged, smiling smugly.

'Sure, Sandy Bay's no catch at all for any woman. He wasn't when he was young and he's well past young now.' For a moment he looked thoughtful. 'Have you any idea who she is?'

'I didn't say there was anyone, I only said all the signs pointed to that.'

'But he's forty-five if he's a day, and he's no oil painting, is he?'

Chrissie said nothing.

'No, no,' he said finally. 'You're making it up so that I'll pass it on and look a fool, Chrissie MacEwan.'

'Since when did you need my help with that?'

'You just want me to go down to the Inn and announce it to everybody, and then I'll be a laughing stock, that's what you're up to.'

'Fine.' said Chrissie. 'Maybe he just suddenly needed a vegetable rack, and two new bedrooms and a set of stairs, and a lot of boxes from Inverness, then.'

It was June and *Ocean Wanderer* had been in harbour for three months. All her minor repairs had been attended to, she had been freshly painted and there was a notice in the *Fishing News* advertising her for sale. They had no idea what she would fetch, but that didn't really matter. The real money, as Sorley Og had mentioned, was in her fishing licence.

Over the years the amount and variety of fish she was allowed to catch had steadily increased. The more she caught, the more she was allowed to catch. It had been decided that one more trip was needed because they were low on the sand eels allowance, and if they didn't catch their quota the amount of the deficit would be deducted from next year's licence, making it that much less valuable to a prospective buyer.

There was a great deal of excitement within Acarsaid about the *Wanderer*'s last trip, and Sorley Mor had decided that he and Gannet would be aboard for the historic event. The present crew had retired to the Inn to become sentimental: Sorley Mor, Gannet, Stamp, the two engineers, Stevie and Eric, Sorley Og, young Pete. Also there, of course, was Father Mick. As they entered Sorley Mor said loudly 'You'll be sticking to the mineral water, Eric?' and glared a warning look around the assembled Inn regulars, a look that said, 'This man becomes violent on booze and he's not a dancer', then he got the drinks in for the rest of them. As it happened, the non-drinking, non-dancing Eric looked like a man with a problem; he had just had a run-in with the law.

'It wis three in the mornin',' he complained. 'Who wis aboot at that time?'

'But someone was?' Sorley Mor encouraged him. These days the Skipper could understand Eric better because, he had convinced himself, Eric spoke properly – like him, in fact.

'Musta been,' Eric sighed. 'An' it was a thing Ah've never done in ma life afore, but it was three in the mornin'.'

'Aye, you said,' said the skipper.

'Ah mean, whit kinda . . . whit kinda –'

'Now, now, Eric,' warned Sorley Mor, looking round the Inn, 'just you keep that temper of yours in check.'

'Maybe someone walking their dog,' Gannet suggested.

'Mibbe,' Eric replied. 'Ah'll tell ye this, Ah widnae huv done tae a fella human bein' whit they done.'

'So what happened, Eric?' a voice asked from across the bar.

'Ah did somethin' Ah swear Ah've never done in ma life afore,' said Eric earnestly. 'Ah ran a red light.'

'Dear God, man,' said Father Mick, 'I thought you were going to tell us you'd knocked someone down and killed them then driven off! A red light? Sure I run them all the time.'

'Ye don't have red lights up here,' Eric reminded him innocently, and a snigger ran round the Inn's clientele.

'Aye, well,' said Father Mick, 'I have been known to go out of Acarsaid occasionally, you know.'

'When?' someone asked.

'Show's how much you know,' blustered the priest. 'Is that you, Sandy Bay? Aye, I thought it might be. Been buying any more bits of plastic recently?'

'Anyhow,' said Sandy Bay, ignoring the taunt with as much dignity as he could muster, 'what happened, Eric?'

'Ah was oan ma wey hame fae here,' said Eric sadly, 'tired an' 'at. Ah wis nearly hame, naebody aboot, nae traffic, nae people, nuthin', so I ran the red light.'

'As I have done myself many a time,' said Father Mick firmly, looking around the Inn.

'An' the next thing Ah know is there's a coupla polis at the door. Said somebody hid reported me, an' wis it true an' 'at? So Ah says aye, it wis true, it wis likely a daft thing tae dae, but –'

'But there was no one about,' said Father Mick impatiently, 'And, and . . . ?'

'Aye,' said Eric, 'but they charged me.'

'You daft sod,' said Sandy Bay. 'You should've denied it! It was their word against yours!'

Sorley Mor glared at Sandy Bay, faking alarm. 'Now, Sandy Bay, that kind of language isn't advisable. This is Eric you're talking to! As a special favour to me I'd be obliged if you'd take no notice, Eric. The bugger's drunk and has no idea what he's saying.'

Eric sighed. 'Fined four hundred and fifty pounds and six penalty points,' he said sadly.

'You're kidding me!' said Father Mick.

'Naw, honest,' said Eric, sipping his mineral water. 'Never been in any kind of trouble afore either.'

'Aye, well,' said Sorley Mor, looking around, 'not in a car at any rate.'

'Well, I don't know,' said Sandy Bay slowly, 'but I would have to say that wasn't called for.'

'Ah know, Ah know,' said Eric sadly.

'If I were you, Eric,' Sandy Bay continued, 'I think I might be dancing with rage at that!'

Around the Inn there were several sounds: Sorley Mor's drink going down the wrong way, Gannet coughing to cover his confusion, but mostly the sound of stifled laughter.

'Well,' said Sorley Mor, desperately trying to pick up the pieces. 'Just because Eric's a big man, there's no need to poke fun at him! I'm sure he could dance with the best of them even if he is that size. If he wanted to dance, that is, though I'm sure he doesn't. Not, mind you, that there would be anything wrong with him having a dance if he felt like it.' Wondering if he might, he just might have gone slightly overboard, he thought it would be a good idea to divert attention in case anyone, that Sandy Bay especially, smelt a rat. 'Donald, man,' he called to the barman cheerfully, 'bring me one of your Ploughman efforts, if you please!'

'There wur two a' them,' Eric continued thoughtfully, 'wanna thum musta knew it wisnae right.' He sighed. 'But ye know whit the polis is like, they likely hid a spite at me for somethin' else, thought they'd kill two birds wi' wan stone.'

'Aye,' Stamp said firmly, 'you're right there, Eric. It was likely, just as you say, they just decided to . . . to . . . hit two ducks with a brick.'

Later, back at MacEwan's Row, slightly the worse for wear and with a bottle of Milk of Magnesia clutched in his hand, Sorley Mor told Chrissie of the near miss.

'I have my suspicions about Sandy Bay,' he said. 'I sometimes think he can't be one of us at all. I sometimes wonder about his mother. She used to be over-friendly with one of those Klondikers, everyone knows that, and he's a sneaky sort, like those Russians – not like a real MacEwan at all!'

'I can see why you'd think that,' Chrissie replied in a mock serious tone, 'and I'd agree with you if it wasn't for the fact that he looks just like the rest of you.'

'How do you make that out?'

'Dark hair, blue eyes, sneaky tendencies. Just as you say, that kind of thing, Sorley Mor.'

'I don't know what you mean,' said the skipper innocently. 'This is a man who sneaks around buying things and not telling people what for or why.'

'Definitely,' said Chrissie, 'keeping from them things they have every right, not only to know, but to be consulted about.'

'Exactly!'

Chrissie looked at him then shook her head. 'You're hopeless, man, do you know that? And what's this I hear about you and Gannet going on the *Wanderer*'s last trip?'

'You hear right, woman,' said Sorley Mor grandly. 'It's only right that we should bid the old girl farewell.'

'You could stand by the harbour and wave,' Chrissie replied.

'I've said it before, Chrissie MacEwan,' said the skipper with exaggerated patience, 'and I'll say it again: you have no soul. Of course we must be with her on her final trip, she would expect nothing less!' He looked at Gannet and the two of them smiled manly smiles at each other. Gannet threw an arm about the skipper's shoulders.

'Spoken, if I may say so, Skipper,' he said emotionally, 'like a true seaman. Like a real man of the seas, like a –'

'Drunk,' Chrissie said tartly. 'Sit down the two of you before you fall down.'

'We will not fall down,' said the skipper, as he and Gannet swayed about. 'You are but a woman and would not understand such things, Chrissie, but we are doing what we have always done, what we have done all our lives. We are supporting each other.'

The skipper and his first mate took an even firmer grasp

of each other to drive the point home, nearly falling over in the attempt, just as Chrissie had predicted. Chrissie looked at them with a jaundiced eye.

'The two of you are about to lose your balance and crash down, so I'll put it another way,' she said. 'Sit down or I'll push you down.'

'Ach, Chrissie, you wouldn't do that, now,' said Gannet, chuckling. He put a hand out to ruffle Chrissie's hair and she slapped it as hard as she could. 'Fair enough,' said Gannet, and sat down on the raised marble fireplace beside the skipper in his corner.

Chrissie shook her head. 'To think the reason we got that slab of marble was to make the place look good,' she said. 'He sits on it that much that there's a big hollow worn away in it by his arse.'

'Language, Chrissie,' said Sorley Mor, taking another slug of his Milk of Magnesia.

'Some people settle for gnomes in their gardens,' Chrissie continued. 'Us? We get a great big arse on the fireplace. That's when he's able to sit. When he's too far gone for that we lose the use of the table in the porch.'

'*Conservatory*, Chrissie!' said Sorley Mor.

'And this daft idea of the two of you ancient mariners going on some mad farewell trip, I still don't understand why.'

'Because she's the last *Wanderer*, Chrissie,' Sorely Mor explained patiently. 'We'll never go on her again. You are watching history in the making here.' He looked as deeply into her eyes as his own could focus, then shook his head. 'I've said it before, Chrissie MacEwan,' he sighed, 'you have no soul.'

'The *Wanderer*'s just a lump of metal, you daft old bugger,' Chrissie responded. 'It's no different from all the other bits of metal on the high seas.'

Sorley Mor bristled. 'Did you hear that, Gannet?' he demanded indignantly, the two of them once again struggling unsteadily to their feet and throwing an arm round each other's shoulders. 'Did you hear her insulting our boat? Why did you let me marry a creature like this who has no finer feelings? I blame it on you entirely, Gannet, you should've stopped me!'

'Ach, Skipper,' grinned Gannet, looking at Chrissie with undying though equally unfocused devotion, 'sure nothing could've stopped you. Isn't she the most lustrous pearl, the most glittering gem of the sea! Doesn't she gladden your heart –' at this Sorley Mor was smiling sentimentally – 'and make you –'

'Fear for your life if you think I'm falling for that crap,' Chrissie supplied acidly.

Sorley Mor looked once more into Gannet's eyes. 'Most of the time she's a bad wee bitch, though,' he said conversationally, and the two of them laughed, their arms still entwined.

'True, true,' Gannet conceded.

'And she's also the only one who'll remember this conversation when you two are sober,' said Chrissie.

'True, true,' said Gannet again, smiling down at her.

'And this mad trip to annoy the rest of the crew: have you stopped to think what Sorley Og might feel about it?'

'He understands these things, woman,' Sorley Mor announced. 'You can't be expected to understand these things: these are things of men!'

'Christ, I don't know why I bother trying to make him see sense when he's had a few,' Chrissie said to herself. 'After all these years, you'd think I'd know it's hard enough talking sense to him when he's sober. And by the way, who drove the Land Rover up here?'

'Can't remember,' said Sorley Mor, 'but I do know it was someone, because I was in the back with the others.'

'Others? What others?'

'My crew, woman!' Sorley Mor shouted grandly.

'Sorley Mor MacEwan, lower your voice. And if you call

me "woman" just once more I swear to Christ I'll remove your kneecaps with a fork. Just tell me, where are the others now?'

'In the Land Rover, wo . . . , Chrissie, where else would they be?'

'All of them?'

'I think so . . .' said Sorley Mor, suddenly uncertain. 'Gannet! Gannet! Where's the crew?'

'Forget it,' Chrissie said, looking at the figure sitting on her hearth, head down. 'The big clown's sleeping.'

A quick glance in the back of the Land Rover quickly proved that Sorley Mor told no lies. There they all were, lying in a heap, snoring – apart from the ever-sober Eric, who had returned to the *Wanderer* alone.

'For God's sake,' Chrissie muttered, and immediately turned and made her way to Rose and Sorley Og's house. There she discovered that her sober, responsible son had driven the vehicle home; given the time it took him and Rose to open the door, though, she guessed being responsible hadn't been on his mind at the time. As she could hardly say, 'Sorry, I didn't realise you were busy, carry on,' she asked Sorley Mor to identify the bodies that were actually in the Land Rover, because knowing her husband and his capacity for collecting people, there could be a few known to no one but their particular God. They were all crew, though, plus Father Mick 'Hooligan', so Rose and Chrissie called their homes, told their wives where they were and that they would be looked after, then they watched as Sorley Og disentangled limbs and dragged them and their owners into Sorley Mor and Chrissie's house.

'Look at Stamp!' Chrissie laughed despite herself as she and Rose dragged him indoors. 'He's still got his old bunnet on! Will we look underneath, Rose?'

'Don't you dare!' said Sorley Og. 'Some deep instinct would alert him that his head had been invaded and he'd never talk to any of us again!'

One by one they were all laid in the beds vacated by MacEwan daughters and son who had left home.

'Father Mick's here as well,' Sorley Mor grinned. 'Do I throw him back or is he allowed in these days?'

'If I say throw the wee bugger in the sea, will you do it?' Chrissie asked. 'Bring him in, he's been avoiding a telling-off for months now. I can hardly wait to see his face when he wakens up and sees where he is.'

'Or who's there with him,' Rose laughed.

'Why did you let them get in to this state, Sorley Og?' Chrissie asked. 'I mean, this is worse than usual.'

'I love the way you think I have any control over any of them,' Sorley Og laughed. 'Besides, it is a special occasion, the end of an era and all that. Everybody wanted to stand them a drink.'

'But how many times are they to be stood a drink?' Chrissie demanded. 'They don't leave for two days yet! Anyway, I've always wondered about that, "stand them a drink" nonsense. Usually it means they can't stand, and tonight is no exception.'

At the skipper's house on MacEwan's Row all was silent that night, except that there was considerably more snoring than usual and then a crash from the porch-conservatory followed by Gannet's voice shouting, 'It's only me! I'm fine!'

'There he goes,' said Chrissie as she lay beside the slumbering Sorley Mor. 'Never fails. You can never really relax till he's fallen off that table at least once.'

Next morning Chrissie had to draft Rose in to cook numerous breakfasts and dole out hangover remedies as the aroma of eggs, bacon, sausages, toast and coffee engulfed the house.

'I feel guilty about big Eric down on the boat,' said Chrissie. 'He was the only one sober, and he's the only one who has to cook his own breakfast. Doesn't seem fair. Rose, give him a call and ask him if he wants to come up.'

In due course Eric arrived, and they all sat together around Gannet's big table in Chrissie's porch, the five-man summer crew of the soon-to-be-departed *Wanderer*, plus Father Mick 'Hooligan', his head down to escape Chrissie's barbs, and the old skipper and his first mate, who seemed unnaturally quiet, even for Gannet.

'I know the cooking won't be up to your standard, Stamp,' Chrissie said, distributing more coffee, 'but Rose and I have done our best.'

'That's all right, Chrissie,' Stamp replied seriously, 'it's not that bad.'

Chrissie exchanged a sarcastic look with Rose. 'He bloody means that, you know!' she said.

'Language, Chrissie,' said a weak voice from the end of the table.

She looked at the silent Gannet. 'You OK?' she asked.

Gannet nodded.

'No, I mean it,' Chrissie said. 'Are you OK?'

'Must've given my arm a wee bump somewhere,' said Gannet.

'Probably when you fell off the table,' Chrissie suggested.

Gannet looked blank. 'I didn't fall off the table,' he murmured.

Chrissie rolled her eyes at Rose. 'No, you never do,' she replied. 'Let me see it.'

'It's fine,' Gannet smiled unconvincingly.

'It bloody isn't,' Chrissie said, looking at his left arm. She put her hand under his forearm and lifted it slightly and Gannet winced. 'Well, either your left side has shrunk in the night, or your arm's grown longer,' Chrissie said. 'The only other explanation is that you've really hurt that arm. Rose, call Gavin.'

'No, no . . .' Gannet protested.

'Call Gavin,' Chrissie repeated.

'If he doesn't answer, try the school,' Sorley Og laughed.

'Stop being snide, you,' Chrissie said. 'It breaks my heart to say it, but in some ways you get more like that old father of yours every day.'

Dr Gavin Johnstone, the local GP, Sorley Og's lifelong friend and best man when he and Rose had married, arrived ten minutes later, a tall, well-built, handsome young man of about thirty, with fair hair and brown eyes.

'My, son,' Chrissie greeted him, 'but you're another one gets more like his father every day.' She glanced at Sorley Og. 'Only this time I mean that as a compliment,' she said. 'How is old Dr Johnstone, Gavin?'

'Great, Chrissie,' Gavin smiled. 'On a Caribbean cruise again, loves them. Spends all his working life beside the sea, then all his retirement on it.'

'Only with sunshine,' Chrissie smiled back.

'Aye, well, there is that, not to mention constant room service.'

'There's some gets that even when they're ashore in these parts,' Chrissie replied, leading him to the porch, where Gannet was still sitting with Rose, his face almost white, but protesting that there was nothing wrong with him.

'So, what's up?' he asked.

'Nothing,' said Gannet.

'It's his left arm,' Chrissie explained, both of them ignoring Gannet. 'He fell off the table last night, and it just doesn't look right.'

'I did not!'

'Hurts when he tries to move it,' Chrissie said.

'Does not,' protested the patient, wincing again as Gavin lifted it slightly.

'Looks as though he's dislocated the shoulder,' Gavin said to Chrissie.

'I have not.'

'How did you happen to fall off the table?' he asked Gannet. 'Is tap dancing popular with your crew, Skipper?' He raised an eyebrow in Sorley Mor's direction and smiled as Sorley Mor turned away and looked into the distance with an innocent expression.

'You'd do better asking the table than asking him,' Chrissie

284

sniffed. 'He was feeling no pain at the time. He was sleeping on the table and fell off, as always.'

'Did not!' said Gannet.

'It's been out too long to just slip it back now. I'll have to take him to the hospital, do it under general anaesthetic.'

'No!' the patient protested.

'Shh, you,' Chrissie chided him. 'This is nothing to do with you, you'll do as you're bloody well told.'

'Bring him out and I'll run him up now. I'll put a sling on just now to protect it a bit, and if you can get some cushions to prop him up in the back seat,' said Gavin. 'And it might be best if we have someone sitting at either side, too.'

All this time the rest of the crew were looking on with interest, but Sorley Mor had been hovering around, being pushed back every now and again as he shoved his way between Gannet, Gavin and Chrissie.

'Is Gannet going to die?' he asked theatrically.

'With any luck,' Chrissie replied savagely. 'How long have I been waiting for this moment?'

As Gannet was arranged in the back of the Range Rover, still protesting that it had all been a mistake, the others trooped out behind him.

Chrissie's eyes settled on Father Mick. 'What about you, Holy Joe?' she asked. 'Do you want to mutter over him a bit? How do you fancy that, Gannet, the Last Rites from the Father Hooligan here?'

Gannet shook his head vigorously, a look of horror on his face. Chrissie laughed, looking around the crowd of anxious faces.

'Back! Back!' she shouted, prodding at them with an imaginary chair and cracking an imaginary whip. 'Bugger off the lot of you, but keep away from the Inn.' She turned to Sorley Mor. 'And you,' she said, 'while you're not in the Inn, *don't* eat any of Dan's food, is that understood?'

'But can't I come too, Chrissie?' the skipper pleaded.

'No, you can't,' Chrissie replied. 'The last thing the good people at the hospital need is you running about trying to tell them how to do what they have to do.'

'I'm fine,' said Gannet.

Young Dr Johnstone looked at Sorley Mor's concerned expression and laughed. 'Skipper,' he said, 'he'll be fine, I promise you. His shoulder's out of the socket, we'll just pop him off to sleep and put it back. He'll be awake minutes later and he'll be home in a few hours.'

'Would that be his official or unofficial home you're talking about, Gavin?' Chrissie muttered tartly.

'He'll be OK?' Sorley Mor asked in a weak voice.

Gavin looked at Sorley Og and the two of them laughed.

'I promise,' the young doctor said, climbing into his car. Chrissie placed herself on Gannet's left side and Sorley Og on his right as the Range Rover began to move off, then Chrissie shouted from the open window, 'Make that a "maybe", Sorley Mor,' and cackled at him. Then she glanced again at her husband's worried face. 'Ach, Rose, will you take the daft bugger in and revive him? What a state for a grown man to get into!'

From between her and her son, Gannet protested, 'I'm fine.'

'I'm not talking about you,' Chrissie laughed. 'I'm talking about the other ancient mariner there. He's in a worse state than you are!'

20

When Gannet came out of hospital that evening he was still slightly becalmed by the effects of the anaesthetic. He wore a sling that supported his left elbow to take the weight off his shoulder joint, his arm was bent up towards his neck, and he was on painkillers that he refused to take until Chrissie threatened to slap his arm. The shoulder was back in its socket, Gavin had explained, but the real damage had been done by tearing of the muscles, tendons and ligaments.

'The soft tissue has all been shredded,' he said cheerfully, then smiled as Gannet's face took on an ashen tinge, 'and, Gannet, I have to warn you that there's a high risk that it might dislocate again. You'll have to be careful; you've got to understand that.'

'Are you listening to this, stupid?' Chrissie demanded. 'And can you,' she asked Gavin, 'spell it out in words so small that not only Gannet here can understand, but also my husband: that there is no way Gannet's going to sea tomorrow?'

'Oh, that's out of the question!' said Gavin. 'I'd have thought that was obvious to anyone.'

'Huh!' Chrissie exclaimed. 'Your trouble, Gavin, is that being a nice lad you think fishermen are of average intelligence. Say it again: *Gannet cannot go to sea tomorrow.*'

Gannet, who had been exchanging horrified looks with his skipper said 'That's not fair!' and Chrissie gave the young doctor an 'I told you so' look.

'Look, Gannet, I know you're being very macho here,' Gavin said, sitting down on the marble hearth beside him. 'Dear God,' he muttered. 'Next time you come into the surgery remind me to examine you for piles, Gannet. As I say, you're being very macho here, but I know how much pain you're in. This is a substantial injury, I saw a lot of shoulder dislocations among rugby players when I was at university, and the pain brought those big guys to their knees. It won't ever again be the same as it was before and it won't get better overnight, or for many nights to come, for that matter. In this case it'll take longer because you're not a fit, twenty-year-old rugby wing-half, you're getting on a bit.'

Beside him Chrissie sniggered.

'It was a bad dislocation, there's nerve damage, that area on your upper arm below your shoulder will be numb for perhaps two or three years, maybe it won't ever regain feeling. You'll probably find sleeping difficult for months, because no matter what position you try, the torn tissue under the skin will open up. You cannot go to sea, is that clear?'

Gannet nodded glumly.

'It's time you were giving up going to sea anyway,' Gavin laughed at him. 'You're well past your prime, even if you do think you're still fifteen years old. And you,' he looked at Sorley Mor, 'should be doing the same, taking it easy.'

'It's the *Wanderer*'s last trip, man,' Sorely Mor protested. 'I'm Sorley Mor MacEwan – do you think I would ever go to sea in another boat?'

'I hope not,' Gavin replied. 'The next time you go fishing it had better be with a rod in your hand at that wee lochan up the hill you keep going on about.'

'You were right, Chrissie,' Sorley Mor said, glaring at Gavin, 'he gets more like his father every day. He liked to order folk about as well. And to think you used to look at me like I was a hero, too!'

'You were,' Gavin laughed, 'when I was ten years old. It was the way you used to swagger down through the harbour at the end of a good trip.'

'Every trip on my boat was a good trip,' Sorley Mor

protested in a shocked tone. 'Would you listen to the cheek of the boy? And I never swaggered.'

At that everyone in the room laughed loudly, including – Sorley Mor was less than pleased to observe – Gannet.

'Get out of here, boy,' he said to Gavin, 'before I put you over my knee and give you a good thrashing for cheeking your elders!'

Chrissie saw Gavin to the door, leaving Gannet and Sorley Mor together in silence. 'And how's Tess?' she asked. 'You two don't seem to be rushing it exactly, do you?'

'Oh, she's gone down to Glasgow for a couple of weeks,' he smiled. 'We're not, you know, joined at the hip.'

'But you'd like to be, right?'

Gavin looked sheepish. 'Well, who knows?' he said. 'One thing's for sure, nobody here will be satisfied till I'm safely married with a bunch of kids!'

'Neither will you, Gavin,' Chrissie smiled, reaching up on her toes to kiss his cheek. 'Men always pretend they've been caught, but what are they without a wife and family? Look at the Gannet there. He's part of this family, but don't you think he would've been happier with his own wife and bairns to come home to? Sure, isn't the reason he spends so little time at his wee house in Keppaig that it's empty?'

'You're probably right, Chrissie,' Gavin replied. 'Make sure he takes those painkillers. He needs them. 'Bye.'

Inside the house, all was gloom.

'Well, that's it,' Sorley Mor said resignedly, 'if Gannet can't go tomorrow, I'm not going either.'

'Don't be bloody stupid!' Chrissie told him. 'Who are you playing now – Sorley Mor the Martyr? He's dislocated his shoulder, the last thing he needs is you loading him with guilt to carry.'

'I've never been to sea without Gannet in my entire life,' Sorley Mor said quietly, 'I'm damned if I'll do it now.'

'Skipper, Chrissie's right,' Gannet told him. 'This is the last trip, there'll never be another one, you'll only make me

289

feel bad if I'm the reason you miss it. You have to go.'

'No, no, it wouldn't be the same.'

'Skipper, I've been trying to get you to take an order, any order, since we were boys together, and you never have, but this one you must take. Go with the lads. You'll regret it if you don't, and you'll make me regret it even more.'

The two men looked at each other solemnly.

'I'll be with you in spirit,' Gannet said and laughed. 'Go.'

Chrissie watched them, wanting to say something funny, but feeling moved by the bond between them. She had known both of them all her life, had taken, as she never tired of saying, both of them on when she married Sorley Mor, but she had never felt jealous of their relationship. She saw every day how much they relied on each other, how much they thought of each other, how much, dammit, they loved each other, and knew both would react with horror if she said so out loud. She knew, therefore, how much it would affect Sorley Mor that on this trip of all trips Gannet wouldn't be there, and she knew, too, how lost Gannet would be without Sorley Mor a couple of steps behind him, fending off the usual banter. Sorley Mor really didn't want to go without Gannet, and Gannet didn't want to stay behind without Sorley Mor, so they would both be making a genuine sacrifice for the sake of the other.

'He's right, Sorley Mor,' she told her husband gently. 'He's giving you this gift, he's your friend, you have to take it. And there's your son to consider, old man. This is the last chance he'll ever get to go to sea with you. It's something he'll want to tell his own bairns about when he has them, how he and his father went on the *Wanderer*'s last trip together.'

Sorley Mor made no reply, but bowed his head as the silence stretched.

'Right,' Chrissie said, 'enough of the glooms. And you,' she looked at Gannet, 'have said more sober words to-night than I have ever heard, you must be exhausted. Let's try and make you comfortable, the table in the porch is out tonight.'

'*Conservatory*, woman,' Sorley Mor said quietly, smiling up at her. 'Will you never get it right?'

They left the next evening amid a great deal of noise: boat whistles screeching, car and lorry horns sounding, people shouting and clapping. Everyone, it seemed, was down at the harbour to watch them depart, including Gannet and Father Mick, who would now never get to set foot on any *Ocean Wanderer*. Their destination was the fishing grounds of the Wee Bankie, near the entrance to the Firth of Forth, where in June there was a short season for sand eel fishing. Catches would be landed at Esbjerg in Denmark, a centre for the processing of sand eels into fishmeal/fertiliser. Once the boat's quota had been filled, probably in two or three weeks' time, they would head home for the last time and the MacEwans would be officially finished with the fishing.

Even before they left, plans were already being made in Acarsaid for Sorley Mor's return, with a large banner under construction with 'The Wanderer returns – for GOOD!' emblazoned on it. It would be hung across the harbour when they came back. Up on MacEwan's Row, Rose had a stone ready to place on the cairn outside her house when Sorley Og returned, a fine big lump of pure white quartz she had found on the shore and kept back for a while. She and Chrissie watched the boat leave harbour from MacEwan's Row, as they always did, waving to the distant figures aboard as they waved back, until it was so far away that they could no longer be seen with the naked eye. This time Chrissie rushed indoors and Rose found her at the sink, furiously washing dishes and blinking away tears.

'Why are you crying?' Rose asked.

'How should I know?' Chrissie answered. 'Relief that that daft old bugger finally went, or that he won't go again, or my son either. I don't know!'

She threw her arms around Rose and cried some more and Rose joined in.

'So why are *you* crying?' Chrissie demanded, laughing at the same time.

'Well, if you don't know,' Rose laughed back, trying to wipe away the tears, 'how on earth do you expect me to know?'

They had been away two weeks when Sorley Mor phoned Chrissie for something approaching the tenth time to say they had caught enough and would be home in about two days, and was there anything happening? Sorley Mor's opinion was always split about what happened to Acarsaid when he was at sea; either nothing of note happened at all because he wasn't there, or bizarre, wonderful and interesting events took place in his absence. Chrissie told him the place had completely stood still without him, as it always did. She passed him on to Gannet and listened while they had a fishermen's conversation, all about crans, tonnes, the weather. The reason behind Sandy Bay's shopping expeditions she decided to keep till the end of the conversation.

'So?' he asked, peeved. 'Nothing happening? Nothing at all? Ach well, we'll be home on Monday or Tuesday.'

'Fine. Oh, there is one bit of news, Sorley Mor,' Chrissie said casually.

'What? What is it?'

'Ach, it's nothing, it'll keep.'

'Woman, I'm busy; either tell me or don't!'

'Well, as you're busy I'll tell you when you come home. It's just idle gossip, really. It's about Sandy Bay. Goodbye now.'

'Wait a minute! Damn and blast, she's hung up. Chrissie MacEwan, are you there?'

Chrissie put a hand over the mouthpiece and laughed, then, 'Aye, Sorley Mor, what is it you're wanting?' she asked sweetly.

'What was that about Sandy Bay?'

'It's not worth taking up your time with,' she grinned to herself.

'Now I know fine it's something, will you damned well tell me, woman?'

'Going to sea does you no good these days,' she said. 'You get so cranky, it's just as well you're giving it up.'

'What about Sandy Bay?'

'Sandy Bay?' she asked vaguely. 'Oh, he never went to sea, you know that fine.'

'Chrissie MacEwan, as sure as God is my maker, when I hit port you're for the divorce courts.'

'Well, funnily enough, he's got married. 'Bye!'

Gannet, witnessing the kind of Chrissie wind-up he normally experienced from the other end, had a mental image of the screeching rage that was coming over the phone as Chrissie laughed at the skipper.

'Chrissie, Chrissie!'

'What?'

'Did you say Sandy Bay had got married?'

'Aye.'

'Ach, away with you.'

'Suit yourself. You asked if anything had happened and I told you the only thing that had happened.'

'Well, I mean, who would he get married to?'

'To Tess, the schoolteacher lassie who was seeing young Gavin,' Chrissie said simply.

'I don't believe you,' Sorley Mor laughed loudly. 'I'll admit it, you had me going for a minute there. That was a good one, Chrissie, but you went too far. Now if you'd said he'd married Batty at Black Rock, I'd have believed that sooner than the wee blonde lassie! Ha ha ha.'

'Well, as I say, Sorley Mor, suit yourself.'

'Let me speak to Gannet again.'

'Can't,' Chrissie lied, 'he's gone to the Inn.' With that she pressed the button to end the call, then released it and called Rose. When Sorley Og phoned she wasn't, under any circumstances, to mention a word about Sandy Bay and Tess getting married. 'That will confuse the old man even more,' she laughed.

'Too late. He called two minutes ago,' Rose laughed, 'but he didn't believe me either!'

Off the coast of Denmark, father and son compared notes, and Sorley Mor came to the conclusion that Chrissie had put Rose up to it. Then he thought a bit more and decided that the only way to prove the matter either way was to call Father Mick, only there was the distinct possibility that Chrissie would have put him up to it, too. It was only when Stamp and Pete, the other locals on board, reported having identical conversations with their own wives that Sorley Mor called Father Mick, who reported that nothing untoward had happened and asked if Sorley Mor hadn't better things to do.

'So,' Sorley Mor asked cautiously, 'nothing's happening?'

'How many times do I have to tell you, man?' Father Mick yelled. 'Now it's Saturday night, I've had one helluva day listening to the dullest confessions this end of a convent, so why don't you leave a poor old man alone?'

'Aye, fine, well.' Sorley Mor hesitated, trying to get the words right, because if he got them wrong and just casually said, 'So I hear Sandy Bay's gone and married that nice wee teacher,' Father Mick would tell the tale of how he'd been fooled for all it was worth.

'And have you seen Sandy Bay at all?' he asked instead.

'Sandy Bay!' Father Mick yelled down the phone. 'Bloody Sandy Bay is it? I'll tell you this, I'll never talk to him ever again.'

'What about him?' Sorley Mor asked innocently. 'Has he been up to something?'

'Has he been up to something? He's gone and got married, that what he's been up to!'

'Surely not?' Sorley Mor said, even more cautiously. 'Married you say. To a woman?'

294

'To that wee lassie at the school, that's who to!' the priest exploded. 'Sneaked off to Glasgow together, had it planned for months, apparently. Came back already spliced. Sandy Bay said they hadn't married in Acarsaid because he knew the lads up here would've done terrible things to him. In a registry office, if you please. What an insult to me, what a snub! Well, I'm finished with him, I'll tell you that. If he wants a blessing he can go back to Glasgow for it! Kin of yours or not, Sorley Mor, he's a miserable skinflint. That's why he got married quietly in Glasgow, to avoid the expense of a decent wedding up here.'

'Are you sure, Father Mick?' Sorley Mor persisted.

'Of course I'm sure! Hasn't he always been a mean bugger who'd cross the road to pick up an old ha'penny long after it stopped being legal tender?'

'No, I don't mean are you sure he's tight, we all know that,' said Sorely Mor patiently. 'Are you sure he's married or did you just hear it from Chrissie? Or maybe you've been drinking *and* talked to Chrissie?'

But Father Mick's pent up fury had been released. 'And he's sixty-five if he's a day,' he continued, 'and she's what? Fifteen?' When Father Mick judged himself to have been insulted, he still had a habit of over-icing the cake. 'Disgusting, that's what it is! Not that there's the slightest hope of it ever being consummated at his age, but it's the vanity of the man, thinking he can take on a young lassie like that, and the thoughts are all there, the carnal thoughts! By God, I'll tell you this, Sorley Mor, he'd better not come to me for confession and absolution. It's not Hail Marys he'll get, but a damned good hiding!'

Next day Sorley Mor was on lookout as the *Wanderer* made her way to land the last catch before returning home. It was just before five o'clock on one of those beautiful, clear, quiet June mornings he loved, the kind where you can see for miles and miles. He had been right about it not being the same without Gannet, he thought to himself as he sat in the wheelhouse. Not that his first mate said much, he thought with a smile – he was more like a silent partner – but he had missed the sight of him sitting in the corner, a stack of books at his side, absorbing information with which to amaze people once he was at home and had had a drink. He laughed out loud at the memory of the big man discussing psychology with old Ina Hamilton the year before.

'I'm determined to outlive you, Gannet,' he'd said later, 'if only to tell that story at your funeral.'

'The trouble with you, Skipper,' Gannet had replied with as much dignity as he could muster, 'is that you don't have a sophisticated mind. Old Ina there might not be nimble on her pins any longer, but she has a quick mind still, she understands deeper things you can't. She knows everything about astronomy, we have some fine talks about it.'

'Away with you, man,' Sorley Mor had doubled up again. 'She couldn't hear a damned word! Poor old soul, sitting by her own fire, the only one not able to get up and run away from you and your theories.'

'They're not theories, they are facts, Skipper,' Gannet complained, 'I read them in a book, and books don't lie, unlike some skippers I could mention.'

'And what do you mean by that?' Sorley Mor demanded.

'Oh, well,' Gannet said airily, 'let's just say if I had a mind to, there's a few true things I could tell Chrissie.'

Sorley Mor wondered how Gannet was getting on with Chrissie, and how Chrissie was getting on with him. He half-expected to find a note on the door when he got home, saying the two of them had been carted off to the separate madhouses. He laughed again, rubbing his chest. Chrissie had been more right than she knew: it was time he gave up this business when even Stamp's food could give him indigestion. The night before, Stamp had served up spaghetti with spicy meatballs, Sorley Mor's favourite, as a special offering to his skipper, and this morning it was giving him gip. Not that he would let on to Stamp. Maybe he should give that stuff young Gavin had given him a try.

Sandy Bay and Tess, eh? Now there was a thought. If it was true, of course, and he was still far from sure that Chrissie hadn't made the whole thing up and convinced or coerced Father Mick into feeding him the same line. And the others; when Chrissie prepared a wind-up she spared no effort. The rest of the crew had all laughed out loud. Now if that wasn't a pointer, he didn't know what was, but a pointer to what exactly?

'She's an awful woman, your Chrissie,' Stamp said admiringly.

'But your Molly said the same thing,' Sorley Mor reminded him, 'and Alison and Rose. And you have to remember, Chrissie wouldn't let me talk to Gannet. Now Gannet couldn't lie to me, that's a clue.'

'But a clue to what, Father?' Sorley Og grinned. 'That's the real mystery.'

'Aye,' Stamp laughed again, 'an awful woman all together!'

He was the only one up on that Sunday morning, apart from Sorley Og, who had gone aft to have a look at one of the pumps before relieving him as lookout. As soon as Sorley Og took over, he'd go to his cabin and look out Gavin's stuff and take a swig. When the boy came back up to the wheelhouse he'd ask him what he really thought about Sandy Bay and the nice young teacher. After all, Gavin was his pal, who would know better than anyone else on board what was going on? He rubbed his chest again and decided not to wait for Sorley Og to come to the wheelhouse; the boy could be a while yet. He'd go downstairs to his cabin now and get Gavin's stuff and be back by the time Sorley Og arrived to take over.

At MacEwan's Row Chrissie got up after lying awake for a while; it was always like this when he'd called to say he'd be coming home soon. She wandered in to the kitchen and found Gannet at the window, staring out to sea, a cup of coffee in his right hand.

'What are you thinking?' she asked him. She lifted the kettle, shook it, then crossed to the sink to fill it up again.

Gannet looked up and smiled. 'That it's quiet without him. And it feels odd.'

'Aye, well, you've spent more time with him than I have,' Chrissie said. She looked across to Sorley Og and Rose's house and, seeing her daughter-in-law at her sink, waved and smiled. 'Great minds think alike,' she said quietly.

Gannet looked across at Rose and waved too. 'Do the two of you always do this?' he asked.

'Always,' Chrissie said.

The next time Father Mick's phone rang was on Sunday morning. He hated being called on Sunday mornings and everybody knew it; the day was busy enough with wall-to-wall masses stretching before him as far as the eye could see. He debated with himself whether or not to lift the receiver, then did, tetchily demanding 'What in hell's name do you want? And I'll warn you now that this had better be good, I am no mood for idle –'

'Father Houlihan?' a strange voice interrupted him.

'Yes,' Father Mick said uncertainly.

'Father, this is the Coastguard at Great Yarmouth,' the voice said. 'I'm calling to tell you that a signal from an emergency beacon was picked up at just after six o'clock this morning and the Falmouth Coastguard has confirmed that it's from the vessel *Ocean Wanderer*. We have you listed as the contact number.'

Father Mick laughed. 'Ah, no,' he said. 'You see, what happens is that they get knocked off. It happens all the time, it'll be a mistake, you know, a false alarm.' In his mind he could hear Sorley Mor chiding him. 'Not on *my* boat, Father Mick. Our beacon is safe and secure, we don't spark false alarms!' When he told the skipper this story he'd have to come up with a different line there, or he'd never be forgiven. 'You really said *that?*' the skipper would demand indignantly.

'Father,' said the voice again, 'I'm sorry, but this is the real thing.'

Father Mick stood still for a few moments more, his mind trying to cope with what was being said to him by this stranger. And come to that, how did he know this man was genuine? How did he know it wasn't some silly prank? 'Dear God,' he said eventually, reaching for a chair to sit on. 'If there is a God at all, please make it that, make it some sort of sick joke!'

'Father, Father?' said the voice, full of concern. 'Father, can I ring someone for you?'

'Just tell me,' he asked.

'The agent's manager in Acarsaid, a Mr Douglas Nicolson, has confirmed that there were six men aboard the vessel, Father. I'll give him a call and ask him to contact you. Is that all right?'

'Tell me first.'

'Well, as I say, shortly after the beacon was activated the signal was identified as coming from the *Ocean Wanderer* and attempts were made to contact them, but there was no answer. Then we were notified of a "Mayday" call from a German freighter, reporting that she'd hit a fishing boat at the same position as the beacon's signal. He didn't know her name then, but said she had gone down bow first in little more than a minute.'

'And the crew, are they all safe?' Father Mick asked, closing his eyes.

'I'm sorry, Father, there are no survivors reported. The freighter launched her own lifeboat immediately and found debris bearing the name of the *Ocean Wanderer*. Her liferafts and a rubber dinghy were recovered and we now have confirmation that her beacon has been recovered, too. There's excellent visibility in the area, but it's now three hours since the boat went down. Rescue efforts are ongoing, but I'm afraid we have to conclude that the crew is lost.'

There was no answer from Father Mick.

'Father Houlihan?'

'I'm here.'

'We did try to contact you earlier, but there was no answer, sir, and no answering machine to leave a message on.'

'I was saying mass,' said Father Mick absently, 'and up here there's no need of a machine. Everyone always knows where I am and how to get hold of me.'

'I see, sir.'

Coastguard officers were used to dealing with shocked people who didn't want to or couldn't take in what they were being told, and often this was made worse because they found themselves talking to the skipper's wife. Even so, they knew how to deal with these situations, though it was never easy. Still, the immediate reality had to be put across.

'The boat went down so quickly, you see,' said the officer gently, 'it looks like they were steaming for port fully laden, so probably the crew would have been in bed, apart from the man on lookout. They would've had no time, no chance. I'm sorry, Father, but you are the emergency contact, and I want you to understand what has happened. I don't want to leave you with any false hope that you then might pass on to the families. That would be worse than the truth. And there's always the chance that the media might get hold of it and break the news before anyone can tell the families. It wouldn't be right for them to hear that way, do you see?'

Out of the window Father Mick saw Dr Johnstone's Range Rover pulling into the driveway. As it stopped, Dougie Nicolson got out, then the doctor. 'Yes,' he said. 'Thank you for your kindness. Mr Nicolson has just arrived. Goodbye.'

Slow motion, that was what those involved in terrible events often described, time moving in slow motion; and in his chapel house, Father Mick realised that it really was how it seemed. Dougie and Gavin slowly came into the house without knocking, slowly looked at him. Dougie slowly opened his mouth, then shut it again, still looking at him.

'Dougie, we're sure about this?' Father Mick asked plaintively. 'Really sure?'

Dougie nodded. Gavin, he noticed, looked as shellshocked as he was himself and said nothing.

'Dougie, what do we do now? Tell me, what do we do?'

'Call Gannet at Sorley Mor's house, tell him we have to see him and not to let on to Chrissie that anything's happened.'

'Right.'

Father Mick didn't move, so Dougie picked up the receiver and handed it to him.

'Couldn't you do it?' he asked.

'No, Father, it has to be you, because Chrissie will probably answer. I'd have no real reason to call Gannet, now would I?'

'You're right, of course you're right.'

Chrissie did answer. 'What the hell do you want with Gannet?' she demanded. 'Can't you let him have a few sober hours, Hooligan?'

Then he heard Gannet's voice on the other end and his resolve broke down. He handed the receiver to Dougie.

'Gannet, it's Dougie here, I'm up at the chapel house with Father Mick. I need you to listen carefully and don't let on to Chrissie. Are you with me?' Dougie said seriously.

'Aye . . .' Gannet responded, puzzled.

'Gannet, something bad has happened to the *Wanderer*. Make any excuse you want, but get out of the house and start walking down towards the village now. We'll pick you up in Gavin's Range Rover. OK?'

When he replaced the receiver he turned to Father Mick. 'Father, we have a desperate situation here. We have to let the families know at the same time. You're the emergency contact, but as we couldn't get hold of you we had to make a few arrangements. There are two lads from the Seamen's Mission ready to visit Molly Stewart and Alison Kerr, and we've arranged for Mission people to visit Stevie's wife in

Fife and Eric's Marilyn in Glasgow as soon as the word is given. I'll phone the Mission now and they can set all that in motion while we go off to pick up the Gannet and explain to him what's happened. Then you and Gannet can go back to the house and tell Chrissie, while Gavin and I tell my sister. Is that all right, Father?'

'Aye, it's fine, Dougie,' he said distractedly, but as he tried to move towards the door his legs refused to obey him. 'I can't do this!' he cried.

'Father,' Dougie said firmly, 'you have no choice. Sorley Mor gave this task to you because he trusted you to do things right if anything ever happened. He decided you were the best person to deal with it and to look after his wife. You can't let him down.'

'I know this, Dougie,' he said desperately, 'I know this,' but for a long moment he considered just refusing to move. What could anyone do if the local priest refused to walk out of his own house? But maybe none of this was happening, maybe the drink had caught up with him as Chrissie kept telling him it would, maybe it was that old cliché, a nightmare, and any moment now he'd wake up and find that there had been no phone call from the Coastguard and no Dougie and Gavin standing in his living room, demanding that he be the one to break Chrissie's heart? One thing was certain, though; sooner than do what was being asked of him, he'd rather lock himself away and never come out again, never. Then 'No,' he said, 'you're right. This is for Sorley Mor. I won't let him down.'

They drove down the Brae. 'Look,' Father Mick said sadly. 'Everything is normal. People walking about, buying papers, talking to each other, laughing. How can that be so when this has happened to us? Take a good look, my friends, because we will never see Acarsaid like this again.'

Dougie was in the front passenger seat beside Gavin with Father Mick behind Dougie as the car turned right and on through the village until they reached the bottom of

MacEwan's Row. They sat in a painful, bewildered silence until the tall, thin figure of Gannet appeared, head down, striding towards them with his left arm still in its sling.

'I don't know how we're going to tell him,' Father Mick said quietly, as all three of them concentrated on Gannet.

'Simply,' Dougie replied quietly. 'Gannet will have worked it out already.'

'He can't have!' the priest said. 'How could he?'

Dougie shrugged. 'He's a fisherman,' he said, 'from generations of fishermen. These things happen at sea.'

Slowly Gannet came nearer till he had reached the Range Rover. He opened the door behind Gavin and got in, taking care with his injured shoulder.

'How bad is it?' he asked, looking directly at Dougie.

'The boat's down, the entire crew's lost,' Dougie said. 'She was run down by a freighter.'

'No one left?' Gannet asked.

'No one, Gannet,' Dougie replied evenly. 'She went down just after six this morning, bow first, in around a minute. She was heading for Esbjerg, fully loaded. They've found liferafts and the beacon.'

'Six,' Gannet said thoughtfully, his head down. 'They'd all have been asleep except for the lookout.' He looked up. 'The lookout would've been in the wheelhouse, he'd have had the best chance. They didn't even get him?'

'No.'

'We'll have to tell Chrissie,' he said, 'but I need a minute. That all right?'

He got out of the Range Rover and wandered about, head down once more, for what seemed like hours but was probably no more than a few minutes; then he got back in again.

'What've you arranged, Dougie?' he asked, nodding as the details were explained to him. 'Pete's wife is six months pregnant,' he said. 'Shouldn't Gavin be with the Mission man when she's told?'

Gavin turned round in the driving seat. 'He's going to

collect her mother first,' he said, 'and if there's any problem he has my mobile number. I'll be going down to see her anyway after Dougie and I see Rose.'

'You've done well, Dougie,' Gannet said, reaching out awkwardly with his right arm and patting Dougie's shoulder. 'You don't think you should get your mother for Rose?' he asked.

Dougie shook his head. Everyone understood; Margo wasn't that kind of mother.

'OK, then, let's go,' he said. 'Our only bit of luck is that it's Sunday morning. We'll have time to shut the village down before the papers get to us. But we'd better get our skates on, they'll still be here sooner than we want.'

They drove in silence up to MacEwan's Row and stopped just before Sorley Mor's house, in a common, unspoken consensus to gather themselves together for the terrible, incredible thing they were about to do. It had come upon them so suddenly that they didn't really believe it themselves, yet here they were, about to pass this devastating news on to people they had known and loved for years, knowing it would destroy their lives.

'You up to this, Father?' Gannet asked him kindly. 'I'll do it myself if you want?'

Father Mick shook his head. If anyone had asked him who would have handled this terrible day best he would have said himself, and he would have guessed that Gannet would be too distraught to do anything, but in reality the roles were reversed. And Dougie Nicolson was a revelation; he had always been a serious boy, but now he had turned into a strong man. Father Mick remembered once seeing him in the Inn and remarking to him that he hadn't ever seen him at mass, and Dougie had replied, 'And if you ever do, Father Mick, better put up an umbrella. They say pig shit makes a helluva mess when it falls from a great height.' Then he'd drained his glass and left, shouting quiet but friendly goodbyes to everyone.

Sorley Mor and Gannet had nearly choked with laughter at what Dougie had said and the fact that Father Mick didn't understand what he had meant. 'You daft wee man,' Sorley Mor had chuckled. 'He means pigs will fly before you see him at mass! You'll not get the better of that one, you might as well forget it.' And to tell the truth, Mick had laughed too, and tucked it away in his memory, hoping an opportunity might arise when he could use it himself.

Chrissie opened the door to their knock, her face with its usual pugnacious expression on seeing Gannet and Father Mick together. 'Well,' she said, 'we've Peter Sellers and Spike Hooligan, all we need now is Sorley Secombe home from the sea and we'll have all the Goons!'

Then she caught sight of Dougie and Gavin on their way to Rose's door, and her face immediately went white and fearful.

'Is it Sorley Mor?' she whispered.

'It's all of them, Chrissie,' Gannet said.

'My son too?' she gasped.

Gannet nodded miserably. 'The whole crew, Chrissie, we've lost them all.'

As he was walking towards his sister's house, out of the corner of his eye Dougie had seen Chrissie falling and Gannet pulling his arm out of the sling to catch her before she hit the floor. He turned away; that situation was being dealt with, he had his own to think about.

When Rose opened the door she looked from Dougie to Gavin and asked, 'Has something happened to Granny Ina?'

Dougie gently pushed her back into the house, shaking his head. Rose's right hand flew to her throat, still clutching the tea towel she had been using to dry her coffee cup when the knock had come. Dougie looked at the pattern of French scenes on the towel and remembered she and Sorley Og had gone to Paris for their honeymoon. As her brother moved towards her, something clicked in Rose's mind and she put her other hand up to stop him.

'Don't!' she cried aloud. 'If you're going to tell me it's Sorley Og, just don't! Get out of my house!'

She dropped the tea towel and pushed hard against Dougie with one hand, grabbing the door with the other and trying desperately to push him far enough to shut him out. Dougie tried to put his arms around her, pushing against her so that she went backwards in to the house, struggling all the way, her feet slipping and sliding, resisting every inch.

'Don't say anything!' she screamed. 'I won't listen! You're going to tell me something bad just because you don't like him!'

Then Dougie got his arms around her, holding her against him, and hushed her like a baby.

'Rose, my little one, you have to listen,' he said quietly, 'because it won't go away.'

'No! No!'

He motioned with his head for Gavin to help him, and between them they half-carried her, still struggling, to the couch.

'Rose, the boat went down this morning. The whole crew is lost.'

Rose managed to free one arm, drew it back and gave her brother a hefty slap across the face.

'Don't tell me that!' she screamed, her voice like a wounded animal. 'It's not true! You'd like it to be true, wouldn't you? Ever since we got married that's what you've wanted, but it isn't true! I hate you for saying that, I'll never talk to you again!'

He turned towards her again, the mark of her hand already showing red across his cheek. He was still holding her, but as she prepared to lash out again she suddenly noticed that tears were rolling silently down his face.

'Oh, Dougie,' she sobbed, burying her face in his chest and hugging him to her. 'Oh, Dougie, Dougie, I'm sorry!'

Gavin stood beside them, trying to control himself, then he broke down in great gulping sobs and ran outside, where he found Father Mick standing crying at the door of Sorley Mor's house.

'I heard Rose crying and . . . ,' the priest said helplessly.

'How's Chrissie?' Gavin asked, trying to steady himself.

Father Mick shook his head. 'Not good. Gannet's magnificent.'

'So is Dougie,' said Gavin.

'Look at us,' Father Mick said, 'a doctor and a priest. The very ones who should be good at handling this kind of situation, and we're no bloody use to anyone.'

21

It was summer, the height of the tourist season. In the days following the sinking of *Ocean Wanderer*, Acarsaid was full of holidaymakers, all in divisions and sub-divisions. There were those from over the Border, where the tragedy had merited no more than a paragraph in the newspapers, or from abroad, where it hadn't been reported at all. Others came from nearer at hand, and had been exposed to the growing media frenzy. Then there were the media themselves. The village was in deep shock, no one was unaffected by the loss of the boat and the crew, and the villagers instinctively put up barriers around their grief. Those visitors who went to Acarsaid year upon year were still catered for; the sun still shone on familiar and favourite spots; the faces about the place were still recognized; but now they were aware of a heavy blanket of devastation hanging over the village that made them feel what they were: outsiders.

In Hamish Dubh's store down by the harbour, remarks about the sinking, however sympathetic and sincere, were met with a polite but inpenetrable blankness and, if pursued, Hamish would say quietly that he was happy to be of service to them, to provide newspapers, ice cream, buckets and spades and postcards, but he did not wish to discuss the *Wanderer*, if that was all the same to whoever was asking. All the boats that had been at sea had cut their trips short and returned as soon as they had been told of the sinking, and over the next few days the harbour had filled up. None went out again, so there were plenty of boats for the tourists to look at, but little activity. Fishermen still carried out routine tasks, but in silence.

They did not wish to engage in conversation; if tourists set foot on the harbour crewmen would disappear below deck till they had gone.

And then there were the reporters, photographers and TV crews. Not that they couldn't be dealt with, but they were an added nuisance, an irritation. In the wider fishing community where other boats and crews had been lost over the years, lessons on the need to contain the media had been learned the hard way, so one of the first things that had been done was to appoint someone from the Seamen's Mission to be the exclusive spokesman for the families. That, however, didn't stop the reporters from trying for a word or a photo that no one else had; no amount of organisation and controlled information would ever do that. In a larger harbour, where a lost crew might be known only by sight, someone would undoubtedly have talked to the press, but Acarsaid was small enough for everyone to feel bereaved. Sorley Mor, Sorley Og, Stamp, Pete, Eric and Stevie were part of their lives, and those who weren't family even ten times removed still felt their loss as keenly as if they were. So anyone approached for information simply looked the asker in the eye and lied. They denied that they had ever set eyes on the crew, couldn't even say what colour the boat had been and had no idea where the families lived, a tactic that discouraged all but the most determined – though unfortunately there were more than enough of those.

At MacEwan's Row on the day following the sinking, the talk was of what to do next. Dougie Nicolson had taken the lead. Normally agents tried very hard to stay out of these events, but this was different, not least because his sister was involved, but partly, too, because Dougie was able to do it when no one else could. He had organised for all the widows and families, apart from Stevie's in Fife and Eric's in Glasgow, to be brought together at Chrissie's house with Father Mick and Gannet; he was anxious to get everything in order before the press hunted them down. The *Wanderer*, he explained to them, was lying near enough to shore and in water that divers could work in. The insurers had already had a team go down to find the boat and attach a line. The insurers had to carry out investigations anyway, and the divers had reported back that they thought it might be possible to retrieve the bodies. It would be difficult, but they were willing to try, and the insurers, to their credit, had agreed to underwrite the extra cost, if that's what the families wanted. What they now had to decide was whether they left their men with the boat on the bottom of the sea, or brought them home and buried them in the little cemetery high above Acarsaid.

It had always been tradition to leave the men with their boats, but times were changing. Technology, developed particularly for the oil industry, was leaving the old ways in its wake, and bodies were increasingly being retrieved from downed boats. In 1990 the Carradale fishing boat *Antares* had been snagged by her trawl-warps by a submarine engaged in NATO exercises and dragged under off the Ayrshire Coast, something that was happening more and more, though Navy policy was to deny everything unless there was absolute evidence that their sub had been involved. In the case of the *Antares* the Navy had been caught red-handed and, as a gesture of regret, had sent down divers to find the bodies of the four crewmen and return them to their families for burial.

From then on the possibility of retrieval had raised questions about the tradition of leaving the men with their sunken boats, and in 1997 the widows of four men lost with the *Sapphire* off Peterhead decided that they wanted them brought home too. Parts of the fishing community were totally against it – many fishermen themselves were known to be opposed to it – but the *Sapphire* had gone down close enough to their home harbour for a lifting barge to reach her. When the Labour Government refused to cover the estimated cost of £250,000, the widows had launched a public appeal for donations. Bad weather caused delays, and the cost rose to

£600,000, but the extra money was quickly raised from a public appalled by the treatment the widows had received, and their men were duly brought home. So it was not only technically possible for the *Wanderer*'s crew to be recovered, but feelings within communities were changing. Even so, as Dougie told the families that Monday morning, they had to make the decision quickly. He was aware that few wanted or were able to make it, and he wasn't surprised that at first no one said anything. It was only twenty-four hours since the boat had gone down, and less since the families had heard the news. The silence continued.

'What do you think, Gannet?' Chrissie asked eventually.

Gannet didn't reply.

'You're as much family here as anyone,' Chrissie said gently. 'As far as I'm concerned your opinion on bringing Sorley Mor home is as valid as mine or his daughters'. The girls haven't arrived yet, so I'll speak for them.' Rose was sitting at the far end of the couch apart from the others, holding tightly to her brother's hand. 'And you too Rose, do you agree?' Chrissie asked.

Rose nodded without looking up. The event had over-whelmed her and she still didn't believe any of it was happening; she felt that just being here, discussing these things, was an act of betrayal.

'It's difficult,' Gannet said at last. 'I've always believed the crew should stay with the boat, but I think if the families want them home, and they can be brought home, then they should be. Sorley Mor would've said exactly the same thing, I know that. He had no time for superstitions or daft traditions: everyone knows that. We never once discussed what we would like if it happened to ourselves. You just don't, because you never think there's any chance it will happen to you. It always happens to someone else, doesn't it? But he admired the *Sapphire* women and damned and blasted the government for refusing to bring their men home. In fact, as everyone knows, he went on about it till we all threatened to hit him.'

He stopped talking and smiled sadly. 'I know he'd say the same as me. If you and the girls want him home, Chrissie, then that's what should happen.'

'That's good enough for me,' Chrissie said quietly. 'I want him to have a decent burial here at home; the girls will agree.'

One by one, those who could gave their painful, halting thoughts on the matter, for and against; the fathers, the mothers and the new widows.

'I want my child to know where Pete is,' said Alison Kerr quietly. 'I want to have a place where we can go together and talk to him. This baby, whether it's a boy or a girl, that's the only chance they'll have of talking to him. I don't want to point to the sea and say, "He's somewhere out there."'

'I want Sorley Og home,' Rose said simply. 'I don't want to discuss this any more. I want Sorley Og home.'

Then came the question of who should travel to Denmark to identify the bodies. The relatives winced as one. It seemed that they were being rushed from one horror to another, without having any time to come to terms with the disaster that had befallen them and their families. They were still struggling to absorb the fact that their men were dead – there was no one in the room who was truly expecting never to see them again, never to hear their voices – yet there was Dougie Nicolson, behaving like a businessman and matter-of-factly going over an agenda. Father Mick saw their looks and felt their pain.

'I know how bad this is for everyone,' he said gently, 'please believe me, I do. I can't think too deeply about it at the moment without losing all control. Like you, I don't believe it yet. I can't, I don't want to, but these things have to be attended to; practical things have to be done. I've known this lad,' he looked at Dougie, 'I should say, this man, nearly all of his life, and I have to tell you that in these past hours I've looked at him with new and admiring eyes.'

Dougie shuffled his feet and looked uncomfortable.

'He's feeling this too,' Father Mick continued, 'you must all know that, in your hearts, but he has some God-given ability the rest of us don't have, to keep going, to keep thinking straight in what is the worst disaster this village has ever experienced. We must try not to resent the speed with which he's moving. He's doing it for all of us and, I suspect, at great emotional expense to himself. We must help him do what has to be done.'

There was another long, heavy silence as first one pair of eyes, then another settled on Gannet until everyone was looking at him. Gannet looked up, shocked, then shook his head.

'Not me,' he said. 'I have to look after Chrissie.'

'It's OK,' Dougie said, still embarrassed and clearly near to tears at Father Mick's intervention on his behalf. 'I wasn't asking for volunteers and I wouldn't ask you to do this, Gannet,' he said. 'I was going to say, if no one objects, that I'd do it.' He looked around the room. 'If this is something anyone else feels they should do, please say so. I'm not trying to usurp anyone's position, I just felt it might be easier on everyone if I did it.'

From around the room came a murmur of agreement.

Dougie hesitated. 'I know this is difficult for all of you,' he said in a low voice. 'I'm sorry if I come over as not caring. I'm trying to get all of this done without giving myself time to feel it. There will be more than enough time for that later.' He swallowed hard. 'Father Mick's right, though, we have to get these things sorted now because it will be easier in the long run. I don't want the press bothering anyone, and the Mission will be handling that side of things, so there's no reason why they should bother you, but if they do, let the Mission know. Unless anyone specially wants to talk to the press?'

He looked round the room; everyone shook their heads vigorously.

'I need to know if you want to handle funeral arrangements

individually or if you trust me to handle them all on your behalf?'

At the mention of the funerals there was a spontaneous outbreak of quiet weeping, and Dougie lowered his head.

'I think you can take it, Dougie,' Father Mick said, 'that everyone would be grateful if you would handle it on their behalf.'

Dougie nodded. 'I'll keep in close touch with all of you,' he said. 'So will the Mission and Father Mick here. I promise nothing will be done without keeping you informed. If anyone else contacts you and tells you things or asks questions, refer them to one of us, and if you have anything you want to say or ask, call us at any time.'

As they were leaving, Rose looked at Alison Kerr. The thought suddenly struck her that the baby the girl was carrying would be born without a father, with a father lost to the sea, as Rose had herself. She reached out and put her arms round Alison.

'How are you?' she asked.

'I'm OK, Rose – or, not OK exactly, but, well, you know. And you?'

Rose nodded. 'The same. I was thinking of the baby.'

'Oh, I'm not going to lose this!' Alison said firmly, putting a hand on her stomach. 'I know everyone is afraid that I might, with the shock and everything, but I won't, I bloody well won't!'

The two young women laughed, then immediately cried.

'It's all I have left of him,' Alison wept quietly. 'I'm not sure *I'll* survive, mind you, but I'll make sure his baby does!'

'And we'll tell the baby about Pete, all of us,' Rose wept with her. 'Everybody has such good memories of him, we'll all talk to the baby about him and keep him alive that way.'

Chrissie watched the two young women clinging together. Wiping her eyes, she turned to Gannet. 'Look at the two of them,' she cried. 'The poor lassies! They've had no time at

314

all with their men. At least I had all those years with Sorley Mor, all those memories to look back on.'

As Dougie was leaving, he turned to Father Mick. 'By the way, I didn't appreciate that,' he smiled quietly.

'What was that, Dougie?' the priest asked.

'This ability you say I have. It's not God-given at all, it's all my own work!'

Father Mick laughed gently. 'Ah, yes,' he said. 'Pig shit, I remember!'

22

As the press arrived, details about the circumstances of the *Wanderer*'s sinking were filtering through. She had been making for port and the freighter had noticed her seven miles away, but as the *Wanderer* was on the freighter's right, the freighter had right of way and the lookout expected the *Wanderer*'s lookout to take note and alter course. The *Wanderer* kept on her original course, though, and the freighter didn't even sound a warning whistle till collision was inevitable. The question was why the *Wanderer* hadn't altered course when her lookout would have been able to see a freighter three times her size on a bright, clear morning, so all attention focused on the subject of lookouts. The inference was that there wasn't one aboard the *Wanderer*. In Acarsaid this was greeted with indignation and disbelief. Sorley Mor was the most disciplined, safety-conscious skipper in the industry, everyone knew that; his crew were of the best and had been with him many years and his boat met every safety and operational requirement. The suggestion that there was no lookout was an insult, nothing less, and, furthermore, it was a slur on the integrity of a dead man who could not give his side of it.

'They can say anything they want,' Gannet told Father Mick as they sat in a subdued Inn, 'and that's the truth of it. It doesn't matter what story surfaces, it will be one-sided and always will be, but I will not believe that Sorley Mor or any of the crew deliberately endangered the *Wanderer*.' He looked around. 'And no man had better suggest it.'

All around heads nodded in agreement; a slur against Sorley Mor would not be tolerated by anyone.

In the village the mood was still one of shock, as if a large black cloud had descended out of that bright, clear, Sunday morning and settled on the entire area, seeping into every crevice, enveloping Acarsaid in pain and grief and sealing any escape route. The tragedy occupied the thoughts and actions of everyone, and when villagers met in the streets they would lock eyes and see reflections of their own feelings. There was little talk; there was nothing to say and no words anyway to describe the loss. Everyone waited for news from Dougie, waited for something they could do, something that could move their minds on from the awful, raw emotion they couldn't see beyond. They fended off the press as best they could: a united front against intruders, they made sure in quiet ways that the families were protected, and they waited some more.

Dougie flew back three days later and immediately met with Father Mick and Gannet. The divers had brought up all the crew, he told them, and he had identified them. All that was, except one. Sorley Mor had been found at the bottom of the stairs to the wheelhouse, fully dressed and freshly shaven. Gannet nodded. 'Sorley Mor was on lookout,' he said quietly. Stamp, Pete, Stevie and Eric had clearly been asleep and were in various stages of trying to escape from their bunks, but Sorley Og was nowhere to be found. Five widows would be told that their men had been recovered and one would be told that her man was missing: Rose. Gannet and Mick closed their eyes; it was the worst possible outcome. For Chrissie the waiting would be only half over. Instead of burying her husband and son together, a fate that was bad enough, she would have to face Sorley Mor's funeral, then later, if he was found, Sorley Og's. Rose was in the worst position, though, and Dougie would tell her himself, he said.

'You don't have to do it, Dougie,' Father Mick said. 'You've already had to break the news of her husband's death to her, you've more than done your bit. Let one of us tell her.'

Dougie shook his head. 'She's my sister,' he said simply.

★　　★　　★

317

The arrangements were the same as before; Gannet and Father Mick would tell Chrissie, the Mission men would tell the others, and Dougie would talk to Rose. She looked at him expectantly as he entered the house.

'News?' she asked, staring at him. Going through her mind was the fantasy that when he got there he had found that it was all a mistake, that it hadn't been the *Wanderer* at all, that they'd headed for some other port and every communication device had broken down at the same time. They'd all laugh over this, one day . . .

'It's not good, Rose,' Dougie said. 'The divers got all the men except Sorley Og.'

At first her heart soared. OK, it *was* the *Wanderer*, but obviously Sorley Og wasn't on board, maybe he'd stayed behind in Esbjerg when they'd landed the previous catch. He'd probably wanted to buy her something special to mark the event; what Dougie was saying confirmed it. Dougie saw what was in her mind.

'Rose,' he said slowly but firmly. 'Sorley Og *was* aboard –'

'But you've just said –'

'I said they hadn't found him yet, but they're still looking. They'll keep looking till they find him.'

Rose shook her head. 'You don't know that, Dougie,' she said brightly, 'you don't know for sure that he didn't change his mind and go off somewhere. He could've arranged to be picked up on the next trip into port.'

'Rose, don't do this to yourself. He called you from the middle of the ocean the night before she went down, don't you remember? He called from the boat and you told him about Sandy Bay!'

'Maybe I got that wrong –'

'Stop it!' he said harshly, moving towards her with his arms outstretched. 'Sorley Og went down with the *Wanderer*. He's still on the boat, he'll be found.'

Rose moved her arms backwards to avoid his grasp.

'So what are you going to do now, Rose MacEwan?' he

asked softly. 'Hit me again? That will make it not true, will it?'

'No, no . . . I . . . I wasn't going to –' she stammered, then she put her head down, wrapped her arms around her body defensively, and sobbed.

Next door Chrissie was taking the news stoically, nodding her head as she was told. 'And the other women have been told?' she asked. 'They're being taken care of?' She nodded, satisfied. 'I'll have to see Rose,' she said.

'No, don't,' Father Mick said. 'Not now, anyway. Dougie's handling it. The Nicolsons have always been a tight lot, better leave him to it.'

'What about her mother?' Chrissie asked, puzzled. 'I haven't seen her up here yet. She lost her own man at sea; surely she should be with her daughter?'

'I don't know if she's offered, but Rose doesn't want her anyway,' Father Mick said. 'She doesn't want anyone. Dougie suggested that Sally could stay with her. Alan's gone down to Glasgow to be with the family – Eric was his cousin, as you know – but Rose won't have it. Things haven't been good between her and Sally, as far as I can gather, since that nonsense over the wedding.'

'But that means she's alone in that big house!' Chrissie said. 'That's not good. Tell her I'd appreciate her company. Maybe she'd come over and stay here with me till this thing's over.'

'I'll mention it to Dougie; he's the only one she seems able to talk to at the moment,' Father Mick said. 'But, Chrissie, maybe we should leave her to handle it in her own way.'

Chrissie thought for a moment. 'Don't mention it to Dougie,' she said. 'I'll go over there later and talk to her myself.'

Chrissie left it till that evening, then she went over to her son's house, where Rose was sitting in darkness by the big window.

'I was wondering if you might like some company, Rose,' she said.

Rose smiled but made no reply.

'It's not good for you to be all alone here,' Chrissie persisted. 'What about one of your family? Your mother, one of your sisters?'

Rose shook her head.

'Well, how about coming over and staying with me and Gannet?' she laughed gently, trying to conjure up something of the atmosphere that was gone for ever. 'Between the two of us we should be able to keep him under control.'

'I don't want to leave the house,' Rose said simply.

'But you've barely left it for more than a minute all week, lassie,' Chrissie said, 'and that was to come the few yards to my house.'

'I can't,' Rose repeated, then her head slumped forward and she wept.

'Oh, lassie,' Chrissie said, moving forward and putting her arms around her, 'you can't stay here alone like this.'

'I can't leave!' Rose sobbed. 'I can't!'

'But why?' Chrissie asked. 'You won't miss any news, it all comes to me first.'

'I have to be here,' Rose said desperately, her voice broken with sobs at every word. 'Don't you understand, Chrissie? What if he phones or comes home and I'm not here?'

The two women stood by the big window, holding onto each other and crying together.

It was, of course, a story tailor-made for press interest. They had several widows, one of whom had also lost her son, while another was due to give birth for the first time in less than three months. Then there was Rose, the one in limbo, the one who had a husband to grieve for, but not to bury; for Rose the anguish spread out without any end in sight. Though information was being fed to the media through the Mission and they had been asked not to contact the families, inevitably some did. Cars sat outside family homes with cameras focused and primed for action at a moment's notice, though they were assured that no one would be saying or doing anything. A relative leaving his house was told by a voice from within a waiting pack of reporters, 'If you don't give us a quote we'll just print what we like!'

Inside the homes of the bereaved, phones were constantly ringing, and every relative felt they had to pick up, because if they didn't they might miss something important. They were in a constant state of waiting for any scrap of news, their emotions unable to cope with delay; they had to know as soon as there was anything to know, and so lifted the phone at its first ring, just in case.

They tried not to read the newspapers, but those who did passed on their outrage at some of the coverage and, inevitably, it got back to those it would hurt most. One newspaper printed a diagram of the *Wanderer* on the seabed, split in two by the impact, and the missing crewman, Sorley Og, floating off into the distance; possibly, it was said, never to be found. The wreck had been found and divers had gone down to examine it very quickly on that terrible Sunday, reporting back that the *Wanderer* was intact apart from damage to the bow. This information had been released to the media, so it had been perfectly clear from the outset that she had been holed, not broken in two. There was, therefore, no possibility of a body floating off into the distance. No one in Acarsaid could understand the need to suggest anything so deeply hurtful, the thing was offensive, and from then on their blank looks when approached by anyone from the press were replaced with abuse.

While arrangements were being made to return the crew of the *Wanderer*, or those who had been found, their funerals were being planned in Acarsaid. Again it was Dougie who took the lead, anxious to have the whole awful experience pass off as smoothly as possible for his sister and the others. The two engineers, Stevie and Eric, would be buried in Fife and Glasgow at the request of their families, and Sorley Mor, Stamp and young Pete in Acarsaid. The families wanted to attend every burial, so they would be carefully co-ordinated, starting with the skipper's first. It was agreed that the relief crew, the men who filled in when a regular crewman was away for some reason, or when more men were needed in the busy seasons, would carry every coffin. From Gannet there had come a measured intervention.

'I want to carry the lads,' he said, as the details were being gone over with Chrissie and the others.

'Don't be daft!' Chrissie replied.

'I want to,' Gannet repeated quietly.

Chrissie looked at Father Mick and Dougie.

'Gannet, son,' she said gently. 'You've got your arm in a sling.'

'I'll take it off,' Gannet said simply, 'and I can carry them on my other shoulder anyway.'

In normal circumstances Chrissie would now have threatened violence, but she knew what was in the big man's mind.

'Sorley Mor wouldn't expect this of you,' she said. 'Neither would the others. You won't be letting him or them down just because you couldn't do it.'

'Aye, I would,' Gannet said, 'and I'd be letting myself down too.'

'But you'll be all off-balance and it'll still hurt.'

'Gavin can give me something so that I can't feel it. If I can't feel it I won't be off-balance.'

The Chrissie of old, of one short week ago, emerged.

'But think what a balls-up you'll make of it if you find halfway through that you can't do it,' she protested. 'What do you think Sorley Mor would feel about that, you great silly sod?'

Gannet shrugged his one good shoulder. 'He'd probably have a damned good laugh at me,' he smiled. 'So what is there to lose?'

The following Saturday, six long days and nights after the sinking, a convoy of three grey hearses drove slowly towards

Acarsaid, holding up the traffic. It was a changeover weekend, when one holiday fortnight finished and the next began, so traffic was heavier than normal, but those going to the village were, in the main, those who – rightly or wrongly – felt a sense of belonging, and so had taken note of the tragedy. On the long, twisting road that led eventually to the new road, not one car attempted to overtake the hearses. Everyone sat respectfully behind the cortège and saw Sorley Mor, Stamp and Pete brought home for the last time.

The following day came news that Sorley Og's body had been found. Sorley Mor had been fully dressed and near to the wheelhouse because he had, as Gannet had stated, been on lookout. The others had been partly dressed and either in their cabins or just outside. They hadn't found Sorley Og in either place, because he was aft, looking at a pump. He, too, was fully dressed, ready to take over from his father as lookout. Before he flew off to identify his brother-in-law, Dougie went to MacEwan's Row to tell Rose and Chrissie. Rose was still by the big window, she had rarely left her usual vantage point for a moment in the last week. She looked up as Dougie came in. 'They've found him,' he said. Rose walked over to her brother, put her arms round him and hugged him, as though he had given her a gift.

It was a bad week to be in Acarsaid, for locals and visitors alike. The villagers were civil, they attended to the needs of the tourists, but they were preoccupied and subdued, and the tourists felt in the way. There were to be funerals every day, either in Acarsaid or in Fife and Glasgow, and notices were posted on shop doors announcing that they would not open as a mark of respect. As Acarsaid closed around itself to bury its dead, most of the visitors did the decent thing and took themselves elsewhere until it was over, but the press remained.

In the chapel house of Our Lady of the Sea, an hour before Sorley Mor's funeral, Father Mick was trying to pull himself together with little success. Conducting the services of friends was something he had had to do often and was bad enough, but this was different. A disbelieving voice in his head kept repeating 'Sorley Mor? *Sorley Mor?*' He hadn't come to terms with it yet, even the awful reality of the coffin lying in the chapel hadn't helped him do that, and now he was expected to preside over his friend's funeral. In the days since the sinking he had wondered over and over again why Sorley Mor had given him as the emergency contact in case of just such an event, because, as he had said himself, he had been of no use to anyone. He had no comfort to bring because he had none for himself to start with. He felt he had failed everyone. If Dougie hadn't been there, if Dougie hadn't been the man he was, it could have been a shambles, and Sorley Mor and the lads deserved better than that.

'I don't think I can get through this,' he said to Dougie fearfully.

'I told you before, you don't have a choice,' Dougie replied matter-of-factly.

Father Mick nodded. 'I've prepared a speech,' he said, 'and every day I've been going over it, but I haven't managed to get through it out loud once. What happens if I stand there and collapse in front of everyone in an embarrassing sobbing heap?'

'Then you let Sorley Mor down,' Dougie said calmly. 'It's as simple as that, and you can't, can you? It isn't an option: you have to hold yourself together for him.'

'No, I know that. But knowing it and doing it are two separate things.'

'Tell yourself they're not, then,' Dougie suggested. 'Tell yourself they're the same thing.'

'You think it's that simple, do you?' Father Mick asked.

'Aye,' Dougie said cockily. 'You priests, you get money for old rope every day of the week, now you're being asked to earn it and you fall to pieces!'

Father Mick smiled wryly at him. 'When this time's over,

boy,' he said, 'you shall suffer for the way you've treated a servant of God, mark my words! Now go away and leave me alone, I still have some time to go over this.'

At that moment Chrissie was having a similar problem with Rose, who had left her home only once in over a week to see Sorley Mor's coffin be accepted into the chapel in a mercifully brief ceremony the night before.

'I can't do this,' she said helplessly as they were getting ready for the funeral mass.

'You have to, Rose,' Chrissie told her gently, 'because there's nothing else to do.'

Rose's shoulders sank and her whole body sagged dejectedly.

'We have to hold ourselves together till this is over, Rose,' Chrissie said, taking Rose's hands in her own. 'Then we can all fall apart for as long as we need to.'

Rose nodded, her head down. 'How are you managing to keep going?' she asked in wonderment.

'I have to,' Chrissie said quietly, 'for Gannet's sake.' She looked behind her to where the long, thin figure was standing alone. 'Look at him. We all have each other, but he's lost everything.'

A few days earlier Father Mick had asked Gannet how he was managing to bear up so well when he himself felt as if he was dissolving. 'For Chrissie,' he replied. When he had asked Dougie Nicolson what trick he was using to keep control, Dougie had replied, 'For Rose.' So that was how they were all getting through this torturous time: they were all doing it for each other. Now Father Mick had to do it for Sorley Mor. When it came to the funerals of Stamp, Pete and Sorley Og, he would be doing it for Sorley Mor, too, because Sorley Og had trusted him to do it and therefore he had, as Dougie said, no choice.

★   ★   ★

Father Mick made his way to his chapel, glancing around at the crowd, knowing there were more people outside, as there had been when the coffin arrived the evening before. He placed his prepared notes on a shelf in the pulpit and went through the familiar rites: what Chrissie called 'the standing, kneeling and – in your case, Father Hooligan – falling-down bits.' Automatic pilot so far, but with a knot of something else tightening inside him: nerves, apprehension, grief too, probably. Slowly he climbed the steps to the pulpit.

Chrissie and her daughters had decided against Sorley Mor's merits being gone over by a succession of speakers. They wanted this to be a normal, intimate village send-off, or as near as was possible, so everything depended on the little gargoyle in the pulpit. He took out his glasses, cleaned them with the hem of his garment, put them on again, then looked up at the congregation. Then he looked down at his notes, took his glasses off again, cleaned them and put them on once more. From his position standing at the very back, Dougie knew he was playing for time and, as the silence went on and the congregation waited and watched, he wondered if Father Mick could pull this off. 'What the hell do we do if he chickens out?' he was thinking desperately, but just then Father Mick looked up, holding his notes in his left hand.

'I was,' he said, 'going to read this prepared speech. God knows, I've sweated blood over it this last week, trying not to miss anything out. I was going to go over Sorley Mor's strengths, his abilities, pay tribute to his discipline as a skipper, his place in this community. But you all know that every bit as well as I do, so to hell with it. It's garbage, anyway. I can hear him now saying, "I'm damned well worthy of better than that!", and he'd be right. Sorley Mor deserves the best, and what I have here isn't it.' He threw the pages of notes over his shoulder where they scattered on the floor beside Sorley Mor's coffin, as a murmur that was almost a chuckle ran round the chapel. 'I've never seen so many people at one of my services before,' he smiled. 'The skipper would be delighted. He'd never let me forget that he'd pulled a bigger crowd than all the congregations I've ever had put together.'

He stopped for a moment to gather his random thoughts into some sort of order.

'I don't have to tell anyone here what Sorley Mor is like.' He stopped, eyes down. 'Was like,' he corrected himself, and hesitated for a moment, biting his lower lip and taking a deep breath before going on. 'I've never met anyone who disliked him, and if there is someone, somewhere, it's only because they didn't know him. Everyone here knew him, everyone knows what kind of man he was, what kind of skipper he was; which makes this event all the more awful and incomprehensible. On occasions like this I'm supposed to tell you to keep the faith, but I'm not sure I have any left myself, and that's the truth. The rulebook says I should give you the usual hogwash about not questioning God's will, that he moves in mysterious ways, but if I did you would stone me to death and I'd probably throw a few myself. The truth is that if I had this God fellow here right now I'd want a few answers I don't think he could give, then I'd tell him what a bloody fool he was and kick his arse out of my chapel. What happened to Sorley Mor and the lads, to everyone who loves them, to this village, well I refuse to mouthe platitudes, to cover the fact that no loving God would inflict such cruelty. Feel free to quote me on that by the way, the Vatican may well get my dog collar in the post before they can demand it anyway.'

He laughed gently. 'All of us here have our memories of Sorley Mor, so forget the eulogies and just remember your memories, that's what I've been doing these last terrible days. How he hated to be beaten at dominoes and refused to accept it; he always accused the winner of cheating. I always did, of course, but he never worked out how I was doing it, he was too busy trying to cheat himself. How he kept eating Dan's "Ploughman efforts" long after the rest of us had thrown in the towel – thrown up, too, come to that; even Gannet. How he was with a drink in him, that way he got where he couldn't stop laughing, he couldn't have stopped to save himself, and you couldn't help joining in though you had no idea what you were laughing at. The sight of him and Gannet arguing over nothing as they made their way up to MacEwan's Row, Sorley Mor, as ever, a few steps behind. The laughs we all had over the years as he tried to keep Eric's dancing from us. He thought we didn't know because we didn't tell him outright that we did; it was too much fun keeping him guessing. I asked him once why Eric looked so suntanned when he spent all his time in the engine room, and rather than admit it was out of a bottle and for cosmetic purposes, Sorley Mor told me it was because Eric's real father was an Egyptian, but that I wasn't to ask him about it, because he was such a wild big man that even his skipper had no control over him when he was angry. Eric angry: he had as much chance of selling us that one as Eric as a hellraising violent drunk; I never met a gentler soul than Eric.

'He was a terrible liar, Sorley Mor — inventive, but terrible. And he was determined to keep me off his boat. I made a half-hearted attempt to get on board one day when I'd had a drop of the falling-down stuff, and those buggers from *Ivy Ann* and the other boats had taken advantage and egged me on. He stood in front of me, arms crossed, and told me he'd knock me unconscious before he'd let me set foot on the *Wanderer* — for my own good, you understand, not because of any daft superstition. He would have done it, too. There are so many pictures in my mind. Watching him chasing Chrissie around as though he was seventeen, hearing the cheerful insults between them that were a sign of their deep affection. Watching him walk through the harbour exchanging wisecracks, planning trips on helicopters to fish in lochans, until Chrissie found out, of course, and blamed me entirely. It never ceased to amaze me that she knew him so well, she could thwart any ploy before he got it going, but she still managed to believe that someone had led him astray — usually me, for some reason, though I never argued, because she has always scared the hell out of me. He used to call her "a sweet, gentle, wee angel", and I really thought he'd lost it, but then he had had a few, and I'm a firm believer in giving a man who's had a few a bit of leeway. I would ask you to take note of that because I intend to get more legless later than I have ever been, and I'm sure to mortally offend everyone.

'So I'm not going to offer moral guidance here today, I'm not going to insult anyone by telling them that time heals. I don't believe that, though I hope we may all come eventually to a place where we can cope with the grief we're feeling, because I for one am hurting more than I would've thought humanly possible. I have no consoling words, nothing like that to offer, because I can't imagine going through the rest of my life without him either. He was my friend, my fellow-conspirator with Gannet, always with Gannet, in trying to outwit Chrissie, something we never managed. He was my brother in every meaningful sense and I loved him – I still love him, love never dies, and I know his toes will be curling inside that box at this very moment. I can give no comfort on this occasion, if someone has any to spare I'd be glad to receive it. All I can tell you is that we have lost the dearest, the kindest, the best and silliest character any of us will ever encounter.

'Priests and the like are supposed to tell people there's a purpose to everything, but there's no damned purpose to this. Sorley Mor deserved more time and we deserved more time with him, but I have been honoured to have known him and have his friendship, to be cared for by him, even if it far too often amounted to waking up in the back of that bashed old Land Rover of his, covered with a tarpaulin and with no idea where the hell I was. I will miss him every day of whatever time I have left. In that I believe I speak for everyone here today and everyone who ever met him.'

Father Mick stopped and bowed his head, then turned to go. From the back of the chapel came the sound of Dougie clapping, then another pair of hands joined in, and another, till the whole congregation was on its feet applauding. Father Mick looked up, surprised, then smiled and executed a perfect curtsey, and a burst of laughter threatened to raise the roof.

From there Sorley Mor was carried to the cemetery high above Acarsaid, Gannet at the front, his skipper resting on his right shoulder as the entire village followed on foot. From some distance away they were conscious of the press, cameras whirring, watching, but the villagers instinctively arranged themselves to shield the relatives from their gaze and that was all the notice anyone took of them. Chrissie spotted Haffa, Sorley Mor's shovel-leaning cousin, standing to one side, his infamous shovel hidden out sight. He had dug Sorley Mor's grave, as he would the graves for the others, and he knew that relatives didn't always feel comfortable seeing him there as they left in their cars, knowing that he was waiting to perform the final task of throwing shovelfuls of earth onto their loved ones. This day was different because it was Sorley Mor, but all Haffa knew to do was what he always did, avoid eye contact and try to be invisible. Chrissie noticed him straightaway, though, and went up to him, taking him by the arm and making him walk with her.

'How's the knee today, Haffa?' she asked brightly.

'Fine, Chrissie,' he mumbled, 'fine.'

'Good,' she replied, smiling at him. 'So that means you did a good job for Sorley Mor, does it? No ancestors behind the dyke? You know what he always said would happen if you didn't give him his money's worth, don't you?'

At that Haffa broke down and Chrissie hugged him, feeling guilty; she had been trying to make him feel less self-conscious but had upset him instead.

'You come with me,' she said kindly, holding onto his arm. 'I need someone strong to help me. We can help each other.'

23

And so it went on, that awful week. They buried Sorley Mor on Monday, Stamp and Pete on Tuesday, Eric and Stevie on Wednesday, their widows taking centre stage in turn, like some awful grisly dance they were being forced to perform. The relief crew, anxious at first to carry their crewmates, were wearying, their exhaustion not caused by the physical effort but by the emotion of it all. But they wouldn't give up; it was doubly terrible, after all, for the families. On Thursday afternoon Sorley Og came home alone and was taken to Father Mick's chapel.

'I want to see him,' Rose told Dougie.

'You can't,' he told her sharply.

'I want to see him!' she repeated.

'Rose, listen to me,' he said sternly. 'You're a grown woman, old enough to be married and to be widowed, but this is a choice I will not let you make. You will not see him, and that's an end to it.'

'I want to say goodbye to him.'

'Then say it,' Dougie replied. 'Are you telling me that whatever existed between you and Sorley Og depended on your seeing each other?'

Rose looked at him, confused, trying to think of an argument.

'All those times he was away,' Dougie continued, 'you never felt any connection with him? That only happened when you were looking into his eyes?'

'No . . . no . . . I mean . . .'

'Rose, you are a fisherman's wife. Conduct yourself like

one. None of the others asked to look at their men; they showed some dignity. You should be doing the same. There are reasons you shouldn't see him; he's been in the water for the best part of a week. Do I have to draw you a picture?'

Rose winced.

'So behave yourself, behave as he would've wanted you to. I know he wouldn't have wanted you to see him.'

'I still —' she protested.

She wanted to see him because she was still clinging to the illogical hope that it wasn't him. In her mind she had done a deal with fate, she had decided to accept that the others had gone — even Sorley Mor, whom she had adored all of her life — if only there had been a mistake about Sorley Og. It could be someone else, someone they had picked up in Denmark. A stranded fisherman, perhaps, needing a lift home; anyone, as long as it wasn't Sorley Og. She wanted to look into the coffin and say triumphantly, 'It's not him! It's not Sorley Og! Didn't I tell you that all along?' She felt on the edges of madness, all her scenarios bordered on hallucination. She knew Dougie had already seen him and identified him, but if there was any chance, however slight, she wanted to take it. Dougie knew what was going on in her mind, but he also knew it was a stage of grief his sister had to go through. Seeing Sorley Og's body would not help: she would still deny that it was him.

'Rose,' he said, 'when it comes down to it the widow's wish is final, but if you are determined to see him then find a screwdriver and prise the lid off yourself, because I can assure you that no one in this village will do it for you. We all knew him, we all liked him, and on his behalf we will not let you do this to yourself, or to him.'

After Sorley Og had been received into the chapel that Thursday night, Dougie had driven Margo to Rose's house at MacEwan's Row. Margo looked neither comfortable nor uncomfortable, but Rose was sure the visit was Dougie's idea.

'So how are you?' Margo asked briskly. She might have been speaking to an old friend who had been gone from the village for a while – if she'd had any old friends, that was.

'As well as I can be with my husband lying in the chapel up the Brae,' she replied calmly.

Margo looked round. She had always disliked this house, thought it far too grand, as indeed it was. And she had never taken to Sorley Og; everyone knew that.

'This house will be far too big for you now,' she said.

'Yes, well, I think, if you don't mind, Mother, I'll bury my husband before I start thinking of selling the house he built for me. If it's all the same to you, that is,' Rose said curtly. She had found that she was being sharper with people, she didn't know why. Maybe she was being a child, knowing that no one would answer back. She smiled wryly and, looking at her brother, saw an expression of stern disapproval in his eyes. Except Dougie, of course, Dougie would answer back. There was a long silence.

'And money?' Margo asked eventually. 'Things are going to be settled soon?'

Rose turned away and stared silently out of the big window.

'She'll be fine, Mother,' she heard Dougie say in an embarrassed voice. 'I don't think that's something she's given any thought to yet.'

Rose couldn't stand it any longer. 'Dougie, how's Granny Ina?' she asked, ignoring her mother.

'A bit confused, Rose. You know, the way she has been, but a bit more so.'

'Does she know?'

'Aye, she knows.' Dougie smiled sadly. 'She was relieved Gannet hadn't been aboard. You know how she likes him.'

Rose nodded and smiled back. 'Take me up to see her when you drop Mother home,' she said, walking towards the door.

'Unless you'd like to spend a minute with Chrissie first?'

Margo shook her head and Dougie and Rose shared a look.

of what Rose couldn't really say. It wasn't surprise or shock, though paying her respects to Sorley Mor's widow would've been the most natural thing for anyone else to do. It was a look of confirmation, Rose decided, an acknowledgement between brother and sister that their mother wasn't like other people, that she lacked something they had.

Granny Ina was sitting by the lit fire. She was always cold these days, even in the warmth of late June, but she wore no slippers on her feet; her cold 'baries' were preferable to enclosed warm feet. When the old woman saw Rose she suddenly remembered what it was she had forgotten, the something that connected Rose to Dolina. It was the sadness in her eyes – and just as suddenly she remembered why it was there. Once it had been filled with Ella's romanticism, but not now. She made to rise from her chair but Rose stopped her, kneeling beside her and taking the old woman's hands in hers. Tears immediately filled Ina's eyes as she freed a twisted hand and reached forward to stroke her granddaughter's cheek.

'Don't,' Rose said gently. 'It's all right, Granny Ina, I'm all right.'

'But look at you lass. So young and in your widow's weeds!'

Rose put her head in Granny Ina's lap, as she had done so many times during her childhood; it was never her mother she sought out in times of trouble or sadness, she remembered, always her grandmother.

'Why them?' the old woman asked, gently stroking Rose's hair. 'Here I am, no good to anyone, not even myself. I've lived far too long as it is. Why wasn't I taken instead? I'd have gone instead of any one of them, especially your Sorley Og, Rose!'

'I know, I know, Granny Ina,' Rose said, blinking away tears of her own. 'But it doesn't work like that.'

'And young Alison, too, about to have her baby! It's too hard, that's what it is, it's all just too hard to bear! A wee baby just like yourself, Rose, born without a father!' The old woman was weeping, the tears rolling unchecked across the deeply wrinkled, translucent skin of her cheeks. 'And I haven't been to any of the funerals, haven't been to see them and give them a word. What must they be thinking of me? It's these old legs, you see, they won't work.'

'It's all right, Granny Ina, everybody knows things are difficult for you. They know you'd be there if you could,' Rose reassured her. 'No one expects you to be there.'

Granny Ina nodded. 'When it's all over, Rose, will you help me to write a wee note to them all?'

'If that's what you'd like,' Rose smiled, 'but you don't have to. I'll tell them all how you feel.'

'No, no, I'd like to send a note.'

Again Margo was bypassed, Rose noticed; Margo wasn't the kind of person you'd ask these things of.

'And Sorley Mor,' said Granny Ina. 'I just can't take it in. He was the life of the place. How will the village go on without him? How will poor Gannet manage on his own?'

'Chrissie's looking after him,' Rose explained. 'He hurt his shoulder and he's got his arm in a sling, so he can't do very much for himself. That's why he didn't go on the trip.'

'How did that happen?' the old woman asked.

'He fell off the table when he was drunk,' Rose laughed gently. 'Dislocated his shoulder.'

Granny Ina laughed too, then immediately wept again.

'Did no one tell you?'

'Maybe they did,' Granny Ina said. 'These days I don't remember things too clearly. Tell the big man I was asking for him, will you?'

'Of course I will.'

'I've always had a soft spot for Gannet. He's a good man, you know; a better man than he's ever known.'

'You really do have a soft spot for him if you think that,' Rose teased her.

'He's always made me laugh.' Granny Ina nodded, managing

a short smile. 'And Chrissie and her lassies as well?' she said anxiously. 'You'll tell Chrissie and her lassies too?'

'And Chrissie and her lassies as well,' Rose smiled.

They buried Sorley Og beside his father that Friday. Once again Father Mick spoke from the heart about the boy he had known all his life, the boy he had christened. He had hoped that after marrying him to Rose little more than a year ago that he would in due course christen Sorley Og's bairns. Father Mick smiled sadly.

'He made me stay sober on his wedding day, then said he wasn't sure it had been a good idea after all, that he hadn't realised till then that he'd never seen me without one in me before and he wasn't sure he liked me after all.' The congregation laughed quietly. 'He even made me shave with an electric razor so that I wouldn't look like a tinker,' he said with a sad smile, 'but he also brought me a half-bottle of the precious Islay Mist, so his heart was in the right place, as I always knew. This week I have presided at the funeral rites of my dearest friends, my family, dearer than my own blood relatives. Watching Sorley Og growing up all these years, so like his father, I often regretted I would never have a son like him. Priestly vows of chastity are stupid, if you want my honest opinion, but I gave up any hopes of being Pope years ago, so it doesn't matter if anyone quotes me. I used to tell Sorley Og that I thought priests should be allowed to marry and he'd say, "What are you talking about? Nothing of woman born would ever have anything to do with you anyway!" It was his favourite insult. He paid me the great compliment of cheeking me as if I was his father, not his priest, and every time I looked at him he made me wish I could have been a real father instead of just a professional one. That's what he was, the son I never had, and I never told him. I should have, but I thought I would have years and years to embarrass him with shows of affection. Now I'll always regret that I didn't tell him, and I can see Gannet, his other father, nodding his head in agreement.' He paused for a long moment.

'I've used many words this week to say the same thing,' he told the mourners wearily, 'but I don't think I have done any of the lads justice. They deserve better than I've been able to give; my only excuse is that they are too close to me and I'm in too much pain myself to give them farewells full of eloquence and word imagery. I can think of little to add: like everyone here I just want to get today over to find out if I can face tomorrow, and all the tomorrows without them. What else is there to say? That we loved these men, that what happened to them wasn't fair, that we wish there was some court of appeal to reverse the tragedy that befell them, that befell all of us, and that we will miss them forever. If I have left gaps you must fill them in by yourselves, though I believe I have said nothing but the truth.

'When the decision was taken earlier this year to get out of the fishing and sell the boat, Sorley Mor said to me that it would be the last *Wanderer*. I told him at the time that he wasn't strictly correct. The MacEwan boats were called *Ocean Wanderer* because the name Sorley meant Summer Wanderer so, even though the boat had gone from Acarsaid and the fishing industry beyond, there would still be Wanderers here, because we would still have Sorleys. Now we are here today to bury the last Sorley, the last Wanderer; maybe I shouldn't have tempted fate – and you can just hear Sorley Mor chiding me about being an old sweetie wife, can't you? On the wall of Sorley Mor's home and in the wheelhouse of *Ocean Wanderer* there was a framed quote called "The Sea", a warning that there should be no error in the ships and the men who sailed in them, that we should send only our best or the sea would punish us. Sorley Mor loved it because he had such a healthy respect for the sea. He was of the opinion that it owed us nothing, and that those who earned their living on it must be on their mettle at all times. Well, we sent our best; we sent a boat and men with no error, and look what happened.

I can't explain that, I can't understand it, I only wish I could.

'When Sorley Og married Rose last year you were all here and saw the boy kissing me. All I can say now, as I have the painful task for all of us of sending him to a premature grave at such a ridiculously young age, is, "Go to rest, my boy, my beloved son, as we return the compliment; all of our love and our kisses go with you."'

For Rose it was more unreal than when the whole saga had begun less than two weeks before. Something told her that every day would bring more reality to an unbelievable situation, but it hadn't; if anything every day was more bizarre. Her only request had been that Gavin, Sorley Og's best friend, and her brother, Dougie, help to carry Sorley Og's coffin. She knew Dougie had done so much for everyone and that he still felt some guilt at what had happened to his friendship with Sorley Og over the wedding: it was her way of making amends and of letting Dougie make his. Dougie had simply nodded his head when she suggested it, but as he took the weight of the coffin to carry Sorley Og out of the chapel, he whispered a request to the others to stop for a moment, because tears were hampering his vision and he had to regain some control to continue. It was only the second time Rose had ever seen him cry, and both times were for Sorley Og. Rose looked at Father Mick, who stepped forward, patted Dougie's shoulder gently and whispered in his ear, 'I meant to say, boy, do you have your umbrella with you today? Those damned pigs will be circling outside!' Dougie smiled, straightened up and walked on with the others.

Rose sailed through it all, barely thinking, barely taking notice. Going down the aisle she couldn't stop recalling her wedding day, but this time there were gaps, she realised, as she looked without intending to at the places where the crew had been. Stamp and Molly had been there; she wished now more than ever that she had stopped to hug Stamp that day. Eric and Marilyn had stood here, looking unnaturally theatrical beside Pete and Alison, who would marry here six short months later. She looked down, trying not to exchange glances with the congregation.

She passed her mother and, looking her straight in the eye, wondered how she could be so impassive. Margo had made no attempt of her own to be with Rose since this had happened – not that Rose wanted or expected her to, but it still seemed strange. And there were Sally and Alan, his face showing the grief he was feeling for his dancing cousin, and feeling responsible, she knew, because he had brought Eric to Acarsaid and to *Ocean Wanderer*. Like everyone else his mind would be full of so many torturous 'what ifs' and 'if onlys'. Remembering how she hadn't hugged Stamp on her wedding day, she stopped briefly and hugged Alan before following the cortège out.

At the cemetery the widows held hands, once again shielded from the media pack, and then it was over, though in other ways only just beginning. That evening she refused all invitations and offers of company and sat in darkness by the window in her own home, as she had done so often. Here she was, the end house on the end of MacEwan's Row on the end of a road that was itself an acknowledged dead end; fitting, she thought, as she was contemplating the end of her life. Nothing mattered any longer; life was meaningless. In the background the phone kept ringing. As the answer-machine picked up each call she would hear little one-sided conversations taking place in the distance. Dougie had been right; the press had all the information they needed, but they still wanted something extra, and the more the families ignored the calls, the more calls came. As the phone rang again she moved to the machine and listened.

'Mrs MacEwan,' said a strange male voice, 'I'm from the –'

Suddenly enraged, Rose picked up the receiver. 'What do you want?' she shouted angrily. 'Tell me, in God's name what is it that you want?'

There was a pause. 'I've been told by my editor to ask if you'll do an interview, Mrs MacEwan,' the voice said.

'That doesn't answer my question!' Rose shouted shrilly. 'What is it that you actually *want*? Not just you, but all of you. Tell me, please, because I honestly don't know!'

The voice paused again and she heard a sigh. 'To be perfectly honest, Mrs MacEwan, I don't know what the hell we want. Oh, I know what, I suppose, but not why.'

'Well, tell me what you do know, then.'

'We want you to cry, Mrs MacEwan, that's the bottom line.'

'And you think I haven't?'

'We want a picture of you showing all your distress for the edification of the entire nation, that's what we want.'

'Why?'

'In the hope that a pathetic, heart-tugging picture or two will entice people who don't normally do so to buy our paper, then our transiently interested readers can view it over their breakfasts before they move on to the crossword. But why, now that's what I don't know,' said the man wearily. 'I'm passing on the request because I've been told to and I have a mortgage and a family to keep, and if I don't do it, someone else will. Lousy reasons, but they're the only ones I have.'

Rose didn't reply at first. 'Look, Mr whoever you are, and don't tell me, I don't want to know. I'm standing here in the dark trying to work out if I'll go on living, because everything I had to live for has gone. If I had something to end it with at this moment, I would. Can you understand that? What possible difference could that make to anyone outside Acarsaid?'

'None. They'd read it, feel sorry in a kind of detached way, and that would be that.'

'So why are you here? It keeps coming back to that. Haven't you seen enough shock and grief in this village to fill all the column inches you need?'

'Yes, and more on top,' said the man. 'The whole thing is cruel and sick, you're absolutely right. I've been here since the news broke, I know how much we've intruded on the relatives and the village; not even a journalist could be left in any doubt about how this place has been affected. We're only talking about six·men, but given the reaction it seems like a hundred. It's as if the village had been wiped out. Maybe that's what keeps us here: the grief is tangible and, to put it bluntly, it makes good copy. Anyone who gets you to say what you've just said would get a pat on the back because, as I say, it might sell a few more papers, especially if we get a photo of you looking grief-stricken. That's how it works.'

'They were special men,' Rose protested. 'That's why the village is the way it is.'

'I know they were, they always are, but here more than most, for some reason.'

'But you're only interested in multiples, aren't you? If it had been one man you wouldn't have bothered. It has to be a group before you take any notice,' she said bitterly. 'Men die in the fishing every day with barely a mention, but their deaths are every bit as valid as the deaths of our men.'

'You're right, I'm not denying it, and it makes no sense to me either. With respect, Mrs MacEwan, no one outside the fishing industry will care one way or the other about the *Wanderer* and her crew. As for people living in the cities, they won't remember the boat's name in six months' time. They'll read about it in their morning papers, then turn the page and never give it another thought.'

'So why are you here, pestering us like this?'

'Damned if I know,' the man said sadly. 'It makes no sense, but this is how these events have been covered over the years, and so it still goes on, mindlessly.' There was a long silence. 'Mrs MacEwan,' he said eventually, 'I've passed on the crass request I was asked to pass on, and you've declined. That's official, OK? As far as I'm concerned, the matter's ended, and everything we've said is off the record. I won't be pestering you again, but please take my advice: do not be tempted to lift the phone again. However angry you feel, and you have every right to feel it, leave the answer-machine on and ignore

341

everything that isn't family. Don't react again, because in their minds you've cracked and they'll never leave you alone once they've done that to you. We'll all go away, we have short attention spans, something else will come along in your place.'

'If this story is important enough to have you all camped out here for weeks, watching our every move, you would go that easily?' Rose asked.

'That's how it is, Mrs MacEwan,' said the voice. 'You're not important, the story isn't important, other than because it might sell a few more newspapers, and I'm not convinced about that. Some other human tragedy will come along in a few days that might sell even more papers, and we'll desert you and sit outside someone else's door.'

'It's not much of a job, is it?'

'You're probably right,' the voice laughed quietly, 'but neither is fishing. Why the hell they do it I don't know. Harassing decent human beings might not be the finest occupation a man can have, but it beats being drowned at sea fishing for pet food, don't you think?' The voice paused. 'I'm sorry; I didn't mean that as it probably sounded. I just mean that it's been such a waste. We've been sitting here watching your lives, your community fall apart, and we've all been saying the same thing: what a lousy bloody reason to lose your life.'

'I know what you mean,' Rose said. 'It wasn't quite that simple, but that's what it comes down to. They go out there to catch fish, for human or animal consumption, it really doesn't matter which, and they die doing it. It's so . . . so . . .'

'Disproportionate,' the voice supplied.

'Yes, I suppose that's it. Do you have any connection with the fishing?' she asked.

The voice laughed. 'No, but I grew up with a mother who always thought about the fishermen on stormy nights, and argued with people who complained about the price of fish. I'd stand beside her in fish shops in the heart of the city and cringe, knowing she would pick up on the slightest complaint and tell everyone within earshot that the real cost was the lives of the men who went out in all weathers to catch our supper. She had no connection with the fishing either, she never travelled out of Glasgow in her entire life, but she always fought the fishermen's corner. I've no idea why she felt so strongly. Maybe she'd read about a sinking once in a newspaper and it had stuck with her,' he chuckled softly, 'or maybe I'm making excuses because I feel guilty at annoying you. Anyway, she passed a little of it on. The things you retain from childhood, I suppose. They do say you never forget what you take in with your mother's milk.' He sighed. 'Now, do as I told you, don't answer any more phone calls. OK?'

'OK, and . . . and thank you,' Rose said uncertainly. 'I . . . I don't even know your name.'

'As you said, you don't want to, it isn't important.'

'Where exactly are you?'

'Sitting on your doorstep, where else? But I'm going now and I promise you I won't be back. All the best, Mrs MacEwan. My sincere condolences for your loss. Goodbye.'

Rose replaced the receiver, quickly crossed to the front door, and opened it just in time to see a car pulling away in the light summer darkness, an anonymous arm waving a slow farewell from the driver's window.

24

In the aftermath of losing *Ocean Wanderer* and her crew, Acarsaid withdrew into itself, trying to adapt, to redraw the map of village life, of its own world, much as Rose and the other widows and families were trying to do. What made this doubly difficult was that the people who had gone were so much part of the place's identity. While Sorley Mor was alive the possibility of losing him would never have entered the villagers' collective consciousness, because it was truly unthinkable. It was only after the sinking that they would look at each other and say, 'You know, I can't think of anything as bad as this, can you?' and exchange sad, shocked shakes of the head.

He would have gone in the fullness of time, of course, but he would have done so gradually, as old Ina Hamilton was doing. As the years went on, some of the villagers would have looked at him and perhaps mentioned that Sorley Mor was getting on a bit, that he was driving or, more likely, getting Sorley Og to drive him and Gannet to MacEwan's Row from the Inn, because the long hike up was becoming too much for them. They would have looked at the pair of them and smiled at the memory of them in their prime, slightly unsteady on their feet and arguing as they went along, the skipper accusing his first mate of treason, mutiny, or anything else he could think of, for disagreeing with him or reminding him of past misdemeanours he wished not to remember. And the older ones would have told the younger ones that they would never see a skipper like him in their lifetime, a man who liked the odd drink ashore, who loved to laugh, who was a decent man; but how once aboard *Ocean Wanderer* there was no stricter skipper; no man ever took the sea more seriously than Sorley Mor.

And then there would have been a slow and, hopefully, long decline as he and Gannet became old men, then older men, then passed on into village history and mythology. By the time they were no longer to the fore of village life, though, others would have taken a greater part. It was as natural and inevitable as the tides ebbing and flowing, so that their passing would be a sad event, but part of the natural order. Sorley Og would have become Sorley Mor, and he and Rose would have had their own Sorley to attach 'Og' to. The torch would have been passed on, and the villagers would have looked at the boy and remarked on how like his grandfather he was, even if he wasn't.

Stories would always be told about the departed Sorley Mor: that was how the memory of a respected, loved, village character would be handled, how the village would close around their loss; first by healing, then by scarring. This, however, was different. It wasn't just the loss of the boat and a popular crew that the villagers were grieving for; it was the loss of that natural progression and future too.

In those first weeks there was no talk about Sorley Mor and his exploits: the wound was too raw yet for healing to begin. Instead there was a painful void, a feeling that things could never be the same again, that Acarsaid had changed forever. It had been too quick, too brutal and too complete. Not only had the skipper gone, but the entire crew covering at least two generations, the people as strongly associated with him as his own family. Some of them would have outlived him had the natural order been preserved, thereby softening the blow when it eventually came. Because they were part of Sorley Mor, they would have led the recounting of tales and the gentle laughter; having them there with their direct link would have been like still having something of Sorley Mor with them. Even worse, Sorley Og had gone, too, his only son, so there would never be another Sorley MacEwan. As Father Mick had said, they had truly seen the passing of the last Wanderer.

Then there were the widows' situations; it was all too hard to dwell on. Who could think of Chrissie without Sorley Mor, Molly without Stamp? Perhaps worst of all, the two younger women: Rose, whose own father had died on a fishing boat before her birth, and Alison, carrying Pete's baby, a child who would grow up in the same way. The villagers counted themselves lucky that the widows of the two engineers, Eric and Stevie, lived too far away from Acarsaid for the sight of the two women to pain them every day; but then they immediately felt guilty, felt like cowards. The grief of Marilyn in Glasgow and Jean in Fife wasn't any less than the distress of the Acarsaid widows; the villagers knew that. They just felt that they had enough to bear at home.

So life in Acarsaid went on in a kind of painful fog, a life that had contracted and dimmed. Where once people looked at where the *Wanderer* berthed and wondered aloud when she was next due home, now they looked away again and tried to turn their minds to other matters. Even in the Inn, that usual hive of banter and noise, the atmosphere was subdued. Men still dropped in, but not for long and not for much, and the dominoes in the corner where Sorley Mor had contested every move and denied every defeat lay silent, edited out of the traditional life of the Inn. It was as though the entire village and its inhabitants had contracted a sudden and debilitating illness for which there was no cure.

Dan, really Donald, maker of 'Ploughman efforts' and brother of Stamp, who was also really Donald, had just settled an argument between two regulars by throwing them both out and banning them for life. He looked around the Inn.

'What the hell is happening here?' he demanded of no one in particular. 'The atmosphere in this place is bloody awful these days. I've never known so many disagreements. I spend all my times sorting people out.'

'People are a bit down, that's all it is,' shrugged Duncan, skipper of *Southern Star*.

'I know,' Dan sighed. 'Do you think we'll ever recover from this?'

Duncan looked up at him, then back at his pint. He shook his head. 'No,' he replied quietly.

'What? Never?' Dan said in a distant, bemused tone.

'Never,' Duncan said. He drained his glass and left.

At MacEwan's Row at the same time, Father Mick was with Chrissie and Gannet, trying to find a way through the terrible, heavy, painful fog.

'Have you seen some of the newspapers?' he asked, and Gannet shook his head.

'I kept a few,' the priest said. 'Look at this one.'

Gannet looked at him sharply and turned his head away.

'No, no, Gannet,' the priest said gently. 'Not those ones. These have photos of Eric. Look, in full dancing trim!'

He unfolded the newspaper clippings he had carefully cut away from the more offensive accounts of the sinking, and there was Eric in all his finery. Gannet looked and laughed quietly. Eric in his tailed coat, white dickie and patent dancing shoes, his beard shorn and his thick, curly hair slicked back, competing in some Old Time event. Eric in his Latin-American reincarnation, wearing a tight catsuit covered in sequins, his hair now caught back in a ponytail, a dangerous expression on his face; Gannet noticed that his 'bits' had indeed been reined in, the elastic drawers really did exactly what he said they would.

'Can you imagine Sorley Mor's face if he'd seen these?' Father Mick smiled. 'The stories he'd have come up with to try to talk this evidence away?'

'He'd say it wasn't Eric,' Gannet smiled. 'He'd say it was a trick done with the camera, that one of the others had got somebody to do it just to annoy him. He'd . . .' Then Gannet stopped and ran from the house, leaving the clippings in his wake.

Chrissie looked fearfully at Father Mick and tried to stop him going after him.

'Chrissie MacEwan,' said the priest with exaggerated patience, 'I've never answered back to you before, but I'm going to do so now. This is between men, you know nothing about such matters.' He was disappointed that she didn't reply 'Bollocks', and wrestle him to his seat again; if she had it would have meant life was going on in some way, however small. He followed Gannet outside to the wall overlooking the harbour.

'Gannet,' he said heavily, 'we must get out of where we are now. This is a bad place, a place we needed to be in for a time, but one we must move on from.'

'That's easy to say,' Gannet smiled sadly, 'but not easy to do.'

'I said something similar to young Dougie,' Father Mick smiled. 'He told me to pretend thinking and doing were exactly the same. Where would we have been without that lad's logic?' He smiled. 'And besides, Gannet, who said it would be easy? We've lost more than any mortals should be expected to bear; who said it *should* be easy? That doesn't mean we have to set up camp in this desperate place.' His words ran out and there was a silence. 'Do you think if the tables had been reversed and you'd gone down with the boat in his place, that he'd be standing here feeling like giving in?'

Gannet turned and looked the priest in the eye. 'Aye,' he said firmly, 'he would.'

Father Mick looked away. It had been a silly question, a ploy he used on bereaved parishioners all the time, but one he should have known better not to pose in this situation. 'I'm sorry about that, Gannet,' he said, 'it was crass, and you're right. He'd be exactly as you are today. I'd be saying the same useless bloody things to him, too, and he'd be reacting in the way you are doing. All I'm trying to say is that there are others to think of, particularly those he would expect you to think of, Chrissie and Rose.'

Gannet nodded. 'And you think I don't know that?'

Across in Rose and Sorley Og's house there was silence. Rose felt adrift from all life, especially her own. She didn't know who she was any longer. Once she had been Sorley Og's wife, about to start a new life, about to start a family, and now there was – well, there was nothing. There was no routine, no pattern to her days and especially her nights, no reason to eat, or sleep, or move, no reason to live. She was in a long tunnel of nothing and the only sensation she felt was pain. She hurt everywhere, every joint and every muscle, that was the only reality she knew. Days merged into night just because they did, and darkness didn't mean turning on a light; anyway, she preferred darkness. Sometimes her brother or Chrissie would bring her food she didn't want and didn't eat; she didn't want them in the house come to that, because they disturbed her pain and if pain was all she had left to connect her to Sorley Og, then she wanted it undiluted, undisturbed, all to herself. She treated their gentle hints as insults. Life did not have to go on, not if she didn't want it to, and she didn't. Fresh air would not be good for her, neither would company. What would be good for her was if they would just go away and leave her alone. Chrissie was so concerned about her daughter-in-law that she called Father Mick, Dougie and Gavin to her house.

'I'm really worried about her,' Chrissie told them. 'I take her over a bowl of soup and next day it's still lying there, untouched. I go over to collect it and she's sitting by the window, exactly where she was when I left her the day before. She doesn't even look up, far less say a word.'

'She's the same with me,' Dougie said quietly.

'What about your mother, son?' Chrissie asked. 'I'm not criticising, but I'd have thought she might spend some time with the lassie. After all, she lost her own man at sea, she should know how that feels.'

'My mother's not really like that,' Dougie replied uncomfortably. 'Granny Ina is, or was, but she's not keeping too well herself. She's not fit to look after Rose.'

'Well, what about Sally? She only lives doors away,' Father Mick asked.

Dougie shook his head. 'She wouldn't let Sally in the door,' he smiled sadly. 'It was something she said about Rose and Sorley Og getting married.'

'But surely all that's forgotten at a time like this?' Chrissie said, aghast.

'Not as far as Rose is concerned,' he said, '*especially* at a time like this.' He looked at Chrissie. 'We all said things then,' he said, 'and Sorley Og didn't really understand. That's what Rose holds against us all, that we hurt him, not that we said what we said. It was this kind of thing we wanted to protect her against, we weren't objecting to Sorley Og –'

'Sure, I know that, Dougie,' Chrissie said kindly. 'You didn't want Rose to be a fisherman's widow, there's nothing wrong with that.'

'But we must've put it badly,' Dougie said, his eyes filling. 'I grew up with Sorley Og, I never knew a finer man. I told Rose that when she said they were getting married. I just wanted her to have a better life than as the wife of a fisherman, or the widow of one, even Sorley Og.'

'You don't have to explain, Dougie,' Chrissie smiled. 'If I'd ever thought you were putting my son down I'd have had a word in your ear with my fist, you know that. I knew why you objected.'

'All the times afterwards,' Dougie said, 'when Sorley Og came into the office to talk business, I always wanted to say I'd got it wrong, that he'd made Rose happy and I knew now that was all that counted, but I could never say it somehow.'

'Bloody men!' Chrissie pretended to explode in something of her normal style.

350

Dougie looked up at her and smiled, nodding his head. 'Aye, that was it,' he said, 'that was it exactly. There was always a barrier between us that I should've broken through, but I didn't, and I'll regret that for the rest of my life. He was my brother-in-law by then, we should've been closer, but we never got past the fact that I hadn't wanted him to marry my sister.'

Gannet, who was sitting listening to the conversation, spoke up. 'It's all right, Dougie,' he said quietly, 'these things happen in life. We're all struggling with guilt, the place is awash with it. I made the skipper go on that last trip. He didn't want to go to sea without me, he'd never been without me in his entire life, but I made him go. I know it's stupid, but I can't get that out of my head.'

'Have you been drinking on the quiet?' Chrissie demanded.

Gannet smiled and looked down. His arm was still resting in a sling and over the last few weeks, he'd developed a habit of fiddling with the material to distract himself, pulling one thread out after another.

'He's right, though,' Chrissie told Dougie. 'I feel the same. I keep going over it in my mind. I insisted that Sorley Mor should go, too; practically threw him out the door. If he hadn't gone he wouldn't have been on lookout; if he hadn't been on lookout maybe Sorley Og would've been and maybe none of it would have happened.'

'That's silly,' said Father Mick.

'So who asked you, Hooligan?' she demanded.

'And he shouldn't have gone,' Gavin said quietly. 'I told him when he came to see me, but I should've been firmer, I should've stopped him.'

'When he came to see you?' Chrissie asked, looking up sharply.

Gavin squirmed. 'Well, he didn't so much come to see me as ambush me on the road a few weeks before the *Wanderer* went out on the last trip. I was on my way back from seeing a patient in Keppaig, and he and Gannet were coming in the opposite direction in the Land Rover. Just past Sandy Bay it was, and he stopped me by executing the first part of a three-point turn and blocking my way.'

'Ah, yes,' Father Mick chuckled. 'He was the devil of a man with those three-point turns. The first part, anyway: never knew anyone do that first part better!'

'Shut up, you,' Chrissie seethed. 'This isn't funny. Go on, Gavin.'

'He climbed into the Range Rover beside me, said he thought his indigestion was getting worse, or that Dan's cooking was – couldn't make up his mind which it was. Or maybe that the old Milk of Magnesia wasn't working as well these days. Said he was a bit short of breath at times, too, especially when he was climbing back up to the Row with Gannet. Thought it was either down to the heaviness of Dan's cooking as well, or to Gannet making him talk too much after he'd eaten Dan's cooking, and asked if could I give him something to sort it out.'

Gannet nodded without looking up.

'You knew this?' Chrissie demanded, catching the movement.

Gannet nodded again, still playing with the sling material. 'Well, I could hardly not know, I was there,' he said.

Chrissie reached forward and tightly gripped his hand. 'What have I told you about pulling those threads out?' she demanded, like a mother to a child. 'You'll be left with nothing but a single thread the way you're going on.' She looked back at Gavin. 'What happened?' she asked.

'I told him it might not be indigestion, it might be his heart,' he shrugged guiltily, trying to avoid Chrissie's gaze. 'I said I'd arrange some tests in the hospital and he said if I wasn't having him on he'd rather go somewhere well away from Acarsaid, so I wrote off to Glasgow. I was waiting for word back when . . .'

Chrissie stare turned to a glare. 'And you didn't tell me!' she accused. 'How could you do that?'

No one said anything.

'I asked you a question, Gavin. You knew he was ill and you didn't tell me. Why?'

'Chrissie, I didn't *know* he was ill, and I couldn't tell you,' he said quietly. 'He didn't want you to know, he didn't believe there was anything wrong with him apart from indigestion, and he only stopped me on the road because his old standby wasn't working as well as it had.'

'You should've told me!' Chrissie shouted angrily.

Father Mick cowered in his chair, but still felt quietly elated; this was Chrissie of old.

'I couldn't tell you,' Gavin tried to explain. 'Chrissie, there's such a thing as patient confidentiality, even here. It's much harder working in a place you've grown up in, especially a small place like this where the patients are part of your private life too. I had to respect his wishes.'

'I can't believe he didn't tell me himself,' Chrissie said quietly in an amazed, hurt tone. 'All these years together. I thought we were close, but he kept this from me! How could he do that to me?'

'He didn't want you upset for nothing,' Gannet said.

Chrissie spun round, suddenly reminded that he was part of this treachery and advanced on him. 'You knew too!' she shouted. 'His wife was kept in the dark, but you knew, and you didn't tell me either?'

Gannet sighed heavily. 'He said there was no use telling you about something that was probably nothing. He was going to have the tests and if there was something there, well then, that would've been the time to tell you.'

'He was my man!' Chrissie shouted. '*Mine*, Ian Ross, not yours!'

Father Mick now felt uneasy. This was a serious situation; she had called Gannet by his Sunday name. Something told him that hell could have no fury like Chrissie calling Gannet by his Sunday name.

'I can't believe he told you and not me,' Chrissie continued weakly. 'I just can't. What was I to him then, if he couldn't even tell me he was ill?'

'You were everything to him, can you not see that, woman?' Gannet asked angrily. 'He didn't tell you because there was nothing to tell, he was saving you worry.'

'It was my place to be worried, not yours!' Chrissie rounded on him.

'Well, I wasn't worried. I didn't believe for a minute that there was anything wrong. He'd had that odd stomach all the years I can remember; that's all I thought it was, just like him. He was right not to tell you! Look at the state you've got yourself into now. Think what you would've been like if you'd known, and likely for nothing, too!'

'And don't you ever call me "woman". Only one man ever –' She looked at the empty corner of the room where Sorley Mor used to sit and put her hands over her face.

For the first time since the house had been built, the big sitting room seemed filled to capacity – with a taut silence. Eventually Father Mick spoke.

'Chrissie, you have to look at it from Sorley Mor's point of view.'

'Oh, aye, you were always good at looking at things from his point of view!' she returned fiercely.

'Listen, Chrissie,' Father Mick tried again. 'If he had come home and told you that Gavin had suggested there might be something wrong with his heart and he needed tests, what would you have done?'

'I wouldn't have let him go on that trip,' she said firmly.

'Exactly,' Father Mick replied. 'But it would've gone further than that, wouldn't it?'

Chrissie looked at him suspiciously.

He put a hand up – either to silence her or to stop her if she chose to charge at him; he wasn't sure which. 'What about his trips to the Inn?'

'I'd have stopped them!'

'And you think you could have?' Father Mick asked kindly.

'And if you had managed it, what then? He'd have sat about the house all day, taking it easy?'

'Aye!'

'And suppose the tests had showed he had something wrong with his heart. You'd have kept him sitting quietly in the corner, too?'

'Of course I would!'

'And that's the Sorley Mor you knew, Chrissie?' he asked. 'Content to live out what was left of his life sitting quietly in the corner without a dram, without a bit of a laugh with the lads, just with the thought that he was too feeble ever to go to sea again? Wouldn't he have escaped time and time again – because he was who he was – leaving you worried sick the whole time in case he dropped dead walking back home again? You know perfectly well that even you couldn't have stopped him living life the way he lived it, and all that time you'd have been a nervous wreck, wouldn't you?'

Chrissie said nothing.

'Isn't that so, Chrissie?' Father Mick persisted.

Chrissie said nothing but she continued to glare at them, her anger and contempt searing them to the bone.

'There was nothing certain about it, Chrissie,' Gavin said gently. 'I knew his father had died young of a heart attack, so did his uncle at Black Rock. I was just trying to be as careful doing my job on land as he was at sea. Maybe all Sorley Mor had was indigestion; maybe it was a case of an active man getting older, not working as often and eating too many of Dan's Ploughman efforts. I just wanted to be sure I wasn't missing something because he was Sorley Mor and I grew up convinced he was invincible.'

'The man was doing you a kindness,' Gannet muttered.

'You be quiet,' Chrissie said viciously. 'You at least should have told me. There was no patient confidentiality where you were concerned, you viper!'

'And what would you have me do?' Gannet demanded in a loud voice that startled everyone. 'He made me promise to

355

keep it to myself and I have never broken a promise to him in my life. And is that what you think of me? That I would sneak around behind the skipper's back and report every tiny detail to you, as if he was a daft child? He was a man, for God's sake, and so am I, and it's about time you treated me like one!'

The taut silence continued as Chrissie walked back and forth in her living room, casting glances at the empty corner.

'So,' she said eventually, looking at Gavin. 'Anything else you can tell his next of kin now that he's dead and you're no longer bound by confidentiality?'

Gavin winced. 'I gave him a different antacid, that was actually all he wanted, and told him it was time he put his feet up anyway, that he'd worked long enough. I said the same thing to him in this room the day Gannet hurt his shoulder, if you remember.'

Chrissie looked thoughtful for a moment, then nodded. 'Aye, you did,' she said.

'He didn't believe there was anything wrong,' Gavin smiled. 'As far as he was concerned a trip to Glasgow was just an excuse for him and Gannet to have some fun.'

'No doubt you'd have gone, too,' Chrissie shot at Father Mick. 'The three of you loose in Glasgow. Dear God, what a thought!'

Father Mick chuckled. 'But I have to say in my defence that he told me nothing of this. He probably knew I'd crack under interrogation.'

'I wish he was here right now,' Chrissie said with feeling.

'I know, I know,' Father Mick said soothingly, 'we all wish that.'

'Oh shut up,' Chrissie responded. 'Keep your sanctimonious claptrap for those fools who believe it! I mean, if he was here now, I would give him such an ear-bashing, such a slapping . . . !'

★   ★   ★

356

When the atmosphere returned to normal, Rose's situation was discussed once more. They would have to call on her, it was decided, regardless of how unwelcoming she was, to let her know that life did go on and would go on, regardless of how much she resented it.

'Dougie, you've been great, but we have to face facts, you have to get back to your work. We can't let Rose go on like this. We really have to convince her that there's a life out there waiting for her,' Chrissie said.

'We could maybe use Gannet against her,' Gavin suggested thoughtfully.

Gannet looked at him in total puzzlement. Gavin laughed, then explained what he had in mind.

Before he left MacEwan's Row, Gavin dropped in on Rose. He wanted to talk to her about Gannet, he said, and Rose looked as puzzled as Gannet had.

'He's taking this pretty badly,' Gavin told her.

Rose looked at him ruefully. 'Among others,' she said tartly.

'I'm not minimising what you're going through, Rose,' he said gently, 'we're all hurting, you know. Point a finger at anyone you see passing in this village and I'll guarantee that they're in mourning too. You've no idea how many more people are coming to me, mostly with minor problems that I know could best be treated with a script saying, "Bring them all back."' He sighed. 'Sorley Og was my best friend,' he said sadly. 'I can't imagine never seeing him again either. Sometimes the only way I can cope with that thought is to pretend that he's on a trip and that any day now I'll look up and see the *Wanderer* steaming into harbour fully laden. That gets me through another day, but there's always the next one.'

Rose held her hand up, eyes closed. 'Stop,' she said quietly.

Seconds ticked past. 'So,' she said, eventually, 'about Gannet.'

'I was just wondering if you might try and spend some time with him, that's all.'

'I don't want company,' she replied, 'and I'm really not much good to anyone else at the moment. Perhaps later.'

'Well, maybe you could think about it,' Gavin said conversationally. 'He really has lost everything and everyone. Did you know that on the day Sorley Og was born, Gannet held him in his arms before Sorley Mor did?'

Rose shook her head.

'My father told me about it. Apparently, when he was told he had a son, Sorley Mor was so excited that the first thing he thought of doing was running outside the house and yelling the news down to the harbour, and all the boats sounded their whistles. Then out came Gannet carrying Sorley Og and holding him aloft for everyone to see, with my father and Chrissie yelling at him to bring the baby back inside immediately!'

Rose smiled wanly.

'I'm worried about him, Rose, he needs company.'

'He has Chrissie.'

Gavin smiled. 'And you know Chrissie!' he said. 'The big man needs quiet company, too, Rose. He doesn't need to be poked in the ribs and ordered about *all* the time. He could do with some peaceful companionship as well, and Chrissie doesn't provide too much of that. It makes things worse that his shoulder is still painful at night; it's going to be like that for months. Even with painkillers it's impossible to find a comfortable sleeping position, and he spends more hours than he'll admit wandering about the house or sitting by himself through the night with all that time to brood.'

Rose looked at him suspiciously; he was describing her existence.

'It's one of those Catch 22 situations,' Gavin continued, ignoring her glance. 'He needs sleep so that the shoulder and all the shredded tissue will heal, and he can't sleep until it has healed. Plus, of course, there's what he's going through; what we're all going through.'

Rose didn't answer for a while, then, 'Maybe,' she whispered. 'I'll see.'

25

They were good companions for each other. Shock hits people in different ways, but Sorley Mor would have been shocked himself to see Gannet's reaction to losing him; he had become teetotal. There was no way of knowing if this state would be permanent, but while it lasted Gannet had been forced by circumstances to go against his nature and talk without the benefit of a single drop of the falling-down stuff, and he welcomed the opportunity to withdraw into himself again. Rose, for her part, didn't want to breathe, far less engage in conversation with anyone. Gannet would wander from Chrissie's house to Rose's and back again, and the truth was that the arrangement was doing him as much good as everyone hoped it would do Rose. He too had been drifting since the sinking, unsure of where he belonged, of what part he had to play in any life, his own included.

Gannet had been part of the MacEwan family practically since birth, but now that Sorley Mor was gone he wondered if he was in the way. He wasn't sure what use he was being, and if he wasn't of any use, should he be there at all? Chrissie managed; that was what Chrissie had always done. She also had her daughters and grandbairns to occupy her. But there were times when he knew she looked at him and the memories he evoked were painful for her, so he wasn't sure if he should clear out and let her rebuild her life. Maybe he was hindering the process; as long as he was around there was a link with Sorley Mor, and in a way that bond would have to at least fade before she could go on without him. Rose, on the other hand, needed something. He wasn't quite sure what it was, or if he could be of any use to her either, but they rubbed along together – in silence for the most part – and that suited his needs, too. Having him there forced her into some sort of routine. She had to get up, she had to cook occasionally, and out of politeness she nibbled the odd bit herself, though she had become painfully thin.

As those early weeks after the tragedy were turning into months, pieces of information about the sinking were filtering back and forth. It had been suggested that there was no look-out on *Ocean Wanderer*, and that's what had caused the accident. By maritime law the freighter clearly had right of way and the *Wanderer* had failed to yield. There was no doubt about that: she had kept steaming ahead on her course as though the freighter wasn't there, and the freighter, expecting the *Wanderer* to alter course, had continued on her course too.

'But surely,' said Father Mick to Dougie in the Inn, 'you don't just run a boat down because you have right of way? What sense does that make? You might have the law on your side, but that wouldn't be much good if you went to the bottom of the ocean too.'

'Of course not,' Dougie replied. 'There's more to it than that. The lawyers are involved now, so the truth will go out the window. It's all about money to them, closing every loophole to stop their clients being sued.'

'The important thing is, Father,' said Duncan angrily, 'that Sorley Mor's character is being assassinated here. It isn't possible that there was no lookout on the *Wanderer*. The suggestion is a disgrace. We can't let them get away with that.'

'What is Gannet saying?' Dan asked.

'Not much,' said Dougie. 'I get the feeling that he's angry about it, angry enough to burst, but he's not saying anything.'

'He knows what they're suggesting?' asked Father Mick.

'He predicted it,' said Duncan. 'He said from the start that no one would ever know what happened, that anything we heard would be incomplete because it would come from one side only. There was no one left of the *Wanderer*'s crew to put their side, so the other side can say anything they want. That's the only truth here; that's the thing will remain incomplete.'

'What do you think happened, Duncan?' Father Mick asked.

The Skipper of *Southern Star* shrugged, looking down into his pint as if it was a crystal ball. 'I think someone on the freighter maybe noticed the *Wanderer* but did nothing because he knew she had right of way and expected the *Wanderer* to yield.'

'But there had to be a limit to that kind of thinking, surely?' the priest protested. 'When you see a boat coming closer and closer, it must cross your mind that there's something wrong and you might have to take action yourself?'

'Well, that's another rule of the sea,' Dougie said quietly. 'If a collision seems likely you must take action to avoid it, even if you are in the right.'

'So why didn't he?' Father Mick demanded.

'Maybe,' Duncan said, looking around the company, 'because there was no lookout on the freighter.'

Father Mick gasped. 'On a big boat like that? Does that happen?'

Around the Inn all the fishermen laughed ruefully.

'Father,' said Dougie, 'do you remember when Rose married Sorley Og and they went to France on honeymoon?'

Father Mick nodded.

'Well, they flew over, even though Sorley Og was scared stiff of flying. He refused to go on a cross-Channel ferry because he knew they were even more dangerous than something he didn't believe could stay in the air.'

Father Mick looked blank and the others laughed again.

'The English Channel is supposed to be the busiest, most congested stretch of water in the world,' Dougie explained, 'but everybody knows that vessels steam about it on auto-pilot without lookouts. There's an alarm that has to be cancelled every three minutes or it gets louder and louder, but they disconnect it and just trust to other vessels that do have lookouts getting out of their way.'

'But that's scandalous!' the priest exploded.

'Aye, well, what are you going to do about it? A few Hail Marys won't cure this one, Father,' Duncan said.

'And everyone knows this?'

Around the Inn, heads nodded in unison.

'So why is it allowed?'

'It's not allowed as such,' Duncan said. 'It's about money, everything's about money, didn't you know that? Vessels are kept undermanned to save money, crews don't always get their seamanship training at Dartmouth, often they come from countries where there are more important issues than safety; they get tired, people take risks when they're tired. My brother's boy works on one of those ferries. He says they come across vessels every night, shine their lights into the wheelhouses and there's no one there. That's the norm, not the exception, it's part of the job now.'

'But even so, the *Wanderer* went down in early morning, in perfect conditions,' Father Mick said.

'What do people do early in the morning, Father?' Dougie asked. 'They either sleep, or, if they're awake, they have a shower, grab a bit of breakfast. And even if you see this fishing boat miles away, you're bigger than she is, so if you can see her, she can see you, right? So you go below for a cuppa, and when you come back, there she is, coming straight at you, and it's too late to do anything.'

'You think that's how it happened?' Father Mick asked.

'It's one scenario, but it's the one that we all thought of first, isn't it lads?' Dougie looked around and all the fishermen murmured in agreement. 'But we're not asking the right question here. There *was* a lookout on the *Wanderer*, it was Sorley Mor. That is a fact, not something up for discussion. Anyone who wants to debate that is throwing us a red herring. Right?'

Once again all heads nodded. 'The question is, had something happened to Sorley Mor before the collision? It's the only explanation. The lawyers are wriggling around, playing with words. "There was no lookout." Well, that's strictly correct if the lookout was already unconscious or dead, but it's not the truth, is it?'

On his way back up to the chapel house, Father Mick felt even more depressed. He knew the fishing was a dangerous occupation; he'd sat in on enough stories to pick that up. The lads always remembered the funny parts even if the tale was a serious one, but he'd heard about bad weather: sudden, unexpected storms with mountainous seas; boats becoming iced up and capsizing without warning as a result; accidents on board and accounts of being adrift in liferafts for hours, wearing very little and knowing that hypothermia was creeping up on you. He knew about all the difficulties of random quota cuts and incomprehensibly stupid decisions being made by people with no knowledge of the sea, the industry or the families being hit. This was different, though, this was an added dimension. It seemed that everyone knew that justice and truth didn't matter. If the crew weren't there to object, anything could be said about them to ensure those who had survived would not lose money. Suddenly he remembered Gavin's suspicions that Sorley Mor's indigestion might be more than that, and he ran into the house, picked up the phone and dialled Dougie's office number.

'Dougie, Dougie, it's me!'

'Aye,' said Dougie.

'Dougie, what you said about the lookout maybe being unconscious.'

'Aye,' Dougie repeated slowly.

'Well, what if Gavin was right and Sorley Mor didn't have indigestion at all? What if he had something wrong with his heart and that morning –'

'My, but you're quick,' Dougie teased him. 'I don't know,

364

Father, you Holy Joes might have a direct line to your God, but you're not so fast on other wavelengths, are you?'

'You mean you'd thought of that?'

'Had we thought of that? You're really a bit of a Charlie on the side, aren't you?' He grinned. 'We've always suspected it. What did you think we were talking about earlier? Of course something happened to him, but we'll have an uphill task to get that acknowledged in the final report.'

'Why? It's bloody obvious!' the priest exploded.

Dougie laughed gently. 'Father Mick, these reports are done in officialese. There's no place for thoughts, suspicions, feelings – or us saying we knew Sorley Mor and he wouldn't have left the *Wanderer* without a lookout. The problem is that there's nothing to prove it. He's not here to give his account, is he?'

'But that's not fair! It's not right!'

'So?' Dougie asked lazily. 'I've always said your lot know nothing about the real world, Father. Welcome to the place where the rest of us live.'

'Isn't there some way of proving it?'

'Yes,' Dougie replied. 'Post mortems on the crew, but there were none performed.'

'Why not?'

'Danish law didn't need them and, as they were working outside Scottish waters, neither did Scottish law. We were all too involved in getting our heads round what had happened to think about it at the time.'

'Oh my God,' Father Mick moaned.

'Ah, I see the light has punctured the halo!' Dougie smiled down the receiver.

'So what are we going to do?'

'Well, as I understand it, Father, the Marine Accident Investigation Branch won't be allowed access to the freighter crew to question them –'

'Why the hell not?' Father Mick shrieked down the phone.

'Come now, Father, it's all in the spirit of European

co-operation. Surely you didn't believe being part of the EC was intended to *ease* the red tape, did you?' Dougie laughed at him. 'You'll have to lose this belief in truth and justice: it's terribly childish, Father. No, all we can do is make sure we submit the right questions and hope they get asked and, more importantly, get answered.'

'And if they don't?'

'Well, then, they don't,' Dougie said simply.

'Oh come now, you're teuchters, you're sneaky, you're wily, you must have something up your sleeve!'

'Father Mick,' said Dougie, 'that sounds very like a racial slur to me!'

'Ach, racial slur be damned, stop buggering about. Can we do this?'

'We'll try, Father, that's all we can do. We'll try.'

Just over three months after the crew died, Alison Kerr gave birth to a son. She named him Peter after his father and added Sorley for good measure, so at least there was a new toehold in the world of Wanderers. Rose was pleased for Alison and envious of her in equal measure. She knew everyone was picking up the pieces, that there was a feeling in the village that a new leaf had been turned with the birth of the baby, and she resented that as well. They had no right to be getting on with their lives, she thought, and she went through a time of hating them all for it. How could they behave as though it had been 'just one of those things' and expect her to shrug, throw it off and go on as if there was any future worth having, worth wanting? It reinforced her instinct to shut herself away from all contact with humanity, to sit in her house alone, simmering with anger.

The terms of the insurance taken out by the skipper on behalf of the crew gave each family £50,000, but the Mac-Ewans also had the proceeds of the sale of the boat's fishing licence, which ran to over £5 million, so there would be no financial worries for Rose or Chrissie – not that it seemed hugely important to either of them. Rose still refused to leave her house for longer than the time it took to call briefly on Granny Ina or her mother-in-law, but the birth of Pete and Alison's baby provided an opportunity for Gannet and Chrissie to coax her out of her exile. A new baby needed to have a present – a new baby carrying the name Sorley more than any other – and Chrissie announced that she wanted Gannet to take her to Inverness for some serious shopping.

Rose understood what was being suggested, and at first she refused; Chrissie could get her something to give to the baby too. Chrissie would have none of it. The baby deserved a gift chosen by the giver; it wouldn't be the same if Rose didn't pick it herself. Besides, this baby was special. It would grow up as Rose had herself, a little orphan of the fishing; there was a bond between them, wasn't there? And so Rose agreed reluctantly and with bad grace and only after extracting an agreement that they would go and return on the same day. She didn't want to stay away for even one night, she wanted to come home to her own bed. However long the journey took, they must be back by that night.

They set off on a bright, autumn morning, with Chrissie talking non-stop, telling stories about her grandbairns, passing comments on the changing colours of the trees, Gannet's driving, the discomfort of the old Land Rover on a long journey. Then there was a long silence.

'I'm fed up with this,' Chrissie suddenly announced. 'The two of you sit there saying nothing while I gabble on trying to make conversation. Somebody speak, for God's sake.'

'Why have we got to speak?' Gannet demanded quietly. 'What's wrong with silence?'

'Because it's not natural, that's why, not this kind of silence. Stop this bloody thing, I want out!'

Gannet pulled off the road at the next layby and Chrissie pushed Rose out first so that she could climb out. Rose immediately got back in again.

Chrissie watched her. 'You see what I mean?' she demanded.

'What?' Gannet asked, looking bemused.

'She's back in.'

'So what?'

Chrissie walked up and down the layby. 'She's not living, that's so what! She's just existing: moving when she has to and no more than that; talking when she has to and no more than that. It's not right!'

'Chrissie, it's up to her how she deals with this,' Gannet suggested. 'Everyone's different.'

'No, that's not it,' Chrissie fumed. 'This isn't natural; it's not normal. Life has to go on, she can't stay like this for the rest of her life!'

From the passenger seat came a low, lifeless voice. 'Who says life has to go on?'

'Ach, Rose, of course it has to,' Chrissie replied, going up to the Land Rover. 'It would break his heart to see you like this.'

'But he's not here to see me,' Rose replied flatly, 'so what does it matter?'

'You're young, lassie, in time you'll meet somebody else,' Chrissie said pleadingly. 'You're luckier than Alison; you don't have any bairns. You can make a fresh start!' As the words were leaving her lips, Chrissie knew she shouldn't have said them; if she could have clawed them back from the air and reclaimed them she would have done so.

Rose looked at her, brown eyes blazing. 'His own mother!' she whispered fiercely. 'That his own mother should say that to me!'

'I'm sorry, I really am, Rose, I shouldn't have –'

'No, you shouldn't have! Luckier than Alison? Is that what you think? She has her man's baby; she has something of Pete. What do I have left of Sorley Og? Nothing! I'd change places with her and be grateful to do it. And just for the record, there wasn't anyone before Sorley Og and there won't be anyone after him. Is that clear?' She looked at Gannet. 'I want to go home,' she told him, and wordlessly he climbed into the driving seat, started up the engine, and waited till Chrissie joined them. They drove back in a silence more complete than the one Chrissie had tried to break on the way out, and when they reached MacEwan's Row they parted without a word being spoken. Rose went to her house and shut the door and Chrissie, seeming smaller and sadder than at any time since the tragedy, turned towards her own house. Gannet walked off in the opposite direction.

'Where are you going?' Chrissie asked.

'I'm going down to the Inn to get drunk,' he said over his shoulder. 'Roaring, falling down, stinking, rotten drunk – if you don't mind me deciding how I want to behave, that is.' He turned towards her. 'Seeing as you think you have the right to dictate to others,' he said savagely, 'I suppose I should ask for permission!' He turned again and disappeared towards the village.

When he arrived back he had had just enough of the Inn's current atmosphere and the falling-down stuff to be in fighting trim.

'Well, I have to say, Chrissie MacEwan,' he told her, 'that you handled that very well.'

'Ach, away with you,' Chrissie said dismissively. 'You talk as if I don't know that myself already.'

'There we were, trying to bring the lassie out of herself, and with one wee remark you've managed to send her scurrying deeper inside herself than she was.'

'I know, I know. What do you want? Blood?'

'I want you to think a bit, Chrissie, that's what I want. You've ruled the rest of us for years and that's fine, because we all know each other, but Rose is different. You don't know her as well as you think you do.'

Chrissie busied herself with unnecessary tasks about the kitchen without replying.

'What a thing to say to her, too! That's the kind of thing

369

most people think but know better than to say aloud, and to Rose herself least of all. What in hell possessed you?'

'Gannet, you're drunk,' Chrissie said in a businesslike tone. 'I won't talk to a drunk man. Goodnight.'

With that she left him, but when she closed the door of the bedroom she had shared with Sorley Mor she put her head against the wooden panel and wept quietly. She had been trying to be supportive, that was all she had meant to do; she had been trying to show Rose that she, Sorley Og's mother, was quite prepared to see his young widow build a new life. It would hurt like hell to see her with another man and with another man's bairns, but it had to happen, it would happen one day, and she had wanted Rose to know that she mustn't feel guilty on her behalf. Somehow it hadn't come out like that. In her desperation it had sounded as if she didn't give a damn about her own boy and, worse, as if she didn't have much respect for the love between Rose and Sorley Og, as if it was of so little consequence that it could be easily and quickly replaced if only Rose would buck up. Maybe Gannet was right. She had spent many years cheerfully insulting everyone around her, and because they understood her they could judge the abuse correctly. But Rose was indeed different, and Chrissie knew she had hurt her.

Next morning Chrissie walked down to the village and into Hamish Dubh's store. Not that she needed much, if anything; it was a case of flying the flag, showing that after everything that had happened she was still part of village life. The shop was busy, all locals at that time of year, and they greeted her and each other. Annie Stewart, Dan's wife and Stamp's sister-in-law, asked how she was, and the other women listened in, all of them part of her concern.

'Ach, you know, Annie,' Chrissie replied brightly, 'up one day, down the next. It can only get better.'

'And the girls?'

'Getting by, Annie,' said Chrissie. 'How's Molly holding up?'

'About the same. We keep an eye on her,' Annie smiled. 'I see you still have Gannet with you?'

Chrissie hesitated. 'Aye, I do. And is there anything you'd like to say about that?' she demanded suspiciously.

'No, no, I was just saying,' Annie smiled a slightly puzzled smile.

Chrissie looked around the women in the shop.

'You're a miserable bunch of old sweetie wives!' she said viciously. 'Is that all you can think to talk about, what me and Gannet might be getting up to now that Sorley Mor's cold in his grave up the hill there?'

The women exchanged glances and Hamish Dubh looked uncomfortable behind the counter.

'Let me make it clear,' Chrissie addressed them. 'Gannet has always been part of our family, and if anything the passing of my man and my boy have made that stronger. Gannet will stay at my house because that's where he's always been, as fine you all know!'

'Chrissie,' Hamish Dubh said, trying to calm the situation, 'I don't think anyone meant –'

'I know bloody fine well what they meant!' Chrissie shouted, her face red with anger. 'Everyone of them in this village has been wondering if Gannet has been sharing my bed all these years –'

Annie Stewart opened her mouth to protest, but Chrissie ignored her.

'Well, I won't spoil your fun as you have nothing else but gossip to occupy your minds,' said Chrissie. 'I won't confirm or deny it, you can just keep guessing, but Gannet will be staying where he is. Now, has anyone got anything else to say?'

Without waiting for a reply she turned and stormed out of the store and home to MacEwan's Row.

Up the Brae, Father Mick had been thinking about the whole situation. He hadn't been able to switch his head off it since that first awful phone call, and though his mind was hurting with constantly running and re-running everything that had happened, for some reason he couldn't stop. He wasn't sleeping well, and Father Mick needed his sleep. A couple of hours at a time, that was all he could manage, long enough to have horrific dreams of himself doing terrible things to complete strangers, running down roads in cities he hadn't seen in decades, stabbing people in the streets, tearing them limb from limb. It was reaction to what had happened, he knew that, and he kept telling himself that it would get better, but he was beginning to wonder when; he was feeling so tired that it was like a physical illness, as if he had permanent 'flu.

There was a knock at the door and, when he answered it, to his utter horror he found Batty and Maddy from Black Rock standing on his doorstep, one looking prim and proper, the other like some mad ex-hooker who didn't realise that her days on the street corner were over. Since their mother's death he no longer visited Black Rock, so they waited in various parts of the village to ambush him these days, or they turned up at his door. He looked at them standing there, his heart sinking as Batty proffered yet another rosary for his blessing, and suddenly he had had it. He grabbed the rosary from her hands and savagely ripped it apart, breaking the links with his bare hands and not stopping when the metal cut his skin and blood flowed. Then he threw the bits on the floor and jumped up and down on them.

'Will you bugger off with your gee-gaws and leave me alone!' he yelled, while in his head another voice was asking him what in hell he was doing, as Batty and Maddy stared at him in shocked confusion. 'I've blessed enough bits of crap for you. You could fill a dozen shops with the rubbish you keep buying. Go away!' he shouted, shoving the bemused sisters out of his doorway. 'Get out! Leave me alone! If I ever see either one of you again I'll blast your arses off with the biggest shotgun I can lay hands on!' Then he locked the door behind them, retired to his sitting room, switched off the light, drew the curtains, got out a bottle of Scotch and sat by the fire taking slugs of it till he was unconscious.

When Chrissie arrived back from her encounter in the village she found Gannet packing the old kitbag he usually took on fishing trips.

'What are you doing?' she asked.

'Packing,' he replied tersely.

'I can see that,' she said, 'but why are you packing?'

'I thought I'd go back to my own house in Keppaig,' the big man said.

'Do you remember where it is?' she asked, laughing.

Gannet kept stuffing clothes into his bag but made no reply.

'OK, I'll fall for it,' Chrissie said. 'Why are you going back to your own house?'

'I just thought I would,' Gannet said loftily.

'Dear God,' Chrissie sighed. 'Look, can we maybe have the short version? What are you doing?'

'I was only ever here because of Sorley Mor,' he said quietly, 'and now that he's not here there seems no reason for me to be either.'

'Now that's just crap!' Chrissie said angrily.

'And,' he said, looking up, 'I was also thinking that maybe we needed a break from each other. Is it all right if I take the Land Rover?' he asked with exaggerated politeness. 'I'll make sure it's returned to you in due course.'

'Sure, what good is it to me?' Chrissie asked briskly. 'I can't drive the damned thing.'

Gannet finished his packing and looked her in the eye. 'I'll be going now then,' he said.

Chrissie returned his gaze. 'Right,' she said after a while. 'Fine. Go then. That's fine by me.'

Then she did what she always did, she put on her pinny and started to work about the house. The front door opened, then closed. She was washing a few dishes at the sink by the window as the tall, thin figure passed, but she didn't look up. As she heard the familiar 'clunk' of the Land Rover door she forced her hands down into the soapy water, shut her eyes and swallowed hard; once that noise meant Sorley Mor was about to bound through the door. The engine started up, then faded as the Land Rover moved off towards the village. Chrissie kept washing her dishes.

As Gannet was passing Black Rock, the man himself stepped onto the road and put a hand up to stop him.

'I thought it must be you, Gannet,' he said in his slow way, his hands fiddling with a metal file covered with sawdust. 'I'd know the racket of that Land Rover anywhere. So how are things with you, then?'

'Fine, fine, Black Rock,' Gannet replied quietly. He knew that these opening pleasantries always had to be gone through with Black Rock, but there were times when you wanted to grab him by the throat and yell, 'What do you actually want?'

'I was just saying to Haffa there, it's not bad weather for autumn.' He blew some sawdust off the file.

'Aye, it is that.'

'No frost to speak of yet, makes his digging easier.' He brushed the sawdust off his dungarees with his other hand.

'Mm,' muttered Gannet, looking at the file and the sawdust. 'Has somebody . . . ?'

'No, no,' said Black Rock slowly, 'nothing like that. Just another job for Sandy Bay, though I always say I'll never take on another.'

'I meant to ask you about that, Black Rock,' Gannet said, 'about the lads. Did you never have an idea?'

Black Rock shook his head. 'Never know if it's family,' he intoned, 'but I was a bit restless for a couple of days before, couldn't explain why. Must've been on account of the other lads who weren't actually family, and the distance. It's a terrible thing, the second sight, Gannet. A curse, to be truthful.'

'Aye, but it has its advantages,' Gannet suggested. 'It gives you a head start on the coffins when it's not family.'

'Aye, aye, there is that,' Black Rock intoned solemnly, 'but it's a terrible burden to bear through life. Aye, aye. And is Chrissie getting by?' he asked kindly.

'Ach, you know Chrissie,' Gannet said diplomatically, 'she's just Chrissie.'

'Aye, aye,' said Black Rock, as though he had heard a great universal truth, which he probably had. 'And Rose?'

'Not so good,' Gannet admitted.

'Terrible, terrible,' said Black Rock. 'It's a sad, sad time we're all having, Gannet, but the lassie most of all.'

'Mm,' said Gannet again.

'I was thinking that Father Mick isn't doing too well either,' Black Rock remarked, getting to the point of the conversation at last.

'No worse than the rest of us,' Gannet murmured.

'Aye, aye, that's maybe true,' Black Rock said slowly, looking off into the distance. 'Except that he pulled a gun on Batty and Maddy last night and threatened to shoot their arses off.'

Gannet stared at him, thinking this was the best joke Black Rock had ever come out with. Sorley Mor would have fun with that one when he heard it . . . He took a deep breath and silently cursed himself for his stupidity, then he looked at Black Rock again and realised that he hadn't been joking.

'You're not serious, man?' he asked.

'Aye, fair out of sorts he seemed. I was thinking of taking a walk down there myself, but I'm not too keen on maybe having my own arse shot off, so I thought I'd leave it till I saw you. He's a bit upset I think, poor man.'

Gannet turned the Land Rover round and headed back towards the chapel house. As he'd passed on the way up he had noticed that the curtains were closed and had decided not to disturb Father Mick. He knew the priest had been having trouble sleeping, maybe with his normal pattern out of kilter he'd overslept, but that would be no bad thing, sleep was sleep. Racing back down again he had a horrible vision of finding Father Mick shot dead by his own hand. He didn't know it had been that bad; they were all still struggling and Father Mick was the one pushing them all onwards; what if he was the very one who needed help most and they hadn't noticed it?

Gannet knocked on the door but there was no reply, so he knocked again and again, his fears rising each time until he felt he might be sick right there on the doorstep. Eventually he noticed the curtain move and was relieved and enraged in equal measure, then Father Mick appeared at the door still clutching an empty bottle and looking desperately hungover.

'Damn and blast, man!' Gannet shouted, trying to stop his fist from swinging. 'I thought you were dead!'

'And I'm not?' the priest asked. 'Oh, bugger!'

Gannet pushed him inside and followed.

'What's all this about you threatening Batty and Maddy with a gun?' he asked.

Father Mick looked blank, rubbed his head, fell over a table in the gloom and lay there swearing. Gannet pulled the curtains back to let in some light.

'Where's the gun?' he demanded, desperately looking around.

'What gun, you silly sod?' Father Mick laughed from the floor.

'You're going around threatening people with a gun and all you can do is lie there holding on to an empty bottle and laughing?' Gannet shouted. 'You don't have a gun licence, the new copper would be in here in an armoured car if he knew that! Where the hell is it?'

'There isn't one!' Father Mick said dismissively. 'I didn't threaten them with a gun. I only said if they didn't clear off I'd blast their arses with the biggest shotgun I could find.'

'Aye, well,' Gannet replied sarcastically, 'I can see that makes all the difference! That'll be your plea in court, will it?

"I didn't have a gun, but if I could've laid hands on one I'd have blasted their arses off."'?'

Father Mick crawled along the floor, grabbed the arm of a chair, hauled himself up into it and sat giggling for a few minutes, his arms clutched across the empty bottle.

Gannet spotted the dried blood on his hands. 'What in hell's name have you been doing to yourself?' he demanded.

Father Mick looked down, turned his hands over and examined them closely from various angles. 'That?' he asked vacantly. 'Ach, I was tearing up a rosary and the damned thing gave me a few wee cuts, that's all.'

'Oh, well,' Gannet replied, 'as long as you were just tearing up a rosary . . .'

'As you do, Gannet,' Father Mick smiled. 'As you do. It was no big deal. It wasn't blessed, so technically speaking it was only a string of beads.' Then he started shaking with laughter. 'Can you imagine what Sorley Mor would've made of this story?' he asked. 'I can see him now, laughing that laugh of his till he couldn't stand! Can't you just see him, Gannet?'

Gannet could; Gannet already had. The big man smiled. 'So what the hell was it all about?'

As Father Mick described his encounter with the Black Rock sisters, Gannet relaxed.

'I'll have to apologise, of course,' Father Mick sighed. 'I'll give them a bit of wood off something.' He looked around the furniture in the room for inspiration. 'I'll tell them it's a splinter from the Cross. They'll fall for that.' He sighed again. 'Well, at least I got a night's sleep out of it, so it was worth it after all.'

'If you can call an Islay Mist–induced coma a night's sleep!' Gannet laughed grimly.

'I can,' Father Mick replied loftily, 'and I do.' He smacked his lips a few times and pulled a face. 'Mouth like a Turkish wrestler's jockstrap,' he muttered. 'Did I ever tell you that I once met a Turkish wrestler, Gannet? He was their Olympic coach, in fact. Huge great chap, built along the lines of our Eric.' He stopped and looked down. 'Only not so light on his feet, of course!' he said with forced brightness. 'Funny how it creeps up and hits you out of the blue, isn't it?' he asked sadly. 'You don't know you're saying it till you've said it.'

Gannet nodded. 'I suppose it's part of the process,' he said quietly.

Father Mick clapped his hands together. 'Right!' he said. 'Let's get out of here! Fancy risking some of Dan's cooking?' He was already moving towards the door.

'Are you not going to shave, man?' Gannet asked.

'I most certainly am not!' Father Mick shouted, already climbing into the passenger seat of the Land Rover.

The Inn was full of regulars, but somehow it still wasn't busy, and the atmosphere, as Dan had remarked, wasn't so much quiet as moody.

'I don't know,' said Father Mick, 'I've never known so many short-tempered people in all my life, myself included. Gavin was just saying the other day that he's got a constant stream of people coming through the surgery door with nothing wrong but insomnia and bad temper – though, mind you, the two tend to go together.'

'It's the same on the boat,' said Duncan, 'and at home come to that. My wife snaps at the slightest thing. I'm beginning to wonder if she'll be there when I come home the next time.'

'There have been fights in here,' Dan said. 'I'm not kidding you, men who've known each other all their lives almost throwing punches over nothing. Not that I'm feeling too bright myself.'

'I'm not talking to Chrissie,' Gannet reported flatly, 'and Rose isn't talking to her either.'

'What happened?' Father Mick asked.

'Ach,' Gannet said, waving his hand in dismissal, 'she said something daft to Rose about there being somebody else out there for her and her being lucky not having any bairns so

378

she could make a fresh start. You know Chrissie, she talks.'

Dougie, who had been silent, drew a sharp intake of breath and raised his eyebrows.

'She didn't mean it, Dougie,' Gannet said kindly. 'Chrissie's had so many years needing to beat me and Sorley Mor up to get through to us that she's likely forgotten how to be sensitive when she needs to. She's worried about Rose, she was just frustrated at not helping the lassie more and it just kind of slipped out.'

'She had a real argument in Hamish Dubh's yesterday, did you hear about that?' Dan asked quietly. Everyone looked at him. 'Annie came back, really upset. She still can't make up her mind if she owes Chrissie an apology or the other way round. She mentioned that you were still up at MacEwan's Row, Gannet, and was going to ask how you were doing, and Chrissie blew up in front of all the other women in the store. Tore them all off a strip, said they were a lot of gossiping sweetie wives and stormed out, saying you'd be staying at MacEwan's Row regardless of what they all thought.'

'Bugger!' Gannet said, wincing.

'What?' Father Mick asked.

'When I bumped into Black Rock this morning I was on my way home to Keppaig. I was so annoyed at Chrissie over Rose that I more or less said I'd had enough of her and needed a break.'

'Bugger indeed,' said Father Mick sympathetically.

'She didn't say a word about what had happened in the store, though,' Gannet protested.

'I think it's still bugger, old son,' Duncan said with feeling.

'And I said I'd shoot Batty and Maddy!' Father Mick said sadly. 'What the hell is wrong with everyone? We should all be pulling together: isn't that what small, close–knit communities are meant to do? Instead we're all carping at each other –'

'– and threatening people with non–existent guns,' Gannet grinned.

'Exactly,' Father Mick said. 'We're falling apart.'

'It's Sorley Mor,' Gannet said after a while.

'You mean he's haunting us?' Father Mick chuckled affectionately.

'Kind of,' Gannet smiled. 'I read about it in a book.'

Everyone exchanged smiling glances; it was an expression they hadn't heard in a while.

'We're over the initial shock o the thing,' Gannet explained, 'and we've come out of the denial part, so now we're in the angry zone. We're all just angry about what happened and we're taking it out on whoever happens to be around. Think about it; if you were asked to picture the village in your head, the first image you'd come up with would be Sorley Mor. He's always been the centre of the place. Is that not true?'

They all nodded thoughtfully.

'Well, maybe he was the glue that held us all together, as they say, maybe that's why we're falling apart now. We were all trying to go on as normal, only we can't do that, it isn't normal without him, is it?' He looked at Dan. 'I'm not forgetting Stamp and the others, Dan, I mean the boat and all the lads, too. When we think of them we see him; when we think of him we see them. They were all part of each other, part of what's missing now, and we're all angry about it.'

'I think you might have something there,' Father Mick said quietly.

'We don't talk about him at all,' Gannet continued, warming to his theme, 'do we? All those mad capers, the laughs, the stories of how different he was on board the *Wanderer*.'

'It's hard,' Duncan stated simply. 'Talking about him in the past seems, I don't know . . .'

'Like we've accepted it, like betrayal,' Dougie remarked.

'Aye, I suppose so,' Duncan smiled sadly.

'Maybe the real betrayal is not talking about him at all,' Gannet said quietly. 'It's like he never existed. What if the only way we have to keep him and the lads alive *is* to talk about them?'

26

Up at MacEwan's Row, other disagreements were forming. After her fall-out with Chrissie, Rose had stayed in her own house, spending the night sitting on the couch, dozing fitfully. She was still drawn to the big window; it was like an instinct she couldn't resist, though she was no longer waiting for her first sight of *Ocean Wanderer*. She had tried to stop, or at least cut down her pointless vigils, because Sally's husband, Alan, still went to sea and came home again, and more than once she and Alan had made eye contact; she didn't know which of them had found it most painful.

She had been thinking of Chrissie's remark about her being 'luckier' than Alison because being childless would give her a more completely fresh start with someone else. She was stoking her own anger, increasing the insult every time she repeated it in her head, when something struck her. She hadn't had a period since – when? She got up and went to her diary, desperately flicking though the pages. They had been trying for a baby for months before that last trip, so she had been meticulous about keeping tabs on her cycle. May, that's when it was, the middle of May, a whole month before Sorley Og's death, and that was, when? Three and a half months ago! Add May and it was four and a half months since her last period! What a fool she had been. So lost in her grief that she had forgotten about their baby plans, too busy being sorry for herself to realise that she was pregnant, that she had something left of Sorley Og, that she was carrying his bairn inside her! Rose dashed over to the phone and called Gavin.

'I need to see you,' she said.

'Do you want me to come up now?' Gavin asked, afraid that Rose had reached a crisis.

'No, no, it's nothing like that,' she laughed, reading his mind. 'How about tomorrow morning?'

Gavin was bemused, he hadn't heard Rose laugh like that in months. He had seen her only a day or so ago and had made a mental note that she wasn't picking up at all, that perhaps he should suggest that she needed some help. He couldn't think of anything that could have legitimately lifted her spirits since then, and that thought increased his concern.

'Rose, you would tell me if there was anything wrong, wouldn't you?' he asked.

'Of course I would!' she laughed, and when he didn't reply she said, 'Oh, well, I'll tell you then, but you mustn't tell a soul. I think I'm pregnant!'

'Pregnant?' he repeated.

'Yes, pregnant! With child, idiot,' she laughed. 'What kind of doctor are you when you don't understand that word?'

'Well, OK then, come down first thing, and bring a sample with you,' Gavin replied in what he hoped was a relaxed tone, but deep inside his own spirits had plummeted. Maybe Rose was pregnant, but if she wasn't he could see a situation developing where she would fall into a deeper abyss than the one she now seemed to have bounced out of.

Chrissie looked up as a figure passed the kitchen window.

'I thought it was the Land Rover that was coming back in due course,' she remarked, drying her hands, 'not you?'

'It's down at the Inn,' Gannet announced slightly unsteadily. 'That big ugly policeman from Inverness was sitting outside waiting for some innocent man who'd had a few to drive off, so I left it there to spite him.'

'So what is this, then? A visit?'

'Ach, don't be daft, woman,' Gannet said, reaching down to ruffle her hair.

382

'Do you want that arm back in a sling?' Chrissie asked.

Gannet laughed. 'As McArthur said, "I shall return." Well, I have.'

'Aye, and he was a bit of a chancer as well,' Chrissie replied. 'The pair of you are well met!' She looked around.

'What are you looking for?' he asked. 'I told you, the Land Rover's in the village.'

'If you were in the Inn, so was Father Hooligan,' she said tartly. 'What's happened to him?'

'Ach, he's not fit to walk up here, totally out of condition – if he was ever in it, that is. I left him in the back of the Land –'

'– Rover, covered with a tarpaulin,' Chrissie finished. 'Aye, I know. Old habits die hard, right enough.'

When he arrived at his surgery next morning, Gavin found Rose already waiting. She had walked down from MacEwan's Row, further than she had walked since the day of Sorley Og's funeral. She was bright-eyed, almost euphoric, and he was aware that he was going to some lengths to avoid making eye contact with her. He unlocked the door, showed her into the consulting room and sat down uneasily across the desk from her. He didn't know what to do first. Did he explain things and then test the sample she was holding so restlessly in her hand, or did he do the test first then explain? Unable to make up his mind he opted to open his mouth and go with whatever came out first.

'Rose, I know how much this means to you,' he started.

'Oh,' she laughed back, 'the serious doctor voice!' She looked excited enough to explode before his eyes.

Gavin smiled back through tight lips. He had been going over variations of this speech in his mind ever since she had called the day before, but it still wasn't coming any easier. He reached for a glass of water. 'The thing is, Rose, that I suppose you've noticed an absence of periods and that's made you wonder if you might be pregnant?'

'Haven't had one since May,' Rose smiled back. 'I hadn't given it a thought till last night, isn't that incredible?'

'Well, no, it's not, that's what I was about to explain.'

'I was thinking about Alison and the baby,' Rose said seriously. 'Chrissie thinks I'm luckier than Alison, and I was thinking that Chrissie doesn't know what she's talking about, it's Alison who's the lucky one if anyone is — and it just hit me!' She leaned across the desk and planted the pill bottle containing her urine sample right in front of him.

Gavin looked at it as though it might be a bomb, then moved it to one side.

'Aren't you going to test it?' Rose demanded brightly.

'In a minute, Rose, in a minute,' he replied, trying to pick up the traces of his badly prepared speech. 'The thing is —'

'That *thing* again!'

'Yes, um . . . Rose?'

'Yes?'

'Be quiet and let me talk.'

'Right, OK, sorry,' she smiled.

'Rose, please listen to me. It's important. Look, there are other reasons for amenorrhoea in young, healthy women of child-bearing age.' Inside his head he cringed, realising he was falling back on textbook language. 'What I'm saying is that bereavement and shock often cause periods to stop for a time, sometimes for a considerable spell, so the fact that you've had no periods for a few months doesn't in itself mean that you're pregnant. Do you understand?'

Rose sat across the desk still smiling at him; she hadn't taken a word of it in.

'Have you had any other symptoms?' he asked. 'Frequency in passing urine, breast tenderness, nausea?'

'I've been feeling sick nearly all the time, I just didn't put two and two together, that's all. Silly, isn't it?' she replied, and he sensed by the way she had avoided the first two symptoms that deep down she knew. The only thing to do was to test the sample.

384

He took the bottle over to a metal table by the window as Rose carefully watched his movements from behind, then he turned to her and said, 'I'm sorry, Rose, it's negative.'

She stared at him for a long moment and he saw her eyes cloud over, then she immediately brightened up. 'It could be wrong, though, couldn't it?'

'Well, a false negative is more likely than a false positive, that's true, but –'

'Well, that's what it is, then!'

'No, Rose, I honestly don't think so,' he said slowly. 'If you've missed three or four periods as you say, then I don't really think we'd be getting a false negative this far along.'

She sat silently for a long time, the muscles in her face working furiously. 'You don't want me to have this baby, do you?' she said at last in a low voice.

'Rose, it's nothing like that!'

'You don't want me to be happy, do you? You have to take this away from me.'

As Gavin was moving towards her, she was moving away. 'Just because Tess preferred Sandy Bay to you, you don't want anyone else to be happy!' Before he could stop her she ran out of the surgery, slamming the door behind her.

Gavin sat at his desk and ran his fingers through his hair. The whole thing was grotesque. He was dealing with his own grief as best he could – losing Sorley Og had been as hard on him as losing Sorley Mor had been on Gannet – but he had no real support mechanisms: no Chrissie shouting at him, no Father Mick carousing with him in the Inn. He was the local doctor, and there had to be some distance between him and his patients, however familiar they were. On top of his own feelings he was trying to cope with the increase in patients coming through his door with minor and fictional ailments. It seemed he had discovered a new illness, '*Wanderer*-itis'. If there was a way of dealing with this massive blow that had hit everyone in the village, he had yet to find it. All he could do was to take one step forward, and two back, if he was lucky. No matter how well he thought he was doing, just around the next corner some other difficulty triggered by the loss of the boat and her crew waited, coiled and ready to spring out and attack him.

That evening he drove up to MacEwan's Row and knocked on Rose's door. When there was no reply, he turned the handle and let himself in. She was standing by the big window, the lights off, looking out over the sea. She turned and looked at him, then turned away again, embarrassed, as he walked over the long lounge floor towards her, glad of the lack of illumination.

'About this morning, Rose,' he started.

'No, don't, Gavin,' she said quietly. 'I've been feeling so ashamed of myself ever since. I'm sorry I said the things I said.'

'That doesn't matter. You were upset,' he replied.

'What if everybody in the village was upset, would that give them the right to go about offending each other? Think of the trouble that would cause.'

Gavin smiled wryly. 'Funnily enough, that's exactly what they are all doing,' he told her.

'Really?' she asked, looking at him. 'Why?'

'Because they're upset.'

'Over the lads?' She sounded surprised.

'Of course over the lads,' he smiled. 'There's hardly anyone in this village talking to anyone else. It's just a phase, it'll pass, but it's hard on everyone.'

Rose nodded slowly. 'I didn't realise they were all feeling so bad,' she murmured.

'Well, your own feelings have been pretty major,' Gavin said. 'It's hardly surprising that you haven't had time to look around and see how they've all been affected.'

She nodded again. 'Listen, what I said about Tess and Sandy Bay, I really am sorry, Gavin.'

He shrugged. 'It's not a problem, honestly. Everybody wanted us to make a match of it; they want to marry me off

386

so badly they'd have been happy if *I'd* married Sandy Bay! But there wasn't much in it with me and Tess. A couple of dates and we knew we were just pals.' He shrugged again. 'I feel sorry for Sandy Bay, though. Father Mick's giving him a helluva time for going to Glasgow and snubbing him, as he sees it. Keeps making the age difference bigger all the time to prove Sandy Bay's nothing but a dirty old man.'

'What is the age difference?'

'Well, she's about thirty and he's late forties, I think, but you'll never get Father Mick to accept that! Thirteen and seventy was the last estimate I heard!'

For a while they talked quietly in the dusk, going over old times and new, and Gavin had the feeling an important crisis point had been passed. As he turned to leave he had one more thought.

'What we were talking about before, Rose,' he said. 'If you want to make absolutely sure I could arrange an ultrasound appointment at one of the city hospitals if you like?'

Rose shook her head and smiled. 'No, that's OK, Gavin. I was clutching at straws; I think I knew that all along. There's no baby, I only wish there was.'

By the time he left, the dusk had grown into darkness, but Chrissie was waiting on her doorstep, arms crossed against the chill of an autumn evening, concerned by the sight of the doctor's car.

'Everything OK?' she asked, glancing across at Rose's house.

'Fine,' Gavin replied, opening the door of the Range Rover. 'It wasn't professional, just a personal call. She seemed a bit upset earlier today. I was just checking, but she's OK.'

'Aye, that was my fault,' Chrissie admitted quietly. 'I went too far, as usual.'

'Don't be so hard on yourself, Chrissie. Everyone's a bit near the edge, it's part of the process. I was just explaining that to Rose.'

'Aye, Mastermind in there explained it to me before he

conked out.' Chrissie motioned with her head to her own house. 'I suppose there's some sense to it, though I'd never admit it to him.'

'Gannet?' Gavin asked. 'Where is he?'

'Asleep on the table in the porch.' She threw her head back and laughed.

'What is it?'

'I just heard a voice from the past, that's all,' Chrissie grinned, her eyes shining even in the darkness.

'What did it say?' Gavin asked.

'It said "*Conservatory*, woman!" Silly sod! Goodnight, Gavin.'

27

As the months passed in Acarsaid, one phase of grief gave way to another, and a new village life began to establish itself. What emerged in the wake of their loss was different from the days when Sorley Mor was at the centre of the village. For one thing, it was quieter, but time, if it doesn't heal, at least forces the most reluctant to move on. Chrissie was forgiven for her remarks to Rose, Gannet took to reading his books again and, gradually, Rose came out of her bitter mourning and was seen about the place. That more than anything helped to restore the village: the sight of Rose – whose suffering they all felt – picking up the pieces seemed to give them permission to go on.

Rose borrowed the Land Rover to visit Granny Ina, spending quiet hours with the old woman, who was asleep more often than she was awake. It suited Rose just to be in the comforting presence she remembered from her childhood. Though her mother was there in the background, there was still little connection between mother and daughter. It was the same with the rest of her family, the gentle, biddable Rose had gone for good; the gulf that had started with their opposition to her marriage to Sorley Og had continued in the months after his death, and apart from Dougie the paths of the Nicolsons rarely crossed. It was the way they were. They weren't like other families, she realised that; probably thanks to Margo and despite Granny Ina's efforts, they understood family to mean ownership. One relationship had flourished, though, that of Dougie and Father Mick. With Sorley Og the little priest had become as near to being a real father as lifelong celibacy would allow, but the meetings and discussions in the wake of the tragedy had brought him and Dougie into closer contact, and they were often to be seen, cheerfully arguing and insulting each other. Gannet would watch them, matching the relationships of surrogate son and surrogate father up to his latest reading matter, and smile, wondering if either understood this new friendship and determined to explain it to them once he had tracked it down. For Father Mick's part he wondered how he could have known Dougie nearly all his life and seen him almost every day without realising what a splendid chap he was. To cap it all, the boy took his dram like a man: what higher praise could there be?

In Sorley's Mor's corner of the Inn, overlooking the dominoes table, a photo of the *Wanderer* was placed on the wall, with another of her crew taken at Sorley Og's wedding, and beside them a copy of 'The Sea', the tract the skipper had liked so much. That made three, counting the one on the wall of his house on MacEwan's Row, and the original where he had put it, in the wheelhouse of the *Wanderer* at the bottom of the sea off Denmark. At first the locals didn't look at the little memorial on the Inn wall, though they were acutely aware that it was there, but slowly they were able to. Then they would smile when they saw it, and in time the stories it provoked came more easily. They laughed when they talked of what Sorley Mor's reaction would have been to Tess and Sandy Bay's marriage, knowing from Father Mick that he hadn't had time to believe it and suspected it was just one of Chrissie's wind-ups.

'I tell you this, Sandy Bay,' they would tell him over and over again, 'but you got off lightly there. Sorley Mor would've put you through hell every time he saw you!'

Sandy Bay would smile sadly. 'I wish he was here to do it,' he'd say. 'Nothing would make me happier than to walk in some day and find the skipper sitting there, ready to make a fool of me. Especially now, with Tess expecting the twins. Think what he'd have made of that! And it breaks my heart that he'll never know them and they'll never know the fine man that he was.' Then Sandy Bay would look away, as once again a moment of jest proved capable of catching them out by turning so quickly to grief.

So there was still the occasional fast blink of an eye at such times, or when a painful lull in the telling of an old story reminded them of their loss, but they were reclaiming their lives and their futures post-Sorley Mor. Boats went to sea and the crews didn't expect to see the *Wanderer* when they returned, and they no longer waited in the Inn to shout 'The Wanderer has returned!' as the skipper entered, even if they remembered vividly the times when they had. In the loft area of the Inn lay a big, yellow plastic banner prepared for the boat's return from her final trip proclaiming that 'The Wanderer has returned — for GOOD!' It lay folded into a large square shape taking up a great deal of room and gathering dust. Annie Stewart, Dan's wife, kept tripping over it; knowing what it was, she hadn't said anything about it. As time went on and the pain receded, though, she would complain to Dan, suggesting that he destroy it or put it somewhere else, but somehow Dan could never bring himself to do anything with it, so there it stayed.

Six months after the sinking there were definite signs of recovery, and one day Rose announced that she was fed up with the bone-shaking old Land Rover, and bought a car. She had never needed one before — the uncomfortable Land Rover had always been there for whatever journeys were necessary — but the car was perhaps as much to do with her growing sense of independence as comfort. She bought a new Beetle that Gannet sniffed at, saying it was 'a lassie's car'.

'Well, that's all right then,' Chrissie remarked. 'I don't suppose the lassie will let you near it, so what's it to you?'

Chrissie liked the odd little car so much, and spent so much time in it with Rose, that she wondered aloud about learning to drive, a thought that sent Gannet into paroxysms of laughter. 'What will you drive?' he demanded, 'a bulldozer?' and she was forced to stand on a chair and soundly box his furry ears. But though new paths were being forged, their eyes were still focused on the results of the probe into the sinking of *Ocean Wanderer*, and the campaign to make sure Sorley Mor wasn't blamed for the sinking. Rose's attitude worried Dougie, though. Her sights were firmly set on having the freighter skipper found guilty of a major crime, and he knew that wasn't going to happen – it shouldn't happen.

'What I don't want,' he told Father Mick and Gannet, 'is for Rose to go back to the state she was in because she doesn't get what she wants out of this – and I can tell you she won't get what she wants.'

'She's pretty angry, right enough,' Gannet said quietly.

'A natural reaction in the circumstances,' Father Mick mused. 'There's been a bit of me baying for blood, too, I have to admit that, and you can see her reasoning. Her world has been destroyed in such a terrible manner: surely someone must be held to account?'

'It's not going to happen, Father,' Dougie repeated. 'I've tried to tell her that, but she won't listen. She's convinced things like right and wrong and justice actually exist.'

'Well, don't blame her for that,' Father Mick smiled. 'It's the sign of a good heart, just like my own!'

As the time drew near for the publication of the Preliminary Inquiry report, there was a heightened tension in Acarsaid. On the day it was to be released, the village widows gathered in Chrissie's house, waiting for Dougie to arrive. Gannet had taken himself off to his official residence in Keppaig for the afternoon. Dougie looked around the expectant faces of the women as he entered and his heart fell. He had warned them all, not just his sister, what to expect, but obviously not one of them had taken it in.

'It's as I told you it would be,' he said, sitting down, 'the accident happened because the *Wanderer* did not alter course as she should have, and the freighter didn't take avoiding action in time to prevent the collision.'

There was a long silence.

'That's *it*?' Rose eventually asked, incredulously.

'Rose, it's just the Preliminary Inquiry report,' Dougie said.

'It makes it sound as if our men were at fault,' Chrissie said. 'We know there was a lookout on the *Wanderer*. Is there no mention of the lookout maybe being taken ill before the collision and not being able to alter course?'

'Chrissie, you're looking for too much,' Dougie said gently. 'This is the initial reaction, the one taken after a first look at the available evidence.'

'They've taken nearly a year to come up with *that*?' Rose demanded. 'We knew that from the minute the boat went down!'

Dougie squirmed. 'I tried to make you understand,' he said.

'So now it's *our* fault, is it?' she demanded.

Chrissie put a hand on her arm and patted it. 'No, Rose, it's not our fault, but it's not Dougie's either, is it?' she asked kindly.

'There will be a fuller inquiry,' Dougie told them, 'one that looks at all the circumstances, and we'll be putting detailed questions into that one.'

'Will it make any difference?' Rose demanded angrily.

'Rose, I don't know,' Dougie replied. 'You have to appreciate that we're dealing with three countries here, which makes everything more difficult and time-consuming. But we won't be giving up. Sorley Mor was on lookout, we know that; he was fully clothed and found at the bottom of the wheelhouse stairs, so we also know something happened to him. Sorley Og was fully clothed too; he was clearly about to take over as lookout. We won't be letting them or any of the crew be blamed, but this report just states –'

'The bloody obvious?' Chrissie butted in.

'As you say,' Dougie smiled sadly. 'I'm sorry if you were all expecting anything else. I tried to warn you, but I obviously didn't try hard enough.'

'It's not your fault, Dougie,' Chrissie repeated firmly. She shook Rose's arm gently. 'Is it now, Rose?'

'No,' Rose said quietly, her face flushed and holding back tears. 'It's not his fault.'

And so the inquiry into the accident continued for another year, with Rose taking the lead in pushing to make sure nothing was missed.

'She's making it her life's work,' Dougie told Gannet. 'I can't get her to accept that, whatever comes out of this, it won't be exactly what she wants.'

'Leave her alone,' Gannet advised. 'If it gives her a reason to go on, then it makes her stronger. Even if it doesn't work out exactly as she wants, that strength will help her to get through it.'

That winter there was heavy snow in Acarsaid for the first time that Rose's generation could remember, and she stayed in her house and cried; Sorley Og had never seen snow and had desperately wanted to. The others all faced identical low points. As with all bereavements the 'firsts' were always difficult: the first birthday, the first anniversary, the first snowfall. Peter Sorley Kerr grew more like his father every day. He learned to walk, unaware that he was a special child to everyone; unaware, too, that he had provided the reason for his grandparents and his young widowed mother to go on with life. Rose, though, still seemed to be stuck in the pattern of waiting that had begun when she and Sorley Og first started going out together: waiting for him to phone while he was away, to start the journey home at the end of each trip, for first sight of the boat as she headed for harbour, for his body to be found and brought home, for his funeral and, now, for the final inquiry report to come out. In the back of her mind she sometimes wondered what would happen when there was no more waiting to be done, but mostly she just waited, feeling much older than her years.

Then the day arrived, two years after the *Wanderer* had been lost, when the official last word on what had befallen her was released by the Marine Accident Investigation Branch. Dougie had warned everyone that it would be couched in bureaucratic language, but he was surprised to find that it read as though it had been written by human beings.

Sorley Mor was, without question or argument, it said, a particularly safety conscious skipper, who ran one of the best regarded boats in the Scottish fleet with strict discipline. The boat was well maintained, every safety device had been regularly serviced, and there were no mechanical or structural defects on her. Likewise her crew had the qualifications they required; as well as the experience and attitude to their work that Sorley Mor demanded. They had all the safety and survival certificates modern fishing asked of them, even the older fishermen and the skipper himself, and they had all been with him a great many years. Why this boat, of all boats, should have sunk with all hands was not only a tragedy, but a mystery, and though the initial report's findings were upheld, the investigators had indeed looked more closely into the accident.

They accepted that Sorley Mor had been on lookout, and they surmised that prior to the collision he had suffered a fatal or life-threatening condition that had rendered him unconscious. The alarm that sounded every three minutes was activated, but because of engine and other onboard noise, it could not be heard in the cabins, not even when it had gone unanswered and grew louder each time; neither could it be heard where Sorley Og had been found. So a picture emerged of the skipper being taken ill, putting his boat on auto-pilot to leave the wheelhouse in an attempt to get help, then collapsing and possibly dying, with everyone else on board unaware of his problems and of the advancing freighter. The lookout on the freighter had spotted the *Wanderer* and, though he denied it, there was evidence that he had then nipped below for some reason, leaving no one in his place, expecting the *Wanderer* to change course as she should have. When he returned the two vessels were less than two minutes apart, too close to avoid collision. There hadn't even been time for the freighter to sound her whistle five times in warning, as maritime law demanded, and the damage she had sustained proved that she was only just beginning to change course at the moment of impact.

Dougie couldn't believe it; it was all Rose could have asked for, and infinitely more than he himself had expected, and he couldn't wait to get to Chrissie's house to tell the women. He took Father Mick with him, but again Gannet had gone elsewhere. The women listened as Dougie read out the relevant passages before he handed each woman a copy of the report.

'And this will go to the press?' Chrissie asked anxiously. 'They'll print that it was a good boat with a good skipper and crew and that something had happened to Sorley Mor?'

'It's all in the report,' Dougie said. 'We'll make sure their attention is drawn to the relevant points.'

'Well,' Chrissie sighed, 'I'm content.'

Around her the women murmured in agreement. There was a great sense not only of relief, but also of anti-climax; the lads had all been cleared, but they were still gone. It seemed only fair that they should now be able to play the incident over again with the ending they wanted – their men safely back home. But no report could do that; nothing could bring them back. They sat for a long time thinking their silent thoughts, then suddenly Rose spoke.

'I'm not content,' she said, throwing the report back at Dougie.

Everyone looked at her.

'What happens to the skipper of the freighter?'

'The MAIB had no control over that, Rose. His own country's maritime authority made that decision after they had carried out their own investigation. They decided the cause of the collision was 50–50, and it was punishment enough that the skipper of the freighter would have to carry the knowledge that his boat was at least half responsible for the deaths of six men.'

'So he just walks away from it, does he?' Rose demanded.

'Well, what do you want to happen, Rose? Do you want him put in prison?'

'Yes!'

'What good would that do?' Dougie persisted.

'At least he wouldn't be on the sea. He wouldn't be in a position to kill any more innocent men!'

'Rose, he didn't kill them, it was an accident,' Dougie replied patiently.

'In that case we should let every murderer go free, not put anyone away, because they'll have to carry the guilt for the rest of their lives and that's clearly enough!' she shouted.

She got up and walked up and down the room, her arms folded tightly around herself.

'You can see what she means,' said Father Mick. 'Do you remember Eric's little run-in with the law before the sinking? He went through a red light in the early hours of the morning with no traffic and no people about, against the law to be sure, but he did no actual harm to anyone, he even freely admitted it when the police came calling. He was fined four hundred and fifty pounds and got six points on his licence. A boat gets run down on a clear day with no other vessels in sight, six men die and, well, nothing, and we're all sitting here grateful that this report has reflected what we knew to be the truth. Where's the justice in that? I'll be buggered if I can see it.'

'How about Christian forgiveness?' Dougie suggested, glaring at him. 'I would've thought that came within your remit.'

'I'm only saying that sometimes there are grey areas and limits, even for Christians, smart arse.' Father Mick retorted.

'I can fully understand Rose's feelings that basic justice has not been served here.'

'But what makes you think justice should even come into it?' Dougie persisted. 'And if it does, maybe this is the nearest we'll ever get to it. I doubt if this man will ever forget what happened, do you?'

'At least,' said Rose bitterly, opening the front door, 'he has a life to carry his guilt through. Our men don't have their lives. They're lying up on the hillside for eternity. And what about the damage to our lives?' Then the front door closed and Rose had gone.

She didn't come out of her house over the next five days, locking the door and refusing to open it, even for Gannet, and ignoring all phone calls. The only way they knew she was alive was because she could be seen at the big window, looking out to sea from time to time. It was the scenario Dougie and the others had dreaded. Chrissie had a key and they debated using it to invade her privacy, but Gannet advised patience.

'Leave her alone,' he said quietly. 'She'll get through this in her own way and in her own time. It's really no business of ours.' On the sixth day, though, Dougie arrived with his mother, took the key and let himself in.

'Well,' said Chrissie sarcastically, 'there's a sight you don't see often, Margo Nicolson going out of her way to call on her daughter. I was wondering what it would take.'

'Now, now, Chrissie,' cautioned Father Mick, as they watched discreetly from behind the curtains at her house, 'that thought doesn't become you.'

'Aye, it does,' she replied. 'You're such a liar!'

Dougie had wanted a reaction, any reaction, even if he had to dodge missiles as he entered the darkened room, but there was nothing. Rose looked up silently, then looked away again, returning her gaze to the familiar seascape.

'We wondered if you might like to talk?' he asked quietly.

'No,' Rose replied flatly.

'Or just some company?'

'No.'

'Rose,' he said helplessly, 'you have to make some effort to cope with this. You've climbed out of the worst kind of despair, you can't let this pull you down again.'

No reply.

Dougie was casting around in his mind, desperately trying to find something that might rouse her.

'Look, this other man, he made a mistake. He didn't get up that morning and decide he was going to down a boat and kill her crew. He didn't choose to do this.'

Still no reply.

'If Sorley Mor or any of the others were here they would say the same as I'm saying now.'

'But they're not here,' Rose said. 'Isn't that the point?'

Dougie sighed with relief; at least there had been some response. He took a deep breath.

'And they're not going to be, Rose, not ever again. No matter how much you may brood in here, they won't be coming back. Even if the other skipper had been sentenced to life imprisonment, it wouldn't change anything. They still wouldn't be coming back.'

'You think I don't know that?' she asked, then she turned towards him, tears coursing down her cheeks. 'The only thing that's kept me going these last two years was the Inquiry report. I wanted to see some kind of justice for the lads, but it's not there, is it?'

'I tried to tell you, Rose, I said it over and over, justice wasn't what it was intended to deliver. It was only ever meant to be an explanation of what happened that morning, and why.'

'And I'm never going to get justice, none of us ever will. So tell me, Dougie,' she asked plaintively, 'what do I do now?' She turned away from him towards the window and her shoulders shook with sobs.

'Dougie,' Margo Nicolson said briskly from beside the front door, 'wait outside.'

399

Dougie looked at her, unsure of what was going on, but Margo opened the door, waving a hand to guide him out, and he found himself obeying as though he were still a boy. Then she closed it and locked it behind him.

Inside Rose's house there was only the sound of her sobbing for a long time then, when she had calmed down, Margo spoke.

'What the hell are you doing to yourself, lassie?' she demanded harshly.

'Just go away,' Rose said wearily.

'I will not!' Margo said, raising her voice. 'I'm your mother, you're going to hear what I have to say whether you like it or not!'

She walked around the immaculate, stylish sitting room. 'So this is it, is it?' she asked. 'This bloody awful barn is to be your resting place? And how are you going to get revenge on the world, a rope over that beam there? I'm sure there must be a rope from the boat about somewhere. That would be nicely theatrical, don't you think?'

Rose stared at her, shocked and angry but unable to answer back.

'Or just starve yourself to death to show us all how you're suffering, to spite everyone who's tried to help you over this. Looking at the state of you, it wouldn't take long.'

'What do you expect of me?' Rose cried.

'I expect you to get on with your life.'

Rose laughed bitterly.

'Aye, I know you've heard it before, but this isn't the life you should've been living in the first place. You're not the first one it's happened to who's had to make the best of it. You should never have married him.'

'That again!'

'Aye, that again. You've got a second chance. Chrissie MacEwan was right, you're lucky.'

'Lucky?' Rose was enraged, her fists clenched.

'That's what I said. I wish I'd had the chance you have

now when I was in your position, but I didn't. I had all you bairns,' Margo said bitterly.

'What kind of human being are you? Didn't you have any feelings for my father at all?' Rose asked incredulously.

'Of course I did,' Margo replied amiably. 'He was quite a nice wee man, that's what I felt about him, but he was a mistake, the whole thing was a mistake, and then I had to watch you repeat it.'

'Just how do you make that out?' Rose demanded.

'Rose, Rose, you're a clever lassie, but you're so daft at times,' Margo replied, patting the couch beside her, and Rose was so taken aback by what sounded like kindness in her mother's voice that she sat where she was invited to.

'Look, Rose, all your brothers and sisters, they're mostly like your father, not in looks, but in nature. There's a slight bit of me in them, though, the methodical bit, which is just as well. It's just odd that you're his double and you're like me.'

Rose gasped.

'Can't have everything I suppose,' Margo sniffed. 'I recognised from the very start that this place wouldn't be enough for you, that's why I made sure everything was pumped into giving you the chance to learn. It was to be your road out of this place.'

'Without consulting me!' Rose protested.

'Ah, so you were planning to be one of those modern parents, were you?' Margo laughed. 'Not violating your bairns' rights by changing their nappies.' She sighed. 'Your brothers and sisters, Rose, they've all turned out decent enough people, though none of them would be where they are if I hadn't pushed them hard all their lives. I could do that with them, I was their mother. Oh, I know, that Margo Nicolson has no feelings, I've heard it all and maybe they're right, but I did all I was capable of, I swear. My other bairns have no imagination, no fire. Look at Dougie. He's a fine man, I know that. They're all so proud of the way he's handled the whole *Wanderer* thing, but he was built for just this kind of event. Solid, that's a good way to describe our Dougie, practical; a decent lad to have around – reliable, but that's it. Just what you'd expect to come out of a coupling between me and Quintin. You're like me, though.'

'Like you? Don't say that again.' Rose was aghast. 'I bloody well am not!'

'Aye you are, you're just like me,' Margo grinned, 'though as I say, you're softer than me, I'll give you that. The way you used to look at Sorley Mor and wish he was your father,' Margo shook her head, smiling sadly.

Rose looked at her sharply.

'You think I didn't notice?' Margo asked her. 'I noticed all right. I used to see how fond of him you were and think back to my father and how I could've seen him far enough, yet there you were, looking for one, and one in this bloody hellish village at that.'

'He's – he was a good man, Sorley Mor,' Rose said quietly. 'I'd rather have had my own father but, as I couldn't, Sorley Mor was the next best thing.'

'I know, Rose, I know,' Margo said wearily. 'I don't understand but I know that's how you felt, but I could've shaken you for not looking outside this place. You always seemed to look through rose-tinted glasses at Acarsaid, and there's more to life than a wee village for the likes of you.'

'I've been happy here,' Rose said defensively, 'this is my home. What more do I need?'

'The world, Rose, that's what you need, the outside world.' She looked at her daughter, trying to find a way of explaining what was in her mind in a way that Rose could accept. 'Look, when I was young I had what was considered to be all. It was money mostly, but that means a lot to most people, and don't believe anyone who says it isn't important. I was odd, I always knew that, I never fitted in, and if I'd had no money I'd have been regarded as a pathetic character, but because I had it I was just eccentric. That's what money does, it smooths over rough edges.' She laughed quietly. 'The trouble was that I was like you. I was bright, I had my eyes on wider horizons. We both get that from Granny Ina, by the way: she knows it, even if you don't. What I should have done was to get away from here. I could have done it too, but I made a mistake.'

Rose looked at her quizzically.

'I got married when I shouldn't have,' Margo said.

'If you're going to start in on Sorley Og again –'

'Be quiet, Rose,' Margo said firmly. 'Just listen. I don't know if we'll ever have another conversation after this one, so make the most of it. In my day, Rose, you had to have a man, that was the size of it. Even misfits like me had to toe that line. It wasn't like now – my God, how I envy this generation of lassies! In my day, if you didn't have a man you were a failure, a "poor old spinster", that's how they talked about you, "left on the shelf". Not that that kind of talk bothered me, but getting married presented a way out, or so I thought. I had my father on one side doing everything he could to keep me here while my every instinct was to get away; that's when I made my mistake. A married woman in those days passed from being the property of her father and became the property of her man, so I looked around and picked the most amenable man I could, the one I could make do what I wanted. That seemed to me to be Quintin.'

'That's a terrible thing to say!' Rose accused her.

'It probably is, but it's the truth and, anyway, he got the last laugh. My downfall was in not knowing anything about men. I suspect you're like me in that respect, too. Quintin might have been quiet and easy-going, but he was stubborn. Nothing would've taken him from this place; he was like all the rest – Sorley Mor, Gannet and Sorley Og, too. By the time I realised I'd got it all wrong, I was pregnant.' She laughed. 'Now there's an irony. All he had to do was wave to me from the boat and I was caught again! I took my fertility from my fisherwife grandmother; she couldn't stop having

403

them to save herself. You're lucky. You seem to have taken yours from your father's mother. So there I was, stuck here, having baby after baby, and don't mention the Pill or abortion, this was Acarsaid, not Hampstead, but I'm telling you truthfully, I would have grabbed at either one. Then my father's business failed and there was little money either.'

'You sound as if you regret having us!' Rose said moodily.

'Now don't be childish,' Margo chided her, 'you're an adult. Of course I regret having six bairns! If I hadn't had them I would've been free when your father was killed. Want to know what I felt when I heard he was dead? Relief.'

Rose gasped.

'Terrible, isn't it? The truth often is, Rose,' she said thoughtfully. 'But I wasn't free, I had five bairns and another on the way. Even then I'd have dumped the lot with old Ina and Aeneas, with old Ina herself after he died, and that's the truth too, but you changed that.'

'Me?' Rose exclaimed.

'Aye, you,' Margo replied quietly. 'From the minute you were born I knew you were different from the others, and as you were growing up I could see that I'd been right. I knew your brothers and sisters would plod along, though I always hoped they'd escape this place. I don't suppose I gave up till they married people with little Acarsaid minds, but that's all I ever had with them anyway: hope. But as I say, there was something in you that reminded me of myself, Rose. You wanted more, you needed more, so I thought to myself, "Better face facts here, Margo. You've blown it as far as your life's concerned, but if you concentrate on this one, get her educated, you could get her out of here, win something back from this . . . this bloody disaster of a place."'

Rose looked at her, too confused to answer.

Margo laughed wryly. 'Oh, I'm not saying your father was a bad man or anything like that, but he bored me, he had one of those small minds, an Acarsaid mind. He was quite happy to go to all those different ports in the name of fishing, but he wouldn't travel ten miles on land – and I wanted to see exciting places in far-off continents.'

'So you didn't ever love him?' Rose asked.

Margo shook her head. 'Don't even know what the word means.'

'And all my life I've heard stories about you and Sorley Mor,' Rose said. 'Was there never anything between you and him either?'

'Nothing,' Rose laughed. 'Everyone here wanted to marry us off, just as they're trying to marry you off to that Gavin –'

'What?'

'Ach, stop being silly, you know fine they have their hearts set on it. It would tie up all the loose ends nicely. But you can't let it happen, Rose.'

'But he's just a friend!' Rose protested. 'Do they think I can forget Sorley Og that easily?'

'That's how it starts, Rose, you drift into situations; everybody does it. Are you really so naive that you think that when every couple here came together there were fireworks in the sky? People marry for convenience, they settle for what they can have. Look around you. Are there many men here who look, think or behave like romantic heroes? For God's sake, for your own sake, stop being a tragic widow, and stop trying to make Sorley Og into a hero. He was just a man, and now he's gone. Make the most of it.' She shrugged and Rose started weeping quietly.

'Be honest with yourself. If he'd lived, would you have been content to sit here in this great, daft house for the rest of your life, being his wife, bringing up his bairns, not using your brain?'

'We were going to travel,' Rose said defensively.

'And come back,' Rose smiled wryly. 'You would never have got him away from Acarsaid, Rose, never. The end of the road,' Margo said dismissively, 'and they're so proud of it they print it on T-shirts without seeing the irony! My God, the end of the bloody universe would've been a better name

405

for the place! Don't fool yourself, Rose, you would always have that need to see other places, to do other things. Even if you did suppress them, it would be within you forever, that regret that you didn't do everything you could have done. And now you have a choice. You can get away from this place and live, and if you ever do come back at least you'll have had enough experience to choose to be here, or you can stay instead and end up like me, a trapped, bitter, twisted old bitch who resents everyone.'

Rose opened her mouth to deny it.

'Don't, Rose,' Margo said, holding her hand up to end any protest. 'That's what I am and that's what I'll always be. All the do-gooders here got it *half* right. "Poor Margo", that's what they said when your father died, then it was "Bitter Margo", because, they thought, I'd been left a widow at that age. Their descriptions were right, but their reasons were wrong. Sometimes I thought of telling them the truth just to see their faces, but then I'd think, why bother? Affronting little minds is no victory.' She sighed. 'I cheated myself of my life all those years ago, and all I have to show for it are my bairns and their bairns. That's just basic reproduction; it's hardly an achievement. First I was trapped here looking after them, looking out for you, and now old Ina has me trapped. She's gone down a lot in the last year or so, I suppose you've noticed that.'

Rose nodded, then looked at her mother and thought to herself that she was indeed 'poor Margo' in ways that she had probably never thought of; that she deserved sympathy precisely because she had been unable to feel anything for Quintin. Poor Quintin, too, come to that. They sat in silence for a long time.

'So you've never been in love?' Rose asked, thinking over the conversation.

'Never,' Margo said simply. 'You have the advantage there, Rose, or disadvantage, depending on your point of view, I suppose. I don't think I was capable of it, but there you are, you play with the cards you're dealt. What I'm saying to you is that you've been dealt better cards. Don't waste them, lassie. Leave. Go. Do it now!'

'But just where do you see me going?' Rose asked.

'I don't know,' Margo said, exasperated. 'Go and look up Uncle Murdo's lot in Canada, or Danny's family: see if they really exist beyond old Ina's imagination. Go and see the land of trees, or whatever the old woman calls it. It's not where you go that's important, just the fact that you do.'

Then she unlocked the door and left, no hugs, no touching of hands, and certainly not a motherly kiss on the brow. Outside the house Margo climbed into Dougie's car.

'What happened?' Dougie asked.

'Nothing,' Margo replied crisply.

'Nothing?'

'Nothing you'd understand, Dougie son. Just take me home,' Margo said.

'Do you want to see Chrissie before we go?'

'I don't do chit-chat, Dougie,' Margo said in a bored voice. 'Just take me home.'

28

Over the next two days Rose did a lot of thinking, but for the first time in two years her thoughts were not about the loss of the boat. In the deepest recesses of her mind she knew that even after she and Sorley Og married there had been a restlessness, a nagging kind of panic that this might be all there was. She felt guilty admitting it, but it was true. She loved him, there was no doubt about that, and if he had lived she would have loved him and only him for the rest of her life, but sometimes it had all felt like an illusion. Just over three years ago she had got her first degree, and had been going to study for another. Her life's ambition had lain within reach, until she had come home on holiday and looked towards the harbour for *Ocean Wanderer*, as she always did. She had been looking for Sorley Mor, that familiar, comforting presence, and there he was, waving to her from the wheelhouse. Then Sorley Og had turned round to see who his father was greeting, and it was like looking at Sorley Mor as a young man. That was it; from that moment her fate had been sealed, and now here she was, standing by the big window, trying to make sense of it.

Sometimes, when he was away at sea, she had wondered whether she had married Sorley Og or a younger Sorley Mor. Even though she banished the thought from her mind instantly, it had still occurred, it was still there. Even while they were both alive, when she dreamt of them she often got them mixed up, as though her mind couldn't decide which was which. There were times, if she was being entirely truthful, when she wondered if any of it had been real. Was that part of the anger she had been feeling in these last two years as a widow? Was part of it at least because she knew this wasn't the life she had wanted and now she was trapped here, without the reason, without the cause, now that Sorley Og wasn't ever coming back? And wasn't she angry *at* him sometimes, bizarre though she knew it was, for leaving her here without him, isolated and deserted?

At other times she dismissed all of it. It was warped thinking brought on by her distress. Her marriage and her life in Acarsaid were the only reality she had, but still the same thoughts kept creeping back. She only realised she had been asleep when she awoke that Sunday morning; five hours she had slept, longer than at any time since the sinking, and her mind was clearer than it had been, too. A shower first, then coffee, then a final thought or two to sort out before she paid a visit to Chrissie.

'Chrissie, I've decided to go away,' she told her.

Chrissie looked shocked, as Rose had expected. 'But where? Why?' she stammered.

'I just need to be somewhere different for a while,' she said, to soften the blow.

'On your own?'

Rose nodded. 'You've got a key, could you empty out the fridge and freezer for me?' Somewhere in there was half of an ice cream she knew she couldn't face seeing again. 'Just throw out what you can't use yourself,' she said. 'I'll give Dougie a key, too. I just want you to keep an eye on the house for me.'

'Maybe that's what you need right enough,' Chrissie said, trying to sound bright, 'a break, a wee holiday.'

'That's it,' Rose lied and, as she looked at Chrissie, she knew Chrissie was lying too.

'So when are you off, then?' Chrissie asked, turning away to dust something, a familiar ploy.

'I've got a few things to do first, but soon. Where's Gannet?'

'He's been off wandering,' Chrissie replied, and they looked at each other and smiled. 'He goes to the Keppaig house sometimes when he wants to do his Greta Garbo routine.'

Rose hugged Chrissie briefly, climbed into the Beetle and drove down to Dougie's office.

'I'll be in touch when I know where I'm staying,' she told him. 'I haven't decided what to do about the house. If you could just make sure it's OK, do any repairs that need to be done, that kind of thing . . . I've written a letter to the bank and one to Gavin, will you make sure they get them?'

'You sound as if you're going to be away for a while,' he suggested.

'I don't know, Dougie, but I want everything covered, just in case.'

Then she drove up the Brae to Granny Ina's house. Her mother looked up expectantly as she walked in.

'If I go, what about Granny Ina?' Rose asked.

'Now don't use the old woman to get out of going,' Margo replied tartly.

'You never give anyone a break, do you?' Rose said.

Margo sighed. 'She's lived longer than Methuselah; she won't even know you've gone. She isn't with us any longer: she's in Lowestoft or Great Yarmouth more often than she's here, lucky bugger! She spends most of her time talking to people who've been dead for years, and seeing supernovas exploding in the sky. She's probably happier where she is than she would be if she knew where she was.'

Rose looked at her sharply.

'Rose,' Margo sighed, 'she's waiting to die, she wants to die, she's had enough of life. Given the way she is, is it any wonder that she's finding escape routes? Everything's disintegrating. She can't hear, she can't see and every bone in her body aches with arthritis.

'She'll just sleep away what's left of her time,' she said quietly. 'You wouldn't be allowed to let an animal linger like this. Go and see her if you want, but you'll only upset her, and, anyway, you'd be far better remembering her as she was. This isn't the picture you want to take away with you.'

Rose thought for a moment then shook her head. 'I won't see her,' she said.

'So you're off?' Margo said.

'Yes.'

That was it, no long farewells, no emotional goodbyes; Margo Nicolson didn't do them either.

Further up the Brae was the chapel house. She had stopped at Hamish Dubh's store to buy a half-bottle of Islay Mist, and she handed it to Father Mick as he opened the door.

'I've always said, young Rose,' he smiled, taking the bottle, holding it out and looking at it admiringly, 'that you have a heart of pure gold!'

'Father, I'm going away,' she said.

'And now I'm not so sure,' he said in a bemused tone.

Rose laughed. 'It's no big deal. I just need to get away for a while.'

'A while,' Father Mick repeated, 'is that all it is?'

'I don't know,' she confessed. 'We'll see.'

He looked at her. She'd had a rough time, he could see that from her face, from her eyes. If ever someone needed to escape it was Rose. Still, he opened his mouth to protest, then thought better of it and shut it again: trying to persuade her to stay would be entirely selfish.

'You'll keep in touch?' he asked eventually.

She nodded. 'Of course. And when I come back I'll make sure I stock up with duty-free!' she laughed.

After he'd waved her off he sat down and poured a large glass of Islay Mist. Life in Acarsaid had gone on for years and years without a thing changing, he thought, and with the deaths of six men it had started to disintegrate. There was no telling where or when it would end. The map of the place had been obliterated as surely as if an earthquake had hit it. The only thing he could count on in the entire universe, he decided, holding up his glass and admiring the falling-down stuff of his choice, was the glorious Islay Mist.

Heading back home, Rose packed a few things, placed another pebble on the cairn outside the house, then picked up the bright lump of quartz she had planned to add to it when Sorley Og came home from the last trip, holding it for a moment before putting it in the car. Then she looked around the house for the last time and found that she didn't feel as emotional about it as she thought she would. She smiled. She was in control; she was handling it. Her eyes fell on the unfinished model of *Ocean Wanderer* in the far corner, Sorley Og's hostage to fortune. She had covered it with a piece of clear plastic two years ago, and it had sat there ever since, looking deserted and forlorn. On a whim she lifted it carefully, collected all the paint pots, brushes, bit of wood and glue and put them in the boot of the car. As she moved away she didn't see Chrissie, but she waved anyway, knowing that she was there. She drove to the cemetery, high above the village, and made her way to the grave where Sorley Mor and Sorley Og lay. She placed the quartz stone at the base of the head-stone: he *was* home. Turning to leave she blew a kiss to all the others lying there: her father, the other lads from the *Wanderer*, all the people she had known throughout her life who were now lying there, too.

Gannet's house was her next stop. He was sitting on a wooden bench outside, a pile of books by his side and a pair of binoculars in his hands.

'I just came to say I'm going away for a while,' she told him.

Gannet nodded in his calm, accepting way.

It was very quiet, the kind of quiet that lulls you to sleep. Keppaig was a backwater; it had none of the noise and bustle of Acarsaid just a few miles up the road.

'What are you doing?' she asked, sitting beside him.

'Well, I'll tell you if you promise not to tell Chrissie,' he smiled.

'Promise.'

'There's some otters down by the shore there. I like to watch them. I watch the birds too these days, I read this book about birdwatching a while back and, once I tried it, I found it very, very, what's the word?'

'Therapeutic?'

'Aye, that's the word. She'd never give me a minute's peace if she found out,' he laughed gently.

'Neither would the skipper!' Rose said.

'Aye, well, luckily it didn't happen till he'd gone, but he'll be laughing at me somewhere, I've no doubt.'

They sat in companionable silence for a while.

'You know what would be good on the side of the house there?' Rose suggested. 'A porch.'

'*Conservatory*, woman!' Gannet corrected her. They laughed, then fell silent again.

'And you'll be all right?' she asked him.

Gannet nodded. 'You?'

'Oh, I suppose so,' she sighed, 'though I'll never understand why you aren't angrier about the whole thing.'

He shrugged. 'That's what the fishing is like, Rose,' he said. 'It could've happened anytime. You could bring a boat out of the water every month and check over every single thing, but a plank could still spring, a pipe could burst in the engine room, the pumps could pack in, you could fall in the winch gear or get run down by a freighter whose skipper isn't as alert as he should be. With the best will in the world, you can't stop these things happening. Your father knew this, so did Sorley Mor and Sorley Og. It's all part of what makes the fishing a dangerous job.'

'Wow!' Rose said, blinking her eyes furiously, 'quite a speech for a sober Gannet!'

'Aye,' Gannet chuckled, concentrating on the binoculars in his hands, 'I've been thinking it was time to get back in character. All this talking isn't good for me!'

After a while she asked, 'Did you read the report?'

'No.'

'Why not?' she asked, surprised.

'Now why would I do that?' he returned, smiling gently. 'I could've told you what it would say from the minute I first heard how the boat had gone down; what else could it say? Besides, I had no reason to doubt Sorley Mor's seamanship. He was the best, and not just because he said so. If I had read the report it would mean I had doubts, and I don't, so I have no reason to read it. Besides, I find I can cope for long stretches if I don't actually believe it happened.'

Rose realised that had been why he had gone elsewhere when Dougie was going over the reports at Chrissie's house. She swallowed and looked away.

'That's why I didn't identify the bodies,' he continued quietly. 'I said it was because I had to stay with Chrissie, but that was a lie. Sorley Mor chose wisely with that one, he always said she could cope with anything, even us. But all my life he was one step behind me wherever we went. I didn't see him dead, so in my mixed-up mind I have it that it might not have been him, there's still that chance, and that chance will keep me from going insane. Sometimes the only way I can get through the day is to believe he's still there, two steps behind me.'

She put her hand over his and they sat in silence again.

'I have something for you,' she said at last, getting up and going back to the car. She returned with the unfinished model of *Ocean Wanderer*. 'Sorley Og has been building this for God knows how long,' she smiled. 'He refused to accept that it was superstition, but it was, just as surely as Sorley Mor's refusal to allow Father Mick on the boat.'

They both laughed.

'Anyway, he thought as long as he didn't finish it there was always a reason to come back. I thought you'd maybe like to finish it for him.'

Gannet looked at it, examining it with a smile. 'He had it to perfection,' he said. 'This really is it, isn't it? The very last

Wanderer. I'll keep it, but I won't finish it, Rose, if that's all right?'

'Why?' she asked.

'That chance again,' he grinned self-consciously. 'As long as it's not finished there's always the chance he'll come back and do it himself. The same reason Dan keeps that banner in the loft at the inn, I suppose.' He looked down at her and shrugged helplessly, and she hugged him.

'Oh, and a couple of things,' she said, 'favours.'

'Anything,' Gannet said, still looking at Sorley Og's model.

'At the house, there's a cairn outside the door.'

He nodded.

'Will you put a wee stone on it every week while I'm away? I believe in that chance, too.'

'I will, Rose,' he smiled.

'And will you look in on Granny Ina sometimes?'

He nodded. 'I always do,' he smiled. 'She's a fine woman, Granny Ina. Sometimes I think she's the only one who has ever taken me seriously.'

'That's because she's always had a crush on you,' Rose smiled. 'She's always said that if she'd met you a generation earlier she wouldn't have let you get away.'

Gannet struck his forehead with the flat of his hand. 'Now you tell me!' he gasped theatrically.

She got back into the car and drove off through Keppaig on the road southwards; then the enormity of what she was doing suddenly hit her like a blow and she pulled in to the side of the road, put her head on the steering wheel and cried for a long time. She had known what she was going to do, it was settled. She would head for St Andrew's to do the degree she didn't do three years ago, the one that would make her a marine archaeologist, exploring wrecks just like *Ocean Wanderer*, where other people's husbands, sons and fathers had lost their lives, and she knew when she did so she would have a different perspective. And there were Uncle Andro and Uncle Danny's descendants ready and willing to welcome her to Canada; there was a whole other world waiting for her out there.

She would probably not return to Acarsaid for many years, if at all; that was what she had decided earlier. But now that she was finally going, all her resolve and control had left her and she began to have doubts about whether she was making the right decision. She could turn the car around and go home, she thought, return to MacEwan's Castle, to the house that Sorley Og had built for his princess, return to the safe life she knew – and for a moment that's what she decided to do. She started the engine, then hesitated.

From the bench outside his official residence, Gannet had his binoculars trained on Rose's stationary car. 'Go on,' he whispered. 'Don't turn back! Go on, Rose!' Then he smiled as he saw the car finally move on, and watched it until it had disappeared from view.

Acknowledgements

Thanks to Colin MacDougall and Michael Currie for sharing their personal knowledge of the fishing industry and their unending patience with all the daft questions; various members of the Marine Accident Investigation Branch for their help; and special thanks to Ann Currie, who gave me some insight into the lives of fishermen's wives and families, and John Crone of C. Crone Ltd and Dr Susan Bowie for their knowledge and experience of kippering.

Also Susan Telford, who wrote an excellent book about her grandmother, who was a Lerwick Herring Lassie, and kindly let me use it as a loose pattern for Granny Ina's working life. I want to stress, however, that the similarities end there, and the family relationships in Ina's life are entirely fictional.

And my gratitude to everyone else who provided answers to odd questions that arrived out of the blue at all hours without blowing up and telling me where to go, and thanks even to those who did.

Sources

'In a World a' Wir Ain', by Susan Telford, published by Shetland Times Ltd.

'Fishing and Whaling', by Angus Martin, National Museums of Scotland.

MAIB for reports and charts.

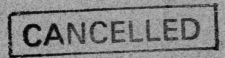